EXPANSION 1

THE ASHEN DOWNPOUR

LARRY GENT

ALSO BY LARRY GENT

Lycotta-Verse

The Benedict Forecasts
Be All That You Envy
Never Been To Mars
To Money And A TV
Bedroom Walls That Save Us
The Future Sold Out (2020)

The TOP SECRET Mac Files
She Who Trains Under Death

Avalon Lost
Lightyears To Go Before I Sleep

Vörissa's Catalyst Online

Expansion 1: The Ashen Downpour
    Patch 1.01:   New Game+
    Patch 1.02:   Escort Mission
    Patch 1.03:   Corpse Run
    Patch 1.04:   In Another Castle
    Patch 1.05:   Silent Protagonist

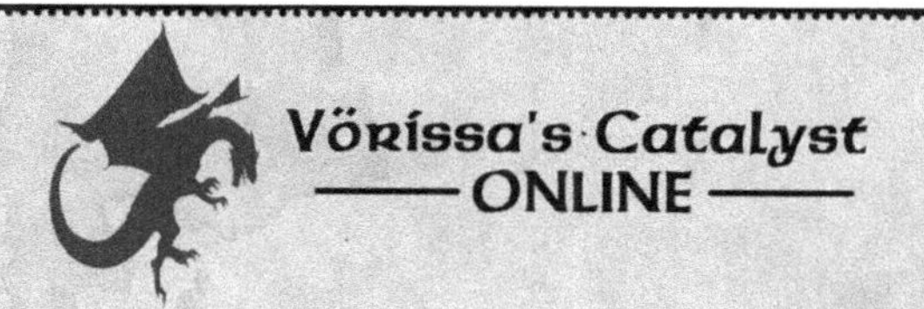

EXPANSION 1
THE ASHEN DOWNPOUR

LARRY GENT

Published in Canada by Midnight Reading Publishing, Ottawa

Gent, Larry, 1983-, Author.
        The Ashen Downpour / Larry Gent
Five novellas.
ISBN: 978-1-989152-06-5

New Game+, *Escort Mission* and *Abother Castle* first published in March 2017
Corpse Run first published in March 2018
Silent Protagonist first published in October 2019

Cover Design: Valérie Gent

Midnight Reading Publishing
511 Brittany Drive
Ottawa, Ontario
K1K 0S1

To Val!

More than any other project, I could not have done this series without you. I love you with all my heart and thank you for all the help and support you have given me.

I love you!

PATCH 1.01
NEW GAME+

LARRY GENT

Chapter 01

"Over the centuries, mankind has tried many ways of combating the forces of evil... prayer, fasting, good works and so on. Up until Doom, no one seemed to have thought about the double-barrel shotgun. Eat leaden death, demon..." — Terry Pratchett

A volley of arrows came from the approaching ship, arcing across the sky until gravity took hold and pulled them downwards. The wooden projectiles, with deadly steel tips, became a downpour of murderous rain.

"Coalition's here," a warrior said dryly.

I turned my head, lifted up my arm and called on my magic. The mana flowed through my body and turned my hair from blonde to a hue of ice blue. The magic erupted from my fingertips, circled around me and formed a protective energy shield. I glanced back at my plate-wearing party member and frowned as the arrow bounced off the magic barrier. Each arrow dropped harmlessly to the ground before fading away. "Yeah, I noticed."

A long time ago, I found myself asking how any game could be so addictive that people would willingly give up their lives. It didn't make sense to me but time and time again, I'd be online and I'd come across a story about talked about some guy - it was always a guy - who didn't work, didn't have any family and did nothing but play a silly game all day, every day. It seemed ridiculous. It seemed impossible. Six months later I found myself lost in a fictional world know as Aspumer. My name is Devon Priestly and I am addicted to Vörissa's Catalyst Online.

VCO is a MMORPG - a massively multiplayer online

role-playing game - that I would pay $15 a month to play. The game was set in the fictional fantasy world of Aspumer, a land of sword, sorcery and adventure. A player would embark on quests, instances and raids in order to obtain gold, gear and power. VCO was about the dark Goddess Vörissa. She fell to the mortal realm and in her descent she either freed, awakened or created the monstrous threats that filled the game's many expansions. The world of Aspumer was filled with such a vast a rich story that the lore for the fictional world had its own wiki, one I had lost countless days simply reading.

The idea behind VCO wasn't new, it was a fantasy MMO. The concept had been done to death in the old style with games like *Rifts, World of Warcraft, Ragnarok Online, Guild Wars* and *Final Fantasy XI* - simply to name a few - but what made VCO different was the system. VCO used a Mark IV Looking Glass immersion brace to put you right in the game. In layman's terms, VCO was a virtual reality game. It wasn't a clunky VR with bulky mitts, large helmets or awkward glasses that filled bad TV. This was true VR. This was the type of immersion that could only be bested by taking the blue pill yourself and seeing how far down the rabbit hole went.

The Mark IV *Looking Glass* - made by Chesire Technology - was a sliver of metallic tech that wrapped around the back of the neck. The brace was filled with several thousand bits of tech, a long wire and one impressive piece of computing hardware. These three pieces, combined with a billion dollar server somewhere in Winnipeg, Canada, was all it took for me to leave my world and travel to Aspumer.

I honestly don't believe that I'm addicted to VCO - my ex-girlfriend did - but I do love it. I love leaving my world and traveling to theirs. I love traveling through their fantasy landscapes, exploring their caves and moving through their dense forests. But even with my adoration of the game, I know my limits. I know when I have been on too long and I know when I have to log-off. The only hindrance is that my definition of limits and too long tend to be vastly different then most people's.

VCO was a serious game to many people. They held major tournaments, annual PVP seasons and raid competitions, each with some serious money as prizes. These players were professional gamers and much like sports stars, they needed the best gear. In golf that means buying a Nike VR S Covert 2.0 Tour Driver with new Fly-Brace technology that allows for higher ball speed, more distance and greater forgiveness with every shot; in VCO that means having the best weapons, strongest armour, and most powerful magic items. A pro-gamer could get the best by spending thousands of hours questing or they could spend real money to buy them online from hard working treasure hunters, treasure hunters like me.

When I started playing VCO, it was purely for fun. Now I spend most of my time hunting down rare swords and selling them for several hundred dollars apiece. The amount I make a week varied on the time of year. When a tournament is a couple weeks away or when the PVP season was in its homestretch, my sales would skyrocket and I would end up making two or three thousand dollars a week; but as the excitement slowed so too did my numbers. I knew that if I would budget my money, I could live off of my VCO earning alone but deep down I knew that I needed more. I needed to get outside and talk with people in RL; real life. It's why I kept my minimum wage job, a crappy part-time shelf-stocker at some Wal-Mart clone, and it is how I knew I wasn't addicted. Then again, addicts are known for making excuses.

The warrior Steelion, drew his two-handed sword and clutched it tightly as he watched the approaching ship. We were in an instance, a dungeon encounter, called Fillmont's Landing and the Collation was bearing down on them. Each instance had a story, a plot surrounding the dungeon. *Fillmont's Landing* had a team of five leading a small platoon of men into a Collation outpost. The first half of the encounter involved the five players taking out the guards and - forcefully - subduing the commander. Then, after pulling a lever to trigger the next half of the instance, the Coalition would show up on ships, with every archer firing, and attempt to retake the base.

VCO, like many games before it, was one based on factions. Players choose a side and fought against the opposing faction. There were the Collation of the Damned, housing Orcs, the blood-thirsty Dhampir, the illusionary Changlings, and the feral Fenririans.

I was part of the opposing faction; I was one of the Descendants of the Eternals, a cheesy name for the human-like races of Aspumer. They were the humans, the elves, the dwarves and the gmones.

The two factions had been at war for one clichéd reason or another. It never really mattered why. Humans versus Orcs; it was a classic battle. I, being a mage of Elven descent, chose the Descendants not for moral reasons or for beliefs. I chose the Descendants for the reason most people do: my friends were already in that faction.

"The ships are docked," Bearcules, the druid, said. I gave him a glance. He was a tall elf with long flowing green hair tied into a ponytail. "They're coming up the main path now."

I nodded and kept eyeing the druid. It amazed me the looks people choose for their PCs. This druid that stood before me, explaining the battle-plan for an instance I'd run literally dozens of times, could have looked like anything. Instead of some young druid he could have been an elderly male, a fifteen year old teenage boy or even a woman. Crossplaying was a major aspect in an MMO, especially when they took the leap to VR, but it was never a practice I subscribed to.

"We'll rush in and start dealing with the trash mobs." The druid continued, "Then we'll head for the first boss."

In RL, I was a tall guy with short dark hair, glasses and a thin frame that was best meant for playing the geeky best friend in a movie. In VCO, I was the Elven mage Stov. I kept my character close to reality. I still chose the tall frame,

I just made minor tweaks. I made my hair blonde and made it flowing, adding life to a mop that had none in reality.

"Stov? Stov?" I blinked and looked at the four faces impatiently staring back at me. "Ready check?"

"Yeah. I'm good. Open the gates and let's do this." Of course I was ready. I was the High Mage Stov; I knew this instance inside and out.

I waved my hand and brought up my party info. Four names and their life bars floated before my eyes. Bearcules, our elven druid-tank, Punchocalypse, a dwarven monk-DPS, Tialla, a human shadow priestess, and my old *friend* Steelion, a human warrior.

I'd known Steelion for a long, long time, ever since launch. He and I ran our first instances together, randomly pugged by fate. PUG, for those who aren't in the know, stands for pick up group; it's a term for when the game puts a group together. Steelion and I exchange friend-codes and we partied together often. The warrior was even the person who introduced me to the world of treasure hunting. That introduction, however, started our rivalry. I was better at farming items then he was, I was better at puzzle solving and I was a better tactician. In short, I was better at the game than Steelion. Add onto that the fact that I've undercut him by at least twenty-five percent every time we had similar items for sale and he started to get a little pissed with me.

Music filled the air as the gates opened. From the bottom of the hill, I could hear a compliment of men, two ships worth, charging up the hill. It was our job, aided by our platoon, to stop them. Different parties approached *Filmott's Landing* differently. Some would order the platoon to the wall and take up bows; this meant more soldiers would survive at the end but make the fight harder. Others would order the men to the front line; this would allow the soldiers to take out the trash mobs - gaining a momentum bonus - while leaving the elite drops for the PCs. Steelion was like me, we wanted to take on the instance's optional boss. That meant we needed as many soldiers surviving as possible but we'd require the momentum bonus to bring down the big bad. Going for the FL's optional boss was an end-game challenge, even fully geared seasoned pros like Steelion and I found ourselves sweating during the fight.

Bearcules let out a massive roar as his body began to shift. His smooth elven skin became jagged and hairy as his arms tripled in size and his face contorted to form a snout. The druid, an avid shifter, was taking his tank form. He was turning into a dire bear. With claws sprouting from his hands and his entire body taking on an animal form, he charged in calling with him the entire platoon. Steelion gave me a look. He didn't have to say anything, I knew what he wanted. Even though we had our differences, he was still one of the best DPS warriors I knew.

Steelion let out a vicious yell and charged in after, his hand-and-a-half sword held high. I watched as Punchocalypse dashed in next. I started to call upon my magic, forcing the magic that flowed through my body to turn cold. I felt my skin chill as I called an ice-spell to my fingers, the cold allowing me to see my breath even in the blazing heat. With a final flick of my wrist, and a twist of my body, I summoned ice from my fingertips and created a wall of ice between me and the charging NPC soldiers.

After Steelion and I were pugged with the other three, we suggested to the group about going for the optional boss but Bearcules and Tialla said no. The monk didn't care either way. Steelion and I were here for a rare drop and we were going to fight that optional boss one way or another, even if we had to trick the rest of them into it. The wall of ice would keep our NPC soldiers busy for ten minutes; ten minutes we had to spend fighting without them. It would keep them alive and still grant them the momentum bonus we needed.

I tapped my wrist and a watch materialized, the time counting down. VCO allowed me and every other player to install apps and mods into the game. Some were simple things like a countdown app, other were vastly more complicated and change the entire interface for the game. I only had five add-ons installed.

Bearcules spun his head around in surprise. "What are you ---arg!!" The sword cut through his hide and pulled his attention. The trash mobs, Coalition soldiers, had reached him. Their blades cut and sliced at his hide but most did little to no damage. With large swipes the druid fought back, pulling threat from the mobs and knocking them back three at a time with a single swat.

Bearcules: What are you doing?

I smirked. His whisper message was expected. Right now he was trying to decide if I was a dick or just an idiot. Chances are he was leaning towards the dick option. I flicked my finger and quickly whispered back.

Stov: We're doing the boss. Deal with it.

I raised my hand and clicked my fingers, twice with the pinky and once with the thumb, and the skin on my hand turned a deeper blue. A targeting circle formed in the air. I moved my hand over the circle and flicked my wrist. The ice erupted from my fingertips, the blue fading away as the spell shot forward. My ice formed a cone, trapping anybody unlucky enough to be caught in it, in a wave of razor sharp shards of ice while slowing down their movements.

Assisted combat in VCO worked by the game presenting targets for you to use in combat. Targeting circles would pop up for attacks and targeting squares would pop up to for defense. You would move your weapon or your foci to the targeting circles to launch a successful strike and you'd move your weapon to squares to block an oncoming attack. It was a little jarring at first but, like most of VCO, it became second nature in no time.

It didn't take long for the first wave, the vanguard, to fall. They were trash mobs; they weren't supposed to be difficult. This meant it was the boss time, but not the optional one.

In any instance there was anywhere from four to upwards of twelve bosses per. FL had seven plus the bonus one. The four of us took out the first five when we took over the outpost. We just had three more to down.

Boss #6: Sergeant Hiram Holdem.

The Sergeant was Fenririan warrior armed with a long spear, a large steel shield, and six like-minded mobs at his side. The Fenririans were a wolfman race; once human, now cursed. Essentially they were hybrid-werewolves who no longer had a human form. Take a snarling wolf-man, give it a spear, a shield and backup and it became a terrifying boss.

Tactic: DPS-Tank and Spank.

AOE - area of effect - meant that Punchocapylse and I would deal with the mobs with big multi-hit attacks. His chi-strengthened fist snapping through their steel shields like they were drywall and my glacier shards tore through their flesh.

Tank and Spank meant that Bearcules, our tank, would hold the boss' attention by making as much threat as possible while Steelion would lay on an obscene amount of damage with his mighty sword swing - essentially laying a massive spanking on him. All this was done while Tialla repaired any and all damage with her swift healing spells.

The Sergeant fell and loot flashed before my eyes. For each piece of loot that dropped, a player had three options. They could choose Need, reserved if a player needed the gear to strengthen their stats or if they needed the supplies for crafting. They could also choose Greed, a choice if they just wanted to sell the stuff or feed it to their alt. The third option was Pass, which gave up their chance at the gear.

I waved my hand over the drops and examined the stats. There was an axe, a decent weapon but not one that would fetch much, a trinket that increased attack speed, Punchocpalypse needed that, and a rare mat drop called the chaos orb. Chaos orbs were used for most high-end profession crafting but only dropped one per boss. They also sold for - on average - forty gold per in game but only four bucks in RL money. On average I sold fifteen orbs per week. It was small money but it was easy money. I clicked need for the orb.

Stepping off the boat was the Orc caster. With a wave of his staff and the Orcish mumblings of powerful arcane words, a grey mist flew inwards and spun, coming together as it thickened until nothing but a grey cloud could be seen. With a final arcane shout, the cloud took a final shift and formed into a massive beast. The earth shook as the newly summoned creature immediately charged.

Boss #7: Mogar the Greyhorn

Mogar was a massive creature, one of the bigger ones in all of VCO. It looked like a rhinoceros had been given the McDonalds Super-Size treatment. It had a hide thicker than most armour, strength that put the most insane warrior to shame and a horn so big and strong that it could easily tear a hole through the side of any ship. Mogar was devastating.

Tactic: Tank and Spank

This fight was a simple one. Bearcules would charge in and face it head on, swinging with every claw and swipe it had. Each attack and each growl; strengthened and enhanced by the mystical power of nature's magic, generated threat by the dozens. While Mogar focused on the tank, and Tialla healed from the rear, Steelion, Punchocalypse and I spanked him. We lay such a massive amount of damage from spell, sword and fist that you could watch entire sections of the boss' health bar vanish. They didn't lower and they didn't shrink; sections just vanished. The only problem was that for every point of strength the developers gave Mogar they subtracted them from its intelligence. This mean that sometimes Mogar got confused.

In VCO, and many MMORPGS before it, threat was an invisible counter that each character wore. Monsters and bosses were attracted to threat. The more of it you had, the more they attacked you. Everything increased your threat. If you attacked, you got threat, if you healed, you got threat. The only difference was that the classes that could tank, like Druids, warrior and paladins, had abilities that drastically multiplied their threat.

When Mogar got confused, he ignored threat.

Every ninety seconds of the fight he would randomly choose a party member, strike them with a powerful three-hit combo that finished with a gore from his massive horn, then all threat counters would be reset at zero. What that meant to us was every ninety seconds, we had a one in five chance of being stabbed in chest worse than Wash from Firefly. The moment our tank took the first swipe the clock started.

Clutching my weapon tightly, so much so that I could feel the wood beneath my fingers, I clicked my fingers and summoned forth the cold. A chill ran through my body and my breath began to form before me, the tip of my fingers turning a shade of light blue. I eyed Mogar and moved my staff over the targeting circle, letting the magic pour out of me with a glacial burst. I started with my favourite opening volley, summoning a massive ice spike and forced it into the side of the great beast. The move barely caused the beast to stagger. I shifted a couple steps and fired another spell, an ice-born debuff that slowed the beast, its hide taking on a slight blue tinge.

The thing about being a range-dps, or a healer, is that you stay back and fire an endless stream of spells from afar. Unlike a melee-dps, who had to be front and center punching, smacking or stabbing their way to victory, a range-dps could watch the battle from afar and study how the other players moved. You couldn't just stop and watch; you still had to blast the baddies with spell after spell or arrow after arrow if that was your thing, but it didn't require the full non-stop attention that a melee-dps did.

As I laid an unending stream of magical violence, I allowed my eyes to wander. Punchocalypse was a monk but he was a brawler. A monk could specialize in numerous ways. Some players became water monks, moving and dancing like bugs on the water, and some became air monks and soared through the sky with high-flying moves. Then there were the rock monks. They were full strength brawlers who were straightforward and hard fighting monks. Punchocalypse was a standard rock monk and acted like one. He didn't dance around foes, he didn't dodge or weave, spinning around punches; instead he saw his target and moved straight for it. He wouldn't move around a bad guy; he'd plow right through them.

Bearcules was the opposite. He didn't charge right in, he'd run to the edge, roar to taunt them, and force the bad guys to come to him. Some bears would barrel inwards like a cannonball and attack from the center, Bearcules pulled them to him. He used their strengths against them.

Tialla was shadow priestess. She used shadow magic to attack and heal. She casted HoTs and over healed. As long as she kept players at full health, her spells granted the players bonus buffs.

Then there was Steelion. I'd watched Steelion fight numerous times and I'd seen his style evolve. When he started he was a sword-and-board fighter, meaning he used a one-handed sword and shield, but as the levels passed and the adventures continued, Steelion switched to a two-handed weapon. He'd swing gigantic blades in wide arcs and deal massive amounts of damage. It was a brutal style and I teased him for it. Eventually, he developed a versatile style. He wielded a hand-and-a-half sword, one that he could use with one hand or two, and switched styles as he needed. He would swing in a wide arc with two hands, landing single blows each with massive damage, or he'd use one hand and swing a fury of smaller blows to overwhelm his target.

Mogar stomped his foot, roared and attacked. For a heartbeat we all paused and worried which of us was going to be chosen. I was first. The horn slashed across my chest, twice, and then gored me through my chest. I stood there, stunned, and stared down at the horn that ran through one side of my chest and out the other.

Crap.

Chapter 02

"The worst thing a kid can say about homework is that it is too hard. The worst thing a kid can say about a game is it's too easy." — Henry Jenkins

Nobody ever felt real pain in VCO but the Looking Glass system sent shivers through my joints. Sometimes it felt like small jolts, other times it felt like the rumble pack in a console's controller but never did anybody feel pain.

My vision shifted and my focus returned to the game. I was lying on the ground while the others fought on. Swirls of holy magic danced around me as my wounds healed and my health bar restored itself. I grumbled as I climbed to my feet. I freaking hated Mogar. Of all the battles and all of the bosses, I hated Mogar the most. He wasn't the most difficult boss, he was just annoying and for some fucked up reason, he always chose me first. I hated him for that. I let the rage flow through me as I started to tap my fingers.

"Don't do it, Stov," Steelion yelled. "You're getting ragey again."

Damn, this guy knew me. I swiped my hand and cleared the spell; I started tapping out another. A flurry of arcane missiles tore through my fingers and collided with the beast's head. Mogar struck twice more before he fell, once to Steelion and once to Punchocalypse. Tialla healed both and we moved one. Bearcules pointed to the end of the ship; the mage stood there waiting.

Final Boss: Liocro'ah the Summoner.

Liocro'ah was Coalition mage, or so we were meant to believe, and he led the forces trying to retake the outpost.

He summoned Mogar, and he was about to summon more. Liocro'ah began to chant in orcish and wave his fingers around. Grey mist rolled in off the sea and began to take form but instead of forming one cloud it formed five. I knew what was coming next, it had been incredible the first time, but after the amount of times I farmed this instance it had started to lose its appeal. Each form grew bigger until they shifted into five separate fury gryphons.

Tactic: Crowd Control - Tank and Spank.

A crowd control battle seemed similar to an AOE battle, it dealt with a larger number of enemies while having a primary target, but the difference was that you couldn't take them out all at once. AOE spells did less damage than a single target one but in exchange, it hit more targets. In an AOE battle, the extra mobs were significantly weaker than the big boss. In a crowd control battle, they were just as strong.

In an AOE battle, you had hit many people at once. In a crowd control battle, you had to disable a baddie to temporarily take it out of the battle. That way it let you focus on one or two bad-guys.   So for the Liocro'ah battle, you had to keep the gryphons busy while you pummeled the living snot out of the caster himself.

COUNTDOWN: 00:00:00

I had another plan. A roar reverberated from the outpost as the glacial wall I erected shattered. The platoon of NPC soldiers charged downward from the base. I smirked. This fight was going to be easy.

"Target the gryphons," I yelled. Most parties would have the tank agro them all to the ground while the DPS took out the caster. I had a different plan. "Keep them in the air."

Tialla struck first, forsaking her holy magic for shadows, and summoned a wave of nightmares. Her shadowy horrors sprung upward and dove deep into the mind of each gryphon. The beasts screamed and turned, two of them flying away as three others shook off the fear and dove downward. I followed suit by summoning all of my magic into my chest only to expel it all at once, forming an explosion of arcane energy that rippled outwards and sent the gryphons fleeing. In the lore of VCO, uncontrolled arcane energy is a dangerous thing. It is highly volatile, extremely dangerous and when expelled at volume can cause severe damage. To flee a build-up of arcane energy meant not that you were a coward; simply you were smart enough to run.

Those few gryphons dumb enough to stay and fight dove towards the ground. Their hope was to pin an unsuspecting melee fighter, Steelion or Bearcules, with the substantial weight of their body. Then, with their razor sharp claws and vicious teeth, they would tear through their victim's steel and flesh. The gryphon's dive was intercepted by the high-flying antics of Punchocalypse. A flying dragon kick, an aerial high-kick, knocked the summoned creature from its path and forced it to the ground. The feral beast turned and lunged at the monk, viewing him as easy prey. It was very wrong. Gryphons were the size of horses or cows, large cat-like beast with wings, and carried with them an admittedly nimble frame, but one that held a great many muscles and a great strength. For any normal mortal, a charging gryphon would have overrun them with little effort. Punchocalypse was, apparently, no mortal and he was far from normal.

In lore, a charging gryphon was horrifying; in game term it was ever worse. Liocro'ah's summoned aerial beasts were devastating fighters with attacks that dealt massive amounts of damage. Their pin-claw-bite-claw combo, which came with the unflattering side-effect of making even the seasoned player look like a stupid noob, was enough to drop most leather-players and below to around 25% health - a whopping 75% damage combo - and even the plate wearers suffered, normally losing anywhere from 15% - 30% per combo. Yet as devastating as that move was, it was still blockable. The charge was not. When anything in VCO stomped it's hoofs, snorted and/or roared and glared at you the way a hungry VCO player glared at cheesies (man, that metaphor hit close to home), the only recourse you had was to try and dodge. Arcane shield did nothing but make it angrier, snares just backfired and sent damage back to the caster and those foolish enough to try and block found themselves as nothing more than a stationary target that ended up with an additional 4x damage. The charge was one of the few unblockable moves in the game. When a beast charged you either dodged or stuck your head between your knees and kissed your ass goodbye.

Punchocalypse did neither. He simply gave the beast the middle finger, cracked his knuckles and braced himself. He moved his arms quickly, moving through a crit-increasing kata and pulled back his arm as he readied for a punch. I found myself staring like a man watching a lion make a stealthy kill on the nature channel, watching and waiting for the carnage. Punchocalypse smirked and at the last moment fired out his fist. The punch connected with the gryphon's head and the beast toppled to the ground.

I stared in surprise.

I was in the middle of picking my jaw out of the dirt as dozens of NPCs charged past, each roaring with a battle-buff that sent their stats through the roof. The soldiers swarmed the gryphons like locus and fell the beasts in mere seconds, only an unlucky few falling to claws and teeth, before turning their sights on Liocro'ah. The orc was nothing more than a massive collection of 1s and 0s; it couldn't show fear unless it was programmed too, and this character was not but somehow as I stared at it, watching the horde of npc soldiers descending upon him, I swore could see fright.

"Punchocalypse?" I muttered, my focus returning to the impossible sight I had just seen.

"Not now; we'll talk later." Punchocalypse dashed in and leapt into the air. He cleared a gryphon and bolted straight for the caster. "I'm going in, cover me."

I nodded and quickly called on my spells. Liocro'ah's aura turned red as he called on fire, an element for a lethal blast he had aimed at the monk. My fingers danced as I fired a counterspell. The two spells met and both fizzled. I smirked and prepared another. From the corner of my eye I noticed Bearcules charging forward, swiping his massive paws at the mage. Liocro'ah dodged the blow and chanted as he tried to throw up an arcane shield. I never gave him the chance. With my counterspell at the ready all his shield did was fizzle, leaving him open and vulnerable to Punchocalypse's barrage of fists. Moments later the mage fell. With his gyphons out of the way, and his shields countered at every turn, Liocro'ah was no challenge at all. Twenty seconds later he fell like every boss before him.

Bearcules looked over at me and growled. I knew what he was thinking. Technically the instance was done. He could loot and leave now and be done with it but as I looked at his animalistic form I could see the debate in him. We had enough minions to do the boss and the rewards would be great but would it be worth the challenge?

"Do it," He growled. I smirked and marched to the ships.

"I have no quarrel with you adventurers," a charismatic, yet frightening, voice bellowed. "I was simply transport, but if you take one more step closer to my ship, to my girl, I will protect it."

It was an in-game script, a hint of the optional boss. "Take your rewards and leave with your life; quit while you're ahead." The speaker walked to the edge of the ship, standing where the ramp met the deck, and grinned down at the adventurers. He was a pirate captain with two scimitars, a wide brimmed hat and a glowing red eye. "You want not of the carnage I will bring upon you if you disobey me."

Steelion and I stepped forward, passing the invisible trigger. We heard a loud sigh. "Fine, taste of my blade. Remember, you brought this on yourself." The pirate flashed an evil grin as he descended the ramp, drawing both blades as he walked.

Optional Boss: Captain Airmo Hau

The roar of a loyal crew filled the air as dozens of men leapt over the edge of the ship and onto the dock below. Each was armed with a weapon, a blade or a pick, a hammer or a knife, and each had a look of murder in their eyes. The rush of pirate mobs were met by the charge of the npc platoon and both forces clashed. The momentum bonus pushed the soldiers onwards, providing speed to their legs while strengthening their attacks. The two factions clashed in a binary battle, lines of code dictating their actions. Men fell on both sides, downed by sword or axe, but the skirmish carried on.

Captain Hau marched past his loyal crew and eyed our party of adventurers. I had run this battle numerous times, I'd studied the wiki and I'd also read the dozens of books and comics set in the VCO world. I knew all there was to know about the pirate Captain. In truth I admired the character. He was the anti-hero of the VCO franchise, the Boba Fett of the digital world. He was a fan-favourite character, both in and out of the game.

He also was one of VCO's greatest fencers.

Hau gave his scimitars a spin and dashed forward, slicing at the nearest foe. His edged blade slashed across Steelion's chest and drew first blood. There was no blood in VCO. There was only a damage number that floated upwards when you were hit, but there was a First Blood buff for the first successful hit and Hau won the buff, he always won the buff.

Tactic: Survive.

In VCO lore, Captain Airmo Hau didn't play by the rules. He made his own. This held true within the game. Captain Hau didn't operate on threat, a legendary rogue wouldn't dare operate on such a common basis, but instead he chose a target at random. In VCO there were two different fights that involved the legendary Pirate Captain. The FL fight was a level 90 fight and one of the hardest in the game. There was an earlier fight, at a lower level, that still proved to be difficult for max level players. When a battle was as randomized as the Captain's it became impossible to plan for.

Steelion switched his stance to a one-handed grip and frantically tried to avoid getting hit. He blocked the pirate's blades with his own steel and even parried a blow with a steel gauntlet on his left arm. The two scimitars moved like lightning as Captain Hau attacked. Most strikes found little but steel or armour but still many dealt damage. The Captain twisted his blades and ripped Steelion's sword from his grip, sending the weapon flying away. Hau flipped backwards, stunned Steelion with a mid-air kick to his head and landed back on the dock, several feet away from the warrior.

"Shini'ka!" Steelion's cry carried across the air. Shini'ka was an arcane command that any melee class could use. It would magically pull a dropped weapon back to their hands. I was happy Steelion had his blade again but I was focused on who the pirate would target next. Hau pivoted on his feet and glanced in my direction. The Captain had randomly chosen me for his next target. I was *clearly* thrilled.

My fingers tapped out a protective spell as Hau approached. A wall of ice shot up from the ground. The wall would normally slow a normal boss character but I had long since realized that the Captain was not normal. His blades cut through the wall in less than a second but it was long enough that I was able to throw up another pair of protective spells. My body was warded against the sting of steel and was protected by the best shielding barrier that arcane energy could provide. It still wasn't going to be enough and I knew it.

A defensive targeting square popped up and I moved my staff to it, blocking the first blow. I tried to bring my weapon down to the second square that popped up but my speed was nowhere near the pirate's. The steel cut through the arcane barrier and dove into my skin. The damage counter floated upwards followed by another and another. My HP dropped like a stone as his blades stung time and time again. A shadowy fog danced over my body as Tialla's magic knotted my wound together. She was keeping me alive but just barely. Captain Hau quickly disengaged and leapt backwards. His foot stunned me as he flipped. My vision became blurry and my targeting reticules vanished. For the next eight seconds, I was useless. Eight seconds seems like nothing to most but during a fight eight seconds meant the world.

When my vision returned, I spotted Bearcules on the ground fighting to get up, as Punchocalypse faced off against the pirate. Somehow he had the rogue on the defensive, Captain Hau was blocking the flurry of punches and kicks with the flat end of his swords. I glanced at Tialla, still un-chosen by fate, desperately trying to cast one HoT after another.

"Get Ragey, Stov," Steelion yelled. "Unleash the Hulk."

I held my staff up high and saw an icon flash on my HUD. I triggered my very *special* ability and watched as my staff transformed into ice. The ice moved up my arm and across my body, replicating as it moved. Inch by inch, the ice moved up and across my body until not an inch of bare skin remained. This was a rare ability I had unlocked called the *Jötnar* form. It transformed my body into an ice golem. I was the digital representation of Bobby Drake and I was ready to do some damage.

I had no magic in my *Jötnar* form but my strength and constitution were through the roof. I barrelled into the fight and fired a punch. The Jötnar form didn't come with any targeting circles or squares. It meant I was on my own for the scrap but luckily a simple punch wasn't that difficult. All I had to do was connect and the Jötnar form would do the rest. My colossal icy fist slammed into Captain Hau's back and dealt a resounding amount of damage. I fired a second punch and smiled as a larger number followed.

The battle was a long one, even with my special ability's added damage and ice effects that came with it, the battle still took a while. The Captain didn't become the legendary character that he was by being an easy fight.

"Steelion: Iron Hulk!" If my *Jötnar* was a Hulk impression, then Steelion's trademark move was clearly an Iron Man impression.

Steelion tapped his chest; activating the move he nicknamed *Reactor Love*. From beneath his armour, his heart began to glow, dimly at first but rapidly growing brighter. Seconds later a bright light filled the instance, blinding those who weren't apart of his party. For two seconds, Hau was stunned. I charged forward with my ice-golem first. This was our Iron

Hulk combo. Bearcules was surprised and didn't know what to do but Punchocalypse didn't hesitate. With a final flurry of blow from Steelion, Punchocalypse and I, we dropped Hau's HP to 1.

The battle ended when Hau signaled his ship. The cannons opened fire and sent the dock exploding into shards of wet wood. My party and I were pitched into the water and everything went black. It was a scripted event that signaled the fight's end. When the world came back into view we were all lying on a beach, washed up on shore by the tide, as Captain Hau sailed away. He laughed as he gave us the finger.

The fight was over and we had won, barely. Bearcules was severely injured, my mana was completely drained, Tialla had used several potions and Steelion's HP read zero. Punchocalypse, miraculously, was unharmed. Tialla finger's danced as she resurrected the fallen warrior.

"What in the hell was that?" Punchocalypse asked in wonder. "I've never seen that move before."

"It's one of Casper's Chache," I admitted slowly. "Kills my magic but give me the temp strength of a giant."

In RL there is a man name Casper Ramirez. He is both a very obsessive and brilliant man. Luckily he was able to take that combination of bane and buff to make a great deal of money. Casper Ramirez was the producer and lead programmer for VCO. He oversaw the project from its earliest stages through to its many expansions. Casper had been the subject of dozens of interviews. During which he's said that his goal was to make VCO a game unlike any other. However, he didn't want to rely just on the immersion tech to set him apart. To do this he spent thousands of hours, alone, programming hidden features, skills, items and abilities into that game. He inserted into his game, into his world, secrets that not even his development team knew about. Some he developed covertly by himself, other he hired outside studios under the guise of a new game but each of his secrets, the dubbed Casper's Caches, were hidden deep within the game. Some, like the legendary rogue blades, had been found and been made public.

Every rogue worth their salt now had those blades. But there were many secrets that were not widely known. One of these secrets was the *Jötnar* Set.

The *Jötnar* Set was a collection of items that when assembled would grant the wearer an additional ability. Armour sets were nothing new; they had been around since Blizzard released *Diablo 2*. The difference with the Jötnar Set was all the items were from different weapons sets. The magical staff was part of the *White Drake* set, the cloak was from the *Morning Hull* set and the gloves - which required a reconfiguration spell - were actually rogue gear that belonged to the *Cat Burglar* set. Together, if worn by an ice-spec mage, they granted an ability that couldn't be found in any book or wiki.

The *Jötnar* Set took me months to discover. There was no quest or pointers. There were only secrets, buried deep within the lore. Each of the items were created by an artificer named Ymillia Heimr. The lore spoke of how she was a travelling artificer, with an affinity for ice magic, on the run with her lover as they tried to escape her father. To make ends meet she hired herself out to whoever needed her skills in the creation of magical items. Mostly she created additions to an existing armour set, an item that would work in sync with spell that had previously been laid. Casper Ramirez adored the lore of his world and everybody knew it. It had taken me weeks digging through his wiki before I even found or saw the name Ymillia Heimr and weeks more before I heard the legend of her miss-matched items. Months passed by before I found them all, collected them one by one. Months that, in the wake of my fight against Hau, suddenly seemed worth it. I smiled.

"How the hell did you stop the charging gryphon? I thought that was unblockable?"

Punchocalypse shook his head. "It is, if it hits. The only way around it, that I've found, is to disrupt it. I had to up my crit and give it a shot. It was like punching a shark in the nose."

I snickered. Punchocalypse motioned behind me and

I turned around. Bearcules - back in human form - stomped towards me. "You shit. My gear's all red because of this shit. I wasn't ready for that crap."

"Dude, I'm sorry. I needed to run the boss." I pulled up my inventory and thumbed down my list. I hummed to myself as my eyes tracked each item that flashed by. "Here. Have this." I opened my palm and a ring digitized before us.

"That's much better than what I got," Bearcules admitted.

"I know. Take it."

"Don't fall for it," Steelion warned. "The great and amazing Stov strokes again. He's got much better gear on him, at this very moment. I promise you that. If he really felt bad he'd give you one of them." Bearcules looked at me and I shrugged. It wasn't a lie. Steelion held open his palm, a different ring digitized. "This is *much* better than what he was offering. Take it."

I hid my smile. I knew what Steelion was doing; he was going after my reputation. The name Stov was famous in VCO, everybody who was anybody knew about me. I was like Zezima from *Runescape* or Leroy Jenkins from *WoW*. Except in many gamer's eyes, I was a source of wisdom and power, not some internet meme about some idiot ruining a raid. Steelion's name was also known but my reputation was better. After a VCO tourney the winner, Madam_Magitek, said my name in an interview. She thanked me for my services and for helping her locate her items. It went downhill from there. Before that day Steelion was the *go to guy*. Madam_Magitek made sure that everybody knew that I was better.

Tialla stood by me and flashed me a casual smile. "Shall we see what we got?"

The group nodded and moved to the large wooden chest that washed up alongside us. I reached out and placed a hand on her shoulder. She looked back at me. I held open my palm as a large staff digitized. "Here."

She took the item and looked it over. "Hilsona's Crutch; it's weaker than my normal staff."

"Yeah but look at the special abilities. You're a shadow priestess, right?" She nodded. "While this staff will weaken your magic overall, the bonuses it gives shadow is massive."

She looked at me with cautious eyes. "What's the catch? You going to demand boob pics like the rest?"

"I wouldn't turn them down," I jokingly smirked. "But no, this is a gift with no strings attached. You're a good priest; this will just help you get better."

Tialla looked at me hesitantly. It was obvious she didn't know what to think of my offer. She reached across and touched the staff. A confirmation of trade flashed before my eyes. I tapped it and the staff transferred to her inventory. "Pay it forward."

I approached the chest and heard Steelion talk. "Last big run I did - OV Heroic - we pulled the mother of drops. We hit three greens, a blue and a purple. So the purple goes quickly, as do the blue and two of the greens, but we all look at the last green and nobody wants it. It's some crappy ring with crappy bonus to damage. It's an item *way* below the raid level. So I grab it; turns out it's one of Casper's Cache. I spend the next week hunting down the right socket gem for the damned thing. You put them both together and bam; sucker turns orange. I'm now holding the legendary *Ram Ring*."

Steelion was spitting bullshit. The Ram Ring granted a PC the ability to make the unblockable charge attack. The ring would sell for four hundred dollars in a slow season; in a tourney season it would sell for a couple thousand. Whenever a Ram Ring went up for sale, it made news. It would have shown up in MMO reports, it would have been all over reddit and I would have heard about. I hadn't heard a whisper.

"So what we got?" Steelion kicked opened the chest and floating screens flashed before our eyes. Descriptions of the items rolled past our eyes. I went down the list.

There were three green items: a cloak, a shield and a plate helm. None of them were class essential to a mage so I clicked greed on each. Seconds later the randomizer distributed the items. Steelion got the helm, Tialla got the shield and the cloak came my way. Next, I looked to the pair of blue items. One was a set of cloth boots and the other was belt. I smiled at the belt.

"Punch, you get the belt." It was the Waistwrap of Emberlock and for a monk like him it was a doozy of a find.

Steelion clapped, Bearcules just snorted and Tialla nodded in approval. I passed on the belt and clicked greed for the boots. Seconds later the belt went to Punchocalypse and the boots went to Tialla. I glanced at the final two items. One was Choker of the Grizzled Crimson, a necklace that granted a bear-druid a flame based breath weapon. It was a good find but nothing compared to what my eyes fell upon next. If a man could cry - for which I was raised to say no, they could not - and if a VCO character could shed a tear, I would have. Floating before my eyes and the eyes of everybody was the weapon I had come looking for.

Whaitiri Edge
Requirement: Level 90
Drop Rate: 0.02%

This blade was built for defense. It had stats like a shield, damage like a shortsword and had an elemental bonus just for kicks. The blade was amazing and it was a treasure hunter's wet dream. It was one of the rarest weapons available in VCO. At that exact moment, Steelion and I were thinking the exact same thing. Dollar signs existed where our eyes should have been. I could sell this blade tomorrow for five hundred bucks, minimum. In one month time, when the next tourney was set to begin, the annual Royal Tourney, I could essentially name my price and people would pay it. His whisper message flashed before my eyes.

Steelion: Holy shit.
Stov: I know.
Steelion: So how do we decide?   Neither of us can

use it.

Stov: Greed it and let Glados decide?
Steelion: Agreed. Just clicked greed.

I stared at the item and smiled to myself. My mind wandered with the possibilities of what I could do with that money. My bills were paid up and financially speaking I was actually in the black for once. This money would be a bonus; it would be a nice addition to my life. I'd been eyeing a new car and the sale of that blade would put a nice chunk towards it. I succumbed to my more basic desires and clicked need. The same words flashed before each of them.

Stov won Whaitiri Edge (Need Roll: 47/100).

I glanced at Steelion and saw rage take hold on his face. I'd just lied to his face; I just ninja'd the blade.

"You sum bitch," Steelion cursed. He drew his blade and started towards me. "You bastard; you just cost me a shit ton of cash. You lied to me."

My finger tapped quickly as I called upon my ice power. I threw up a wall of between the two of us and quickly pulled my recall scroll from my bag. I activate the scroll and vanished. I was running and there was no shame in it. Every character had a recall scroll; it teleported a person to the last inn that they'd synced too. I kept myself synced to the Grey-wind Inn, deep within Havenhold. The city, which acted as the human capital, was the hub for the Descendants and it was also my home.

Chapter 03

"Henshin a go-go, baby!" - Viewtiful Joe (Viewtiful Joe)

The familiar blue walls were the first thing I saw when my vision returned. In a teleportation spell the world went black for a few moments while the computer dissolved one landscape and loaded another. Whenever I used a recall scroll the first thing I always saw was the blue walls. They were wooden walls with cracked blue paint and a single canvas painting of a ship sailing across the Northern Sea of Aspumer. I stumbled to the bed and fell back upon it. I didn't need to look to know where the bed was. This was room 13c; this was my room. I paid for it and I lived in it. Lived was a *weird* term in a video game but it was as close of a term as any.

I lay on the bed and allowed my stomach to calm itself. A recall scroll was a teleport spell. I don't know what it was about teleportation spells but they always left me feeling ill. I stared up at the ceiling but found the knotted wood disgusting. I turned my head to the right and stared at the canvas of the ship. The imaged soothed me. It reminded me of my younger days when I used to sail on my dad's fishing boat off the east coast. I *hated* being on that boat when I was younger, I hated the sea and I hated the water, but now things were different, things changed and I changed with them.

When my stomach finally settled, I sat up and ran my hands through my hair. Not a single strand moved, each piece snapping back into place as my hand passed through it, but the motion made me feel better. I waved my hand and brought up my inventory. It was nearly full; I only had two slots remaining. I could sell my vendor trash and throw a couple items up on auction but this was the slow period and I didn't want to waste my time. I wouldn't get much money for my sales right now, everybody was desperately questing on their own to avoid spending the big coin but a few weeks down the road and it would be a completely different ballgame. Instead I had to mail the items to myself.

Every character had a private bank in which they could store items. I - or Stov - was no exceptions. The only difference was that Stov's bank was full. Banks could be upgraded, for some hard earned coin, and I had done so. I had upgraded Stov's bank to the fullest and yet I still needed more space. This was the curse of a treasure hunter. The solution was simple: a bank alt.

In VCO, every account had fifteen slots for alt characters. This meant I could try out all the different race/class possibilities I wanted. If I wanted to be a Paladin (as if), I could try it as either a human or a dwarf; neither race was better but each offered different path, items, quest and various other unique experiences. Of these fifteen slots I had used six as real alts. I had tried being a hunter, a warrior, a priest and even a warlock. I had even tried playing for the Collation as a Fenririan and a Dhampir but I kept coming back to Stov again and again. He was my main so I never strayed far. Yet one of my alts, a rogue named Rake, was my bank alt. I originally built him with every intent of playing him, and even constructed him to save the kick-ass name I came up with, but I just never got around to it. Instead of deleting him, I gave him enough gold to max out his bank, then I started mailing him my extra gear to store. VCO - like most MMO - allows a player to mail gear from one character to another. It's mainly used for trade between friends or random gifts but it can also be used to twink out an alt. Imagine raiding on warrior and coming across an *amazing* bow. A warrior can't use a bow, not since patch 4.2, but it would be *perfect* for your alt-hunter when he reached level 50. So you grab it, rush to the nearest mailbox, ship it to your alt-hunter and switch characters. Suddenly your hunter has a bow much stronger than he should have and he's ready to pull of his best Legolas impression when he hits 50. This meant that Rake, my bank alt, was still a level 1 rogue with nothing but a few copper in his pocket, the most basic of gear on his back and a bank full of items he couldn't use for next 89 levels, if ever. All the rogue did was walk from the bank to the mailbox and back again. I never even gave him a room to sleep in.

I exited my room, the door automatically locking behind me, and I exited the inn. I didn't bother talking to the NPC in the bar; they could only speak with specific pre-written scripts. I stopped at the mailbox and quickly crafted a letter to Rake. I filled it with my new blade and several other items that had been accumulating in my bag. Then I hit sent. I smiled and glanced at the time. It was almost time to hit the hay and sleep for the night. All I had to do was switch characters, store my items and then I could log off.

Slashlore: Hey you up for a QO run?

I glanced at the whisper. Slashlore was another guy I ran with. He was a sword and board tankadin. He was raider. He loved nothing more than to clear an instance and leave nothing but bodies in his wake. He wasn't a treasure hunter and loathed puzzles but he could sop up damage like nobody's business. When I needed a tank, I called him.

Stov: Can't; switching to Rake then logging for the night.
Slashlore: No worries, mate.

I waved open my menu and tapped the logout button. I confirmed my decision with a second tap and watched as the world melted away. Everything then went black.

I opened my eyes and found myself *inside* a picture. I

stepped through the frame and landed on firm ground. I looked around. The character selection screen from VCO was essentially an art gallery with dozens of painting hanging on the wall. In each frame was a picture of one of my character, their names etched on the name plate at the bottom. To log into any character all I had to do was walk up to a frame, pull of my best *Mario 64* impression and leap into the picture. The world would melt away and I would be reborn as whichever character I chose. I stepped away from Stov and walked across the room to Rake. I stood before the picture and admired it. Rake was a piece of art. Unlike Stov, who was an elf, Rake was a human and stood a head taller. He had jet black hair that fell before his purple eyes. He was lean but strong and had the symbol of the Whispers organization tattooed on his left arm. The Whispers were a organization of spies that existed in VCO. Their symbol was an incomplete chakram with a demon eye in the middle. In the lore those who wore the tattoo were members, in the game the tattoo was simply cosmetic. I had spent hours creating the rogue, he was meant to be my second main but I never got around to it. He simply became my bank alt. The picture began to ripple as I stepped closer, the glass morphing into a liquid state. I stepped through the frame and into the water and the world went black

Havenhold came back into view. I was standing by a mailbox in the middle of the city. The gaslights lanterns flicked, showering the city with light to combat the invading darkness of the evening sky. A flashing icon blinked before my eyes, signaling that I had unopened mail. I took a couple steps and nearly tripped over my own feet. There was always a couple seconds of adjustment when I went from Stov to Rake. The bodies had different builds and had different styles of walking. Longer legs meant longer strides. I tapped the mailbox and watched as a screen popped up before my eyes. I looked at the long list of items I had waiting for me and one by one I slid them into my inventory. I closed the windows and walked towards the nearby bank. The buildings that housed the bank were massive. They were each virtually unique. They were daunting towers that held thousands of boxes and employed dozens of guards.

I walked into the bank and approached the nearest un-occupied teller. She was a non-descript human woman, with features that didn't stand out. She was a dime a dozen NPC and moments after speaking to her I had already forgotten her. She said something to me but I ignored it. The bank tellers were NPCs, they didn't say anything but their pre-scripted speech. She opened up the bank and a screen flashed before my eyes. I transferred my equipment in, exited quickly and stepped out into the Havenhold streets.

"The end is nigh!" I turned at the sound of a voice crying out in the street. I raised an eyebrow as I recognized the crier. He was Admiral Galen Crowley, the man who led the Descendant Fleet in the Battle of Northern Isles. He was an upstanding figure in the human Kingdoms but looking at him now, one would never believe it. Gone was his Royal Navy uniform, instead he wore a grey ragged and torn cloak. "Our enemies have united and they will now come for us. We cannot fight them."

I blinked at the famous crier and pulled up my calendar. This was the release date for Patch 7.0.3. This was the in-game event to signify a new threat emerging from the shadows. I shook my head. How could I have forgotten this? This was a major lore event. For most players, a new patch meant possibly a new raid, a new instance, new loot and/or new bad guys. Basically, it meant new content to enjoy and exploit. For the lore fiends, it meant a new chapter to the ever growing story. It meant I had new facts to learn and, knowing Casper Ramirez, I had something new to discover.

"They have conquered the heavens and not even the gods could stop them," Admiral Crowley yelled as he pointed to the moon. Etched upon the face of Aspumer's satellite was a half-mask, glowing red in the evening sky. It was the left half of an angry mask, with a single narrowed eye, a downward frown and a symbol on the cheek that could only be described as a melted question mark. Within the mask's eye and between its lips were arcane runes that I didn't recognize. The runes glowed in a purple hue. I frowned. I wasn't familiar for which faction the half-mask stood, it was new, but the blood red hue seemed familiar. I pressed my index fingers against my thumbs and help my newfound square up into the sky. I stared through my finger frame, like a clichéd director, and make a clicking sound with my mouth as I winked. This was a macro I'd built to take a screenshot. I snapped a picture of the moon and smiled to myself. I knew that come morning I'd pour over the image for any clue that Casper would have left. I knew that within days, if not hours, the enemy that Admiral Crowley spoke would reveal themselves and the half-mask would have meaning, but that was the facts on the surface. Casper Ramirez didn't deal in surface facts.

I waved my hand and brought up my menu. I tapped the logout button and watched the world fade away. When my vision returned I found myself once again in the character selection screen. That's when things started going haywire. I stepped out of the frame and let my feet touch the floor. I expected firm ground to step on, instead the entire room started to shake violently. It felt like there was an earthquake but that was impossible. The character selection screen wasn't a part of the game world. There were no digital plates deep beneath the earth or fault lines. There was nothing but fifteen photographs and an exit door. Something was wrong, something was seriously wrong and I had to get the hell out of dodge.

I bolted for the exit. I reached the door but never made it through. The wooden door frame shattered, the fragments vanishing mid-air. I slid to a halt, the ground still rumbling beneath, and stared in shock. What the hell was going on? Where the fuck did the exit door just vanish to? I snapped my head around frantically and quickly tried to figure out a plan. The floor began to break apart. It started with the far corner but slowly crept inwards. I bolted towards Stov's picture. I wasn't sure logging further into a collapsing VCO was the best idea but honestly, I didn't like the idea of falling into the abyss, vanishing alongside the floor. I slid once more to a halt when a fissure ripped from one end of the floor to the other, tearing the room in two. The two ends pulled apart, like chunks of ice breaking apart on a frozen lake, and took Stov with it. I spun around and glanced at the nearest picture: Rake. I ran towards it and dove into the frame.

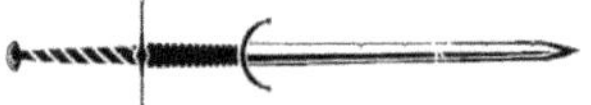

Havenhold came into view but the city, normally safe and secure by the city's guards, had suddenly become a warzone. The ground didn't shake like in the character selection, instead legions of men and women, dressed in onyx-black armour with purple highlights and with a half-mask upon their face, assaulted the city. They cut down guards and other NPCs with sword and spell and went into combat with any PC that dared to challenge them. I saw paladins and warriors downing the midnight menace with sword and axe, monks and rogues felling foes with swift attacks while priests healed those in need.

A midnight assailant noticed me, pivoted on his feet and dashed towards me. My screen locked onto his approaching form and flashed me a quick tidbit of information.

Mysterious Attacker: lvl 77

As the attacker approached, he pulled daggers from his chest and flung them at me. I dove to the right, the daggers whizzing my head, and rolled to knees. The fingers on my right hand quickly tapped out a spell as I thrust out my left hand. I expected a burst of frozen flame to erupt from my finger, sending the attacker to whatever hell computers feared.

Nothing happened.

I cursed my idiotic behaviour. I wasn't Stov; I wasn't a mage. I was a rogue, I had no spells, and to make matters worse I was roughly 70 levels away from even having a chance against this attacker. The midnight attacker, clearly a rogue by his dagger use, slowed his approach as he drew a falchion. I eyed the blade carefully. I had no way to fight him.

I had no rogue skills, no good weapons, not enough stats and worst of all I had no practice in hand-to-hand fight in VCO. It had been years since I'd played anything remotely melee. My head whipped around as I looked for a way out. I spotted the bank and bolted for it. The bank had lots of guards and they would slow the attacker long enough to for me to use my recall scroll. Stov kept his scroll synced to Havenhold: Rake's was still synced to the Vineyard Valley. I never bothered to sync Rake to Havenhold because he never left the city. For the first time I was glad of my laziness.

I entered the bank and watched as two guards rushed out to stop the approaching assailant. I ran as far inwards into the bank as possible and crouched down in the corner. I fished out my scroll while keeping my eyes on the murderous rogue. I didn't know who these half-masked murders were but the one who was after me took no time in cutting down the city guards. They were not Collations; the ones attacking Havenhold were clearly the Descendant races. I activated the scroll and watched as black took hold. My vision returned and I found myself near a large stone building. The structure overlooked the massive wine vineyards that echoed outwards. There were no half-mask killers here but the moment I took my first step I felt the ground start to shake. Just like in my character selection screen, the world shook violently. It caught me off guard and pitched me into the side of the stone building. My skull slammed against the side and pain took hold. I stumbled away, my head hurting and my vision blurring, and felt the usual sickness that came with teleportation. My feet, my human feet, tripped over themselves and I tumble to the ground. I slammed hard against the land and felt my stomach turn. I climbed to my knees but made it no further. My stomach screamed out and I doubled over as I violently vomited. Toppling over, thankfully not in my own vomit, and I lay on the ground. My head spun and stung, a terrifying combination, until my body gave way and I passed out. My final thought before the darkness took hold, random as they were, was me marveling at how nice and soft the grass felt on my aching head.

When I came to I noticed two peculiar things. First was my head hurt like a bitch. The second was that it was nearly eighteen hours after I passed out. I looked around and realized that I was still logged into VCO. That wasn't supposed to happen. The Looking Glass immersion gear was built to recognize when someone had fallen asleep and forcefully - but safely - log them out. It was dangerous to leave someone logged into a VR game for hours on end, especially while dreaming. I climbed to my feet and felt my body object. It was stiff and sore. I shuddered at the thought that I was getting older. One of these days I'd be super old, like over thirty, and be forced to collect a pension and use a walker. Truth was if any part of my body felt pain, it was all being ignored in favour of the migraine I was currently suffering. In the world of pain and suffering, the head took precedence.

I waved my hand and brought up my menu. I scrolled down until I found the logout button. I gave it a tap. Nothing happened. I tapped it again. Nothing happened. I rolled my eyes. My net was lagging and VCO was suffering. I reached for the side of my head and touched behind my ear. Every immersion gear had an automatic exit button. If you tapped behind your ear, where your ear met your skull, the gear would instantly - and safely - log you out. Nothing happened. I pressed it again. Nothing happened.

I waved open my menu and looked for the logout button. It no longer existed and I started to panic. I scrolled to the very bottom and looked for the emergency help button that normally resided there. It was gone as well. My heart raced as I realized what was happening. I wasn't able to log out. I was stuck in a video game.

My brain scream at me, not in panic or fear or even in pain, but in nerd rage. This was such a trope. Everybody and their mother had used this very plot in dozens of stories, both good and bad, over the years. In books Piers Anthony used it in *Killobyte*, Tad Williams used it in the *Otherland* series and Vivian Van Velde used it in *Heir Apparent*. It was used in *X-Files* and *The Matrix*, and *Tron*. There were dozens of animes and comics that used it as well, like *.hack*, *Sword Art Online*, *Log Horizon*, *Nth Man: The Ultimate Ninja* and *Over Lord*. That wasn't even counting *He-Man*, *Filmation's Ghostbusters*, *Centurions* and *DuckTales* (Woo Hoo). Don't even get me started on *Saints Row 4* and *Star Ocean: Till the End of Time*.

I was stuck in a video game and couldn't log out. I fucking hated this trope. Suddenly I froze. I cursed loudly and started kicking the ground and anything I could find. I had just realized that that the situation was worse than I had thought, much worse.

I wasn't just stuck in a game with no way out; I was stuck in a video game in my damned bank alt.

Chapter 04

"Reality is broken. Game designers can fix it." — Jane McGonigal

Panic slammed into me like a van being driven by a texting teenager. I frantically tried to log-out with every way possible. I tried all my options and even tried to get in contact with a GM but nothing worked. I looked around and felt my chest start to heave. I was going to die here. I was never getting out. Fear was setting in and it was starting to affect my mind. I couldn't focus and I couldn't think straight.

"Fear is the mind-killer." Frank Herbert wrote those very words in *Dune*. I love that book, it meant a lot to me growing up. The words have always hung in my head. Even now, as my lungs fought to gasp for air and my head spun in pain, I felt the words in my heart. I had to calm down. I had to relax before the panic attack took me out.

1:   Relax.
2:   Stop Negative Thinking.
3:   Use Coping Statements.
4:   Accept Your Feelings.

I knew the steps; I just had to follow them. I had to relax. I dropped to my knees and tried to calm my breathing. I started to reassure myself. I wasn't going to die here; I was going to find a way out. This was just a glitch or a puzzle. I was good at puzzles. I had taken some of the most difficult puzzles Casper had thrown at me and walked away with money, lots of money. This was just another puzzle. It was okay to be afraid, I just couldn't let the fear own me.

My panic attack started to fade as I let my mind focus and think. If I was living in a trope then I had to start thinking like a trope. Stuck in a video game wasn't new, it was its own genre and it came with its own rules.

1: Death in the game meant death in real life. DO NOT DIE.
2: I couldn't be forcibly removed from a game. I was stuck here.
3: I was under a time limit. I still needed to eat and drink.
4: Winning meant I could leave. Find the boss and beat him.

Every different show had its own rules, some had more and some had less, but these were the common ones that spanned most. That meant until I could disprove one of these rules, they were law. I thought about each one and tried to figure out how to prove or disprove each of them. I didn't want to risk dying on the *off chance* that I'd simply respawn. That meant I would have to avoid death at all cost. I glanced down at my hands and shuddered at the thought that passed next. What was the limit of *at all cost*? Would I kill another to stay alive myself? Could I kill another? I was balling at PVP in the old days but now it was PVP with consequences. I pushed the thought out of my mind, I *really* didn't want to think about it, and moved to the next point.

I couldn't be forcibly removed from the game. This was another point I couldn't prove on my own -- or could I? All I needed to do was find a way to contact someone outside the game. VCO had some methods built into the game engine that allowed a person to reach out into the real world. The GM was one way to reach out into the real world and I'd heard of rumours of others that existed. It would require some investigation but it was a possibility. I'd have to investigate quickly as I still had the third point to deal with.

I still had the time limit. I had three days to find some way to get a drink of water. I could last longer without food but without water I was up shit creek without a paddle. I sighed again, if only that creek had more water and less - what I assume to be - cow feces. Also how did I lose my paddle? Regardless of the creek's makeup, and the whereabouts of my hand-powered propulsion device, I needed to get the hell out of VCO and quickly, but how?

I needed to win to exit. This was one of the biggest tropes in the trapped in a computer genre. I had to find the big bad, shove a plasma grenade up its rectum - assuming it had one - and walk away as everything exploded, never once looking back as the flames. Cool guys walk away from explosions after all. The only problem was I had to find the big bad; I had to find out how to win VCO. How did someone win a game that never ended? I had to figure out who the big bad was and slay them. It seemed easy except for the all damning fact that I was level 1, again. It was infuriating. This entire ordeal would be easy on Stov, but no. I was stuck on Rake and I had to start all over.

I looked around and frowned. I was in the human starting zone. The Vineyard Valley used to be a regular vineyard, with rows upon rows of growing grapes, but in lore it was burned to the ground in an Orc attack. During the assault, the vineyard owner was saved by a band of heroes. He knew he could never help others like the heroes had helped him, so he decided to help those who helped others. He transformed his land into a training ground for heroes. I'd been here before, with other alts, and basically knew this area by heart. This was the starting area for all human characters. It's where a player would learn to use their character and the VCO system. I knew how to use a mage; I had no clue on how to use a rogue. I couldn't die and the only way to stay alive was to level up. So fate had found it fit to make me max-level grind yet *another* character. I approached the first quest giver, a meaningless human with a giant exclamation mark over his head, and activated the quest. This was the first step in a long journey.

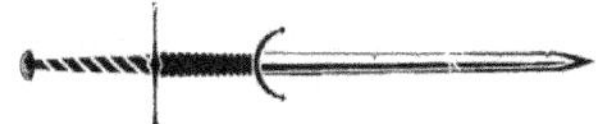

I was approaching the armoury when the waving hand of a player caught my gaze. I paused and look over at him. The man, with a green Mohawk, wore leather armour. My screen flashed as a threat icon appeared over his head. I raised an eyebrow in confusion. A threat icon only showed up on PC and NPC that I could attack. This player was an Elf, and therefore part of my faction. In VCO it was impossible to attack within your own faction outside of a friendly duel. I turned off my threat icon and smiled. "Sup?"

"Hi. I....um...," he scrunched up his lips as he tried to form words. "Can you log out?" I shook my head. "Me either. It's weird. I tried to call the GM but the button didn't work."

He still had a GM button, I didn't. I needed to keep him in mind. I added his name to my friend list. "Keep trying." I glanced at him and saw his name and stats appear before my eyes.

Name: Hizzous
Class: Hunter Lvl: 1

"I...um...I'm powering through until they fix it. I'm just going to leveling up some," he explained. "I just started this game and I'm kind of lost." I felt bad for the guy. His first day in the game and he couldn't log out. "I'm trying to find out where I get my weapons."

"This way," I led him to the armoury and approached the guard. I activated the quest and stepped inside. A weapon master showed up and escorted me into the armoury and pointed to the wall, each with dozens of various weapons hanging from the racks. I looked at the room with wonder. Mage School didn't have this stage of the character. They simply gave you a wand, an orb and a staff and sent you on your way to learning earth shattering abilities. The martial classes, rogues, paladins, hunters, warriors, shamans and, to a lesser extent, druid and monks, all required a weapon and for that player to become proficient with it. I blinked at the selection and began to ponder. Not only would I need to choose a weapon style but I would have to learn *how* to use it. VCO guided a player when they attacked, so to not make it pure combat, but it also allowed those who knew how to use a blade or how to punch, the option to do so unaided. I, however, had no skill in either. I flipped on the targeting guide and approached the weapon master's table.

"No bows," I demanded. I'd tried a hunter in the past and found myself to be *terrible* at archery. I decided to avoid it.

"So be it." The weapon master grabbed something off the table and spun towards me. "Catch!" He flung two coins towards me. I let out a startled yelp and twisted to the side. The coins flew past me and bounced off the floor, skipping across the stone until they came to a halt. I looked back at the master and flashed him a sheepish grin. The master shook his head in disgust. "Perhaps you should become a milkman instead."

"Hey!"

"Quiet." He grabbed my right arm by the wrist and turned the palm downwards. He placed a coin on the back of my hand. He released my hand and held out his in the same fashion. He placed a coin on the back of his hand. "Do as I do."

He flicked his hand upwards and sent the coin into the air, watching as it fell back to earth. He moved his hand, his palm still downwards, beneath the falling coin and raised it quickly to meet the descending currency. He bounced the coin off of his hand Land began the process anew. He repeated it three times, bouncing the coin back up, before snatching it out of the air. Then, he held up his left hand, palm downwards, placed a coin atop of it and re-did the entire exercise. When the coin returned to his left hand he glanced at me. "Go."

I nodded and tossed the coin into the air. I frantically moved my right hand around, each time bouncing the coin but sometimes just barely, until after the third bounce I snatched the coin from the air. I smiled in pride but found only a scowl from the master. My smile faded as I set my left hand for its attempt. It did not go as smoothly. After the first bounce the coin shot outward and flew towards the master's face. He didn't blink or even budge his head. He simply snatched the coin from the air and scowled. "No even blades."

I was fine with that. Rogues could dual wield, it was a major class feature, but they could do so in many fashions. One way was to use two weapons of equal size, like two short swords or, more popularly, two scimitars. This style meant that each hand could move independently of each other, providing true ambidexterity. I did not posses that as a person.

"Catch." The weapon master spun around and pitched two balls at my head. I yelped again, louder than I dared admit, but this time I reached for them. I easily grabbed one ball with my right hand but wasn't fast enough to catch the second. Instead, in an attempt to avoid being hit, I twisted my body and slapped the second ball away with my free left hand.

"No distraction." This style of dual wielding was based around using one weapon to keep an attacker busy, swinging and attacking with one hand, while the other dove in for a kill. This was a step down from the even blade style. The master grabbed two swords off the table and handed them to me. One was a long sword, I took that in my main hand, and the other was a shortsword. I grasped the second with my off-hand. "You'll learn a defensive style."

This style meant that my left blade, my off-hand, would block most of the attacks while my main hand would attack. It was a simple style but an effective one. It was one I could learn. The weapon master drew a longsword from his belt and took a fighting form. "Now we learn: strike."

I tapped my fingers as a shroud of stealth surrounded my body. I crouched down, hugging the wall, and quietly crept down the watchtower's hallway. NPCs resided around me, chatting quietly as they drank and ate. They paid me no heed as I passed by unnoticed.   Each man and woman was a heavily armed soldier of the Royal Army. It was my job to sneak past them and steal a map from the briefing room. The quest was from the thieves' guild. In the lore, this was a test of my abilities. In the game, this was how human rogues learned how to sneak around. The quest was almost impossible to fail, unless you were a true noob, but it was good practice on how to move. If I walked too quickly, my shroud would fail. If I attacked anyone, my shroud would fail. If I used a device or item, my shroud would fail. If my shroud failed, I was in trouble. The thieves guild, while still loyal to the crown, were not the most liked people in the kingdom. Soldiers topped the list of their enemies. I bolted past a doorway, barely avoiding the gaze of a guard, and vanished into the shadows. I crept down the hallways and snuck into the briefing room. Sitting on the table, ripe for the taking, was the desired map. I bolted inward and reached for the map.

"Halt!" I spun around and spotted a guard standing by the wall. I cursed. I didn't look at the room before I entered it, rookie mistake. The guard drew his longsword and lunged. I back-stepped and quickly drew my blades. I brought my shortsword up to the square and blocked the guard's attack, quickly sidestepping. My longsword dashed in to meet the circle and caught the guard on the leg. Another square emerged and my steel moved to meet it, blocking another strike and I pivoted to the side. My body moved on its own as I spun backward and fired a kick. My boot caught the guard's chest and sent him backwards. I lunged in and struck with my longsword, the blade diving into the guard's shoulder. Stepping in, I slammed the butt of my shortsword into the side of his head and watched the guard fall to the ground.

Fighting with VCO's assistance system was an experience that some had trouble adapting to. A hero would strike with a blow and then find that their body would automatically perform the next two attacks in the combination. A hero's body would move on their own, punching and kicking or slashing and stabbing. Some found the effect incredibly disconcerting and had trouble dealing with the lack of control. I was getting used to it. I had lost a majority of life control in the past day that giving up a little bit more seemed like no big deal.

I sheathed my blades, grabbed the map then headed to the door and once more vanished into the shadows. Once I cleared the watchtower, I returned to the guild hall. I was met by Sly Zolton, the recruitment officer for the guild. He stood there with grey hair, an eye-patch and a yellow question mark hovering above his head. I nodded to him and handed him the map. I was bathed in golden light as the words *LEVEL 8* flashed before me in bold golden letters. Sly handed me a pocket full of copper and a leather bracer. I examined the bracer's stats, found them better than the ones I currently wore and swapped them out. I glanced at the clock. I'd been at the grind for twenty minutes and had jumped up eight levels. This was pretty good but it wasn't my best time. Players leveled quickly in the opening area and faster still if you knew how VCO worked.

My stomach growled, reminding me of the looming time limit. I needed food and relatively soon. There was food in VCO but it existed only in lore. In game, food was a one-use consumable that gave stat bonuses. It would do my character good but it wasn't going to affect my RL hunger. I tried to ignore the pain and push onwards. Taking the next quest, I headed towards the inn. My quest was to meet a contact in the inn and play courier with his notes. It was a simple quest, one that started an interesting chain that would lead to the thieves guild into the northern continent for the eventual war outbreak. I always enjoyed the lore quests that build up the story of the various factions. It was quest chains like these that made VCO an immersive world. I entered the inn and slid into the assigned seat. I glanced around the room and spotted a trio of PCs at a far table. One was a mage like me --- like I was, the other was a female warrior and the third was the familiar face of Hizzous. The hunter had on better armour than his starter rags and even had a shiny new-ish bow on his back. I hunched down, my head hidden beneath my hood, and listened as the three talked.

"So you guys can't log out either?" Hizzous said.

"Nope," Jhaara, the female warrior, added. "Stuck like some stupid anime."

"I never would have taken you for an anime kid," Boomizle, the mage, replied. "Let me guess, you're a reverse-harem girl who adores yaoi and ships everybody."

"Bite me, doughboy. Give me shonen or give me death."

"So what will we have to do to log out?" Hizzous asked hesitantly.

"Find the secret, slay the boss and fall in love," Jhaara laughed. "It's standard anime rules."

"Oh man, you know who will probably do get us out, Stov." Boomzile eagerly added. "That guy is booming. I partied with the guy once. He knows everything about everything in this game." My ears perked up at the sound of my name. It always surprised me how people knew me and how they talked about me. "Shame he's been a no show. He's hiding."

"Because of the bounty?" Jhaara nodded. I snapped my head towards them.

"What bounty?" Hizzous sheepishly asked.

"Big guy on campus Steelion put a bounty on Stov," Boomzile explained. "Apparently, the mage ninja'd something good from him and the warrior calling for his head. The offer is a fuck ton of gold, a rare item and protection."

Gold, an item and protection; I had to think in genre tropes. If this game had become some sort of digital prison then I was going to see your standard post-apocalypse scenarios. Some big-headed idiot was going to start a gang and start terrorizing the low-level noobs. Despite our differences, Steelion wasn't an idiot and he wasn't the bad guy. If he was offering protection then the gangs had already started. Steelion was good at what he did and he had the gear to back it up. If anybody could play the hero it could be him. The bounty, however, called into question the whole he wasn't the *bad guy* aspect.

I had to hide from him and luckily I'd already found the easiest way to do that. I would just be Rake. Steelion didn't know the name of my bank-alt and I wasn't about to tell him. Hell, if I was crazy enough, I could even join his gang as Rake and hide in plain sight. As much as I liked the idea, I wasn't crazy enough to risk it.

"Having a rough day?" The dwarven waitress' voice pulled my attention. I just nodded at the NPC. "Having trouble logging out, all you player types been complaining about that."

I snickered. "It's been weird, alright."

"You need anything to eat or drink." I shook my head, instantly regretting the motion. It was pointless to order food. "Just give me a holler if you need me." I glanced back at the table of PCs.

"So I ordered you some steel pie." I snickered as Jhaara slid the pie towards Hizzous. Steel pie was an in-game prank that experience players played on noobs. You gave them a pie - a rotten pie - and they ate it. The pie, instead of giving a stat boots, would knock your stats back 75% for two hours. It was horrible prank but it was an effective one. The noob quickly learned about stats, de-buffs and they'd learn the most important lesson of all: don't trust people on the internet.

"Is this good food? It smells weird." I bit my tongue as I tried to stifle my laugh.

"Yeah, it's cool."

"O...okay." Hizzous took a bite and instantly spat it out. "Oh god, it tastes rotten."

The two players hysterically laughed. I wanted to join them but I couldn't, my mind was too focused on what the hunter had just said. It tasted rotten. It tasted rotten; taste. There was no taste in VCO. I stood up and walked to the bar. I scrolled down the food list and clicked on the red apple option. It materialized before me, I grabbed it and lifted it to my lips. I took a big bite and froze. I could taste the sweetness of the fruit, I could feel the juices running down my chin and I could feel my body hungrily demanding more. I could taste the apple.

Suddenly my brain caught up. I was dizzy, my body was stiff, I was sore, I had a headache and I vomited. None of that was supposed to happen in VCO, those aspects were beyond the immersion tech. Somehow, I was able to do and feel things in the game that I was never before able to do. How had I missed the signs before? The headache: I had smashed my head on the stone building. Shit; I had a concussion.

That conclusion left me with more questions than answers. How the hell does somebody smash their head off of a digital wall and get a real concussion in the process? How did digital food have a taste? How did I throw up and how did I feel pain in my digital body? None of it made any sense unless.....

The *unless* reason sounded crazy, it sounded crazier than crazy. It was impossible. The only way any of this was possible was if the game world was is if this was the real world. VCO was becoming real.

I let the words hover in my head. VCO was becoming real. What did that mean? Why was it happening? How was it happening? Was this the reason why I couldn't log out? Was logging out still a possibility? The questions continued to build as my answers did not. So what happened now?

Chapter 05

"There is safety in mindfulness." — Fawkes (Fallout 3)

I sat by Emerald Lake and stared into the glistening water. Whenever I was lost in a puzzle or bored with VCO and RL combined I would fly to Sparkling Falls and just watch the water tumble down to the earth. Stov had a wide variety of flying mounts, Rake did not. Rake had two feet and a heartbeat and that was it. Rake -- I -- couldn't reach the falls, so I was forced to use the lake instead. It wasn't as magnificent but it would have to do.

I was a city boy, through and through, and sadly I rarely made it out camping. Perhaps that was why I found myself drawn to the glistening waters of Aspumer. I fished out another apple from my bag, the food digitizing in my hand, and rubbed it on my sleeve. I took a bite. My hunger was gone, the digital food somehow silencing my rumbling stomach. Unless my body was operating under a placebo effect, starving was no longer an issue.

"Hey'ya, Rake." I looked up from the water and saw Hizzous standing by me. "How's it going, man?" I gave him a shrug. "Right; dumb question." Silence hung between us. "I'm doing a quest involving the fish-men. Do you wanna join me?"

I knew the quest he was on. By endgame standards it was a nothing quest but by early game content it was difficult. Having a second person would limit the amount of risk we took. Before the Glitch, I would have done the mission alone.

I would fight and possibly die. Then I would respawn, march back in and kill whoever was left standing but now I didn't want to risk death, especially not if things were turning real.

"Why not?" I sighed.

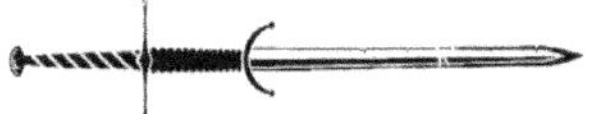

We approached the camp and stared at the fish-men. They were brutal creatures, with monstrous visages the like of the writings of H.P. Lovecraft. They moved in packs, swarmed like wolves and killed with the brutality of a savage barbarian. I pointed at the small coastal camp. "There's the target. The big guy in the middle is their leader and he's the target for the mission."

"Sweet," Hizzous eagerly replied. "So we march in, fill them with arrows and stab wounds, loot their corpses and dance our way out of there."

I eyed him with concern. He blinked at me for a moment. "You have a better idea?"

"We have to be careful. We don't know what happens when we die," I explained. "So I think we have to be more tactical. Do you know what kiting is?" Hizzous nodded. "Good. I'll get into position and while you take aim."

I activated my stealth and vanished amongst the trees. Kiting was the practice of luring a target away from its position into one that was more favourable for the attacker. Kiting was often done by a range DPS like a mage, warlock or hunter. A single spell or arrow would catch the spawn's attention. Experience had taught me that kiting was dangerous. One wrong shot or spell and suddenly it wouldn't be one spawn chasing after you but an entire mob.

I moved from tree to tree, slowly approaching the fishmen camp. The slimy creature were known as the Nthlai. They were born from the dark abyss that existed beneath the ocean's depth. They had always existed in Aspumer, swimming to the surface in small clusters, but in recent years they had emerged from the ocean in greater numbers. The deep ones were massing but nobody knew for what reason. I had theories, Casper always liked dropping hints, but I hadn't dug to deep into their mythos. Truth was the Nthlai made me uneasy.

I knelt behind a tree and waited. I didn't have to wait for long before an arrow flew across the air and landed in the chest of a surprised fishmen. It moved away from the rest of them, numbering nearly fifteen, and moved towards Hizzous. As it passed me, unaware of my position, the targeting circle popped up and I struck. My longsword dug into its side as my shortsword fed upon the fishmen's neck. I struck again, both blades striking quickly. A pair of arrows dove into the creature's chest and it fell over dead. The plan went off without a hitch. I messaged Hizzous and we restarted. As I waited for the next to approach, I eyed the timer for my combo points.

Each class in VCO played a little differently than the one before it. Warlocks, mages and priests used mana for spells. Bear druids and warriors used rage. Cat druids, monks, hunters and rogues used combo points. As a rogue, this meant I got points for using my attacks and abilities. When I used my finishers, which were bigger and flashier moves, I did more damage based on the number of points I had built up.

As a lowbie rogue my move choices were limited. I had my basic bladework, a saber slash and only a single finisher move called cross slash. So as the next couple Nthlai came at me I called on those abilities to fight them off. My blades were slow but there were accurate. I cut at the next fishmen, each hit creating another point, and used my saber slash to fell it. The third approached and struck again, filling my combo meter. I activated the cross slash and watched as my body moved on its own, striking with both blades in an X fashion. My combo meter emptied but the damage was enough to defeat the fishman in a single blow.

One after another, we clobbered the Nthlai. We had slain three of them when the plan exploded. Hizzous was kiting the fourth when a blue ball of magic fell from the sky and landed directly in the middle of the Nthlai camp. The arcane ball exploded, sending each of the fishmen into a furious rage.

The creatures roared and turned towards me. Stealth was only as good as the one spawn that was lucky enough to roll high in their spot check. When one fishmen saw me, they all did and at that moment eleven fishmen were staring directly at me. Shit.

"Hizzous! Incoming!" I yelled backwards as the Nth-lai charged at me, a bizarre spear in each of their hands. I back peddled through the woods, my swords at the ready. Hizzous' arrows rained downed on the charging fishmen as my steel danced. My shortsword met the defensive squares as they popped up and I slapped aside each of the thrusting barbed spearheads. When the circle would pop up I'd move to meet it, causing my longsteel to dive in. I watched as red numbers floated in the air, a new one emerging with each strike. I'd fell one only to take a strike from a second. I would strike the second only to have the third and fourth each score a hit. I struck down the third as the fifth and sixth join the fourth, with the seventh and eighth not far behind. I was being swarmed and I was running out of options. Stov could have handled this fight with no problem but Rake was something different. My skill with steel wasn't great, my speed not enough to fend them off.

My screen began to fill with squares but they were too many to meet. Spear after spear dug into my flesh. My HP was dropping rapidly and I was well below a quarter health. I had nowhere to run and nowhere to hide. I wasn't able to fight them off. In short, Rake was about to die and I was about to find out what happened when he did.

Shit; I was about to die.

A shadowy fog crossed over my body and my wounds began to knit together. My HP suddenly jumped to full. I blinked in surprise and gave silent thanks to whatever healer happened to be walking by. A second later a wave of shadowy energy shot up from the ground, grabbed the raging fishmen and slammed them against the ground. One blow was all it took before the lot of them died, their bodies crumpling to the dirt before lying still.

I let out a sigh of relief and dropped to my knees, gasping for air as my heart raced a mile a minute. Looking up across the fields, I spotted Jhaara and Boomizle standing on a hill, the pair laughing loudly. The blue ball of magic was a mage spell. It was an AOE spell meant to enrage the spawns. It was a spell that was normally reserved for dungeons or raids and it was only meant to be used when the mage had a party behind him. So when Boomizle casted the spell, it was for no other reason than to be a dick. He was trying to troll noobs by swarming them with spawns. In normal gameplay the act was little more than a nuisance; in normal gameplay it made the caster an asshole. Now it made Boomizle something darker.

I looked behind me and spotted the familiar face of Tialla. She held aloft her new staff, my gift towards her, and gave her a nod of thanks. I waved Hizzous over and together we looted the bodies. There wasn't much in the way of treasure but there were coins and a fair amount for our levels. With my pockets full of coin, I bolted after Tialla. I chased her down, calling out her name as I ran. She stopped and looked back at me.

"Tialla," I said between pants."I owe you thanks. We wouldn't have survived that without you."

She smiled at me.

So how you been? You hear anything about all this?" She gave me a confused look and raised her hands into the air. She stood there silently, moving them to and fro. Eventually, with a surprised look, she spoke. "Stov?"

"I...wha....how...." I stammered.

"I have an app installed," she explained. "It lets me see who's alt belongs to whom. I got it about a year ago when some guy started stalking me in the game. BTW - thanks for the staff. You were right; it's really helping my healing."

"My pleasure."

"So what are you doing as a rogue and a low level one at that?" She asked.

"This is my bank alt. When things went tits up I got stuck in this."

"Everybody is stuck in a video game like some bad

TV," she laughed, "and you're stuck in your damn bank alt?" I nodded and she laughed even louder. I stood there awkwardly for nearly five minutes as she laughed. My face held a large frown upon it. The joke was quickly wearing thin.

"What are you doing in low-level territory?" I asked, hoping to dissuade her laughter.

"Havenhold is no longer safe. Gangs have showed up, like some damn *Mad Max* movie, and are turning things to shit. I'm hiding out here until things die down." she said, her laughter dying immediately.

It made sense. It also partially verified what I was worried about. Gangs had shown up. Now how Havenhold went from *Gangs of New York* to *let's obey Steelion and hunt down Stov* was still beyond me.

"So what has the great and powerful Stov learned about this glitch?"

I leaned up by the nearest tree and frowned. "I haven't found out much. All I know is that I can't log out, I can't call for help and this isn't entirely a game anymore. I can get seriously injured, I can get sick and food suddenly acts like it's real." She gave me a curious eye so I explained.

"Shit," she said after a moment of silence. She pulled up her menu and materialized a sandwich in her hand. She took several bites and quickly downed the food. A look of relief crept across her face. "Food has become real." I expect a look of concern but from someone who looked like she hadn't eaten in a couple days, relief was more important. Tialla materialized a second sandwich and silently ate it. The first one she wolfed down, the second she savoured.

"The taste," she said suddenly. "It taste like it should but it taste kinda off."

"I've noticed," I explained. "It reminds me of bread that's about to go bad. It's like the game hasn't gotten food just right." I paused. "You hear anything about what's happening to people who die in the game?"

"All I know is people fall and they aren't coming back. The game still shows that they're logged in but they aren't reappearing," she said. "And I think things are messing with people's emotions. When people get mad, they get *really* mad. When people get sad, they're getting *really* sad. Some are even taking their own lives."

"Shit." That wasn't what I wanted to hear. Dead in the game essentially meant dead in RL. Fuck; that was the *worst* case scenario.

"Do you know what triggered this?" she asked. "If food is turning real and you're concussed and throwing up, then this is more than some simple glitch." Her logic made sense to me. "So what triggered it?"

"I'm not sure yet," I explained. "I mean, there was lore shit going on with masked mages and shit but in the real world, I don't know."

"What if this is some magic shit," Tialla said quietly.

"Magic, really?" I said with a smirk.

"I mean there is nothing in the real world that can turn 0s and 1s into actual food and damage. So what if it actually is magic?" Tialla shrugged. "When you have eliminated the impossible, whatever remains, however improbable, must be the truth. Sherlock Holmes said that."

Magic. Well shit. How the hell was I going to deal with magic?

"What do you know about this bounty?" I sheepishly asked.

"Steelion is pissed at you," Tialla said. "What is the deal between you two? This bounty can't just be because you ninja'd him. What's the story there?"

I breathed deep. "Steelion and I met shortly after launch. We pugged together, found out we worked well together and became friends. He starts recruiting me to hunt treasure and it turns out I'm good at it. Steelion teaches me about selling weapons and gear for RL money. He takes me under his wing and shows me the ropes. It's going well until I blow past him. It turns out that for a lore fiend like me, treasure hunting is the perfect job.

"So I get good at treasure hunting. I get *very* good at

it. I find shit the people didn't even know existed in the game. I decipher Casper's puzzles and sell some of the best shit. I run through dungeons and raids and sell what I find. Most of what I sell is rare and is being sold by others. What makes me special is I got a rep and a good one. Steelion doesn't. Add into the fact that I *seriously* undercut him on every sale means he's has a *serious* chip on his shoulder towards me."

"So the sword?"

"Just the straw," I explained. "I mean a seriously expensive straw but just a straw.

"Well I'd keep your head low," Tialla warned. "He's got people all riled up. Everybody and their mother are out hunting for Stov. I know we've just met but I'm in no rush to see you in the dirt."

Chapter 06

"If only I could handle my problems like a video-game style battle against a boss. But there are no power-ups in real life. No FTW moment when I can declare total pwnage. I don't even know who the bad guys are." — Kat Kruger, The Night Has Claws

Waking up in the game was still a new experience. I wasn't used to opening my eyes and seeing endless blue sky, vibrant green trees and sparkling water. I wasn't used to hearing the chirp of birds and the sound of nature. I was used to a crappy apartment, stale air and the sounds of a whirring computer fan and the echoing siren of a cop car. Aspumer definitely won in the wake up department but the city boy that I was still missed the sounds of cars and sirens.

I climbed out of my sleeping bag and looked at the firepit. Gone were the flame and wood, replaced by the remaining black ashes. I rubbed my head and winced. Pain still emanated from my head, the concussion still reminding me of its existence. The pain had lessened but luckily the nausea, vomiting and dizziness had gone the way of the dodo bird.

I climbed to my feet and started to dismantle my camp. As I rolled up my sleeping bag, I began to plan out my day. It had been five days since the game changed and I was still unable to log out. Five long days had passed with me being stuck in the game and I still hadn't figured out why or how. I had zero leads as to what made things change and even fewer leads on how to get out of VCO. I was still operating under my original four trope rules, albeit with edits:

1: Death in the game possibly meant death in real
　　life. DO NOT DIE.
2: I couldn't be forcibly removed from a game. I
　　was stuck here
3: There is no time limit. Food and Drink are not
　　an issue.
4: Winning meant I could leave. Find the boss and
　　beat him.

I still hadn't confirmed the first point but evidence was pointing in that direction. With food becoming real I had disproved my original third point. Point two and four were still in full effect. With my camp dismantled I opened up the world map. I plotted a course for the Stenha Library. It was a place of learning that existed outside the human starting area. In game terms it was the hub for the next layer of quests. The Vineyard was meant to take players from level 1 to level 12. The farms would bring the player from level 12 to 24 and the library would take player from level 25 to level 30. At my current level, 25, the library would be perfect to continue my grind but my urge to go there had little to do with that.

In lore, the Stenha Library was built by Lord Dorian Bullmourn. He was a seeker of knowledge and believed that intelligence was more important than magic or steel. Lord Dorian Bullmourn was also the head of a spy organization known as the Whispers. While this fact was known to every player - he doled out several quests - in lore it was a closely guarded secret. In this corner of the world, the library was small but it held a wide and varied collection. The royal library, located in Havenhold, was one of the biggest libraries in all of Aspumer. However, with the bounty on my head, I was less than eager to return to city.

I materialized some food and ate a quick breakfast before setting out. My plan was to make it to the Stenha Library and continue my investigation. If I was still working on rule four as a fact, then I needed to find out some lead about who triggered this change in VCO and - to a lesser extent - why.

Without access to the internet, the best place to learn anything was a library.

Tialla was waiting for me in the library. It was a surprised because I wasn't expecting her to be there. She smiled as she saw me enter and waved me over. I passed by Lord Bullmourn, ignoring his quest icon, and slid into a chair across from the priestess.

"What's a guy like you doing in a place like this?" she said with a smile. I smirked back at her.

"Of all the gin joints in all of the cities," I began. I didn't need to finish the quote before she laughed. "So what are you doing here?"

"I'm doing the same thing as you," she declared. "I'm here playing detective like some fantasy Jessica Jones."

"Technically, you're trying to decipher ruins and uncover a puzzle," I corrected, "like some fantasy-based Lara Croft."

She looked down at her chest and thoughtfully stared at her breasts. After a moment she shrugged. "I don't know if I have the assets to be Lady Croft but I'll take it." We laughed together. "Okay, Ben Gates, let's see what we have, shall we?"

I winced at the Nic Cage character but pushed past it. Tialla told me of the investigating she had been doing. She'd been asking around, talking to players and seeing what stories they had to tell. Most of the stories were the same. People were as shocked and surprised at the glitch as we were. Word of food turning real had quickly spread - something I was thankful for - but little was known of exactly what had happened. There were rumours, everything from a glitch in the Matrix to some government conspiracy, but nobody knew anything for a fact.

"A lot of these could be plausible leads," Tialla explained, "but all I have is unverified reports from second and third sources. There is nothing to go on. So, what have you got? Since our investigation into plausible explanations has run dry of leads, I think we should look into our less plausible theory."

"Our?" I mocked. "When did this become our theory? When did you take up my investigation?"

Tialla just shrugged. "We all have a life to get back to, Rake. I want to get back to mine just as you want to get back to yours. There are just as many theories about how we get home as there are about what happened. Most sound crazy. Yours isn't any better but it is easier to grasp. So until someone comes with a better theory, I'll tag along with you."

"If you find yourself in a trope you can complain or you can hang a lantern on it and play by its rules," I explained. "So do you have experience in an investigation?"

Tialla shrugged again. She remained silent. I took the hint and moved on. I held up my hand and materialized the screenshot I took of the moon. I handed it to her.

"Right before the glitch, there was a world event in progress. It was for Patch 7.0.3."

"Yeah, the pre-expansion patch for the upcoming *From Perdition to Rapture*."

"I see Admiral Crowley doing his best *the end is nigh* impression. He points out the moon and I see *that* etched on the damned moon." I tapped the picture with my index finger. "Then the city gets attacked by these mobs. They're dressed in black armour and were wearing half mask that look identical to the one etched on the moon."

"I faced a couple," Tialla explained. "So who are they?"

"I have no clue," I explained, "not a single fucking clue. But I think I could change that. Casper loves his riddles. Nothing is simple; not his puzzles, not his factions and not his villains. This is the sixth expansion. You can't just throw a new bad into the world. Things have to be built up. He would have dropped hints about who this bad is."

"So how do we find it? I mean these masked attackers would have been the first wave in a long list of hidden attackers. This was supposed to be Casper's big mystery expansion.

He revealed the shadowy threat but not who was behind it."

"Casper loves his hints," I explained. "He won't just spring a bad on us, he'll drop crumbs and award those who follow the trail. I think the first clue is here." I tapped the picture once again. Tailla pulled the picture toward her and carefully studied the snap.

"What does the mask mean?"

"No clue."

"Okay, what does the runes in the eye and mouth mean?"

"Haven't the foggiest."

"So what good are you?" Tialla asked in jest.

"I'm here to find those out." I pointed at the legion of books. "I'm hoping that if food is real, then so are books."

Tialla looked at the library and let out a small chuckle. "I love me a good library."

My hunch proved true and hours passed as we studied. I started with scrolls of crests and symbols and moved from there. Tialla decided to study the arcane runes. When one scroll or book proved fruitless, we moved to another. We studied until there was a mountain of books, tomes, journal and scrolls between the two of us but still we found nothing.

"I have another tome that may help," a voice said. I looked up and saw the figure of a female NPC standing over me. Her name was Garruil and she was one of Lord Bullmourn's legion. I took the tome from her and quickly thanked her for her assistance.

Garruil, along with the rest of Bullmourn's men and women, had been incredibly helpful. It was surprising. I had started to see the NPCs begin to act more like *real* people but I hadn't expected them to be so helpful and forthcoming. I had expected them to be hesitant and scared of players.

"I have other books that may prove helpful but truth be told, Rake, for arcane symbols like the one you search, the Royal Library would hold your answer. If you need an introduction, I could provide you with one. I know one of the curators there."

"Thanks," I stammered, once again caught off-guard by her friendliness. "I'll keep that in mind." I nervously rubbed my arm, bare from the sleeveless vest I wore. I opened up the book and started to flip through it. It was a book on dark mages and their cults throughout Aspumer's violent history. I thumbed through the pages, scanning through names and looking at the sketches of mages and their signatures. A symbol caught my eye and forced me to pause. The symbol looked like two Us atop each other, the top one right side up while the bottom was upside down. The two Us crossed over each other, like a Venn diagram. I glanced at the mage's name: Kahail Voltair.

Kahail wasn't a mad mage with his own cult; he was a wizard who had sacrificed his morality for his work. He believed that each man held lightning within them and he longed to find a way to use it against the dangers that threatened the world. Kahail worked with the best intentions, believing the ends justified the means, but he went too far. He joined the Nohorian Brotherhood for their resources and continued his work. Kahail was a man who was obsessed with lightning and laced his personal current within all weapons he forged.

I ran my fingers over Kahail's symbol, his arcane signature and found myself frowning. Why did the Kahail symbol look familiar? Why did I know it? I took a deep breath in and let it exhale loudly and I rubbed my forehead. Pain still resided in my skull and my thought process was fuzzy. Nothing was clear.

"You okay?" Tialla asked. I nodded. She saw the look on my face and didn't push further. Instead she changed the topic. "You know I still owe you thanks."

"For what?"

"The staff," she explained. "It's been a big help."

"You're helping me here," I defended. "That's thanks enough."

"I'm here for my own reasons. I still owe you. What

do you need?"

"Well if you're in a charitable mood, I won't say no to twink gear."

"How about a lucky dagger?"

"I'd love one," I laughed. "But it can only be wielded by someone level 50 or higher."

Lucky daggers were off-hand weapons that were built to help raise the critical percentile of that attack. Good rogues used it as a throwing weapon. Great rogues used it as an off-hand damage monster.

"Are you sure? It doesn't say that on the weapon." Of course it did. Lucky daggers were a decent seller for me. I knew the blade by heart. Tialla slid the dagger across the table and I glanced at it. I tapped the hilt and watched the stats appear before me.

Lucky Dagger
Requirement: None
Drop Rate: 38.62%

WTF? What the *actual* fuck? There was no level requirement. What was happening? I looked up in shock. "Quick - check your gear. Is there a level requirement?" She looked. Moments later she shook her head. Was this part of the Glitch? If so, then this was a game changer.

"Thanks," I said, pocketing the dagger. "This will seriously help."

"My pleasure," she said with a smile. Silence filled the air between us until she pointed at the book "What's that?"

"Just some write up about some mage. I recognize the wizard's signature but I don't know from where."

Tialla grabbed the book and gave the book a scan. "What's the Nohorian Brotherhood? They in the game?"

"Simply put, the Nohorian Brotherhood is a power hungry cult," Garruil said. I spun around. I never heard the woman approach. How the hell was a librarian so quiet? "They've allied themselves with some frightening powers in the past. After the Dragon Wars, the cult was presumed destroyed or disbanded..." Her voice trailed off.

"But?" Tialla asked.

"But Lord Bullmourn thinks otherwise. He says he hasn't seen proof that they still exist. So they probably do." I looked confused but Tialla smiled.

"How many reports of MJ still being alive popped up? How many stories that Tupac is still alive do we hear every year?" Tialla explained. "When people are dead and gone we always hear rumours that they aren't. So the fact that they haven't heard anything about this cult means somebody is trying *real* hard to stay hidden." Tialla's words made sense. "So what has the Nohorian Brotherhood been involved in?"

"There are unconfirmed reports that --" I interrupted Garruil's words with a wave of my hand. I materialized my brown journal and placed it on the table. I tapped it twice and activated my second add-on. I sighed in relief as the journal glowed and flipped open.

My second add-on was the VCO wiki. I couldn't install the full wiki into the game, that was stupid and ridiculous, but my add-on did allow me to build a direct link to the online database. The add-on, which looked like a journal, allowed me to dive directly into the wiki without having to logout of the game.

Normally when the journal add-on activated, a small keyboard would pop-out but this time it didn't. The journal acted like a regular journal, with nothing special about it. It did, however, give off a golden glow and allowed me to search the wiki simply by touching the journal's pages and guiding it by thought. I ran my fingers over the pages and willed the journal to bring forth the Nohorian Brotherhood information. The empty pages glowed for a moment before they filled with paragraphs and pictures on the cult. I pushed the journal towards Tialla.

"The Brotherhood are assholes," I laughed. "They played both sides during the Dragon War, unleashed the Crypt Walker's curse on both factions and even betrayed the Fallen

Goddess for a hint of her god-spark."

"Rake."

"Man, I loved the Wurm Nest raid," I said.

"Rake."

"I ran that raid so many times that I could have timed when every crow flew by."

"Rake!"

"What?"

I looked at Tialla. She pushed the journal back at me and pointed at the image. "Look at the Nohorian Brotherhood's logo."

I glanced down. The Brotherhood's logo was four lines that emerge from a center point and curved outwards, each in a different direction. I blinked. The top left line, which curved to the right but ended facing the left, looked like what could only be described as a melted question mark.

"Am I seeing things, Rake, or does that line look like the mark on the moon's mask?" Tialla asked. I cursed. The last thing I needed was for the Nohorian Brotherhood to be involved with the Glitch. The Brotherhood's involvement seemed like the worst thing that could happen. Suddenly a private message popped up before my eyes.

Slashlore: U at the Stenha Library?
Rake: Yeah - why?
Slashlore: Steelion knows you're Rake. He's sending a strike team against you.
Rake: Fuck!

It never ceases to amaze me how quickly I can be wrong.

Chapter 07

**"Wonderful craftsmanship, Simon decided with the expert eye of one
who had played enough computer games to know art when he saw it."**
— Sorin Suciu, The Scriptlings

I blinked the PMs and found myself without words.
I was stunned. How the hell did Steelion learn about my alter ego? Anonymity had been my only armour. I was under-
geared, under-leveled and in no way ready to fight Steelion. I
had been counting of anonymity to stay alive. Now I needed a
new plan. Now I needed to run.

 Rake: WTF man? What happened?
 Slashlore: I think I screwed up. I think it's my fault
and I'm sorry.
 Rake: Your fault? What did you do?
 Slashlore: Dude, I fucked up. I'm sorry.
 Slashlore: Blame me later. Hate me later. But get the
fuck out now.
 Slashlore: Run!

"I gotta go," I said suddenly.
Tialla looked at me with concern as I grabbed my journal and
shoved it into my backpack. "What's wrong?"
 I looked at Garruil. "I need a couple books, that
okay?"
 "Anything for a member." Her words struck me as
odd but I ignored it and kept packing.
 "Rake, what's wrong?" Tialla asked again.

"Steelion knows that I'm Rake, he knows my location and he just sent a strike-team to kill me."

"Shit, how did he find out?"

"I don't know. I think a friend fucked up."

"Who is this Steelion?" Garruil asked.

"He's a warrior who hates my guts and put a bounty on my head," I said as I packed. "He wants me dead."

The look on Garruil's face changed from confusion to anger. Without another word she stormed off. I didn't waste time watching her go.

"What now?" Tialla asked.

"I don't know," I admitted. "I'm going to run and hide and try to grind while I can. Eventually, I have to make my way to the Royal Library but I need this heat to die down first and in order to that I need to survive that long."

I grabbed my bag and moved for the door. I took a couple steps and paused. I looked back at Tialla. "You need to get the hell out of here. You don't want to be seen with me. There is no telling what Steelion's been doing to people he thinks are helping me."

I bolted out the door and slid to a halt. Standing before me was a group of four heavily gear players being led by a familiar face: Bearcules.

"Hello, Stov," he said with a grin.

"Bear! How you doin'? How's that ring working for you?" I stammered.

"Shut the fuck up," he snapped. "We're bringing you to Steelion, alive or dead. It's your choice."

"I'll pick the *or* choice?" I laughed. "It'll help with my blacksmithing."

"Do you know what Steelion did when he found out you were stuck in your bank-alt?" Bearcules asked. "He laughed for five minutes straight."

That reaction was beginning to wear thin.

"Why are you working with him?" I asked, stalling as I tried to formulate a plan. It was hard to come up with anything clever when you're staring at a druid, two rogues, a warlock and a priest. It was a party of five without Matthew Fox, Neve Campbell or Jennifer Love Hewitt. I didn't even think that was possible.

"Sides are forming, gangs are starting and Steelion is the biggest and the loudest," the first rogue said, speaking in an honest to God Jersey accent.

"Siding with him is just good business," the female rogue added with an accent that sounded like Snooki.

"And that bounty can't hurt either," I laughed.

Nobody laughed with me. I sighed. Comedy is dead.

"So here's what I propose," I began. "It's a little out there so bear with me....."

I bolted back inside and slammed the door shut. I dashed to the nearest table and grabbed the chair. I bolt back towards the door. I was going to wedge the chair into the door but never got the chance. The library's door exploded as a familiar bear barrelled his way through. I slid to a halt and whipped the chair at Bearcules. I turned around and dashed further into the library. I grabbed Tialla by the arm and dragged her with me.

"Okay," I yelled. "Things have taken a turn for the worse. The whole situation is a little more grizzled then I would like."

Bear puns. I am totally proud of that one.

Tialla looked over her shoulder and cursed. "Bearcules?"

"Apparently Steelion is doing his best *Warriors* impression and now has a gang. So I suggest getting the fuck out of here." My ears perked as I heard the familiar sound of a spell being cast. I grabbed Tialla and dove to the floor as a green ball of arcane flame flew past our heads. It hit the far wall and exploded in sickly green flames. "Fucking 'locks. Who the hell *willingly* plays a whorelock?"

We scrambled to our feet to see the pair of rogues descending upon us. Pauly D and Snookie moved as a well trained pair. The male went left as the female went right. They were flanking us like a group of raptors.

"Clever girl," I muttered as I drew my blades. "Welp - we're boned."

Tialla raised her hand and called upon the shadows. Tendrils of darkness rose from the ground and lashed out at Pauly D. I moved to meet Snookie. Defensive squares popped up quickly and I spun my blades to meet them. Her steel bounced off of mine. I spotted the attack circles as they emerged, openings from which I was to strike, but I could never reach them in time, my blades being forced to deflect and defend instead of attack not that a strike from me would do any damage at all.

Fighting in VCO was based off of levels and stats. At level 25 my attack was so low that even if it landed a hit on Snookie it would never get past her armour to do damage. Her attack was high enough and my defence low enough that if she did as little as lightly scratch me, she could do enough damage to drop me.

Tialla raised her other hand as she called upon a shadowy shield, deflecting another incoming blast from the warlock named Fleyming. Her hands moved quickly as she faced off against two opponents. She called upon shield to block the warlock as she ordered her shadowy aberrations to attack Pauly D. Then she'd switch, directing her attack at the unsuspecting warlock.

A battle cry rang out as the familiar form of Garruil dropped from the rafters and slammed her foot into Snookie's side. The female rogue flew across the room. Garruil quickly pivoted and fired a second kick into the legs a surprised Pauly D. His legs buckled and he crumpled to the ground. I stood there stunned.

"Run," Garruil snapped. "Run now."

Tailla grabbed my arm and pulled me away. I looked back as we ran and spotted the two guidos and the warlock descending upon the librarian with swift attacks from their daggers and dangerous spells but Garruil stood firm. Her arms and legs jetted out, blocking an attack from one as she would slap away the strike from another, all the while dodging spells and striking back with attacks of her own. Her limbs were a blur as she fought. Garruil was a monk and a damned good one at that. She fought using a style similar to Wing Chun. She looked like a female Donnie Yen. She was one with the force and the force was with her.

Tialla pulled me through the library as Bearcules chased after us. There is something terrifying about being chased by a bear. It's hard to put my finger on what exactly makes it terrifying but if I had to guess, I would say it's because bears are godless killers and they run hella fast. Tialla slid to a stop, spun around and once again called upon the shadows for assistance. Darkness crawled across the floor, consuming the light until it had created a dome of darkness. She lowered her hand.

"That should give us ---" her words were cut off as a beam of divine light pierced the dome and quickly dissipated the darkness. Tialla cursed. She spotted the dwarven priest and frowned. The dwarf approached us; his hands covered in a golden glow, and started to tap out another spell. I moved without thinking. I grabbed the lucky dagger from my belt and delicately held it between my fingers. I arched my hand back as an attack circle appeared before me. I flung my hand towards the circle and released the dagger. The dagger flew through the library and collided with the priest's right shoulder. The dwarf stumbled backwards and held a stunned look on his face. His tapping stopped and his spell fizzled. The dagger dematerialized and returned to my hand.

"Enough of this shit, Stov," Bearcules roared. "I'm tired of your games."

"Why? Do you find it em-bear-assing?" I flashed a panicked grin. "Just bear with me a second; I mean what pawsible benefit is there for you bring me to Steelion with your bear hands? I mean then you're going to have to listen to him roar about his accomplishment while he treats you like some cub. Nobody deserves such a grizzled fate. I mean come on, Honey, you're better than that."

Bearcules stood there stunned. For a moment he did

nothing but blink. Eventually he spoke, asking in disbelief. "Are you making Bear Puns? Do you think this is funny?"

"Wakka Wakka?"

I was about to die but it was *totally* worth it.

They attacked by surprise and saved my life. The librarians emerged, led by Lord Bullmourn, and attacked in full force. They were twelve of them in total and each fought with a high amount of skills. Bullmourn swung with his onyx-blade longsword as others attacked with pairs of daggers or staves. He charged Bearcules, his NPC sword cutting deep into the tank's hide. Bearcules stumbled backwards in shock. His shock mimicked my own. Why were the librarians coming to my defence and more importantly, did all librarians fight like this?

"Take him out the back," Lord Bullmourn yelled. Garruil yelled out a verbal confirmation and grabbed my arm. She pulled me and Tialla by our arms and escorted us through the back. We cleared several hallways before Garruil stopped at a bookshelf. She reached up, pulled out a book and watched as the bookshelf gave way to reveal a hidden door. I smirked. Never mess with the classics.

"Thank you for your help," Tialla said. "You have gone above and beyond to help us."

"We would do the same for any member of our organization." Tialla looked at me with a look of confusion but Garruil never gave her the chance to speak. She pointed to my tattoo. "You wear our symbol. Only those who have sworn our oath dare to wear our symbol and those who have sworn that oath will do whatever they can to protect one of our own."

I stood there, speechless. My tattoo was purely cosmetic. They meant nothing in the terms of the game. NPCs never noticed them and they never granted access or allegiances. They just looked cool. Now it was different. Now librarians-spies were coming to my defense.

"Many thanks to you and M'Lord," I said, choosing to speak like them for a moment. "Tell Lord Bullmourn that if he needs me, he needs only send for me."

I bow before the NPC, before my fellow spy and exited through the hidden door. I started to breathe lighter as I saw daylight but the moment I stepped out of the library I noticed the dwarf priest was waiting for me.

Name: Holmiarty
Class: Priest Lvl: 90

"That was a good play, Mr. Rake," the dwarf said calmly. "I'm not sure how you were able to get the NPCs to defend you but it caused a retreat."

"And yet you're still here," I said carefully. I glanced behind me and saw Tialla slowly exiting. "So what made you stay when the others ran?"

"The others didn't know how to respond to such an alteration in a plan. They weren't willing to adapt. I was." It made sense. Holmiarty was a strategist. VCO attracted all sorts of players. Some like to slay endless hordes of bad guys like Legolas stuck in *Groundhog Day*. Some liked to quest, others liked to PVP, some liked to treasure hunt - like me - and some liked to plan the perfect run dungeons and raids. They were the strategists. They were the ones who liked to plan for every attack and every possible outcome. For every attack that happened, they had a counter. When Tialla filled the room with darkness, he assaulted it with light.

"So what happens now? There are two of us and one of you," I asked. "I'll admit I'm under-leveled but the odds are still against you."

"I assumed that you wouldn't be alone. The great Stov doesn't get as big as he did without making friends. So I came up with a couple ways to remove your potential allies from the combat," Holmiarty explained. "Since Ms. Tialla is primarily a shadow priestess, I will use burst of holy energy to stun her then cast a purifying spell to temporarily drain her of her shadow energy. Then I'll assault you. By this time she will have regained her spells and she will attempt to fight back. I will dissuade that course of action with threat of violence upon your person. In short I will threaten to kill you."

"That's a lot of spells to cast in a short period," I said, speaking from knowledge. "What stops me from stunning you like I did earlier?"

"I will have to dual-cast. It will be difficult but I calculated a 72.8% chance of success in my dual-casting." It was a good plan. Fuck, it was a great plan.

"Why are you telling me this?" I asked.

"Because there is no way that you can avoid this fate," Holmiarty said. "You will go through a moment of defiance and attack me but between your low level and my defense it will do no good. I have accounted for all possibilities."

He wasn't lying. With his defense and my low attack, it was highly unlikely I could hit him, let alone do any real damage or act as a threat. His defense was nothing compared to a warrior, a paladin or a bear druid but compared to me, it was an impossible amount.

"So draw your swords, Rake, and let us end this resistance."

I reluctantly drew my blades and took a fighting stance. My mind raced. Was I simply going to let Holmiarty's plan unfurl as he described it? There had to be a way out. I wanted to blast Holmiarty with a spell, I wanted to shape the battlefield or slow him with ice but I couldn't. I wasn't Stov. I scolded myself. No longer was I was mage; I was a rogue. I had caught myself thinking like a mage. It was high time I started thinking like a rogue. Mages came prepared and could shape the battlefield. Rogues didn't have that power. Rogues simply won, regardless the cost and if there was no win possible, they rewrote the rules. If I was going to be Rake then I needed to start figuring out how to think like Rake. I needed to win at all cost and if winning wasn't an option, then I had to cheat.

I charged in and attacked. My longsword met the attack circle and struck hard but the steel bounced harmlessly off of Holmiarty's enchanted robes. I thrust with my left blade but it too had no effect. Holmiarty clicked a spell with his left hand and thrust the magic into the air. A burst of holy energy collided with Tialla and stunned her. He clicked a spell with his right hand and thrust his right arm forward. Three things happened next. First, Holmiarty screamed out in pain. Second was that the purifying spell went wide and missed and the third, and in my opinion the most important, was I came to an amazing realization. Pain was real and not everybody knew that fact.

Holmiarty clutched his right shoulder, the same shoulder I threw a dagger into earlier. The dagger might have caused some HP damage and it would have shown up in Holmiarty's life bar but the damage would have been so low that he would have ignored it and not healed himself. If he had, then he would have stitched together the cut and repaired the internal damage to his shoulder. Now as he tried to move his arm, he was assaulted by cries of pain from his body. This was my impossible mission, this was my Kobayashi Maru and I was about to Kirk the hell out of it. I stepped in and kicked with my left, assaulting his knee with the blow. The stunned Holmiarty watched as his leg buckled and he dropped to one knee. I slashed with my left steel and ran it across his bleeding shoulder wound. Holmiarty screamed again. Red numbers appeared in the sky, floating reminders of the miniscule HP damage I'd cause, but the real damage was the unexpected pain I was the inflicting. I grabbed the back of Holmiarty's skull and held it tight and I kneed him in the nose. I smiled at the crunching sound. The dwarf let out a very un-dwarf like scream. I sheathed my blades and withdrew my dagger. I pressed its point against his shoulder wound and pressed. Holmiarty screamed in pain.

"You're working for Steelion," I yelled. "Why? Why him?"

"He's big, he's bad and he's the best course for survival," Holmiarty cried. "Gangs are forming and the biggest and baddest are asserting their dominance. It's like we've all descended into prison rules."

"What about Steelion?"

"He didn't want any part of the new way of life but he was forced into it. Gangs came after him and he smacked them down. Nobody is as well geared as Steellion." Holmiarty quickly stammered a correction. "I mean Stov *was* but...."

"Stov is gone."

"Steelion defended himself, took down some big bad and suddenly found himself in charge. People flocked to him and now he has a following."

"And his first order of business is to come after me," I spat. We had been stuck in the game for less than a week and already anarchy had taken hold. Was I surprised that Steelion was at the center of it? Not at all; Steelion craved attention, he craved admiration and he craved power. I robbed him of that in the past. I wasn't a shrink but to me it seemed like his desires seemed to stem from more than just the game. Now that he had what he desired, he was coming after me. This was not going to be something that *died down* if I left it alone. This was more than some bounty based on revenge. I had become the trigger for the guy's psychological issues. Tialla was right. When people got mad, they got *really* mad.

I pushed Holmiarty to the ground as I fell deep in thought. Food was real, people could get hurt and now nothing was cosmetic. The world was changing and I was struggling to keep up. I needed more information and I wasn't going to find it at Bullmourn's library. I needed to go elsewhere.

"So what now," Tialla asked.

"Now," I reluctantly said, "I need to sneak into Havenhold."

Chapter 08

**"I burned through all of my extra lives in a matter of minutes, and my
two least-favorite words appeared on the screen: GAME OVER."
— Ernest Cline, Ready Player One**

I entered Havenhold through the rear entrance. It was
a small entrance with very little protection, guarded by a pair
of NPCs. The rear entrance was mainly used by the Coalition
as a way to get into the city for attacks on the factions leaders.

Every race in VCO had a leader, an iconic character
that represented their people. They were favourites amongst
the fandom and often the subjects of books, fan fiction, fan
speculation and endless shipping. They were also the subject
of endless attacks from the opposing faction. The orcs would
go after the human Queen and the humans would hunt down
the Orc Leader. The victors would brag, the leaders would respawn and the process would restart all over again. If the rear
entrance was good enough for orcs, then it was good it enough
for my needs.

Once in the city, I headed to the large cathedral that
stood at Havenhold's center. I was meeting Slashlore and there
was no better place to do that than the cathedral. I needed to
decipher the mystery runes and the information I needed was
in the Royal Library. I knew that it was unlikely that all of my
answers were going to be solved in a single trip. Several trips
into Havenhold would be needed and the only way I was going to achieve that was with someone on the inside, someone
who could keep track of Steelion's crew.

"This is gutsy." I heard the voice as I crossed over

the threshold into the place of worship. I looked over at the familiar elf paladin and smiled. He sauntered over to me with a wicked smirk and kept talking. "You have a massive gang on your tail and you sneak into their hometown so you can break into a library? I'm not sure if there are proper words to describe this situation but one does come to mind."

"Oh?"

"Nnnneerrrrrrrrrddd!" Slashlore thought himself a funny man. His humour tended to lean towards funny insults but it still drew laughs from time to time. I shook my head. Despite his humour, Slashlore was still a solid friend. He also got real serious when the time called for it. "So what now?"

I eyed Slashlore and shook my head. Slashlore was an Elf paladin. He was tall fellow with a swimmer's build. It was the standard Elf build, however the spiky blue hair and multiple piercings was not standard Elven fair. He wore full plate armour and carried an axe and sturdy shield on his back.

"Tell me about the gangs."

"Tell me about physics 'cause *that's* about as simple of a question," Slashlore laughed. "Short version: it took about a day after the glitch for the *real* gangs to show up but there were small ones almost instantly. Most were parties that just didn't disband. People were scared and wanted safety in numbers. Then the real assholes showed up.

"So some nobody warrior named Browntown comes along and learns that he can attack his own faction. So he starts PKing. He starts with lowbies then moves on. I mean he starts acting like some post-apocalypse bully. It's textbook psychological behaviour: you remove the rules to the world and there will always be some asshole who will claim power. It's some straight up Negan shit." For I moment I can't help but be surprised at the change in Slashlore. He talked like someone who knows what he's talking about. In truth, Slashlore could be a psychologist or someone who studies human behaviour. At the moment, I am reminded that I know little if anything at all about my VCO friends. I know them in Aspumer, I know them in VCO but in RL, I knew shit all. The way Tialla spoke about her interviews and the investigation, she could be a journalist, a police detective or just someone who spends way too much time watching *Law and Order* and *The Newsroom.* "A couple players stepped up to stop him but he either sent them packing or he killed them. I don't know what it was but nobody could lay a blow on the guy. Browntown must have focuses entirely on defense because he walked away from every fight with little to no damage. TeenyGoku even tried to take him out. Somehow he lost as well." Slashlore's voice trailed off. "TeenyGoku is dead, man. He's gone and Browntown barely had a scratch."

I swore silently. TeenyGoku was a halfling monk - hence the name - and was a massive Dragonball fan. He even wore a cosmetic tail on his character to make himself look more like the famous fighter. He started out as most did, a fan just having fun. Then he got really good at PVP and turned pro. TeenyGoku was a professional player, he was unbeatable. He was our digital Muhammad Ali. TeenyGoku was known to take a hit or two but when he struck back, it was devastating. He could go eight rounds getting pummelled but still end the fight with one punch. TeenyGoku was a household name in VCO. Hearing that he died, I found myself wondering if this feeling, this despondency, was what the people of Metropolis would have felt upon hearing that Superman had died. If a hero that great can fall, what hope was there for the rest of us?

He was also a repeat customer.

He was also a friend.

"So Browntown starts being a bigger asshole. He bested the best and now wants to crush the rest. Then Steelion shows up," Slashlore continued. "He didn't want to get involved but had no choice. He faced off against Browntown and killed him. I don't know what Steelion did or what items he had but he was one of the only people to get through Browntown's defenses. He killed the guy and people loved him for it.

"After that, people start flocking to Steelion and begging him to be their champion. They are fucking throwing themselves at the guy. Girls are tossing panties at him, guys are flinging their boxers at him and there is a line up around the block, of both men and women, to be next in his bed. They offer him whatever he needs to protect them and asks him what he wants."

"And he says my head on a pike?" Slashlore nods. "So begins the witch hunt."

I go silent as I try to piece together all of the information I'd just learned. Thinking still caused my brain to hurt but it's slowly getting easier to keep my thoughts straight. Like a compiling program, I start from the top and work my way down.

Browntown: the warrior with the horrible name.

He was impossible to hit. This made sense to me. Each class in VCO had a standard build. These would allow a player to focus their stats where they were supposed to. It made sure tanks had enough defense, attack and HP to properly play their class. However, VCO also allowed players to customize their stats and put focus where they wanted. A player like Browntown, going by Slashlore's description, focused primarily on defense. This meant he took points from his stamina and HP in order to up his defense stats. That, accompanied by the right gear, would make it nearly impossible to hurt him but those who could hit him had the potential to hit him hard.

Steelion: the warrior with a hard on for killing me.

What allowed Steelion to break through Browntown's defenses? I knew the guy; I knew what he could and couldn't do. His attack was good but it wasn't that good. What did he have that made his attack unblockable? What ----

Then it hit me, like a stonewall against the side of my skull, and I felt like a total idiot. He had it. The mother fucker actually had the ring. Steelion had the Ram Ring. How did an idiot like him find the legendary ring? I was flabbergasted; so much so that I *actually* thought the word *flabbergasted*.

"So what now?" Slashlore asked. I shook my head. Did the ring change anything? Did it alter my plans? The truth was it really didn't. If he and I came to blow Steelion would have no trouble killing me. The Ram Ring just made it so he could do it quicker.

"So now," I finally said, "we get me to the library. Queue the danger music; I have some studying to do."

We snuck through the city, using every back entrance and alley way we knew, until we arrived at our destination: the Royal Library. According to the lore, the human ruler - and leader of the Descendants - was the Witch Queen Theresa Archona. The library had been commissioned by Theresa's grandfather, it was meant to be an illustrious source of knowledge. Yet during her years as a princess, Theresa ordered the library to be expanded in order to better store magical writings of all schools: arcane, divine, nature, shadow and dark. The princess spent years essentially living in the library, studying magic. By the time of her coronation, a result of the tragedy that befell her parents during the Dragon Wars, she was a powerful caster of both arcane and shadow magic. She was crowned the Witch Queen and the library was her lair. She still lived in the castle but it was rumoured that high atop the library, hidden in a room only able to be seen by those as skilled as her, was her true home. It was rumoured that in the Witch's Nest were the most powerful magical secrets in all of Aspumer. The nest had yet to be discovered by players but if there was lore written about it, especially to that extent, than one could assume that it was true.

As we entered the royal building, I found two familiar faces waiting for me. It was the two rogues from earlier, the ones I nicknamed Pauly D and Snookie. My eyes narrowed as I stared at them.

"What do you want?" I asked, my hand slowly dropping to the hilts of my swords.

"It ain't what we want," Snookie started.

"It's what the big man wants," Pauly D finished, "and he wants you." He double gunned me and in that moment I realized why my generation got such a bad name.

"Well how about this," I began. "Tell Steelion to go fuck himself."

"Who are the guidos?" Slashlore asked.

"Stay outta this, failadin," Pauly D spat. "I don't want to have to hurt you."

"Yeah, my man will fuck you up."

"Your man is going to fuck Slashlore up?" I said in a ridiculous tone. I was mocking her now and it wasn't going to end with just that. "Well Slashlore is *my* man and *my* man ain't gonna take shit from *your* man. So why don't we step aside and let these men just beat each other off."

Snookie stared at me in confusion for a long moment before realizing I was seriously making fun of her.

"You think you're better than me or something?" I really did but somehow telling her that wasn't going to make things healthier. "I should fuck you up myself."

At least I didn't make things worse.

A burst of light came off of Slashlore and we three rogues found ourselves blindly stumbling around. I hear the sound of thumping, gasping, coughing and the distinct sound of swords being drawn. I expected a fight to be underway but as my vision came back I found Pauly D on the ground, gasping for air with a shield-shaped bruise on his neck, and Snookie on her knees with Slashlore's axe pressed against her throat.

"What was your plan?" Slashlore demanded.

"We were to grab Rake and bring him to Steelion," Snookie said quickly.

"And if that didn't work?" The paladin asked. Snookie tried not to answer but Slashlore pressed his blade tighter against her neck.

"We...we were supposed...to pass along a message," Pauly D said between coughs. A look of concern was on his face. "Please don't hurt her."

"Tell me the message."

"The message is that Tialla is being held captive.

Steelion wants to meet you between the bank and the auction house. He'll let her go if you come." Slashlore pressed the blade tighter still. A trickle of blood ran down Snookie's neck. "He's going to ambush you there. He's going to show up with as many people as possible. He wants to ridicule you in front of everybody. He wants to crush Stov while everybody watches."

Slashlore pulled the blade away and let the female rogue go. She crawled over to her man and the pair embraced. Slashlore looked over at me, curious as what to do next.

"We aren't cold blooded killers," I said. "We don't want to hurt you or anybody else but if you come after us again, you sure as hell better be waving a white flag because I won't let you attack me a third time." They nodded eagerly and I let them go.

"Who's Tialla?" Slashlore asked as the rogues vanished from view.

"A friend: shadow priestess." My answer was quick and curt.

"A Face Melter; max level?" I nodded. "Ha, then she'll be fine. In fact I'm more worried for Steelion."

I knew she would, I'd seen her fight, but what were my options? Steelion was going after people who were helping me. Who was next? Was I responsible? Did I have to intervene?

"I need to face him," I said suddenly. "I need to fight Steelion."

"This is Hero Bait 101," Slashlore argued. "You won't survive."

"I know but I'm going to try and even things out. I have a plan." My mind raced as I tried to figure things out. "I need to get to the bank."

A city like Havenhold has multiple banks. There were two main ones and a third hidden one if you knew where to look. Sadly, Steelion knew where to look. Every bank was crawling with big dumb brutes standing watch. They were Steelion's flunkies. He was guiding me to the main bank, the one that stood in the center Havenhold Square. The city was split into nine districts. Havenhold Square was the epicenter of the city - and the Descendant's - commerce. It would have the biggest crowd and the potential for the biggest audience. I stood perched on the rooftop of a nearby inn, keeping low and staring down at the town square.

Tialla was in the center of the square, bent over and locked in a set of stocks. She didn't look angry or scared. Simply put, she looked bored.

Bearcules stood nearby, her jailer. He, on the other hand, looked *very* angry. He didn't want to be guard but he sure as hell didn't want to miss my humiliation.

A group of players stood nearby in gaggles. I recognized the Guido couple and the familiar face of Punchocalypse and Hizzous, spread out amongst the gaggle. Neither of them were there for me but it was nice to know that my name was such an audience draw. Amongst the rabble were NPCs, some I recognized and some I didn't. They mostly stayed amongst themselves, still not sure what to make of our PC gathering. I glanced at the bank. That was my target but there was *literally* no way to get there without being seen.

With a wave my menu appeared. I opened the command bar and a small keyboard appeared in the air. I typed in the /whois command and hit enter. It brought up a list of the players currently in the area. A couple more commands and I narrowed the list to my immediate area. They appeared before me.

Anize
Arese
Bearcules
Birdboy
Burststop
DaretobeStupid
DumbMage

Fletch
Fleyming
Forscythe
FreddyVoorhes
Jonezz
MillennialFalcon
Noran
Pendleton
Punchocalypse
Punter
Reit
Skiplug
Slayme
Starbomb
Tialla
Trill
WendyWitch
Whatisitgoodfor
Zygazza

I stopped the list there. It was still too data much to take in at once. I gave up and waved the list away.

"Now what do I have here?" I spun around to see a malicious looking monk - FreddyVoorhees - standing behind me. I smirked.

"Would you belief I was bird watching?" He wouldn't. He didn't. I bolted. Or at least I tried to run but a spinning foot caught me in the chest and falling to the ground, two stories below. Falling took forever, on account of the feather fall spell Slashlore had casted upon me. A minute later my feet touched the cobblestone and all eyes were upon me.

"Hello," I said. "I'm Rake and I'm here about the nanny job. So while I have your attention let me give you my qualifications.

1: A Cheery Disposition: I am never cross
2: Rosy Cheeks: Obviously
3: Plays Games, all sort: Well I'm sure the children will

find my games very diverting.
4: You Must Be Kind: I am kind but extremely firm."

Nobody said a word. They just stared at me andI shook my head. "Really? A solid *Mary Poppins* reference and I get not a single reaction? How have you all not seen *Mary Poppins*? I mean do you realize how hard it is to work a *Mary Poppins* reference into everyday life? I should make it a point to never make references. It seems like such a very old fashioned idea to my mind." I let out a big smile and waited. Nobody reacted. "Really? Another one goes by and nothing? I quit."

I turned to walk away. Comedy was dead.

"Ladies and gentlemen," Steelion cried out. "Nobody does an entrance quite like the famous Stov."

Steelion emerged from a building and walked towards me. He wore full plate armour and carried an evil grin on his face. Flunkies followed behind him. He stopped a couple paces before me and stared into my eyes.

"Or I could call you Rake?" Steelion sneered. "But I think I'll call you *Dead Meat* instead."

The crowd erupted in laughter. I stared at them in disbelief. "Really? That gets a reaction?" I shook my head and mumbled a curse. Comedy was rolling in its grave. I looked back at Steelion and put on my game face. "You wanted me, so here I am. What now?"

"I'm here to humiliate you. I'm here to crush you. I'm here to ruin the great reputation of Stov,"

"You sure about that," I taunted. "You've sent parties of max levels after me twice now. I spanked each of them and sent them crying to their Mommy. What makes you so sure that you'll fare any better?"

"I'm going to do to you what you did to me," he snapped.

"What? What did I do to you that have you so pissed at me?"

"I introduced you to the world of treasure hunting, I

taught you about Casper Caches and I taught you how to sell, I taught you how to price an object and I taught you how to make money in this game. So how do you repay me? You betray me, you steal from me, you undercut me in sales and you humiliate me at every turn." Steelion shook his head. "Stov becomes a hero to the people and I became some joke. I deserved the same respect you got; I deserved to be a name that people looked up to, not you."

His voice was getting angry. That was good. I needed him angry.

"Do you know why people came to me over you? Do you know why I got the respect and why I became the household name?" He glared at me, daring me to say it. "It's because I am better than you. In every single possible way, I am better than you. I. Am. Better. Than. You."

"It doesn't matter now," he said with a smirk. "They need me now. They flock to me now, not you. They respect me."

"Bullshit; they're afraid of you." I was pushing him over the edge now. I was so close to having him completely lose it. "They didn't come to see you beat up some little guy. They came to see me slap you around Havenhold like the bitch you are,"

His feet were on the edge of reason and anger, his body teetering on the ledge. All he needed was one final push.

"So I came here to do just that. You don't think I could have snuck up here without being seen? Of course I could. Instead your floozy just *happens* to find me on the roof looking over the square and I just *happen* to be here at the right time and I just *happen* to have feather fall cast on me so when he kicks me off of the roof I land harmlessly onto the ground." This was it, this was my final push. "I knew what you were doing so what did I do? I used your own spectacle to lay out a trap for you and you stumbled into it like a big dumb idiot."

Steelion fell off the cliff of reason and plummeted down into the chasm of rage. A defense square popped up but I never had the chance to react before Steelion's fist slammed me into the ground.

Holy fuck, that hurt; I knew pain was now real in VCO but that punch was beyond anything I'd ever felt. With one punch, he knocked me off of my feet and sent me crumpling to the ground below. I wanted to wince or groan in pain but that wasn't possible. My body didn't want to react. Truth be told, I might have been dead.

Steelion grabbed me, pulled me to my feet and punched me again. This time, his fist ended up in my gut and I coughed up blood. He tossed me against a wall. I slammed into it, doing my best to protect my head, and fell back to the cobblestone below.

"This is the great Stov," Steelion called out to the audience. "This was the hero that you'd hope free us from VCO. Well let me tell you the truth. This isn't you hero. This isn't your saviour. This is nothing more than a piece of shit.

"That all you got, Asshole?" I mocked as I climbed back to my feet. "You call that a throw? It's no wonder nobody gives a shit about you."

Steelion stormed towards me and fired another punch across my face. Once more, I found myself on the ground and not sure how I got there. For a moment I began to question if I needed to change tactics. I never got the chance to properly examine it. Steelion grabbed me, hoisted me into the air and flung me. I always enjoyed flying. I loved planes and I loved flying mounts. What I didn't like was flying via Air Asshole. My body crashed through the large wooden doors and I fell into the bank.

From outside I could hear Steelion prancing about, yelling at the crowd like some WWE heel. "I am your hero. I am your protector. I am your saviour. If any of you dare think otherwise or you dare challenge me on the fact then speak up now."

Nobody replied.

"None of you dare?" When people got mad, they got *really* mad. Steelion had succumbed to his anger and was making mistakes. PCs no longer trusted him; they feared him.

And on top of that, Steelion had just made the worse mistake he could. He threw me into the bank. "None of you will face me?"

"Fine," I called out as I emerged from the bank. Steelion spun around and stared in shock. I stood in the bank's archway, dressed almost entirely in new gear. Gone was my mundane leather armour and cheap wooden swords. As I stood there - looking awesome BTW - I wore epic level armour, magical boots and gloves, an enchanted bandanna and in my off hand I held the greatest rogue off-hand in all of VCO: the Whaitiri Edge. "I guess I have to do everything myself."

"What the hell?" Steelion stammered.

"If there is one place you should never throw a treasure hunter's alt, it's into the bank." I gave him a *90s-cool-whatever* shrug. "It's where we keep all of our good stuff."

Chapter 09

"I burned through all of my extra lives in a matter of minutes, and my two least-favorite words appeared on the screen: GAME OVER."
— Ernest Cline, Ready Player One

Steelion was flabbergasted, so much so that I had no other choice of descriptive words *except* for flabbergasted. Murmurs of disbelief rippled through the crowd as I stoically descended the stairs. I wore a confident smirk, one that infuriated Steelion further.

"End this, Steelion. Walk away now and there'll be no hard feelings." This was his way out, before things got worse. I prayed he'd take it but I knew he wouldn't. Steelion stared at my blade and simply got angrier.

The Whaitiri Edge was hard to miss. It had a curved build, like a small scimitar, made with Azure stained steel. Its pommel and quillon were made with gold and its grip was made with red velvet. Etched upon its quillon block was the Kahail symbol.

"You hacker-scum," he spat. "That's how you beat me. You hacked the game for those items. That's the only way you can wield *that* blade at your level." He drew his sword and advanced on me. "I'll cut you down for this. I'll fucking kill you."

He dashed towards me, his sword held in both hands. A defense square popped up and I brought my off hand to meet it. The Whaitiri Edge deflected the attack and sent a bolt of electricity into the warrior. An attack circle popped up and I moved my longsteel to meet it, thrusting deep against his armour: +1 combo point. My longsword dove between a chink in his steel and dug into his flesh. Steelion cried out in pain as he retreated a couple paces. He stood there, angry and confused, as he moved his gaze back and forth between me and his wound.

I had to be careful. I couldn't fight like Steelion did, going all out. I had to be smart. I had to maximize my combo points and use my finishers strategically. Level 25 had given me a new move - shadow strike - but I longed to be five levels higher. A rogue at level 30 got a range finisher called between the eyes.

Steelion came at me again, his sword coming down at me with the full strength of the angered warrior behind it. Once again I moved to meet the defense square but this time I moved both blades to block. Steelion's longsword bounced off of both of my blades and my body moved quickly to finish the combo. Whaitiri Edge slashed against Steelion's right leg, sending an electrical jolt through his body and giving me another point. My left leg slid behind me and I spun around, using both swords in a baseball swing to sweep both legs out from under the warrior: +1 combo point. Steelion fell backward and collided with the ground, hard. I cautiously back stepped. Steelion looked up from the ground, angry and confused.

"H...how?" I linked the weapon in chat and showed Steelion the stats. He shook his head in confusion.

<u>Whaitiri Edge</u>
Requirement: None
Drop Rate: 0.02%

"The level requirement," he stammered, "it's gone. How? What did you do?"

"I didn't do anything," I said calmly. "The world's changing and you missed it. Food is real, pain is real, death is real and level requirements are gone. This isn't a game anymore. VCO is becoming real."

Steelion climbed to his feet and gripped his sword tightly in both hands. He glared at me. "Then we're battling as equals." He shifted his posture to a one-handed sword stance.

"You *wish* we were equals," I spat.

"Mortal Kombat!" I turned around as The Immortal's familiar beats emerged from a boom box that Punchocalypse held in the air John Cusack style. I realized two facts at that moment: Punchocalypse had a music player app installed into VCO and I just met my new best friend

"This is serious," Steelion roared, his rage returning to volcanic levels. He dashed towards me, his sword was a blur. A defense square rapidly popped up before me. The speed of his attacks was impressive and should have proved difficult to deflect but I knew Steelion's style. I introduced him to it and I'd fought alongside him time and time again. I knew what he was going to do next before he did.

I moved my blades to deflect and block each attack, favouring the Whaitiri Edge. Each time his blade came into contact with mine, the Whaitiri Edge sent a wave of electricity through Steelion's body. Each jolt was little more than a bee sting, causing small red numbers to emerged from atop his head, but, as Macaulay Culkin can attest to, even a bee sting could kill in great numbers.

Steelion's one-handed stance allowed him to attack with great speed but as the jolts increased, his body slowed as well as his blade. As his speed decreased, the rate at which attack circles appeared began to increase. His slowed arm allowed for more fencing openings. My longsteel dove in when it could, feeding on his flesh like a hungry piranha. I struck with my shadow strike, my blade moving faster than my eye could follow, and followed up with a powerful saber slash. Each strike added another combo point.

Steelion dropped to one knee as he panted for air. He looked up at me and growled. "Get him!"

Steelion's flunkies all moved at once, preparing to come to his aid. Bearcules shifted to bear form and readied a charge, Fleyming called upon her dark magic as she prepared a spell as FreddyVoorhes called upon his chi. Six other flunkies didn't need to prepare, they just charged forward. The guidos, however, didn't move an inch.

They weren't the only ones to react to the warrior's order. The stocks suddenly exploded as Tialla freed herself from her confinement. Her shadow tendrils lashed out and wrapped around Bearcules. A bolt of golden lighting fell from the sky and zapped the ground before Fleyming. The warlock spun to see Slashlore emerging from the crowd and walking towards him. A female hand clamped down on FreddyVoorhes' shoulder. The monk spun around and struck with a punch but the NPC easily deflect the attack, grabbed FreddyVoorhes' arm and twisted. The monk cried out in shock as pain forced him to his knees.

"Make one more move," Garruil hissed, "and you'll declare war against the Whispers."

Punchocalypse leapt over the rushing six and landed between them and me. He punched the ground and the earth shook slightly. Everybody froze and stared at him. Punchocalypse stood up and spoke loudly. "I really don't give a crap who wins this cock fight but this is their fight. If anybody else feels the need to interfere, then step up because you'll gotta go through me first."

Nobody else moved.

I looked down at Steelion. He was tired, anybody could see it. He had hoped to end this quickly and relied on fast and heavy strikes. He hadn't expect me to fight back and to last this long. He hadn't expected the fight to last this long.

"End this," I said, calmly now. "I'm sorry for what I've done to you. Truth is, I'm an asshole. Anybody who's spent any real time with me knows this. I shouldn't have treated you the way I did. Business is business, but it shouldn't get in between friends. I know this now. You are my friend but more importantly, I don't want either of us to get hurt."

"It's too late for this," he snarled. "You can walk away with your head held high, you're the damn hero. I can't.

I have to prove myself. I have to be the champion."

He stood up and clutched the sword with both hands. The blade began to glow red as Steelion slashed the air. A wave of red magic shot off the sword like some damn Reinhardt ability. The wave rocketed towards me. I brought both blades up to block. The blast collided with my blade and, while leaving me mostly unharmed, sent me flying into the air. I flew backward and collided with the nearest wall, falling to the cobble stone and found my lungs void of air. I fought for oxygen as I stared up at him. As air returned to my lungs, I quickly swore. Steelion had a magic sword but somehow he'd found a way to use the magic as a projectile.

"Fucking Casper," I swore.

"You aren't the only treasure hunter," he reminded me with a cocky smile. "Shall we try this again?"

This no longer was a straight up duel. This was a treasure hunter duel. This would be a test of our gear, our secrets and how quickly we could figure a way to use them in battle. So be it. This was my forte.

I dashed forward, using the minor boost in speed that my boots gave, and leapt into the air. I cartwheeled mid-jump and struck with the cross slash. Both blades slashed across his back and Whaitiri Edge sent another jolt of electricity through his body. Every combo point I had vanished with the cross slash but the damage I'd just inflicted was well worth it. The combo point's damage added alongside Whaitiri Edge's phenomenal weapon stats and the damage was incredible. I landed behind Steelion and willed the true magic in my boots to activate. My feet turned to stone as I fired a kick into the warrior's back. The blow sent him toppling foreword. I couldn't let Steelion recover. I deactivate the stone feet and slashed again, this time with my longsteel.

My longsteel was a blade called Splinter's Bite. It wasn't an *exceptional* blade, my best longswords were kept on Stov, but it wasn't one to ignore. The longsteel bit with exceptional sting. Steelion cried out in pain as he felt the sting. He recovered his footing moments later and spun around, his blade slicing horizontally. I ducked down, only barely missing the deadly bite of his blade. I tried darting to the left but was sent tumbling to the ground as the warrior stamped his enchanted boots. The Tremor Boots sent a small quake through the ground that assaulted my footing. I skipped off of the cobble stone but quickly recovered, rolling back to my feet. Looking up, I expected to see Steelion several feet away from me but he wasn't there; he was behind me. I cursed to myself. He had the Yardrat Helm, an item that could allow him to transmit himself, instantly, across the battlefield.

Steelion's swung his blade down upon me and I had no choice but to activate my epic armour: the Feore Shell. My body became an impassable mist, causing Steelion's blade to harmlessly pass through me and bang against the cobblestone, and I rocketed forward two feet. I hadn't wanted to use the shell's ability so soon. It was a great *get out of jail free* trick but it was a once-per-day ability. My body reconstituted and I turned around. Steelion ran towards me, his blade aiming directly at my skull. I swung Whaitiri Edge around to deflect but I realized too late that the warrior was trying to disarm me. The azure blade was torn from hand and flew across the square. I called upon my boots once again and tried to kick once more but Steelion saw it coming. He quickly sidestepped and brought his left hand to his chest.

There it was, *finally*.

His heart began to glow brightly and a blinding light filled the square. This was *Reactor Love* and it was going to blind and stun everybody who wasn't a part of his party. I was not a part of Steelion's party but I was prepared. I had seen my one-time friend use this ability time and time again. I knew it was his favourite move and I knew how to counter it.

Steelion stepped in, with his sword ready to finish me off, expecting to find me stunned. Instead he found me with my enchanted bandanna covering my eyes and my vision un-hindered. I smirked as I gave Steelion the finger. "You are not prepared."

I called upon my boots once more and leapt into the

air. I was going to flip over him, slash with Splinter's Bite and then dash to retrieve Whaitiri Edge. My plan didn't work out. Murphy's Law says that no plan survives contact with the enemy. So when Steelion grabbed me by the feet, slammed me against the ground a couple times Hulk-Loki style before flinging me across the square, I had a single thought go through my mind.

Fuck you, Murphy.

Once again I skipped across the cobblestone, like a skipping stone across the lake, before the audience parted to allow me to crash into the auction house. I tried to stand up but my legs cried out in protest. My left leg buckled and I dropped to one knee. Realizing that Splinter's Bite no longer resided in my hand, I looked around for it. My arms protested at the thought, they were tired and sore and, much like the rest of my body, just wanted to sleep for the ninety years. I didn't see my sword, instead I saw Steelion in the distance. He was standing, staring at me. He stomped his right foot three times, snorted and roared as he began to run towards me. Time seemed to slow me for as I took in all the details. The stomp, the roar, the run and the glowing ring on Steelion's hand meant one thing: he had activated the Ram Ring. Steelion was performing an unblockable charge attacked. I looked around for a place to dodge but with all of the people around, there was nowhere to run. With nowhere to run, nowhere to dodge and no way to block I was ready to stick my head between my knees and kiss my ass goodbye.

Then I saw Punchocalypse.

I ignored the awkwardness of thinking about the monk during my thoughts of self-ass-kissing and begged my legs for enough strength for one more moment. One way or another, this fight was all but over. I stood up and held aloft my right hand. I snapped and my lucky dagger appeared in my fingers. Gloves of storing: able to hold any item I needed.

I slid my right leg back, put my left hand forward as my right hand cocked backward in preparation of a throw. An attack circle appeared before me. I took a deep breath and moved my right hand forward. I lined my hand with the circle and fired the dagger forward. I instantly started praying. I'm not much of a religious man but at that moment would it do me any harm?

The dagger flew forward, flipping twice in mid air, until it collided with Steelion's head. The warrior's roaring face suddenly morphed to a stunned one - which was hilarious to see in slow-mo - as he stumbled twice before tripping over his own feet and toppling to the ground. He slammed against the cobblestone, hard. The lucky dagger dematerialized and rematerialized in my hand. I snapped my fingers and it vanished into my glove. I kept my eyes on Steelion's body as I limped toward my Whaitiri Edge, retrieving Splinter's Bite along the way.

For several moments Steelion didn't move but eventually his body twitched and he groaned. I approached him slowly, kicking away his blade as I came across it. I sheathed my weapons and knelt by the warrior. Steelion looked up at me and saw my offered hand.

"You okay?" I asked.

Steelion groaned as he accepted my hand. I helped him to his feet. Steelion looked at me. It was clear that, much like my own, his entire body cried out in pain.

"I'm calling it: this is over." I shook my head. "I'm sorry for what I've done. I've lied and betrayed you. We can't do this anymore. Look around; we're stuck in a god damned VR game like some cyberpunk anime shit. Up until now, I've been looking out for me above anybody else. I realize that's wrong. Now, more than ever, we need to work together. All of us do because the only way we're getting out of here is by working together and sharing what we know.

"If this feud goes on any longer, then one of us is going to get seriously hurt or worse, one of us will end up killing the other. None of us wants to be a killer but both of us have the ability to do so. I'm walking away, Steelion. If you want to follow, do so as a friend because...." my voice trailed off. I had no words that didn't sound like a threat. "Just please, come as a friend."

I turned my back to Steelion and limped away. This was it. This was the hero moment. I'd spared my opponent and I let him live. I was walking away. In a movie this would be where the villain would pull out a hidden gun or knife and try to kill me. Then I'd be forced to kill him. This was the position I'd just put Steelion in. Would he try to kill me or would he let me walk away? As I limped away, I silently counted in my head.

1

If I could make it to five then it would be okay. If I could make it to five then he would be okay. If I could make it to five then I would be okay.

2

3

Please, God, please let me get to five. Inside my head I yelled to him, begging for one more second, for just one more.

4

"Shini'ka!" My head dropped. Shini'ka was an arcane command that I knew well. It was a retrieval spell that could be put on any weapon. It was magic but could be used by even the most arcane-impaired warriors and Steelion had just yelled it.

As his sword flew to his hand like Mjolnir, I looked up to the heavens. Why? Why couldn't you let me get to five? Steelion ran towards me, roaring loudly with his sword held high - ready to strike. I raised my right hand and snapped my fingers. The lucky dagger appeared. With despair and sorrow, I pivoted around and fired it. In less than a second, the lucky dagger found itself in Steelion's neck. He came to a halt and dropped to his knees. For a moment nobody moved; not me, not Steelion and not anybody in the audience watching. Everybody knew what was about to happen. The dagger was deep in the warrior's neck. Steelion was fine - relatively - as long as it remained there but this was a lucky dagger and they always returned. In just a second, the dagger would dematerialized from his neck and rematerialized in my hands. When it did that, there would be nothing to hold the blood in. The moment the dagger dematerialized was the moment Steelion would bleed out.

The mere seconds it took felt like an eternity but eventually the moment came. I didn't look away as the dagger vanished nor did I pay any heed to when the weight of the weapon suddenly appeared in my hand. I simply looked my friend directly in the eyes and I whispered an apology. Slashlore and Tialla both rushed over and tried to heal him. Even Bearcules called upon his rarely used nature magic in an attempt to stitch the wound together but neither spell had an effect. Moments later Steelion died and only then did I look away.

I limped to the entrance of Havenhold, not saying a word to anyone. I paused at the city gates and looked once more to the heavens.

Why couldn't you let me get to five?

Epilogue

As a child of the internet there is something off about spending all of my time in a library, even one as vast and amazing as the royal library. It is amazing the difference a few years can make. My sister is seven years older than me. When she went to school, they did all of their research in libraries. They had lessons on how to use a library and they looked up books using file cards. Fast forward seven years and the library is basically a computer lab with books. So, to say the least, sitting at a desk surrounded by tomes as I lose hour after hour studying is weird. It's not a bad weird but it is a new weird.

"You finding everything you're looking for?" I glanced up and see a woman standing by me. She is an NPC who looks familiar but I can't place why. With the amount of time I've spent in the royal library, she is probably from there but for some reason that still feels off.

My brain hurts. The pain is minimal now, the concussion all but gone, but still threads remain broken, thoughts not making it to their logical conclusion.

"Thanks," I smile. "I think I've got what I need."

"As you wish," she steps back. I expect her to walk away but she doesn't, she simply stands there. "May I ask you a question?"

"Um...sure." I look back at her. She wasn't a stunningly beautiful woman but she was good looking. She didn't look special but something screamed in my brain. It was like when a word is on the tip of your tongue but you can't find it. I felt like that. A thought existed at the tip of my brain and yet I couldn't find it.

"I don't mean to forward, but are you okay? I've seen you here every day for the past week. You spend nearly every waking moment here and some nights you have even passed out in that very desk." She pulled out a chair and slid into it. "What makes a man do that?"

Her questions threw me for a loop. In the two weeks since the Glitch the NPCs had developed into real people with real personalities, observations and lives. I wasn't used it. I don't think any of us were.

"A week ago I killed a friend," I explained, unsure why I was telling her this. "I gave him every chance to end it but he didn't. He died by my hand."

"I'm sorry to hear that," she said softly.

"The worst part is that it didn't change anything," I explained. "We're still stuck here and killing him brought me no closer to the solution. So why did it have to happen? Why did I have to take his life?"

My anger started to rise, again. I found myself without control of my emotions. Anger and rage seemed to flare at the drop of a hat.

"After that stupid speech now I'm some big damn hero. People want me to save them, the Whispers need me for work, my friends are looking at me for direction and I don't know what to tell them. I don't know what to do." I shook my head, trying to combat the anger. "So I hide here, in these books, hoping that something will guide me."

The librarian reached out and placed her hand atop of mine. Suddenly I felt the rage fade away. I looked up at her and suddenly felt myself lost in her eyes. For the first time in a week I found a smile creeping up on my lips.

"You must be patient," she said to me. "The answer will reveal itself. You have a long journey ahead of you." She giggled softly. "I know that sounds like trite advice but trust me when I say it."

Our hands separated as she stood up. She smiled at me. "You remind me of someone."

"Oh?"

"I met this man only once, when I was teenager," she explained. "It was early in my schooling and I made a grave mistake. I ended up lost when pirates descended on me. An Elf saved me that day. He was tall mage with ice blue hair. He was so gentle and kind but wielded such power and determination."

I blinked rapidly as the broken threads suddenly began to mend. The Elf she spoke of was familiar to me. No, I was wrong. That Elf was me. But if that story was about me then this would make her....

"He returned me to my father and then left. He didn't ask for any great reward or my hand in marriage. He simply took a small amount of gold, nothing worth speaking of, and vanished. What mage saves a princess and asks for nothing in return? He has always stood in my memory as the one who got away."

I tried to stammer a response but got nothing but random sounds that were as far from words as possible.

"Perhaps it was just a teenage crush but how cliché would that be, the princess pining for her saviour?" She laughed. "The world has changed recently and to be honest, I hoped that this would draw Stov from hiding but he has yet to show himself. So in the meantime, I will take the same advice I just gave you: Be patient. The answer will reveal itself. I have a long journey ahead of me."

"H...h...how?" I stammered. Of the literal thousands of people who'd completed that quest why did she remember me? I had so much more I wanted to ask but all I could get out was that single word.

"There is no path for patience. It simple comes." The librarian took a step back from the table and snapped her fingers. A stream of magic twirled around her like she was Cinderella and Bibbidi-Bobbidi-Boo: her librarian clothes magically transformed in royal robes. She smiled at me. "Trust me; a Witch Queen knows these things."

Then Queen Theresa Archona, ruler of Havenhold and leader of the Descendants of the Eternals, teleported away in a blink.

VCO 2 Cover

Vörissa's Catalyst
— ONLINE —
PATCH 1.02
ESCORT MISSION
LARRY GENT

Prologue

Glitch: Day 3

Her footsteps moved silently through the darkened forest, the mindbending fog moving through the trees like water through a creek. There were many spells at her disposal that could silence her feet further, but they would have proven useless. It had taken years of practise, stealthily creeping around the dungeons and forests of Aspumer, to perfect her level of stealth. It was an impressive feat for a rogue; it was an outstanding feat for a mage.

Scova kept watch as she ran her fingers across the forest floor. She was looking for someone, a group of people to be specific but tracking them in the fog would be impossible. She frowned as her fingers tapped out a spell. Seconds later her eyes began to glow orange, as if her irises burned with an everlasting flame. The trail illuminated before her, each footstep glowing blue for her eyes only.

"Your reliance on the arcane troubles me." Scova hid a smile. Damn, she had snuck up on her again. After all this time she didn't know why it still surprised her. Scova was quiet, she prided herself on how quiet she was, but she was in a whole other world. "You should learn to see with your own eyes, not those granted by magic."

"You should learn what tact is." Scova hid a smile as she turned around. Her enchanted eyes fell upon the lithe figure of Lady Adelaide Bullmourn. She was tall and athletic with long onyx hair and wore a ninja's keikogi with a matching tabi. A ninjatō was on her back, along with several kunai on her belt. "You're late."

"We have been here, waiting," Adelaide smirked. Scova opened her mouth to protest. She saw only Lady Bullmourn but after blinking, six more appeared. Each wore ninja garb like Adelaide and were just as well equipped. "Shall we continue to waste time with idle flirting or should we attend to the mission at hand?"

"Flirting?" Scova asked. Adelaide's stoic nature cracked slightly as a slight blush crossed her cheeks. In the darkness, accompanied by the fog, Scova would have missed it save for her enchanted eyes. She smirked.

Adelaide raised her hand and the team came to an abrupt halt. She pointed to her scout and he vanished. Moments later he reappeared. He leaned in and whispered to Adelaide. Scova watched and marvelled. The Whispers were nothing short of amazing. Some were spies that gathered intelligence, others were field agents who worked the missions and some were ninjas. They were the assassins, the killers and the masters of shadow. They were the arbiters of the Whisper Lord's will.

Lady Adelaide turned to her troops. She never spoke, she simply pointed in various directions. Her ninjas simply nodded before vanishing into the fog. She then turned to Scova.

"The Nohorian Brotherhood's camp is across the bridge. We see fifteen, so we expect thirty," she explained. "My team is flanking the camp as we speak. You and I will take the bridge. We will move swiftly so hasten your feet if you feel the need."

"Trust me," Scova boasted, "I'll keep up."

"Good. Then let us attack."

Glitch: Day 4
The cart bounced along the road, forcing Scova awake. She jolted upright but instantly regretted the move-

ment. Pain shot through her side. Her left arm reached across to cup her wound but it did little to help. Her fingers touched wool bandages, soaked through by her blood. Scova looked around the cart she'd woken in. She was in a cage being transported across the continent to some unknown location. She looked around and saw two unmasked ninjas, each Whisper agents, and the familiar - albeit cut and bruised - face of Lady Adelaide.

"You've finally awakened," the Lady said. "You've been out for nearly a day. I was worried about you."

"What happened?" Scova asked.

Adelaide scowled and Scova suddenly got worried. The noble lady wasn't happy. She was mad, not just on a professional level but on a personal one. Someone had emotionally cut her and the wound was deep.

"Lady Bullmourn, please tell me." She shook her head. Scova asked once more, "Adelaide, please."

"I was betrayed," she spat, "by one of my own."

"Why are we still alive?" Scova asked.

"They want me," she explained. "Those two are to be torture to get to me."

"Why am I still alive?"

Adelaide didn't answer. She simply looked out the cage and watched the world pass by.

Glitch: Day 9

"186, 187, 188," Adelaide counted loudly with each of Scova's kicks.

"You know what I miss?" Scova asked as her legs came to a halt.

"An excuse to stop your training?" Lady Adelaide scolded. The pair were locked in a stone cell, deep within an unknown castle. They had been there for days. Aside from occasionally removing Adelaide to torture her for information, the pair never left the cell.

Scova smirked. "I miss my sword."

"I expected you to speak of your mother, your brother or yet again of your sister, Notian," Adelaide said with surprise. "I did not expect you to speak of your blade."

"My blade was the Thean'melorn," Scova explained. "It was one of the few blades that could be wielded by a mage. It was built by Elven royalty, forged with the heart of a burning elemental. It is an epic blade with 1.75% drop rate. I hunted for weeks to get it."

Adelaide smiled. The woman's enthusiasm was infectious. Her words often made little sense but she didn't dispute them. Scova had told her how she'd come from another land and how her, and thousands of others, were trapped. She told her how this world was little more than a game or a story being told. Some of what she said made sense, other aspect seemed impossible. As far as Adelaide was concerned if Scova and others like her were trapped in Aspumer, then it made little difference where they came from.

"My father's blade, the Dark Murmur, is something he greatly cares for. It is the weapon of his power and the symbol of his order." Adelaide frowned, "I often belief that he cares more for it and his Whispers then he does for me."

"That's not true," Scova said.

"He didn't care when my mother passed," Adelaide continued. Scova paused. Adelaide was an important NPC and a fan favourite amongst the VCO community. Her mother's identity was a massive VCO secret and an often theorized and debated topic. So as Adelaide began to talk of her mother, Scova found herself unable to look away. "She was a mage. She died when her magic was suppressed. Father barely mourned. He simply continued to run his order."

It suddenly made sense to Scova. Adelaide had always been insistent on her being more than simply her magic.

"At this moment it matters not," Adelaide declared. "What matters is you still have 312 kicks left to go."

Adelaide, never one to simply sit and do nothing, decided to train Scova. The mage was strong, unlike any mage she had ever seen, but she could be stronger. Especially since the castle was somehow suppressing Scova's magic and her own. Every day for five days, twelve hours a day, Adelaide trained the mage. In order to escape they both needed to be strong. Training kept them both strong.

Glitch: Day 17

Adelaide's hand abruptly shook Scova from her slumber. The mage bolted up and tried to cry out but suddenly found a firm hand covering her mouth. Scova's eyes blinked as she adjusted to the darkness.

"Something has changed," Adelaide whispered as she removed her hand from the mage's mouth. She pointed to the window. Scova looked out and saw only the midnight noir that encompassed the land. "This is midday, so why is it night out?'

Scova looked around, unable to answer. A tingling feeling moved through her hand. She glanced down at it in surprise. Adelaide spoke. "Your magic is returning. Whatever was suppressing it has been weakened. Can you cast a spell?"

Scova stood up and raised her hand. She tapped out a spell with her fingers. Her hand turned bright red but nothing happened. Eventually the red fizzled. Scova shook her head.

"You spoke of a town portal," Adelaide whispered. "Can you access it?"

Scova brought up her commands. For the first time since she'd entered the castle, her town portal wasn't greyed out. "I can use it but I can't take another with me."

"Then go, Little Flame," Adelaide ordered. "Go, find help and come back for me."

"I can't," Scova protested. "I can't leave you here, Ade."

"Do as you're told, little one," Adelaide said, gently caressing Scova's cheek. "I'm not worried because I know you will return for me."

Chapter 01

"There's two ways to deal with mystery: uncover it, or eliminate it."
— Andrew Ryan (Bioshock)

For as long as I can remember I have been an advocate of reading. I love diving into a good book and I love the benefits that come from reading. So it pains me that the words had even crossed my brain but my name is Devon Priestly and I think I hate libraries.

For the past tenday, I spent nearly every waking moment in Havenhold's royal library. I told myself I was studying arcane runes. I told myself I was trying to decipher the runes hidden on the moon's mask. I told myself a lie. I was in the library for one reason and one reason only.

I was hiding.

It had been ten days, ten long days, since I had stabbed a dagger deep into the neck of friend. It had been ten days since I'd become....

I couldn't say the words out loud, I couldn't even think them. The mere thought of the word, the dreaded word, would be me accepting it as fact but I wasn't ready for that. I wasn't ready to accept the truth. So I hid in a mountain of books, obscured from the world and the truth. I spent my time researching, looking for a truth I was more prepared to handle.

Since the early days of Vörissa's Catalyst Online I had become quite proficient at research. To be a treasure hunter you had to be good at research. The gear - the stuff that really made money on the resale market - required a player to decipher the endless hints and riddles. These were the Casper Caches and these were my goals. While, admittedly, most of my research was done online and through both the official and fan-made VCO wikis, the principles were still the same. I had to set my goals, set my topics and keep on target. When I became a VCO treasure hunter, my research habits were sloppy and undisciplined. I'd start by researching magical swords, click on a link to get me into blacksmiths and two hours later I'm reading about an Orc's marriage ceremony. The lore was fascinating - Aspumer was brilliant with depth - but it was horrible time management. Since my early days, I have become a more disciplined researcher and in turn a better treasure hunter.

For the current research project, I started by setting out my goals. The goals would serve as a written reminder of what it was I was trying to learn. Having a written reminder was essential, especially in our world where a single internet link could take a person from a page about cats to a page about communism. The goals kept me on track.

Ultimate Goal: Discover How to Get Out of VCO

Ever since the Glitch, I was a man stuck in a virtual reality video game. I was stuck in a massively multiplayer online role-playing and I couldn't log out. If it sounded like something you'd read on tvtropes.org it was because you would. They called the trope Trapped in Another World and/ or The Game Comes to Life.

I was stuck in a trope and I had two choices. I could complain about it or I could accept and use what I know to my advantage. If I was stuck in a trope then at least I knew what rules I had to play by.

1:   Death in the game possibly meant death in real life. DO NOT DIE.
2:   I couldn't be forcibly removed from a game. I was stuck here
3:   There is no time limit. Food and Drink are not an issue.
4:   Winning meant I could leave. Find the boss and beat him.

These were the rules for the Stuck in a Game trope and until I could prove them false, they were my rules. I couldn't do anything about the first three rules, they were beyond my control, but I could figure out who was the boss was and I could figure out how to beat it. I had leads, barely, and I had questions. What I needed were answers and I was going to research until I found them.

Research Goals:
- Discover the meaning of the mysterious moon runes.
- Discover the Nohorian Brotherhood's plans.
- Discover who is behind the VCO Glitch.

The only theory I had, the only actionable theory, was that the pre-expansion event triggered the Glitch. The truth was there were other theories out there but they were unconfirmed, second-hand knowledge at best and there was nothing I could about them from inside the game. So I focused my attention on the pre-expansion event; when an army of men with weird half masks assaulted Havenhold while a half-mask symbol was burned onto the moon for all to see.

In my mind, the moon etchings were the key. It was the left half of an angry mask, with a single narrowed eye, a downward frown and a symbol on the cheek that could only be described as a melted question mark. Within the mask's eye and between its lips were unknown arcane runes that glowed purple. It was the mask on the moon and its cheek symbols that led me to the Nohorian Brotherhood.

This brought me to my research topics. Much like my goals, I wrote out the topics I planned to research. This helped keep me focused and on-track. My list contained what I thought to be the best choices of topic for my research and the topics I felt held the best chance for finding my solution. Experience had taught me that during my research I wasn't allowed to stray from these topics unless I found solid reasoning to. Focus was the key to success.

Research Topics:
- Magical Runes with focus on Arcane, Shadow and Dark
- Magical Rituals with focus on Arcane, Shadow and Dark
- World Spells
- Vörissa's Domain and Power
- Effected of a Fallen God
- Effect of a corrupted God-Spark
- Power Magic and the signs
- Aspumer Astronomy
- History of the Nohorian Brotherhood

The Nohorian Brotherhood was bad news. Ever since vanilla VCO, the Nohorian Brotherhood had always been around. They envisioned themselves a power hungry cult but they were little more than pilot fish, metaphorically eating the ectoparasites off of the game's bigger villains. They were forgettable henchmen for the Crypt Walker and disposable trash mobs for the Hellforged. Yet in the past few expansions they had stepped up their game. When both factions made their final push against Vörissa, during the *Babellian Ascent* expansion, players tore through the creatures and factions loyal to the Fallen Goddess. Among them was the Nohorian Brotherhood. After fighting their way through eleven bosses, in the *Babellian Spires* raid, the PCs faced off against the goddess herself only to find that she had been weakened just enough to be killable. Vörissa had been betrayed by the Norhorian

Brotherhood. The cultist drained a hint of her power and then vanished.

They had resurfaced in the next expansion, *Scaleborn Scism*, and participated in the Dragon Wars. The cultists were less of a fighting force and more of background manipulators. They played both sides during the Dragon War, pitting the mortal races in the middle, while promising each Dragon army the fraction of the god-spark they possessed. Their plan exploded in their faces during the *Wurm Nest* raid and the neither the spark nor the Brotherhood had been seen since. That was a full expansion ago. They were thought to have be wiped out but few believed that. Then weeks before the launch of the sixth expansion, *From Perdition to Rapture*, part of their symbol appeared on the moon in a pre-expansion event. The Nohorian Brotherhood was back and somehow they were a part of the Glitch.

Apophenia is the human tendency to perceive meaningful patterns within random data. Could I have been seeing a conclusion that didn't really exist? It was possible but then again, I was also dealing with Casper Ramirez. VCO's creator was a puzzle fanatic. If there was a needlessly complicated puzzle he could insert into the game, he would. If there was a mystery he could lace into his lore, he would. Casper loved a mystery and he loved leaving hints in their wake. So if I thought there was connection, chances were there actually existed one.

It wasn't a comforting thought.

Chapter 02

"Alright, go away. I have a tiny world to save." — Bryan Lee O'Malley, Scott Pilgrim's Finest Hour

"Rake?" The familiar voice hit my ears and I looked up from my books. I blinked in surprise as I spotted the familiar paladin. Slashlore smiled as he approached. "So this is where you've been. The whole city's been looking for you and you've been under our noses the whole time."

"What are you doing here?" I asked.

"Questing: doing some gopher mission and ended up here," he explained. Slashlore pulled out a chair and sat across the table from me. He looked at the books and frowned. His frown wasn't of sadness or sympathy, it was because he didn't know what to say. None of them did. Despite my best attempt at hiding, in the past week I'd also seen Tialla and Punchocalypse. Both had stumbled across me throughout the city and neither of them had known what to say.

"So, what's all this?"

For a moment, I did nothing but sit in silence. Eventually I started to explain. I told him my theory and showed him what I had been researching. I would have shown him my results but after a week, I still had nothing. I knew more about the Brotherhood then I cared to but still I had no actionable intelligence.

Slashlore remained silent as I talked. He intently listened, nodding in certain places and shaking his head in others, but he never interrupted. When I finished there was silence. Once again Slashlore frowned.

"Is this the best use of your time?" He eventually asked. "Have you been getting the letters I've been sending you?"

VCO, like most MMORPGs, had an in-game mail system. In the past week I had received dozens of letters, a large number of them from Slashlore, Tialla, some guy name Reit and, surprisingly, Bearcules. I'd read each and every one of them and then promptly deleted them. The letters were cries for help. Ever since my meeting with Steelion, people had viewed me as some sort of hero. Some thought of me as their sheriff, some thought of me as their champion and some thought I'd be the saviour who would free us all. I wanted to be none of that. I simply wanted to find a way out.

"It's not my problem," I said quietly.

"They seem to think it is," Slashlore rebutted.

"They were also the same idiots who were fine with hunting me down because Ste...." I took a deep breath, "Because someone told them to."

"People are dumb," Slashlore defended. "They're stupid and scared but they can also change. Do you know why you get daily letters from Bearcules?" I shook my head. His mail had been updates on the city's status. They included problem areas, possible solutions, threats to Havenhold and a brief description of any current rumours. "He's become Havenhold's make-shift sheriff. It started out with him helping those who needed it and then word got around."

"Yeah," I scoffed, "People voted for Trump so why the hell not, let's vote an angry bounty hunter as sheriff."

"He's trying to make amends," Slashlore defended. "You showed him that power wasn't the most important thing. You showed all of them that. What was it you said during your grandstanding speech? The only way we're getting out of here is by working together."

"It's been a fucking week," I snapped. I didn't care that Slashlore was using my words against me. I didn't even care that care that Bearcules was trying to redeem himself. All of these were good things, all of these needed to happen but it didn't happen this quickly. Bearcules didn't get to be forgiven in a week. He didn't get a second chance in a week, nobody did.

"We have to get out there," Slashlore said. "This world is dangerous and people are just making it worse. Trolls are running rampant - picking on whomever they can -, PCs are mysteriously vanishing and now there are assholes out there that are hunting and killing people." He became silent. The last one cut deep. "The only blessing we have is that the Descendents of the Damned are keeping to themselves. I figure they're off licking the same wounds we are. Rake, the PCs are divided. They need a leader and the whispers going around say they want you."

"I'm no leader," I said. "They need someone diff---."

Slashlore suddenly raised a hand to silence me. He turned away as his eyes quickly moved from left to right as he read words that were only visible to him. It was obvious he'd just gotten a PM. His lips silently mouthed words as he sent his reply.

A devilish grin crossed his lips as he lowered his hand. I raised an eyebrow. He wordlessly retreated a couple paces as a ball of fire suddenly appeared in the middle of the library. I narrowed my eyes and reached for my blades. The ball rapidly grew until it became the size of a portal. A familiar Elven form tumbled through the flame portal and landed before me Terminatrix style. I eyed the Elf and shook my head. She was tall and thin, with flowing flames where her hair should have been. She stood up and looked around, looking right past me, until her eyes fell on Slashlore.

I sighed and let my head thud against the desk. This was why he was smirking. Fire Mage Scova, the Burning Typhoon herself, had just arrived in my post-Glitch life.

"Hey, Scova," Slashlore began. "How goes? How hav--"

"Shut up, Failadin," she snapped. She stormed over to the paladin, the flames transforming into long brown hair. "Where's Stov?"

"I'm good too. I mean adapting to the Glitch is hard on all of us but we're working together to make it easier. Thanks for asking." Slashlore looked at Scova expectantly.

His gaze shifted as he noticed her lack of weapons and armour. He looked at the tattered rags that she wore and found his attention being drawn to the bloodied bandages wrapped around her chest. "Wait, what the hell happened to you?"

He stepped in and let his hands run up her sides. She winced at his touch, not out of repulsion but at the pain. She tried to pull away but Slashlore didn't let her. He called forth the divine magic and let it pass through his fingers and into her wound. Seconds later Scova could feel the wound stitching together.

"Seriously, what happened?"

"I went head to head with the Nohorian Brotherhood," she explained quickly. She shook her head. "I'm grateful for the heals but I need Stov. I don't have much time. I need his help and I need it yesterday."

Scova was a fire mage and a damned good treasure hunter. She did, however, have the ability to draw chaos. Wherever she went, explosions followed. After years of working together I had learned that if you play with fire, you're going to get burned. You couldn't control Scova's chaos but you could point it, like the Hulk, and hoped that it was only the bad stuff that got destroyed.

"He's behind you." She spun around, stared past me, and turned back.

"Seriously; where he at?" she said in an East Coast accent. "You said he was in the library with you."

"I'm Stov," I said. She spun back around and looked at me suspiciously. I smiled. "Hero ain't on my résumé." It was a joke between her and me. I was ice and she was fire. We were VCO's Captain Cold and Heat Wave. She stared at me with wide eyes.

"WTF?" She blinked a couple minutes. "Rake: that's your bank-alt. Are you trying to tell me that when we all got stuck in some video game that you got stuck in your bank-alt?" I sheepishly nodded.

She laughed for five full minutes.

I was growing tired of that reaction.

"I...need...your...help," she said between giggles. She coughed and tried to stop laughing. She took several deep breaths and calmed herself. Then, like a dying flame that suddenly had a fresh log put upon it, she reignited in a flurry of urgency. "Get your shit, Stov -- I mean Rake. I need to do an emergency instance run and you're coming with me."

"Slow down, what's going on?"

She rolled her eyes. It was obvious that she thought that she didn't have time for this but I needed to figure out what was going on before I jumped into anything, especially with her.

"Okay, like two weeks ago I was questing with Whisper NPCs," she said quickly. "I was studying the pre-expansion event and traced it to the Nohorian Brotherhood. The Whispers and I tracked a Brotherhood camp. We attacked it but shit went sideways and Lady Adelaide Bullmourn and I have been held captive. I just escaped and came here. Lady Bullmourn is still there and I have to go back and save her."

"Why didn't you PM us?" Slashlore asked, "Or town portal out of there?"

"Neither worked," she said quickly. "I couldn't cast a spell either. Something was suppressing my abilities."

Slashlore looked at me. That was a frightening fact. Not only could the Nohorian Brotherhood suppress magic, which wasn't unheard of in lore, but they could also suppress our ability to port and PM. If the world was becoming real, did that mean that those features were becoming magic?

"You don't have to worry about anything," Slashlore said. "NPCs can't die. If they do, they respawn. They don't have perma-death like we do. They respawn in their homes like it never happened."

A fist flew out and connected with Slashlore's face. The paladin, caught by surprise, toppled to the ground. "Don't you fucking say that; of course it matters. She can't die!"

"The hell, Scova?"

"What happens to their memories after they respawn? Do they remember who they were before or do they reset? If they remember, do they remember dying? 'Cause I ain't putting her through that."

"Scova!" I leapt from my chair and moved towards her. "Calm down. I'll help you but we can't go running into... wherever she is. Things have to be done more carefully now."

"You don't think I know that?" she said. "I've been healing for a week, in a god damn video game, because the Nohorian Brotherhood infiltrated the Whispers. They had someone on the inside and they turned on Lady Bullmourn. Now she's there, alone, and expecting me to come save her."

I eyed her for a second. This was something different. This was personal and I didn't know why. "Okay, I'll help. Where are we going?"

"We're going to need numbers. Who do we got? You, me, Failadin," she rubbed her head as her mind raced. "We'll need a good spanker so ring up Steelion." I froze. She looked at me curiously. "What? Where Steelion?"

"He's not available," Slashlore said, coming to my rescue. She opened her mouth to ask more but Slashlore glared her to silence. He looked at me. "What about Tialla? We'll need heals. I could ask Bearcules, he'll be mo--"

"No. You're our tank. I'm not going to him." I shook my head as I thought. "Okay, give me an hour to get ready and find allies." I looked at the rags Scova wore. "What about you? Where is your gear?"

"Brotherhood has it. I got backups in my bank. They're not as good but they'll have to do."

"If he's not coming, then I'm telling Bearcules and others where I'm going." Slashlore paused. "Where are we going?"

"They were holding us in the Crypt Walker's Keep." I walked over to my table, sat back down and let my head fall to the desk with a loud thud. The Crypt Walker's Keep, of course it was the Crypt Walker's Keep.

Fire Mage Scova, the burning typhoon of chaos, had struck again.

Chapter 03

"Be aware of the present moment" — Fawkes (Fallout 3)

I sat in a chair and stared at the painting on the wall. It was of a freshly painted brown barn next to a field of vibrantly green grass, with blooming red flowers and an orange cart. It was a common painting but each time I saw it, I couldn't help but stare. It was a meaningless painting, used to add details to rooms and building but something about it felt warm. Perhaps that was a sign of good game building, when the smallest and most meaningless details felt real.

I sat in the Stenha Library, outside the room of Lord Dorian Bullmourn. I was waiting for an audience so I could tell him of our plans. I don't know what it was about the Whispers that I felt loyal to. They didn't exist, they weren't real and I wasn't a member. I was just some alt with a flashy tattoo. But here I was, patiently waiting to speak to my Lord so I could tell him of his daughter and of the betrayal in his organization.

The door opened and Garruil emerged from the Lord's office. She gave me a warm smile, one that showed her genuine interest in seeing me. I smiled back. "The Lord will see you now."

I climbed to my feet and entered the office. Lord Dorian Bullmourn sat behind a large oaken desk. He looked up at me. I clumsily bowed. Bullmourn nodded away my attempt and offered me a seat. Garruil stood by the door, behind me. Bullmourn was an older man, with greying hair, but still held a well kept body. A black blade longsword sat on the wall behind him, held aloft by a pair of hooks.

"My girl says you wish to speak of Adelaide?" Lord Bullmourn said.

"Yes M'lord," I said quickly. "I have received word that your daughter discovered the Nohorian Brotherhood in a camp. They assaulted the camp but were defeated. Your daughter has been taken hostage and is being held in the Crypt Walker's Keep."

Lord Bullmourn's body tensed up. I waited for a response but none came. Instead I continued speaking. "My allies and I are planning an attack on the Keep. We will be attacking it within the hour, with your blessing, M'lord."

He sat silently for a moment but eventually he spoke. "Thank you, Mr. Rake. This is very damaging news indeed. I had long suspected the Nohorian Brotherhood was still operational. This proves it. You have permission to undertake this mission. I will assign Garruil to you. She will lead a team to assist you."

"I don't mean to be rude, M'lord," I said cautiously, "But according to your daughter, the reason she was taken was because the Nohorian Brotherhood had turned members of your organization; she was betrayed, M'lord. The Nohorian Brotherhood has infiltrated the Whispers."

Lord Bullmourn looked to Garruil with a stern gaze. "That is *more* damaging news."

I walked through the royal library and moved to my desk. It wasn't mine but I had claimed it. I slept there, I ate there, I stored gear there and I basically lived there. I came to a halt as I found it cleaned off and my gear gone. My heart began to race as I became frantic. Where was my bag? Where were my notes? Where was my stuff?

"Master Rake?" I turned around and saw a librarian standing there. I nodded at her. "Please follow me."

She moved through the library and I silently followed. We headed to the rear where she ascended a staircase and stopped at a door. Smiling, she turned to face me, handing me a key. "I received orders today from Queen Theresa Ar-chona. She asked me to prepare this room for you. If you need books or food we will be more than happy to help."

I stood there stunned. My mouth opened to protest or to ask a question but the librarian simply walked away, leaving me speechless. I looked at the key and watched as it dematerialized into my hand. Tapping the doorknob, I heard the distinct sound of the door unlocking. I opened it up and stepped inside. It was a large room with a sturdy desk, a large bed, an armoire and dozens of books placed on a set of three bookshelves. I walked to the armoire and opened it up. Inside was my gear and my supplies. Walking back to the desk I saw a leather bound jotter and note lying atop it. I picked it up and gave it a read.

Rake;

I started my studies into the world of magic when I was a teenager. From then until the days of my early adulthood, I spent thousands of hours in this library; studying every piece of writing I could find. For years, this was my room. I live in the castle now, or some-where else if rumours are to be taken as fact, which means this room no longer has a use. Is a room still a room if it doesn't have a use? Don't let such a good room become something else.
Look after this room for me.

The Witch Queen

P.S. Your notes seemed very disorganized. The jotter will help.

I stood at a large conference table staring down at my *magic* journal. The journal, which was an installed app that gave me access to the VCO wiki, was opened to a map of the Crypt Walker Keep. I pushed the journal into the center of the table and looked at those standing alongside me. I was accompanied by seven others. There were the Elves, Scova and Slashlore, the humans, Tialla, Garruil and Fleyming, a gnome, Skith - Son of Zook, and the craziest dwarf in all of existence, Punchocalypse.   I looked at each, one after another, my eye lingering on Fleyming, the warlock who had tried to kill me.

"Um...excuse my interruption. I am aware I am the new gnome in the group - and thanks goes to Ms. Tialla for inviting me, so I am aware that much will go over my head." Skith started giggling at his own joke. "So pardon my ignorance but is there something going on between the rogue and the warlock? Are they Exs? Are they...um...bumping uglies? Will their sexual desire for each other cause conflict? Are we allowed to watch when they do? For scientific reasons, of course." Tialla shut the gnome up with a quick elbow.

"So who is the little guy?" Punchocalypse asked. "He's fun!"

"I am Mast Skith," he explained. "I used to be a Master but the E and R fell off my sign."

"Just say it," Fleyming said abruptly, ignoring the introduction going on. "Just say whatever it is you want to say."

"I don't want you here," I said.

"I know."

"You tried to kill me," I threatened.

"Yes, I did," she replied.   "But I'm sorry. I'm trying to change."

"Oh my, this is intense indeed," Skith said with a giggle. He pulled out a notepad. "I have always wondered how human boinking differs from the superior gnomes." Tialla elbowed him again.

"I trust everyone here with my life," I said. It wasn't exactly true but it was close enough. "Tell me why I should trust you?"

"Because you taught me that I can't just fear the big guy," Fleyming said. "I have been so afraid since the Glitch, my fear controls me, but you showed me that I don't have to be afraid. You showed me that I can be something other than my fear, that I can be a good person."

It's been two weeks.

"Fine," I scowled. I looked at the rest. "This is a rescue mission. Our target: Lady Adelaide Bullmourn. Our mission is to get into the Crypt Walker's Keep."

"Ade is...I mean...Lady Adelaide is being held in the Keep's prison cells." Scova tapped the on the map. She dragged her finger across the paper until she came across the Keep's east entrance. "We'll enter the keep here and," she tapped the roof, "here. We'll strike on both ends."

"We'll be plowing through the Brotherhood. It'll be easy," Slashlore said.

"No it won't. The Brotherhood's up their game. They've been up-leveled, better armed and even enchanted. They ain't the Brotherhood we saw in WN, they are much worse," Scova said.

"Sweet," Punchocalypse said. "A good fight is a good fight."

"Let us fight together, Mr Biggums," Skith laughed.

"Our second objective is to find any intel on the Brotherhood. I think they're behind the Glitch. Anything we find about them will help me get us out of here," I explained. It wasn't as simple as that but it'd be a start. "Any questions?"

Tialla raised her hand. I nodded at her. "No offense to Ms. Garruil but what makes Lady Bullmourn so special? Why is she worth risking our lives for?"

"How the hell could you say that?" Scova yelled. I placed my hand on her shoulder.

"I was wondering the same myself," I explained. "But I don't think we can walk away from this. We need to know everything about the Brotherhood if we want to get out of here."

"According to your theory," Fleyming added.

"My theory, actually," Tialla corrected her.

"Getting out will require intelligence. However, none of us are super spies and we don't have satellites and wiretaps. To be honest we don't know shit about getting intel in this day and age." I pointed at Garruil. "The Whispers do. They have the knowledge, they have the knowhow and they have the infrastructure. We need an alliance with the Whispers."

"We as in Havenhold?" Tialla asked.

"We as in the PCs," Slashlore interjected. "We don't know where the Witch Queen stands on the Brotherhood let alone the Glitch. We don't know if she even registers the Glitch." He eyed Garruil. The librarian listened intently but said nothing. "So until then we are basically our own people. We are the PCs living amongst the Descendants."

"You are the Enclave," Garruil offered. We all went quiet. That was a damn good name.

"So, they aren't going to boink?" Tialla's elbow began to hurt from overuse.

I stepped out of the portal and instantly felt an urge to vomit. I dropped to my knees and tried to settle my stomach. I felt Scova's presence above me. I looked up at her. She no longer wore her tattered rags. Instead she wore a suit of padded armour, with a reinforced chest plate, specifically built to be worn by mages. She wore a red cloak that fell over one shoulder. Her gear was mismatched, with various belts, buckles and object laced across her body. This was the style of a treasure hunter, equipping what they could, where they could.

"Still get air sickness?" She asked as her hand fell upon the hilt of her sheathed katana.

"It's not *air* sickness," I snapped at the mage.

"Fine, *portal* sickness," she corrected. "Have you tried cake?"

"What?" I asked in confusion, not getting her reference before it was too late.

"This is a triumph," Slashlore sung as he passed by me. "I'm making a note here: huge success." I groaned at the pair of them.

"How old is that reference?" I groaned. I felt a hand reach down and take me by the shoulder. I looked at Garruil as she helped me up.

"I wouldn't listen to Ms. Scova," she said. "The Whispers have a saying that we all live by: the cake is a lie."

The group exploded in laughter and I was left scowling. This was what happened when game developers put memes and references in their games.

We stood on a cliff and stared down at Crypt Walker's Keep. The castle was daunting and was the colour of bleached bones. It reminded me of Castle Greyskull. I don't know who thought that Greyskull would make a cool base for a childhood good guy because truth be told, it was frightening as all hell.

When Vörissa fell to Aspumer, she caused a great amount of damage. She ransacked the world, destroyed magical gates and even created a tear between the celestial realm and the mortal realm. Vanilla VCO was about the players fighting against the Goddess but being unable to kill her. Instead we locked her away, sealed her in a prison but the damage had been done. The first of her Catalyst, the game's name for the horror that followed, was the Crypt Walker.

In VCO lore, there were the gods, the masters of the various domains. Beneath them were the archons, powerful beings who toiled away as assistants to the divine. The land of the dead was ruled by a god called Helruss and his archon Diaduus. As Vörissa killed, souls travelled to the death realm in great numbers. Each soul carried a hint of Vörissa's corruption. Diaduus carried the corruption, in increasing numbers, until the archon succumbed. He became a bastardized version of himself and transformed into a creature of evil. He became the Crypt Walker.

The Crypt Walker stepped through the tear and ashes rained from the sky. The Crypt Walker raised a castle, built his skeletal throne and raised an army of undead. He spat insane rhetoric about how the dead no longer needed to leave the mortal realm and how he could rid the world of the disease of life. This became VCO's first expansion: The *Ashen Downpour*. The expansion brought a new foe, new raids and instances, a bump in the level cap and a new playable class: The Revenants.

In lore terms, Revenants were made from men and women who were within their last moments of life when Helruss came to them. He restored their bodies, filled them with necromatic energy and sent them out to fight against the Crypt Walker.

In game terms they were a hybrid class. They were part tank and part mage. They were great teammates and had quickly become a significant part of raids and PVP. Skith was a revenant and apparently a decent PVPer.

"Okay," Slashlore said. "We all know the plan. So everybody mount up."

Like Dollarstore Power Rangers, each of us grabbed an item from our belt, held it aloft and cried out an animal's name. One after another, our mounts materialized before us. Gryphons, wyverns and Pegai appeared. Skith summoned an undead horse with dynamite instead of horseshoes.

"What in the living fuck is that?" Punchocalypse asked.

"It's my Dead-A-Pult. It's a flying mount that is exclusive to gnome Revenant-Engineers," the gnome explained. There were professions in VCO that allowed players to craft items. Engineers built impossible devices that tended to explode, even when they weren't supposed to.

"But how does TNT on its feet make him fly?" Punchocalypse asked.

"Trust me," Tialla warned, "it's easier if you don't ask. Skith is......an RPer."

We all gave a playful winced.

RPers - role players - built a persona and then played VCO as that persona. Some used RPing for ERPing - erotic role playing - while others did it as an escape. Whatever the reason, RPers and PVErs never meshed well.

"Enough chit-chat," Slashlore ordered. "Let's ride."

I summoned my mount, a simple horse, and climbed on. I didn't have access to either my rare or flying mounts.

They were level dependant and I was still clawing my way back up to the max.

Fleyming, Tialla, Skith and Garruil - the monk sharing the priest's mount - took to the air. Skith's undead steed was propelled into the air by an explosion. As they departed, Scova, Slashlore, Punchocalypse and I moved to the east entrance. I stared at the two doors, built from thick wood. We came to a halt.

"I could use my armour and try and phase through it," I offered as Punchocalypse dismounted. "I could open it from the other end. I mean it --"

"Kamé-Doken Blast!" Light formed from Punchocalypse's hand as he summoned a gigantic ball of ki energy. He thrust his hands forward and watched as the blast collided with the doors, transforming them into thousands of burning splinters.

"Kamé-Doken?" Slashlore asked.

"Copywrite issues," the dwarf replied with a grin.

"Let's kick some ass!" Scova cried out as she pushed her wyvern forward. I kicked my horse forward and followed along behind her. Slashlore, on his pegasus, and Punchocalypse, on his gryphon, flew ahead as I followed behind. The gryphon breached the castle first. Punchocalypse leapt off the flying beast, letting it tackle a pair of surprised Brotherhood members, and landed before before a pair of mobs. His fists were blurs as he struck, streams of ki forming bright energy trails like American Hockey. It took mere seconds for the first two to fall, leaving a cocky dwarf in their wake.

The sounds of approaching reinforcements filled the Keep's hallways. Scova dismounted her wyvern and drew the katana from her belt. "That sounds like a lot of them."

Slashlore drew his axe and shield as I quickly drew both of my blades. Scova scowled as her brown hair began to smolder as it morphed into brightly burning flames. "Make them suffer!"

The mobs came around the corner and Scova was the first to strike. A ball of fire erupted from her fingertips and crashed into the mob of mobs. The ball detonated and sent the first couple rows flying backwards. Punchocalypse let out a battle whoop as he charged forward. His fist regained their blur status as they struck. I reached the mob next, my blades moving swiftly as I struck.

My Whaitiri Edge danced quickly as it moved from one defence square to another, deflecting the Brotherhood's blow, sending jolt of electricity back through them with each parry. Splinter's Bite, a formidable dance partner for the Edge, leapt from attack circle to attack circle. The blade fed on the Brotherhood's flesh, hungrily consuming their health. I activated my boots and called upon their speed, propelling my feet faster and I weaved in and out of battle, striking and cutting as I did. With each strike my combo points increased. The Brotherhood members were above my level so I had to be clever and I had to rely on my team. I would strike with my shadow strike or my saber slash and build up my combo meter. Then I would strike with my cross slash and do devastating damage. My team would finish them off.

The four of us quickly started to work together. When Punchocalypse would duck, I was there with swinging blades. When I would weave, Scova would appear with fire at the ready. When she pivoted to the right, Slashlore would appear at the left, covering her rear and when he drew the mobs back, Punchocalypse would flank them.

I found my blades moving quicker, my body getting used a two-weapon style. It helped that I didn't need to kill each mob myself. I could stab and wound one or hamstring another and my party would be there to help finish them off. There was nothing more satisfying then slicing at an enemy's leg, stepping back to deflect a second attack, only to see a tongue of flame shoot past my head and into the face of the first attacker.

Teamwork.

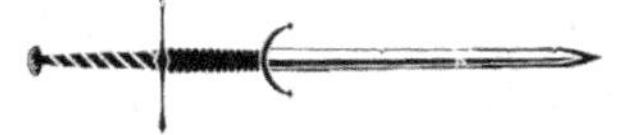

With each Brotherhood member that fell, my experience bar ticked up a little more. In VCO, and most RPGs, a player got stronger by gaining enough experience (EXP) and increasing their levels. EXP gain was normally done slowly and steady but having a gang of PCs ripping through mobs that were well above my level meant my exp jumped at an incredible rate. It was called power-leveling and it was glorious. I had already jumped to level 26 and I was expecting to jump at least one more level, two if I was lucky.

The Keep shook as the shockwaves of explosion, originating from above us, went off in rapid succession. I smiled. Only a gnome could explode with that efficiency. I hope that the roof team was okay. I didn't know what Skith was capable of but I did know what Fleyming was and that was what scared me.

"Go left," Scova screamed as we reached a fork in the hallway. I glanced to the right as a pair of Bortherhood douches charged at me. I deflected the spear of one, Whaitiri Edge slapping it aside, as Slashlore's shield blocked the hammer of the second. My longsteel and his axe struck at once and the two fell. Truth was the axe fell in one hit while Splinter's Bite fell in three. It wasn't the weapon's fault; it was the difference in attack between the paladin and I.

We bolted to down the left hallway for several moments, attacking as we ran, until we exited into the courtyard. We ran across the square, past the benches and weapon racks full of spears, but came to a sliding halt as a giant suddenly materialized before us. I stared at the giant and noticed the silver aura emanating from it. Of all the times for a fucking rare spawn to show up my luck said it had to be now. The giant swung its club down at us but we quickly scattered.

"Punch?" I asked quickly.

"On it," he replied. His hands moved quickly as a ball of ki started to form. "Kamé-Doken Blast!"

The ball of energy collided with the giant's chest. The beast stumbled and roared but it didn't fall. Scova stepped forward, her hand raised and her hair burning brighter than before. She shouted loudly as a set of six fiery blast shot from her palm and into the giant's face. Once again, it roared in pair but it persevered.

"For America!" Slashlore yelled as his shield glowed. In his best Evans imitation, he tossed the golden shield and watched as it swift crossed the courtyard and collided with the giant's neck. Seconds later, it returned to Slashlore's hand.

Scova quickly began to tap a second spell when a lucky dagger flew past her and ended up in the giant's eye. The beast screamed in panic as it desperately tried to pull it free. The giant frantically ran back and forth in the square until it tripped on a bench and fell forward, landing on a weapon rack, the spears having ripped through its neck and emerged out on the other end.

The three other looked back at me in shock. The lucky dagger rematerialized in my hand. I snapped it back into my glove and looked as the words LEVEL 27 appeared before my eyes.

"Well, I think that counts as my kill."

"Like fuck it does," Punchocalypse argued.

"Ade!" Scova cried out as she slid up to the door of the familiar cell. She smiled as she looked inside and saw the familiar lithe form of Lady Adelaide.

"Little Flame," she replied with a smile. "I knew you'd come for me."

"Little Flame?" Slashlore asked with a chuckle.

"Stand back," Scova explained. "Punchocalypse is going to pick the lock."

"Kamé-Doken Blast!"

I marveled at Punchocalypse's lock picking skills.

Scova ran through the smoldering remains of the door and inside the cell. She took Adelaide into her arms and the two embraced. "I knew you'd come. I knew you'd come."

I blinked in surprise as Scova gently ran her hands Lady Adelaide's cheek before leaning in for a kiss. The pair tenderly kissed, their emotion radiating outwards like ripples in a pond.

I looked away.

Punchocalypse did not.

"You have to stop them," Lady Adelaide said when her lips were freed. "They're going to attack Havenhold!"

Chapter 04

"When my dad was young he shot marbles. When I was young I played Marble Madness on my Nintendo Entertainment System."
— Kevin James Breaux

"Tell me what you know," Slashlore said quickly.

"They are going to launch another attack on Havenhold," Lady Adelaide said. "They're preparing a portal attack; Havenhold isn't ready."

It was true. The NPC citizens of Havenhold would be caught off guard but they could respawn. PCs could not and Havenhold was home to hundreds of lowbies. We needed to stop or delay this attack.

"Where?" I abruptly asked.

"Upstairs," she explained. "They are launching it from the battle room."

"Start heading there now," Slashlore ordered. "I'll PM Tialla and tell them to meet us."

We took the stairs two at a time as we ascended the keep. The battleroom was where the Crypt Walker's mages summoned arcane magic to launch their assault. They would create large portals that allowed the troops to cross large distances. Portal warfare allowed troops to launch devastating attacks from the other side of the world. It was a powerful tool but a costly one. Small portals were easy to maintain and could be done by a solo mage. Army sized portals required nearly a dozen mages working in unison.

Slashlore slowed us to a halt as we reached the battle room. I crept to the front and peered inside. Dozens of armed men and women stood around as they waited. Each were dressed in onyx-black armour with purple highlights and wore a half-mask upon their face. Every Brotherhood member in the army stood around doing nothing. They impatiently waited for the mages to finish their arcane machinations. Internally, I smirked. *Hurry up and wait* was universal, even in the fantasy realm.

The room had an elevated platform at the head of the room. Standing on it were two men. One was a full-plated warrior who was big AF and was scary, Jason Momoa scary. He wore onyx armour like the rest but for some reason, Khal Drogo's armour looked scarier. The second was a Lord of some sort, wielding a hand-and-a-half sword, dressed in black chainmail armour and wearing the half-mask. He wasn't as physically intimidating as Drogo, but The Phantom of the Opera held an aura of power and corruption about him. The Phantom stood before a magic mirror, talking to an apparent superior. I ducked back behind the corner and looked to Slashlore. He huddled us together as he laid out his plan.

"This room has an east and west entrance. Tialla just PM'd me. Bravo Team are waiting at the west entrance. We're going to breach the room together." Slashlore seemed different when he laid out a plan. He seemed more composed and sure of himself. "I'm going down the center: Rake and Punchocalypse will follow me. We're going to rip a hole through their numbers. Scova and Adelaide: go for the mages. Take them out. If enough of them fall then their portal to Havenhold will fail."

We all nodded. Slashlore placed a hand on my shoulder and gave me a concerned look. "Stay safe man," It made sense. While levels were quickly becoming less and less relevant, they did still exist and they were important.

Slashlore checked the binding on his shield and adjusted it slightly. He smiled at us. "Okay, get ready." He counted down as he PM'd Tialla. "3, 2, 1 - Breach!"

We stormed in from the east as Bravo Team entered from the west. Slashlore's shield glowed as he Evansed. It bounced off the first surprised Brotherhood member and attacked another. It hit a total of five targets before returning to the paladin. By that time, Slashlore was a mere two feet away from the Brotherhood masses. He smirked, held his shield before him and barreled through their numbers, sending members flying by the trio. Punchocalypse leapt forward, landing in the middle with a ground punch. The ground shook as he sent Brotherhood members tumbling to the ground. I used my boots to propel me forward, using the speed to weave in and out of their numbers as my blades danced. Whaitiri Edge leapt up to meet the defence squares as Splinter's Bite connected with the attack circles, feeding on blood and flesh with each strike.

Bravo Team, not to be outdone, struck just as vigorously. Fleyming launched a volley of sickly green balls of death into the room as Garruil charged into the horde, her hands and feet moving in their usual blurry fashion. Skith charged forward, a glaive firmly wielded in both hands. He swung at the Brotherhood, piling dead bodies faster than a live grenade would at a Storm Trooper/Red Shirt union meeting. His glaive, if it could be correctly called that, was little more than a giant's cleaver tied to a stick. However unconventional his weapon's appearance, I couldn't fault its effectiveness.

Tialla stood back from the fight but was intricately apart of it. Her hands moved swiftly as she summoned healing spells to mend our wounds while calling upon her shadowy apparitions to lend aid.

Scova entered the room and targeted the first mage she saw. With practised speed, she tapped out a spell and launched a tongue of fire. It quickly consumed the unsuspecting mage, the flames hungrily feasting on the Elven flesh. Two warriors, realizing the danger she possessed, charged Scova. The mage smirked, the flame of her hair burning brighter, as she shifted her stance. She held her katana high in the air and she waited. The blade, Keshim's Fang, was made from the tooth of a red dragon. The blade began to glow as Scova willed the weapon's enchantment to life. She quickly sidestepped, missing the Brotherhood's hungry blade, and struck with hers. The Fang dove across the warrior's side, the blade's heat searing the wound close as she cut. The first warrior, still feeling the weapon's burn, pawed at his wound as Scova pivoted to meet the assault of the second. The first looked at his wound, confused, and noticed that it was glowing from the inside. Suddenly, the glow exploded and propelled the first warrior into the air. Scova smirked as she quickly fell the second. While Keshim's Fang wasn't as strong as Thean'melorn, it did have an interesting effect. It could plant a small fireball spell *within* its target's skin that would explode, from the inside, seconds later.

Lady Adelaide entered the room and instantly vanished from view. She reappeared second later, running her stolen sword through a surprised mage. I tried to figure out where she'd obtained the weapon from but as I noticed the path of dead warriors and rogues in her path, I decided against asking too much.

Our initial attack was proving victorious but so far our success had been limited to our surprise. Realizing what was occurring, the Brotherhood began to organize and fight back. Atop his platform, The Phantom began to bark out orders, sadly not in a singing voice as I had hoped, and the platoons responded. Some moved to defend the mages while others attempted to swarm us. We looked to Slashlore for advice. Did he want us to retreat? The paladin ordered us forward.

"Cut them down!" he cried out. "Give them everything you've got!"

"Kamé-Doken Blast!" Brotherhood members flew everywhere as the blast ripped through the room. Not one to avoid the fun, Skith cried out as his face took a disturbing look.

"No gear ticks alone!" Skith whooped as he drew a small figurine from his belt. He tossed it onto the ground and, in some *different enough as not to be sued but we all know what it really is* Pokémon action, the figuring vanished as an eight-foot undead orc materialized in its place. The undead orc (un-orc as Skith called it) stood there with putrid flesh falling off of its body and a massive club in his hand. Skith leapt onto its back and, in the most messed up Groot-Rocket imitation I have ever seen, rode the undead brute as he attacked from atop. The un-orc lunged forward, roaring as it swung it scary AF club, while Skith rode by the brute's head, stabbing with his cleaver-glaive while giggling incessantly.

Fleyming's spells grew bigger and bigger. She'd rain down death and damnation in one instance then she'd reach out and drain the life from a Brotherhood member - which I'd feel sorry for - in the next.

Scova moved her hand back and forth as flames emerged from her palm. She was a living flamethrower and the Brotherhood was suffering. She paused long enough to strike with her Fang or ignite the floor before she returned to casting fire spells.

Garruil moved her way through the masses until she found herself beside Punchocalypse. The pair of monks took a quick look at each other, instantly sizing each other up in some Monk-on-Monk action. Neither spoke, each simply smiled at one another before shifting their stances. Suddenly they were back to back and nobody was getting close to them. Four fists and four feet moved and dozens died. Monks were scary OP.

I ducked as a blade came knocking at my neck and watched as it passed inches over my head. I rolled backwards and came back to my feet. Whaitiri Edge flew upward to block an attack and Splinter's Bite followed. The longsteel dove deep, freeing the soul from the husk that trapped it. The member's body fell to the ground as two more descended upon me. I activated the second enchantment in my boots, slowing me back to normal, and my feet became stone. I spun with a back kick and sent the Brotherhood member flying backward, crashing into four others and causing them all to topple to the ground like a bad set in bowling. My boots returned to normal as I felt the speed return to my feet. My boots held two abilities but only one could be used at a time.

A golden shield flew past my head and knocked back another pair of Brotherhood goons. Slashlore stepped towards me and nodded to the dais. I looked up and saw The Phantom calling out new instructions. He ordered the mages to forgo the large teleport spell, the one that would allow them to breach Havenhol's walls, and instead make dozens of smaller ones. I wondered why until I realized what was happening. This wasn't a shift in plan, they were jackrabbiting. This was a retreat. We were far from a victory but the Brotherhood's losses were too great.

"Telis'un," The phantom called out. Drago raised his head and looked at his master. "Rend them in two." The brute smiled.

Khal Drago stepped down from the platform with a smirk on his lips. He drew the greatsword from his back and let out a menacing chuckle. The blade sliced across the air before him and sent a wave of magic into the room. The blast sent the nine of us flying backwards and we slammed against the wall. I hit the wall first, a painful experience, only to have Slashlore slam against me. We crumpled to the ground, wincing in pain as I forced myself to my feet. I looked around and spotted Tialla. Her hand moved as she tried to hold back Khal Drogo but his blade proved too strong. It easily ripped through her defenses. The brute smashed his fist against her and slammed her against the ground. He stabbed his blade downwards and into Tialla's chest.

Our priest tried to scream but couldn't.

She was dead.

Chapter 05

"I hate guns.   Which isn't to say that a bit of fantasy violence can't be therapeutic." - The Doctor (Doctor Who: Winner Takes All)

Tialla lay on the ground, unmoving. She was dead but perhaps there was a chance to save her. In pre-Glitch combat, if you died in a battle you really didn't until the soul left the body. This gave healers a chance to rez the players. If these same rules applied now, perhaps we could save Tialla before we lost her forever.

"Priest is down," I winced. Slashlore looked over and swore. "Can you battle-rez her?"

"Not with him around," the paladin said as he nodded toward Khal Drago. I looked up and saw the boss confidently approached us.

"I'll deal with Khal Drago," I said. "You save Tialla's life."

"Khal? What are....oh. Got it."

I looked around to see who was on their feet. I spotted Skith and his un-orc, Garruil and Fleyming. The rest were still picking themselves up. I cursed. I didn't want to deal with Fleyming but I had no choice.

"Skith: Tank. Garruil: Spank. Fleyming:" she looked at me expectantly but frowned as she saw the hesitation in my eyes. I shook my head. "Slow him down and don't hold back."

The four of us readied ourselves as Khal Drago approached. I smirked and channeled my cockiness.

"Telis'un," Khal looked at me. "You know that's Elven for *bitch* right?"

Fleyming raised her hand and tapped out a spell. She channeled a beam of sickly green energy into Drago. The warlock's spell drained life from him while replenishing her own. Her spell slowed Drago's step. It only debuffed him with a 13% decrease in speed but every bit helped. Skith climbed back upon his un-orc and the pair charged forward. The un-orc slammed it's club into Drago's side and Skith struck at his face. Garruil and I charged forward. I struck first, using Splinter's Bite for a saber slash across Drago's chest. I quickly dropped to the ground and rolled aside as Garruil filled the space that I'd just vacated. Her hands returned to their blurry state as she slammed her fists and feet against him. I rolled around the brute and returned to my feet behind him. I struck at his back but my shadow strikes barely seemed to faze him.

Drago struck at Skith and the un-orc, hacking away at the putrid flesh as he assaulted the gnome tank. His attacks were large and wide, the greatsword striking Garruil and I with each swing.

A blast of green energy slammed against Drago's head as ravenous tongues of crimson flames jetted up from beneath him. I didn't need to look to know what was happening: Scova was back on her feet. The mage didn't need me to order her what to do, she knew her role. She was DPS and she had to teach Drago how to really lay the D. She had to lay so much D that Drago would be sore and walking funny. Scova loved the D.

That sounded different in my head.

Two more fiery blasts slammed against him as the sickly green magic assaulted and drained his life essence. Garruil continued her blurry assault as my own blades struck, Whaitiri Edge dove deep and sent jolts of electricity through the brute's body. I emptied my combo meter to fuel my cross slash. My blades struck in an X and massive damage poured into Khal's back. The damage drew his ire and Drago retaliated. With a sweeping strike he turned towards me and assaulted my form. He attacked in threes. I brought both blades up to the defense square to block the first strike and instantly regretted it. My arms screamed in pain as they held their own against the powerful assault. I moved them again to the new defense square to block the second. I didn't want to but I had no choice. The pair of blades once again met the greatsword, Whiatiri Edge sending yet another jolt through Drago's body, but this time my arms buckled. They could take no more and there was still another strike to come. I fell backwards and tried to roll away but Drago still came at me. Then, I saw a Dwarven fist.

Punchocalypse charged in and struck. In some d*iffer-ent enough as not to be sued but we all know what it really is* Shoryuken action, Punchocalypse struck with an upwards-spinning punch. The blow stunned Drago for 1.5 seconds but that wasn't enough to change the battle. Drago struck again and again, his assault ripping through our HP like a Zerg Rush through a newbie's base. Drago's HP fell as well, in chunks as the *invisible* force that was Lady Adelaide struck but it wasn't enough. I watched as our team HP plummeted. We were not going to survive.

Suddenly a golden circle surrounded us and our health started to quickly restore itself. I looked back and found Tialla, very much alive, and back on her feet casting every ultimate healing spell she had. We were going to survive.

The battle ended by Skith's glaive. The un-orc trapped Drago in a grapple and the gnome leapt from his un-orc's head onto Drago's. Skith thrust his glaive deep into the Jason Momoa wannabe's neck over and over. He thrust deep with his final strike and then twisted the glaive, making sure that Drago felt his blow.

Skith rode the body down as the brute fell to the floor, then whooped and began to dance. I spun around to see who remained but the room was empty save for a portal, a mage and The Phantom.

"This was unexpected," The Phantom admitted, "But it changes nothing. Havenhold's streets will be filled with blood by evening's fall."

The Phantom and the mage both stepped through the

portal and vanished. I let out a sigh of relief as my blades fell to the floor. I let my arms, tired and sore, hang by my side.

"Okay - that was a good fight," Punchocalypse boasted.

"We came, we saw, we kicked its ass!" Slashlore added.

"One should never revel in battle," Skith said solemnly before breaking a smile. "But we are beyond amazing!" The nine of us high fived and congratulated each other. Our revelry was cut short as the sound of loud eating filled the air. We all turned towards the sickly disturbing sound and stared in horror as the un-orc ate Drago's body. We looked at Skith. The gnome just shrugged. "What? Were you going to eat that?"

Chapter 06

"Every puzzle has an answer." - Professor Layton (Professor Layton and the Curious Village)

I stood at the desk in my room. I stared down at my newly acquired painting as I quickly ate. Slashlore was busy organizing the defenses. I returned to my room to eat, change gear and get ready. However, I was drawn to the painting. A knock at my door suddenly pulled my attention. I walked over and opened it, smiling at Scova as I let her in. She looked around my room and whistled.

"Nice digs," she said impressed. "How did you get this?"

"Long story," I said. "What's up?"

"I got my armour back!" She held her sword aloft to show me. "The Brotherhood fuckers stole my sword but the rest of my gear is intact."

"Small wins," I replied.

"Ade says she'll commission a new sword for me. I don't have the heart to tell her that it won't be a good as Thean'melorn."

"About that," I started. "What *exactly* is going on between you and the Lady?"

Scova nervously shrugged. She paced around the room as she tried to find the words. "Who is your lore crush? Everybody has one."

"Lore crush?"

"It's the character in a MMO that you *really* like. It's the character you know more about than anybody else. The

character you cheer for in a story. It's the character you em-
pathize with when they suffer."

Witch Queen Theresa Archona.

"When people make a MMO so in-depth as this, you
care for the characters. You have your favs and you have your
connections. You have your lore crushes. Adelaide has always been mine," Scova admitted. "I spent two weeks in a
cage with her. We talked, we chatted and we opened up." She
walked to my food and stole a bite of potatoes. She quickly
chewed it and swallowed. "I think I'm love with her."

"It's only been two weeks," I said cautiously, "and
she's a NPC. She's not real."

"I can't explain it," she defended. "But they are real,
Rake. Look at these people. They aren't just dumb NPCs
walking around saying shit like *bad times are a commin'*.
They act real now. I mean look at what happened. I wave my
rainbow membership card loud and proud but Adelaide was
never written as a lesbian, never even subtly, but she made the
first moves on me."

"So you two kissed. That doesn't mean---"

"We've done *way* more than kiss," Scova corrected.

It had only been two weeks.

"In my pick-up experience, girls are like spaghetti"
Scova joked. "They're straight until you get them wet."

I chuckled. That was a good line. "This is....I mean
I'm happy for you but things are changing."

"I'm done talking about this."

"This is important. We need to talk everything that's
happened and figure out what to do next."

"Fine," she said. "You killed Steelion."

I froze.

"You killed him while defending yourself," she continued. "Now you've locked yourself in this tower like some
damned Rapunzel."

"I'm looking for a way out of the game."

"Bullshit," Scova said. "Slashlore says you've been
ignoring mail from people. You've ignored his; you've ig-

nored emails from other friends and from people needing your help.”

“I’m....”

“Check your mail. What do you have?”

I opened my mailbox and looked inside. “There is my daily letter from Bearcules. There is yet another message from some guy named Reit. There is one from Hizzous asking for help again.”

“How many times has he asked for help?”

“This will be the third time,” I said. I looked back at my mail. “And there are a couple more letters from names I didn’t recognize. They want help or need advice and shit.” I knew where she was going with this. I used to help people. Now I didn’t. “I’m not Stov. I’m not the hero anymore. I’m.....” my voice trailed off. I was a k---. I was a ki----. “Steelion was all my fault.”

“It wasn’t,” Scova replied, speaking softly now. “Slashlore told me the whole story. He said Steelion went off the deep end. He put a bounty out on you and you had to put him down. He said you gave him many chances to walk away as well. He didn’t take them.” She put her hand on my shoulder. “Its sucks and I’m sorry you had to go through this but it wasn’t your fault.”

Scova talked for a few moments longer, speaking of guilt and transference. For a moment, I paused and wondered who Scova was outside of VCO but I didn’t dare ask. It had become an unwritten rule. It had become *The Rule*: don’t ask about the real world.

Scova changed the topic by pointed to the painting. “What’s up with that?”

“I’ve been following a Casper Cache and this painting is a part of it,” I explained. “I’m just stuck on what to do next.”

“Well walk me through it, I might be able to help.”

“Don’t you have get ready to skip the spell?” I asked. Scova shrugged.

“The mages are ready to go at a moment’s notice. I

don't have much to do until they actually cast the portal." She pointed to the painting. "So walk me through it. What makes this painting different from the literal thousands of identical ones that exist across VCO?"

"The colours are off." I pointed to the brown barn, the green grass, the purple flowers and the blue cart. "These colours are not what they're supposed be. This one has an obviously different green and brown and the original doesn't even have the purple or blue."

"It's a hex-puzzle," she said. "You taught me that one. Just pull the hex-code for the colours and work from there."

"I *know* that," I scoffed at her. I had figured out the hex portion almost instantly. "My problem is I don't have the tool that can read the hexcode from the colours. The last time I came across a puzzle like this, I took a screenshot and then logged out. I examined it in RL."

"Why?"

I shrugged. "I like doing it by pencil and paper. It also gave me an excuse to log out and get fresh air."

"Addict," she mocked. Scova dug a magnifying glass from her pouch and held it over the painting. "I have a colour-code reader app installed."

I handed her a piece of paper and a functional pen, something that didn't used to exist in VCO before the Glitch. She moved her glass over the colours in question, one by one, and wrote down the numbers that appeared before her.

Brown:	DC9C43
Green:	34B30E
Purple:	B83F7E
Blue:	2F8DBD

I smiled at the list. Now I had room to play. I grabbed a pencil and began to decode it. Hexadecimal is a positional numeral system with a base of 16. It uses 0–9 to represent values zero to nine and A, B, C, D, E, F to represent values ten to fifteen. It is used primarily in mathematics and computing but us treasure hunters simply call it hex. VCO creator Casper Ramirez often used hex, binary and other numbering systems in some of his puzzles. Number puzzles weren't my forté, I was more of a lore junkie, but I knew the basics.

Scova watched as I slowly deciphered the codes. I took the individual numbers, turned them into base 10 and added them up. In Brown's case, D became 13 and C became 12. So when I added up all the number the sum became 53 (13 + 12 + 9 + 12 + 4 + 3 = 53). Green added up to 35 (3 + 4 + 11 + 3+ 0 + 14 = 35), Purple added up to 58 (11 + 8 + 3 + 15 + 7 + 14 = 58) and the sum of Blue was 62 (2 + 15 + 8 + 13 + 11 + 13 = 62).

"Please tell me you have a good map installed?" I glared at Scova and unraveled my map add-on. VCO had a map but treasure hunters had a better one installed. Aspumer was split into four continents. Each of those continents was split into state-like zones. There were seventy-six zones in VCO. My good map had the zones numbered. The map also had coordinated for every spot in the game. I moved my hand across the map until I found zone 62 - Coress Ridges. I tapped on it and watched it expand. I looked at Scova.

"You're the number girl, what now?"

Scova stared silently at the map and the numbers. She was a math girl. In the world of number puzzles, she could do in mere moments what would take me hours. After several minutes, a smile crept across her face. She reached for the pad and pencil and began to break down Blue's hex. Beside each number she wrote a combination of zeros and ones.

```
2:  0001
F:  1111
8:  1000
D:  1101
B:  1011
D:  1101
```

"If you convert them into binary," Scova said, "and

place those numbers on the map..." her voice trailed off as she traced her finger as she studied the ever-changing numbers on the bottom. She came to a halt on the dungeon entrance to *Fillmont's Landing*. I glanced at the numbers: 0001, 1111. The numbers were map coordinates. Scova tapped on Fillmont's Landing and the map shifted to that of the dungeon. Once again, she followed the fingers until they landed on the passage to the dungeon's second half: 1000, 1101. She tapped that and the map shifted once more. She followed the number until she reached her final destination: 1011,1101. I looked down to where she was pointing. This was the location of Captain Airmo Hau. This was also the drop point of the Whaitiri Edge.

"It's a map," I said stunned. "This isn't a painting; it's a map to one of Casper's Caches. I already have the item associated with the Blue Cart. This map will show me where the next three items are. I just have to figure out which items they actually are."

"Pitter Patter," Scova said with a smirk. "Let's get at'r."

A couple hours had passed and I was entering Old Hold. The district was filled with mages, eagerly working. Off to the side was Slashlore. He stood studiously, simply watching but his expression was one of concern. I approached the paladin and nudged him. Startled, he spun around.

"What's wrong?" I asked. "You have that look. You worried about the attack?"

"Nah," Slashlore admitted. "We have that part on lock. I'm worried about something else. If you were going to attack this city, where would you do it?"

"Depends; if I was going for devastation then I would march towards the front gate, big and loud and then portal into the Docks so I could cut off their escape," I said. "If I was trying to take the city quickly, I would do like the Nohorian Brotherhood is doing. I would portal into Old Hold because it's never guarded. I mean who would honestly think about attacking Old Hold?"

"Exactly my point," Slashlore said. "You and I would attack it in that fashion because we know the city inside and out, but how does the Nohorian Brotherhood know to attack there? How do they know the city's guard rotation and placement as well as PCs do?"

"Are you suggesting a player is attacking the city?" I asked. The idea sounded insane but then again, trolls were trolls. It wasn't out of the realm of possibility.

"Maybe...but that doesn't feel right." The paladin shook his head. "This feels more story driven." He looked at me. "That's *your* territory. Any guesses?"

I thought for a moment, racking my brain as I tried to replay the events of the Glitch onwards in my mind. Many events were hazy due to the concussion but I recalled what I could.

"Admiral Galen Crowley," I said suddenly. "I saw him before the attack. He looked like Rorschach did in *Watchmen* when he wasn't wearing the mask. He was all doom and gloom. They probably got to him and pried it out of him, waterboard style."

Slashlore feel deeper in thought. "If that's true we may be in worse shape than we thought."

He began to explain but we were interrupted by Scova's cry. "We have incoming!"

Slashlore quickly PM'd Tialla. The priest was waiting by the docks, making sure the mages were working there as well. Seconds later she replied.

"Scova: you have a go," Slashlore said. "Do your thing."

At the paladin's command Scova went to work. She instructed every mage in the district, from level 10 to level 100, to expel their magic upwards. Portals were an exact science. If a number was off, the portal didn't land where you hoped it would. What Scova's plan was doing was shifting the perception of the ground, just slightly. This would force the Brotherhood's mages to incorrectly adjust their spell. It was like in Die Hard 2 when William Sadler made the plane's computer to think the ground was further down than it actually was. The major difference between the two was that the portal would simply skip to outside the city whereas the British Jet crashed and horribly killed 230 passengers and crew.

The sky didn't change colour but it did began to sparkle, like someone had littered thousands of diamonds into the afternoon sky. I stared upwards, until my neck began to hurt, and suddenly found myself getting bored. Nothing was happening. The thing about magic was the attack spells were all flash and Michael Bay-like but the big important spells that shaped reality rarely took some visible form.

"So how will we know when it start work---" The city shook, cutting the paladin's words off. "I guess that was it." Slashlore froze for a second as he read and replied to a PM. He looked at Scova. "It worked."

"Of course it did," she boasted. Slashlore looked at me.

"Rake, you're with me." He turned back to the fiery mage.   "Scova: you're in charge."

My soul hurt as he said those words.

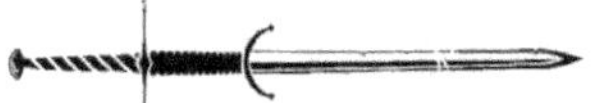

It only took five minutes for Slashlore and me to race and climb Havenhold's gates. We slid beside Bearcules and Tialla. I did my best to focus on the battle but a scowl still emerged. The druid pointed out over the field. We looked as hundreds of Brotherhood members stood in the field, a little confused but quickly regaining their composure. Mages stood to the side as they summoned in a contingency plan. Some ported in catapults and battering rams while others quickly summoned giants and brutes to assault the gates.

"We are in total Helm's Deep mode aren't me?" I whispered.

"Except there isn't going to be a Gandalf coming to our rescue," Slashlore replied. "To be honest, I'd prefer an Elminster or Nanfoodle."

"I wouldn't say no to Dumbledore," Bearcules said as he approached.

"I'd welcome a Ron Weasley," Tialla said. We all looked at her.

"I would take Dobby over Ron," I said. "I would take a dead Cedric Diggory over Ron. I would take a couple broken hockey sticks and half a puck over Ron *Scabbers watched me masturbate* Weasley."

"I had a crush on Ron when I was younger," Tialla admitted. She paused. *"Scabbers watched me masturbate?* What the hell?"

"He was a teenage boy going through puberty. It makes sense in a kind of creepy way," Bearcules said, "especially when the rat isn't a rat but a damn 40 year old man."

"Can we stop ruining my childhood?" Tialla asked. "Why don't we *all* just focus on our imposing doom, shall we?"

I looked at Slashlore and I could see his mind quickly racing. Suddenly he ordered all PCs into the Square. Word had spread quickly that Havenhold was under attack and every PC in the area had shown up to defend our capital. I looked out and saw dozens of familiar faces and hundreds more I didn't. I looked out over the masses and amongst those I had fought alongside, I saw the the Guidos, FreddyVoorhes, Hizzous, Jhaara, Boomizle and Holmiarty, amongst others. I even saw the NPC Guards running to take up position. Everybody was scared and nervous. Slashlore decided to solve that.

"The Nohorian Brotherhood is at our door," Slashlore began. His voice boomed across the Square. Every PC looked to the paladin and even several NPCs slid to a halt to listen. "You're asking yourself *is Havenhold really our door?* We are not citizens, not for real. We are not her children. We are something different. We are a nation of people surrounded by a larger and vastly different populace. So what are we? Are we united? Are we different? Are each of us out for ourselves or are we here to work together?

"Today marks the day we come together as a people;

today marks the day that the PC nation rises as one to defend Havenhold. Why? Because we are the adventurers who crave battle and excitement, we're the explorers who rise to the challenge every time a new bad shows its ugly ass and because we're the players who pay $15 a month for this shit. We are the heroes of this story. We are the players who live amongst the NPCs. So believe me when I say that Havenhold is *definitely* our home and we'll kill any who think to take it from us.

"So I look out over the wall and see the forces that mean to come for us, do you know what I feel? I don't feel fear. I feel pity; I pity the Nohorian Brotherhood. Why? Because we are the Enclave, Havenhold is *our* home and they're the unlucky fucks trying to take it from us. Why do I pity the Nohorian Brotherhood? Because they have no clue what hell they called upon themselves!"

The players cheered! Some used the /dance command but mostly they cheered. Slashlore wasn't finished. He had them riled up, now he needed them in order.

"Everybody group up in fives. Standard raid rules apply; I want a tank, a healer and three DPS." His orders were crisp and organized. "I need all range DPS on the wall. When they breach the wall you retreat to your party and help your tanks because they will be the first thing they see."

Hunters, warlocks, mages and a handful of druids and shamans bolted for the wall. Warriors, paladins, Revenants and some druids ran to the doors. The remainder of the DPS waited behind their tanks, eager to stab; behind them stood the healers.

"Healers: you'll be in charge of comms. If something changes, message me. Keep party chatter to /p, otherwise I want all communications on /3 LocalDefense. If a line is being breached, put it on there. If something big pops up, put it there. If you need to retreat, put it there." Slashlore looked to the lowbies. "I need you guys as runners. You're being assigned districts. Go there and keep a lookout for things. You guys are the few who have permission to PM me. I want check-ins every five minutes. If things get hot - run.

"All battle commands will come from me or Tialla. Keep an eye out from them, do as they say and we'll make it through this alive." Slashlore looked out over the troops, over his troops. "Remember: this is no different than a raid. So let's kill these fucks and loot their corpses."

Chapter 07

"Courage is the magic that turns dreams into reality."
— Richter Abend (Tales of Symphonia Dawn of a New World)

I stood on Havenhold's wall, acting as Slashlore's lieutenant. Scova stood beside me, a fiery grin on her face. I raised my eyebrow but she nodded behind her. There, dressed in her ninja clothes and holding a bow, was Lady Adelaide. I rolled my eyes. Scova just smiled.

"I'll take incoming, you deal with outgoing?" the mage suggested. I nodded. "Don't worry though; the Burning Typhoon won't miss a chance to lob a spell or two."

Oh great, she knew about her title. That wouldn't go to her head at all. I looked over our numbers, my eyes falling on Hizzous. The hunter was now level 60. He had blown past my level 27. He had been grinding some serious exp and it was paying off. I looked back at my fiery partner.

"Ready to be big damn heroes?" she asked.

"Hero ain't on my resume."

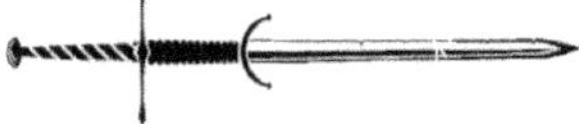

The Nohorian Brotherhood charged Havenhold with a scream. Their roar rippled across the field and assaulted the moral of every PC nervously waiting. It harmlessly bounced off of some but for others, it cut deep.

"Ready!" With a raise of my hand every bow, crossbow and gun raised, cocked and notched. Staves and wands were next at the ready and several hands began to eagerly tap out spells. I waited a moment more, for the troops to be in range before, dropping my hand. "Fire!"

In some *different enough as not to be sued but we all know what it really is* 300 action, arrows soared across the battlefield in such numbers that, for the briefest of moments, they blocked out the sun. I smiled as they rained death down upon the forces. The spells were next. Blast of ice, balls of fire and downpour of corrupted energy assaulted the troops. Screams of pain cried out as the magic ate away at their flesh and souls. I ordered the archers to reload as they prepared for the next volley.

"Incoming!" Scova looked upwards and saw that the Brotherhood's catapults had fired a volley of their own. A dozen boulders came soaring through the air, barreling towards us.

"Mages:" Scova yelled as she took a blaster's stance. "Take them out!"

The mages assaulted the boulders with spells. Some threw up arcane shield in the air, causing the rocks to bounce off of and fall back onto the troops below. Others blinked the rocks away, causing them to land harmlessly in the harbour while some mages resorted to simply blasting the rocks apart with cold or fire.

"Little Flame," Adelaide called out. I looked at Scova with a snicker in my eyes but she gave me the finger and looked to her love. "Giants are charging."

"Coolers: stop the biggums." As I watched the ice mages casted slowing spells down upon the ground, I felt nostalgic. I missed being Stov.

The ice slowed the giants' movements and I ordered the archer to fire upon the beasts. The first couple giants fell but others kept storming forward. The mages continued their assault but Havenhold's gate shook as the giant slammed its club against it. Archers looked to me in worry.

"All hands: fire at will."

Slashlore and Tialla stoically stood in the Square. They looked like they were ignoring the battle but they weren't. Each was quickly reading the /3 channel updates and going over all the PMs that came in. I could see how Tialla would read a message, reply quickly and then order a party or two to move from district to district. Slashlore looked up whenever the gate shook but he never responded out loud. He simply stood there, managing his troops and controlling the battle.

I watched in wonder as clouds began to assault the sky. They weren't white or grey clouds, as was normal. They were a combination of red and orange, like the clouds were aflame. They began to cyclone, eventually causing four tornadoes to touch down on the battlefield. What I found most surprising was how the tornadoes weren't made from wind, they were made from flame. The fiery spirals of death each ripped a swath of destruction as it tore through the Brotherhood's forces.

I snapped my head over at Scova. The mage, whose hair was brightly aflame, simply smirked. "The Burning Typhoon strikes again!"

Yep, it went to her head.

The gate shook again but this time it was accompanied by a loud cracking sound. Slashlore looked up and saw parts of the gate smashed opened. The Brotherhood was about to breach the city. Two seconds later, a message appeared before my eyes.

Slashlore: Get them down. Bearcules will march them out.
Rake: 10-4

I turned to my archers and started to yell. "Okay, get the hell out of here. Return to your parties and get into the ground game."

The gate shook again and this time the door broke even more. I looked over at Scova. She nodded and turned to

Lady Adelaide and gave her a passionate kiss. "See you later, babe. I gotta go do my thing."

Scova and I didn't bother with the stairs, instead each of us leapt off the edge. Scova's cloak wrapped around her and morphed her into a fiery ball. She fell fast and dive-bombed the Brotherhood's forces, landing with a burst of flame. The fire spun around her, revealing a woman with burning hair, a ball of fire in her left hand and a blade made from a dragon's tooth in her right. As I fell I activated my ring and blinked forward, gracefully landing onto the ground below. Before my discovery with the map, I had changed one of my magic items and added a couple more to my arsenal. The blink ring was one of my new additions. It gave me three short teleports, blinks as we called them. Blinks were quick, fast and, best of all, didn't cause me nausea. I stood beside Scova, with both blades out, and smirked.

"Any words before we start?" Slashlore said as he approached the gate, his sword drawn and his shield at the ready.

"I can think of some," Punchocalypse said with a grin.

"What are you doing here?" Scova asked.

"If I'm leading these troops," Slashlore said, "then I will lead from the battlefield." He looked to the dwarf. "Let's hear those words, Punch. Say them loud and say them proud."

"Kamé-Doken Blast!"

"For what seemed like hours, the battle raged on. The Enclave army fought at Havenhold's gate but as the Brotherhood's numbers swarmed us, Slashlore pulled us back to the Square and to our second line of defence. The second wave of troops charged forward, led by Skith atop his un-orc. The first line took a moment to regain our breath as the second line took up the slack. During the brief moment of reprieve, I watched as the wave of PCs tirelessly fought. The Guidos moved as a pair. She would strike first, then vanish, only to have him show up and slash hard. One would be the person while the other acted like the shadow. The pair weaved in and out, switching from person to shadow and back again. Fleyming grabbed the Brotherhood with her tendrils of sickening green magic as she drain the life of those near her. Freddy Voorhes, unlike the skills of Punchocalypse, fought defensively. He waited for the Brotherhood to approach him. Those that came in range suddenly found their own strength being turned against them. Hizzous was a nonstop stream of arrows. Each one that left his bow found a home and each home was deadly. He didn't rely on the special abilities that some hunters chose, Hizzous simply preferred accuracy and precision. Holmiarty kept his party of five healed as he moved and positioned them across the battlefield. The calculator that he was, he'd order his DPS into flanking positions as his tank plowed forward.

Slashlore pointed to the right. Strands of the Brotherhood's members had broken off from the horde and were making their way towards the Mage District. We bolted after them, calling upon the magic and allowed the speed in my boots to propel me forward. I leapt forward and attacked with a downward slash from both blades. My steel cut through the unlucky rear member and I instantly forgot about him. My mind had already moved to the next target. A golden shield Evansed through the Brotherhood platoon, stunning some and slowing others.

They turned to face us but our blades were at the ready. Whaitiri Edge moved to deflect the blade, knocking the enemy steel aside as it sent a jolt through the wielder's body. I thrust forward with my longsteel and ran it through his body. The masked man fell and I moved onto another.

Scova ran up beside me, her hair brightly ablaze. Keshim's Fang swiftly cut through a helpless Brotherhood member as a blast of fire erupted from her palm. The flames hungrily feasted on those unlucky enough to be in her way. Scova and I moved closer covering each other as we fought. To my side was Slashlore, his axe felling any who came close to him, all while Punchocalypse introduced his fist to anybody who would listen. In that moment I realized what I had been missing since the Glitch: teamwork. Stov had friends, he had teammates and he had an online family. Rake didn't. Rake didn't have anything to fight for but in that moment I realized that Rake and I did. It wasn't the same family as Stov but it was a family nonetheless.

Slashlore slid to a halt as the last of our strays fell. His eyes moved quickly as he read the incoming messages. /3 was full of updates. The Brotherhood had splintered into several divergent strands, much like the one we had just taken down, and were making runs for the various districts. Tialla's voice suddenly filled the air as she barked orders across the city.

"Groups 1, 2, 3, 4 and 5: You stay on the door. Hit them hard and keep them busy. Lowbies: I want callout of any and all stragglers. Groups 6 through 11: you're on containment duty. Turn those stragglers back or turn them to corpses. All Remaining Group: Hit them hard."

"I want Pwnage!" Slashlore added.

A roar echoed across the sky and our head snapped in its direction. We stared in shock as a dragon flew over the gate and into Havenhold. It was a small, as black dragons go, but even small were massive compared to an Elf or a Dwarf.

"Shit," Slashlore spat. "They're summoning dragons. I need the mages to start dispelling them to stop--"

"That's not a summon," Scova said in disbelief.

"Oh." Slashlore just stared into the sky, watching the wyrm circle in the sky. The man had devised a plan for every aspect of the battle but it was obvious that he hadn't devised a plan for that. "So...we should probably deal with that then."

"Dibs!" We all snapped our heads toward Punchocalypse. My face had a look that could only be called the offspring from a threesome between horror, disbelief and wonderment. "I haven't punched a dragon in like days."

"Alright then," Slashlore laughed. "We have a plan. Punchocalypse: blast it out of the sky."

"My blast is too slow to fire it at a dragon as a weapon," Punchocalypse said as put his back to the dragon. A ball of brightly glowing energy formed in his hands as the dwarf aimed it at the ground. "Kamé-Doken Blast!"

The ki blast slammed against the ground and shot the dwarf upwards into the air. Punchocalypse had used his rare monk ability, meant for range combat, to slingshot himself into the air. Like a pissed off Red Bird, he flew toward the dragon. His fist glowed as he barrelled towards the wurm.

And what happened, then? Well, in Havenhold they say - that the Punchocalypse's small fist grew three sizes that day. And then - the true meaning of combat came through, and Punchocalypse found the strength of *ten* Dwarves, plus two!

"Punchocalypse Smash!" The Dwarf screamed as loud as he could, his words somehow reaching every inch of the human city. It denizens, PC and NPC, looked upwards to see the Dwarf's glowing first connecting with the dragon's chin. The punch stunned the beast and sent it falling back to the earth. Somehow, and to this day I'm not entirely sure how, Punchocalypse grabbed the dragon's neck and rode the dragon down like he was Major Kong riding a bomb in Dr. Strangelove. Yet, instead of simply waving his hat and cheering, Punchocalypse decided to continuously punch the dragon all the way down. The pair crashed into the ground with a massive thud that shook the city. We all stared in wonder as the dust settled to reveal a grinning Dwarf standing over a fallen dragon. But Punchocalypse wasn't done. He stood over the dragon's skull and dramatically pulled off his elbow guard. With a dramatic flair, he elbow-dropped the wyrm. Punchocalypse had just used the People's Elbow on a dragon.

If anybody asked, this was why we paid $15 a month for this game.

The dragon lashed out and snatched Punchocalypse between its teeth. With a roar, it flung the Dwarf aside and tossed him into a wall. The dragon rolled to his feet and drew in a deep breath. It let loose with his acidic breath, the blast aiming directly for the stunned Punchocalypse.

"No!" Slashlore cried as he slid before the Dwarf. The paladin held his shield aloft, using it to block the acid breath. As the breath weapon ended, Slashlore stood there, an angry look on face and axe in his hand. He glared at the beast and started to charge at it. "Not today."

I started to bolt for the dragon but slid to a halt as something else caught my eye: The Phantom. He sauntered into the city, dressed in his noble armour with his long flowing midnight cloak and half-mask upon his face. He held a wand in his left hand and his bastard sword in his right. The jewel at the end of his wand glowed as tongues of flames erupted forward. I bolted toward The Phantom, my blades hungering for the mystery man's flesh. The Phantom was the leader of the Brotherhood. This meant that if someone tortured Admiral Galen Crowley for city intel, like I believed, then this was the man that ordered it.

The attack circle flash before me and my longsteel moved to meet it. The strike was accurate but it only met steel. The Phantom spun around to block my attack and lashed out with his foot. His kick connected with my chest and sent me flying back onto my ass. He leveled his wand at me and, from the uncovered side of his face, I saw a devilish smirk.

Chapter 08

"Video games are always half real." - Jesper Juul

I had a less than a second to act before I became something that resembled Freddy Kruger's Face. I snapped my Lucky Dagger to my hand which stored my longsteel in my glove, tossed it at The Phantom and, most importantly, prayed to the gaming Gods that I would hit the wand.

I didn't.

My dagger went wide and I missed The Phantom by at least a couple feet. It was embarrassing. It was so embarrassing of a shot that The Phantom didn't shoot. He stood there and laughed at me. The Phantom was an asshole.

His moment of mockery, however, did give me a chance to use my magic ring. I blinked behind him and slashed his back with Whaitiri Edge. It wasn't a deep cut but it was enough to stagger him. I back stepped away and snapped my longsteel back into my hand. The Phantom turned around and glared. I struck again, hoping to rip that smug look off of his face.

His bastard sword rose once more to parry my strike. The Phantom snapped his fingers and his red-jeweled wand vanished in his gloves. He grabbed his hand-and-a-half sword and struck back. His speed with the bastard sword was impressive, my arms straining to meet the defense squares in time to block his attacks. With each strike of the Whaitiri Edge, another jolt travelled through his body, each was little more than the prick of a pin but even en masse they didn't slow The Phantom. I blocked what I could and dodged what I couldn't, trying to use my speed but he wouldn't let me move. When I tried to move right, his blade would force me left and vice versa.   The Phantom was a man of great skill and experience, moving in ways that only could be learned in hard fought battles.

He slapped my blades aside and kicked at my chest. His boot ignited in flame as it connected, the blow searing my skin as it shunted me backwards. I fell backwards but quickly rolled to my feet. The Phantom once again held a wand in his offhand except this one was green-jeweled, not red. The emerald jewel glowed and suddenly vines shot up from the ground and wrapped around my leg, rooting me in place. The green-jeweled wand vanished as The Phantom clutched his blade in both hands and charged me.

"Distraction!" The Phantom turned to see an Elf with burning hair strike at him. He slid and pivoted, bringing his bastard sword up to deflect a katana. The two blades met and sparks formed. Scova struck hard and fast, holding Keshim's Fang in both hands, pushing The Phantom back. The Phantom turned the tides, moving from defense to offense and slashed across Scova's chest. He hit only her after image as she shifted yet again. With her arsenal of combat spell in full force, she moved before her image did. It only worked once every two seconds but it was a powerful spell. Fire flowed through her body and into her sword, the blade causing more devastation with each hit.

She wouldn't be able to keep up her assault for long; she was only a mage - albeit a melee one. A mage could never stand toe-to-toe in a melee fight against a warrior, they had to be clever. They had to use spells to even the score but even arcane machinations had their limits. I hacked at the vines until I freed myself and then charged in. A rogue wouldn't fare any better than the mage but, perhaps, against a warrior of The Phantom's caliber a mage and a rogue could come out victorious.

We struck together, Whaitiri Edge and Splinter's Bite lashing out before I stepped aside as Keshim's Fang came in hard. Scova would attack hard, than step to the left. I would come in from the right and lash out with my longsteel and parry with my short. With each strike my combo meter filled and her hair burned brighter. For a while we held The Phantom at bay but the warrior wasn't without his tricks. He pushed us back and slammed his blade against the ground. A burst of energy rippled through the ground and for a moment both of us were stunned. The Phantom lashed out with a burning kick and sent Scova stumbling backwards. He snapped his fingers and a third wand appeared in his hand. He leveled the yellow-jeweled wand and me and let loose a bolt of electricity. I didn't have time to think; I just reacted.

I raised Whaitiri Edge and used it to block. The blade absorbed the lightning and for a moment I was left unharmed. For a moment I felt stronger and faster, like the lightning had empowered me, but then I felt the pain. I fell to the ground, screaming as every inch of my body was being electrocuted. The pain was unbearable. Spotting a patch of dirt I did the only thing I could think of: I grounded myself. I stabbed the blade into the dirt and let out a sigh of relief as the pain dissipated. I stared at the blade and for a moment found myself wondering what the hell that brief boost in power was. Was it the hidden blessing of the Casper Cache? If so, what went wrong? I shook off the thought, Scova was fighting alone. I willed my new headband to activate Second Wind and felt the wounds I'd suffer start to heal.

When I was preparing for the invasion, I switched out the headband I used on *him* for a Third Eye headband. It was primarily a monk item but some had abilities that could be used by any class. Each Third Eye headband had two spells attached to it. Mine had Sight Beyond Sight and Second Wind. The healing of Second Wind wasn't enough to raid without a healer but it was enough to keep me alive in the heat of a moment.

"Yo, Gerard Butler," I yelled. "Christine Daaé is only 15 years old, pervert!"

I charged back into battle. Scova fingers tapped

quickly as she summoned a fiery blast. She slammed the flames into The Phantom. The warrior's chainmail reacted to the heat as strands of chains separated from the chest and formed long tendrils. They lashed out at Scova. Two strands wrapped around her arms and held her as three more lashed at her neck, like serpents striking at their prey. Scova screamed as she struggled to free herself but the more she moved, the tighter the sentient chains got. Her chest plate began to glow brightly until it was blinding. I unleashed a burst of uncontrolled arcane energy. Nothing was more dangerous or unpredictable then a burst of uncontrolled arcane energy. The blast sent the chain tendrils receding back into its chainmail and send both mage and warrior flying backward. The Phantom was first on his feet but I was there to greet him, using the speed in my boots to dash towards him. I leapt into the air and switched enchantments in my boots. I struck with my stone-foot and kicked The Phantom across the face. The Christine-obsessed villain crumpled to the ground as his half-mask flew off of his face and skipped across the street. I landed on my feet, switched back to speed and dashed once more at The Phantom. I struck with both blades but both were blocked with by The Phantom's bastard sword. For a moment our blades were locked and I stared at The Phantom's uncovered face. My jaw dropped. I recognized the face behind the mask; every PC did.

The Phantom was really Galen Crowley, Admiral of Havenhold.

"Crowley?" I muttered in disbelief. He pushed me back and swung again. Whaitiri Edge moved to the defense square and I blocked the strike. "What are you doing?"

"Havenhold will fall," he spat. "The Descendants and the Coalition will both fall to their knees before the Nohorian Brotherhood."

"You're with the Nohorian Brotherhood?" I asked. "Why? You're one of Havenhold's most treasured heroes."

"And what has that gotten me? I have spent my life fighting against one threat or another. I lost my son to the chaos; I lost everything to this kingdom. Why? They told me because it was the right thing to do? They were wrong." His blade moved faster now. Scova slide beside me, her blade aiding mine in keeping his attacks at bay. "We can sit here and wait for the next horror or we can stop them from happening. No longer will we sit and wait, not when we have the power at our disposal to stop them, to stop them all.

"The Nohorian Brotherhood will be our saviours. They will bring about the eternal darkness but when it is over, there will be the brightest dawn we have ever witnessed. The Nohorian Brotherhood will save us all. Nightfall is coming." His speech didn't sound normal. It sounded like it was the remnant of his expansion speech. Like this very speech was planned before the Glitch.

"He's been radicalized," Scova said. "He can't go on like this. He's too dangerous. We have to put him down." I shook my head. It wouldn't help. He was a NPC. If he died, he would respawn. This war wouldn't end if he simply respawned. We had to stop him but we couldn't kill him.

The pair of us continued to fight against Crowley. The Admiral was quickly running out of tricks but so were we. He caught me with his blade and sent me flying backwards. He leapt into the air as his cloak transformed into black wings. The wings pumped as it elevated him into the air. He flicked out the red-jeweled wand and fired a fireball towards me. I activated my armour, the Feore Shell. My body became an impassable mist and shot me two feet forward. The fireball harmlessly passed through me and detonated, none of the flames touching me. Crowley flicked out a fourth wand, a blue-jeweled one and shot a stream of ice at Scova. The blast caught her squarely in the chest and covered her into a glacial tomb like an unlucky Mei forced to relive her Antarctic entrapment. My body reassembled itself and I glared at Crowley.

"Accept the Brotherhood and welcome their peace." He yelled from high above me. "Standing against them is futile. Would you stand against a god?"

"Yes," I spat. "I did once and so did you. We all stood against Vörissa and we won."

"And we've paid the price for it, again and again. The Brotherhood will make sure it shan't happen again."

"At what cost?" I asked loudly. "I will stand up to God, over and over, for the sake of this kingdom. I will protect all of us and I will die doing so."

"Those are foolish words."

"They were yours," I said as I slowly couple steps forward. "You said those very words as we charged the Goddess' spires."

"A lot has changed," he growled. "Those words may have been mine but they were the words of a naive man. I am no longer that foolish."

"You're wrong," I said as I took a couple steps more. "You are still a foolish man. You haven't recognized that I was just distracting you as I got into position."

He opened his mouth to speak but I never gave him the chance. I activated my ring and used my final blink. I landed on his back, high in the air and emptied my combo meter. My blades cross slashed across his back. He screamed and fell to the ground. I leapt off at the last moment and rolled to safety, his transforming cloak no longer on his back but in my hand. I tossed it aside and glanced at Scova, breathing a sigh of relief as I saw Lady Adelaide freeing from her from the ice. I turned back to Crowley and charged at him.

Crowley stood up and touched the amulet that hung around his neck. His body shimmered and suddenly there were five of him. I slid to a halt. He had used an illusion spell like some Blademaster Samuro wannabe. The Five Crowleys charged me, but I didn't strike and I didn't flee. I willed my Third Eye headband to life and activated Sight Beyond Sight. No longer were there five, there was but one so I struck and I struck hard. Catching him by surprise, I let my blade feast. Hungry was my steel and Crowley was a buffet. The battle finally ended when I ran Splinter's Bite through his chest.

The former Admiral fell to the ground, bleeding out

from his wounds. I dropped to my knees, exhausted. I looked and saw hundreds of PC and NPCS staring at me. Apparently when the dragon fell, the Nohorian Brotherhood had ordered their retreat. That left nothing much for a PC to do but watch the climactic battle between Crowley and me. Once again, I found myself in the eyes of everybody and once again, I hated it. The only difference was I could change how this one ended.

"Healer," I yelled. "I need a healer." A shaman named Reit ran towards me. I pointed at the body.

"Don't let him die." He opened his mouth to speak but I cut him off. "If he dies, he respawns; if he respawns then this war won't end. Do. Not. Let. Him. Die."

Reit just nodded.

Chapter 09

"Why, that's the second biggest monkey head I've ever seen!"
- Guybrush Threepwood (The Secret of Monkey Island)

The PCs changed after the war. We transformed from a population of solo players to a community. We had a name. We were now the Enclave and we were gathering in the Square. Slashlore stood on a makeshift dais and looked out over the PCs who stood before him. People's minds were changing. Some stood confused at the possibilities that lay before them, some stood eager to fight but most were just lost. They needed hope and they needed a hero. He looked at his notes and glanced at the in-game clock.

"Five gold says he chokes on his speech." I turned around and smiled at the human healer. Tialla looked as tired as the rest, but unlike others she had a glimmer in her eye, she had hope. She knew something that I didn't.

"Why do you look guilty?" I nervously asked. "What are you scheming?"

She didn't answer, just smirked. I shook my head. I didn't like this side of her. It was unsettling, like a silent cat.

"So, Colonel Tialla," I said while changing the topic, "how does it feel to be a war hero?"

"Looks who talking?" she laughed. "You're the man who beat the Brotherhood's leader. Hell, we're all war heroes now. People are talking about the Valiant Bearcules, the Unbeatable Slashlore and the Insane Punchocalypse. These are the name people are saying."

"What are they calling me?"

The smile vanished from her face. "You don't want to know."

We stood there in silence.

"Congrats on level 32," she said. "War's good for you."

"Bite me," I laughed.

"So have you heard what everybody is talking about?" Tialla asked. I shook my head. She pointed across the Square to Scova. The fire mage stood to the side, her hand delicately holding Lady Adelaide's. "After the Whisper Princess freed Scova from the ice, she kissed our mage."

"Yeah, I knew they were an item," I began but Tialla cut me off.

"She kissed our mage while thousands looked on. Hundreds of PCs saw that and within hours every single player heard about it. The first ever PC-NPC romance and people are abuzz about it."

"Sounds like a can of worms," I replied with a chuckle.

"A really big can." We stood in silence for awhile, not saying anything. Tialla spoke first, biting back a snicker as she set up the joke. "At least Scova doesn't have to worry about catching an STI."

"Only a virus."

We both burst out laughing. It wasn't dignified.

"Every *Fallout* game starts with the words 'War. War never changes'," Slashlore said to the audience. "I don't know if it's the topic matter, the setting of the games or the fact that it's Ron Perlman's voice saying the lines, but those words have always rung true with me. We have just fought the first battle in a war, a war between us and a gutless villain.

"The Nohorian Brotherhood struck and when Havenhold call out for help, we answered. We are the heroes. Whenever evil rises, we step forward to put it back down and we will always be there.

"Yesterday we stood as a people and fought as one. We are the Enclave and we are a nation far from our home. We all want to get back home but we can't do that alone. Yesterday we proved we could fight as one; today we prove we can act as one.

"Today we choose the man who will lead us, who will guide us on our journey home. We are a ship adrift amongst the stars; we need a captain to guide us home. We need someone worthy, someone who has proven himself and someone who will go the distance.

"I have heard you talk and I have heard your whispers. You think the man who should lead has already stepped up. You think the man who should lead us has already proven himself. You think the man who should lead us has already shown that he's worthy. You think that man is Rake."

The crowd erupted in cheers and chants. I just hung my head. I glanced at Tialla and saw her knowing look. Both Slashlore and Tialla knew I didn't want to be leader but they both thought me the right choice. Perhaps they were right; perhaps I was supposed to lead them. They said that those who wanted power probably shouldn't have it. Perhaps the theory also worked in retreat.

I walked to the dais as the crowd chanted my name over and over. They called out with hope. Yet as I got closer the chants changed. What started as a chant of *Rake* quickly morphed into *Reaper Rake* and eventually it simply became *The Reaper*. This was what they called me. This was what they thought of me. A part of me died.

I reached the dais and climbed atop of it. The masses of PC cheered. I held up my hands and the cheering stopped. I stood in silence for a moment, trying to find my words.

"I have never thought myself a leader," I began. "I have never thought of myself as the person who others would flock to. I never thought myself as the person who could lead a nation of people like this but then again neither do all of you.

"You call me The Reaper. Whether your realize it or not, that is the scathing truth of your opinion of me. I am The

Reaper and one like me should not be put in charge. A Reaper is meant to do things that are necessary but horrible. I am here to fight for you but I am not meant to lead you."

Murmurs ran through the crowd. The joy and hope that held in people's eyes started to fade away. I couldn't let that happened.

"We still need a leader and one does exist. Who stepped up when we needed help? Who led us in our defining moment? Who convince each and every one of us to climb out of our holes, to take up arms, to line up beside each other and to fight? Who already thought of us as a nation and not some gaggle?" I let my words ripple out through the crowd. "There is one among us who is meant to lead and he is already here: Slashlore."

The crowd erupted once more and I stepped down from my dais. I returned to Tialla and glared at her. She shrugged. "Well, there go our well laid plans."

"I....I ...." Slashlore was speechless. He tried to speak but choked on his words. I rolled my eyes and handed Tialla five gold. "I never planned to be your leader. I honestly thought Rake was the perfect choice but I did plan on being his advisor. So what I say next, I say because I truly believe it.

"To my people, I make this promise. We will find a way home, of that I am certain. Until then we must make a life for ourselves and we must survive. It won't be easy because of the Nohorian Brotherhood. If we want to live, if we want to survive, then we need to take them out. Both parties cannot live together in this world. So as of this moment, we are at war with the Nohorian Brotherhood. And much like the Cambodians and the Thais, only one of us will be victorious."

Murmurs of confusions moved through the crowd. Slashlore laughed and hung his head. He needed a better reference.

"Think of us as the Avengers and the Nohorian Brother as Hydra."

The sound of understand rippled through crowd before quickly being replaced by the sounds of cheers. Now they understood.

I walked with Tialla and President Slashlore. We headed back to the library. I wanted to get rid of my gear, including my new cloak I'd won from Crowley. My mind raced as I walked. I was no closer to investigating the runes or the Brotherhood but I had discovered a map to my Casper Cache. I had three instances I had to run, *Under Way, Dragon's Legacy* and *Warlord Notice*. From there, I would find the items I needed. Now I just had to figure out which items they were. I let loose a long sigh. Tialla looked over at me with a curious expression.

"I was just think how all of this - the battle and our new president - came about because of one thing."

"Please don't call me president." Slashlore thought for a second and laughed. "The Fiery Typhoon; she always has a way of stirring things up."

"Not this time," I said. "This time it belongs to that stupid quest of yours. If that quest hadn't brought you to the library you wouldn't have found me."

Slashlore nodded as he thought about it. "The funny part is I didn't even know she was giving out quests again." I gave President Slashlore a curious look. "Who?"

"The Witch Queen." I came to a stop.

"What did you say?" Slashlore and Tialla stopped. The pair turned around and gave me a concern look.

"The quest came from Queen Theresa Archona," Slashlore said. He chuckled. "It's almost as if the Witch Queen wanted me to find you."

Epilogue

Galen Crowley sat in cell, alone. There was a cot in the room but he ignored it. He'd stripped it of blankets and instead laid the covering on the floor. He sat in the middle of the cell, cross-legged with his hands in his lap.

"I am but a servant," he said out loud. There was nobody to hear his words, or so he thought, but he still spoke them. "I will guide the Army of the Dusk and prepare the world for the coming Nightfall. The Superior has called upon me and I will answer the call."

"You never do shut up, do you?" Crowley looked up at the entrance to his cell and frowned. He recognized the woman that stood before him but he held no enjoyment at her presence. "You revealed things that you shouldn't."

"The Superior is our truth. We reveal only what the Superior desires. We exist only by the Superior's desires," Crowley recited.

"You revealed the Brotherhood's existence," the woman began, "you revealed the coming of Nightfall and, worst of all; you revealed the leak in the Whispers. Your only saving grace is that amongst your endless blathering, you didn't reveal anything about the Superior. Why The Superior chose you to lead the Brotherhood in this venture in beyond me but that is no longer the issue. The Superior had decided that your usefulness is over."

"Had I taken Havenold, you would be thanking me,"

Crowley spat.

"But you didn't," she replied. "You failed and now here we are."

"So you have come to slay me then," Crowley said. "You came to use death as a method to silence me?"

"You haven't being paying attention," the woman said in disbelief. "The world has changed. There are two types of people now: us and them. They can die, we cannot. Killing you will not change anything."

"Then why are you here?"

"Our plans are too important for you to reveal the identity of the Whisper double agent," The woman said. She opened the door and entered the cell. Crowley stood up and smiled.

"You have come to free me?"

The woman shook her head. Her hands moved as a blur as he snatched Crowley by the arm, twisted it and slammed the former Admiral onto the floor. She reached to her belt and drew a dagger.

"Ms. Garruil, what are you doing?"

"Silencing you," Garruil snapped. She forced Crowley's mouth opened, grabbed his tongue, pulled it from his mouth and cut it off with the blade. She released him and watched the man flail on the floor, crying out in pain. Garruil retreated out of the cell. "You have played your part, Admiral. Now the rest of us may play ours."

Vörissa's Catalyst
ONLINE
PATCH 1.03
CORPSE RUN
LARRY GENT

Prologue

Garruil watched as steel collided with steel. She stood silently as watched her apprentice spar. He was one of the other people; the PCs as they called themselves. She studied her apprentice's form as he fought. He was an archer and a brilliant one at that but when she found him, he was atrocious at anything else. She was changing that.

He wielded a double-bladed sword, a product of her tutelage, as he desperately fought against his opponent. She assigned Jerril, a Whisper agent loyal to her, to train with him. Jarril fought with two ninjatōs. She needed her apprentice to be familiar against duel wielders. She needed her apprentice to be able to best them.

Her pet PC spun his double-blade as he deflected away the ninjatōs. He stepped forward and tried to move from defense to offense but tripped over his feet in his attempt. Jerril saw the opening and took it. He slashed with his left, pulling across the PC's leg and stabbed with his right, running the blade through her apprentice's gut. Her apprentice's body stiffened at the pain. It wasn't a new feeling, he'd felt it over and over, but it was his motivator, one she choose to exploit.

"You have been ignoring your footwork," she scolded. "Why do you disappoint me?"

Garruil choose her words carefully and watched as they hurt more than the blade did. Those of the Enclave, those who called themselves PCs, were powerful creatures. They could re-align the stars given the right motivation. They were stronger than regular folk and they learned skills at an unheard rate. They were also psychologically fragile. Their emotions were all over the board. One moment they were happy and suddenly they were in a fit of rage. There were no half-way markers for the PCs. Their emotions seemed to live in extremes.

She knew how to manipulate that.

"Look at what I've given you. I provided you shelter, a safe haven from your troubles and I agreed to teach you. Yet you fail to learn, you fail to succeed. Why do you choose to make me suffer like this? Why do you choose to waste my time?"

"I am sorry, Mistress," he said from the floor.

"I promised you that I would make it so you would never have to feel weak again, I promised to make you strong and I promised you that when we were done you would never feel pain again." She approached her apprentice and knelt beside him. "That pain you're feeling now, that is your choice. You failed and now you feel pain. Use it; make it your motivation."

She nodded at Jarril. He drew a healing stone from his pouch and waved it over the fallen PC. His wounds knitted together and the pain vanished but the memory lingered. She stood back up and returned to the edge of the sparring floor. "Again, but this time," she ordered," don't disappoint me."

Isolation, insults, abuse and ignoring him simply to hurt him: these were her tools. She controlled who he saw, controlled what he did and controlled who he felt attachment to. She broke him down until there was little left and then she rebuilt him, in her desired image. She was going to mold him from this pathetic mess he was into what she needed him to be: a hunter.

His body was silent as he ran through the woods. His footsteps were like that of a stag; swift and light, never fracturing the grass, twigs or dirt beneath them. A stag moved through the forest with the intention of committing no harm. Ironically, he moved through the trees with the express interest of committing a lot of it.

The Hunter came to a halt as he found his spot. He crouched by a tree and looked out over the road. This was Hermi Pass, a well used road that ran between Havenhold and Hammer Forge, one of the three great Dwarf cities. Everyday hundred of NPCs and hundreds of PCs passed along this road and now they would pass before him.

For hours on end he watched the road. He studied the routine of the NPC guards, tracking their movements and marking how often they went on patrol. He watched the PCs walk by, some alone and some in groups. The Hunter let them pass by. He watched how they travelled the road. Most went by mounts, some flying and others walking, but some walked by feet. He tracked their speeds and studied their paths. For hours he watched, learning as much as he could.

Then, he was ready

He took his dagger carved five lines into the bark of a tree. He picked up his bow, a gift from his mistress, and notched a red-fletched arrow. He drew back on the arrow and lined up his shot with the attack circle. For a moment, he was filled with hesitation. He looked at his target, a Gnome priestess. She was accompanied by an Elven mage and Dwarf warrior. Most were lowbies, under level 30. Did they deserve what was happening next?

The only reason anybody feels pain is because they allow it. The memory of his mistress' words rang through his head, reassuring him. He was here for a reason, he was here for a mission and he didn't dare disappoint his mistress.

The arrow fled from his bow and travelled across the forest. It passed by several trees before emerging onto the road and diving deep into the Gnome's head. The Gnome died instantly. She never heard the dwarf and human scream and she never felt any pain. The second arrow that emerged, a mere second later, dove into the Elf's neck. The Elf felt a lot of pain.

The Dwarf warrior grabbed his shield and held it before him. He aimed it at the assumed direction of the sniper. He called out a warning as several other PCs traveling along Hermi Pass turned to see what the commotion was.

A paladin, human female, ran over to the fallen pair to see if she could provide assistance. She never made it. A third arrow slammed into her side and sent her tumbling to the ground. The paladin tried to move, to climb out of the way but she never got a chance. A fourth arrow landed into the side of her head and finished her off.

Nobody else tried to help. They just scattered. The hunter stood up and retreated into the woods. He vanished before anybody could see him. His mistress' words ran through his mind.

"You would never have to feel weak again."

Chapter 01

"Proper story's supposed to start at the beginning. Ain't so simple with this one." - Bastion

I am not a violent man but as my blades cut down the umpteenth member of the Nohorian Brotherhood, I found myself struggling with original declaration. I stepped away from my fallen foe and pivoted to my left. Whaitiri Edge leapt up to greet the defense square as my steel deflected the oncoming blade of some other masked lackey. I slapped the rapier aside and moved Splinter's Bite towards the attack circle. My longsteel dove into the lackey's gut as I ran him through until it emerged on the other side. I pressed my foot onto his chest and kicked him off, withdrawing my weapon in the process. I looked at the *literal* baker's dozen of corpses that lay at my feet and thought once more that I was not a violent man.

At that moment I was trying to convince no one but myself.

Incessant giggling filled the air as a revenant Gnome named Skith - Son of Zook- entered the room mounted on an undead orc. He waved his glaive around with glee and I snickered as I found the entire event funny.

I may not be a violent man but I was clearly a twisted one.

"My Un-orc and I cleared the next room with much vigor and zeal," he said, "though I must say that we are fortunate that I wield a glaive and not a club."

"Why?" I asked, fearing the answer.

"I've heard that many frown on zeal clubbing."

My fears were justified.

"Are we really going to allow that pun?" Punchocalypse asked. I glanced at the Dwarf monk and shrugged.

"He's an RPer," I explained. "You try telling him what he did wrong."

"Easy," Punchocalypse said. He walked over to the un-orc and stared up at Skith. "You're not me."

"And you, Mr. Dwarf, are way too tall," Skith retorted.

Both Dwarf and Gnome stared at each other. Their eyes were locked and the said not a word. Somewhere in the distance, I could heard the standard Clint Eastwood western music playing. Then both burst out laughing. Why was I assigned to work with these two?

"Slashlore told you to work with us," Punchocalypse said, somehow answering the question I hadn't actually asked out loud. "Aren't you happy at that?"

"Has our leader chosen a title for himself? If he a king? A minister of prime?"

"We've been calling President Slashlore," Punchocalypse said, "but he hates that title. It's why we do it."

"Actually General Tialla ordered us to work together," I corrected. As part of the Enclave's war against the Nohorian Brotherhood, we had been launching attacks on their strongholds and bases. For the last week my days had been filled with military strikes, my duties as the Reaper and running the Wurm Nest instance over and over. It was tiring but it was great for leveling. Last night I dinged at level 58. "She's the one I have to blame for our grouping, Skith."

"How many times must I request that you call me Mast Skith?"

"Why is it Mast Skith again?" Punchocalypse asked, eye me with a devilish look. I loathed Punchocalypse at that moment. Skith always gave the same answer to that question.

"I used to be Master Skith but the E and the R fell off my sign," he said with a sad expression on his face. I glared. I hated that answer.

"If you were a master before, then you're a master now. Just because letters fall off your sign doesn't make you any less a master," I snapped.

"Yes it does. Without the E and the R it doesn't say Master. It says Mast. How can I be a Master with the E and R?"

I hated RPers.

The three of us moved further into the base. The building was a former Damphir Den. Dens were once small Damphir shelters. They were scattered all across the Aspumer and typically held 45-80 of their kin. In Vörissa's Catalyst Online lore, the Damphir weren't a unified race until the arrival of Vörissa. She controlled the half-breeds with her god-powers. Entire dens would fall and become her thralls. A Damphir named Loken Reign rose to power in her den. With the help generously offered by kidnapped mages, Loken created a blood spell that protected her den from the Goddess' control. Loken moved from den to den, freeing them from the Fallen One's control and uniting her people. Loken started a city and named it after her mother: Malthe Nest. The Damphirs now stood as one of the major races in Aspumer and were major members in the Coalliton of the Damned. With their new city firmly set, dozens of dens were left abandoned across the world, many of which were now being used by monsters, thieves or the Brotherhood.

The Enclave-Nohorian Brotherhood War was going poorly for the Brotherhood, which meant it was going swimmingly for us. Our attacks on Brotherhood bases had resulted in many Brotherhood deaths, none of which were permanent. Since the Glitch, NPCs couldn't die. They could be beaten and slain but they would respawn. Many wondered the wisdom of going to war against a foe that wouldn't stay dead but despite that our efforts proved fruitful. With Galen Crowley gone, the Brotherhood didn't have the leadership it needed. When we assaulted a base and dismantled that cell's operation, it stayed dismantled. Whatever it was that radicalized an NPC into joining the Brotherhood, vanished upon their respawn.

"How many Brotherhood strongholds will this make for you guys?" Skith asked from atop his un-orc.

I scratched my head, "Six, I think."

"Eleven," Punchocalypse said without hesitation. I snapped my head over at the Dwarf and stared in disbelief. He shrugged. "I guess I'm Tialla's favourite."

"General's pet," I mumbled.

The un-orc came to a halt and began to shriek. I stared at it in shock. The un-orc was an undead brute of an orc that Skith rode into battle, like a twisted version of Nunu and Willump. The un-orc didn't talk. It moaned, roared and let decaying flesh fall from its body. It never ever shrieked.

"Skith?" I asked but the gnome didn't answer. The un-orc started to run about wildly, like a woman with a bee in her hair. It flailed its arms wildly and caught me in the face. I flew backwards and slammed into the wall. Punchocalypse ducked beneath the un-orc's arms and rolled away. Skith tried to hang on for dear life.

Then we heard another sound. It was clacking sound, like a woman with long fingernails typing on a computer. I drew my blades as the sound grew closer. The closer it got, the more the un-orc panicked. Whatever it was that was approaching, it had an undead brute of an orc freaked the fuck out.

They lunged from the darkness and attacked and I struck before I knew what they were. My longsteel cut one in two and I eyed the remains. They were dog-sized bugs with razor sharp claws and hungry mandibles. I swore; these were the Errosites. They were what looked to be the crossbreed between a spider and an ant and were as terrifying as a Flood controlled Zerg. They were a hive-like bug creature that lived beneath the ground. What they were doing inside a Brotherhood controlled den was beyond me.

"Cut through them," I ordered. I willed to life the

speed in my boots and shot forward. Splinter's Bite swiftly saber slashed any bug I came across as Whaitiri Edge did it's best to deflect the Errosites' deadly strikes. Punchocalypse was behind me. His fist slammed into anything that got close, making them fly against the wall or sent them crumpling to the ground like discarded trash. Skith pulled up the rear. He de-summoned his un-orc and ran along the ground. His glaive - a giant's cleaver tied to a stick - hacked off any limbs it came across.

The Errosites attacked in great numbers. Their method of attack was to outnumber and swarm, the VCO equivalent of a zergling rush, but as Skith hacked the legs off of the final bug we were shocked at how small their numbers were.

"What the actual hell?" Punchocalypse yelled. "Errosites? Here? WTF?"

I shook my head as I followed the hallway. I winced with each step; the Errosites strikes had taken its toll on my form. The hallway led into a larger chamber. This room, known as the feeding room back in its Damphir days, had several broken eggs and numerous empty cocoons all surrounding a large table.

"Well that makes sense," Skith explained. "My un-orc was slain by the Errosites. That is why he still fears them."

"You wrote back story for your zombie-bitch?" Punchocalypse asked in disbelief. "Crazy RPers."

"Actually, most summons like that have a hidden history and a back story to them," I said half-heartedly as I approached the table. "You just have to look."

"Crazy lore junkies," Punchocalypse said with a roll of his eyes.

I ignored him as I started at the table. There was an arcane circle, a spell book and tiny glowing jewel. I frowned.

"We have to get back to the president."

Chapter 02

"The possibilities are infinite!" - Notch, Minecraft Developer

"The Brotherhood is trying to control the Errosites with magic," I said to the room. Nine faces looked back at me. "The bug race?" Slashlore asked. I nodded. Our President frowned.

I stood in Slashlore's home. He'd used his gold to purchase a large house which now acted as his home and the capital for the Enclave. This was his digital White House. Punchocalypse, Skith and I stood before President Slashlore and his cabinet. There was General Tialla, the newly appointed Commander Mystylz, Sheriff Bearcules, Lady Adelaide Bullmourn - The Spymaster and Ms. Garruil.

"We haven't seen this before, have we?"

"No, Mr. President," Tialla replied. Slashlore rolled his eyes and a small chuckled crossed the room. "This is the first I've seen of it. We don't know what their level of success is."

"Two questions: how big of a threat is this and what do we do about it?" Slashlore asked.

"VCO hasn't seen a full fledge bug attack so it's hard to say," Mystylz said. "Judging off what we saw in *Sound of The Cuprric Echo*, if they could build a bug army of any decent size and control it, we'd be fucked. We couldn't fight against that."

"This brings up question two. What do we do about it?"

"Nuke them from orbit," Mystylz said with a shrug.

"It's the only way to be sure."

"M'lord," Lady Adelaide spoke up. "With every Brotherhood stronghold we destroy, their numbers diminish. We are running out of bases to raid. The Brotherhood will soon be on its final legs. We cannot allow them to regain ground."

"If I may," Garruil said suddenly. She looked at Slashlore and then Lady Adelaide, "with your permission of course." Both Adelaide and Slashlore nodded. "The Brotherhood is falling. They are desperately looking for anything to even the battlefield. This could be one of many possible weapons they are experimenting with. I understand the need for caution but this is the first we've seen of it. Putting excessive resources into finding more about this could prove costly in your war effort. If M'lord and M'lady allow it, I could take what notes we have and put the resources of the Whispers upon it."

Slashlore nodded. "I like that idea. Thank you, Ms. Garruil. I'll get what we found to you."

"There is a third question," Punchocalypse said suddenly. The Dwarf monk had been to a couple of these meeting but he never spoke. Punchocalypse wasn't a politician; he was a brawler. "Is this even the Nohorian Brotherhood's doing?"

Eyes turned to the monk. Slashlore spoke first. "Explain."

"We've never seen the Brotherhood try something like this before. We also know the Brotherhood is either working for or with someone else," he said simply. "Maybe it's not them trying to control the Errosites, maybe it's this mysterious third party."

Nobody spoke. I smirked. Leave it to a monk to take a room full of politicians and leave them stunned with one idea. The room felt like a living example of the Stunned Keanu meme.

The meeting ended and the parties went their own ways. I stopped by Tialla as she was talking with Mystylz and a hunter named Santiago. I paused and let the trio speak. Tialla eventually noticed me and I flashed the priestess a roguish smile. She smiled back, in her priestly ways. (That sounded dirtier then I intended)

"Hell of a find," she said. I shrugged it off.

"Where you want me next?"

"We have four more Stronghold Strikes in progress," Mystylz said, reading it from a journal. "We have three more scheduled for tomorrow. They have been assigned to experienced teams. We foresee no complications."

"Do they need backup? Safety in numbers?" I asked.

"Relax, Super Trooper," Tialla laughed. "It's like you want to tear down the Brotherhood single-handedly."

I shrugged it off and she didn't press. We both knew what I was doing. I was hiding in combat. If rogues know how to do anything, it was how to hide.

"If things get worse, I promise I'll PM you," Tialla said. "But it's been slow. The Brotherhood has attacked the Dwarven cities of Hammer Forge and Diamonfax, nothing more than lane pokes though. They went after the human city Wavmouth but have left the Elven and Gnomish cities alone." She shrugged. "So in short, it's quiet."

"Then maybe, if you're not busy..." I was mumbling.

"Have you met Mystylz?" Tialla asked, not hearing my poor attempt at speech.

"Not officially," I said. I extended my hand to the Dwarf Paladin. He took it.

"I...er....it is a pleasure, Mr. Rake." Mystylz looked like a big, tough manly Dwarf but he talked and acted like squirrely, demure man. "Your efforts have been a big help in the war effort."

"I do what I can." Tialla hired Mystylz as her military 2IC. She needed a tactician and an organizer to help in her war campaign. She had asked me but I said no. What she needed was beyond my skills. I had no problems spending hours behind a desk studying, but planning dozens of attack, managing resources and controlling units were not area of expertise. If I wanted to do that, I'd be a *Starcraft 2* player, not VCO.

"This," she said as she pointed to the hunter, "is Santiago."

I knew of Santiago but I had never met him. He was the one who led Tialla's troops. He'd been on the front line with Enclave's army, small as it was, and the volunteer fighters like me. I reached out and shook his hand.

"Mr. Rake," he said gruffly. "I know Tialla and Mystylz have made an offer but feel like I should be asking you myself. We could really use you in the force. I'd make a soldier of you yet."

"A Reaper has no place in an army," I replied. I hated the name Reaper but it did come with a handy excuse for situations like this.

Santiago spoke like every soldier in every war film. He was big, loud and full of hoorahs. It was bad form to talk about our lives outside of VCO but I had my theories on most people. My running theory for Santiago was he was either a military goon or some wanna-be soldier.

"Perhaps not," he said. He turned to Tialla. "General, this bug problem is exactly what I was talking about earlier. The war is going well so far but it will turn on a dime. We need to press our attack. We need to push harder."

"Commander," Tialla snapped. It was a tone I hadn't heard from her before but one that immediately made me straighten up and stand taller. It also, surprisingly, sent a tingle through my body. "I've heard your thoughts and I've made my decision. Now drop it. Am I understood?"

"Yes, Ma'am."

Tialla turned back to me. "How goes the hunt for your latest Casper Cache?"

I let out a loud exaggerated sigh. "I ran WN like six times. I got every drop the final boss had on him and spent hours studying the damn things."

"And?"

"I got a rope. It's a damn rope." I shook my head. "It's actually an intricately woven belt but it's a damn rope. It's called the Meging Cord."

"What does it do?"

"The Megingjörð was the belt of Thor. It doubles his already prodigious strength," Mystylz said. He paused and looked at the two stunned faces. "I...I mean.....I'm sorry."

"Now I know where they got the name," I laughed at the pun. "This is called the Meging Cord. It gives me a big strength boost and gives me the Mighty Strike ability twice per day." Mighty Strike was an ability that did just as it sounded: Rake hit hard! It was a dumb warrior belt but that didn't stop me from wearing it. I knew how Casper worked. It took me forever to discover the final piece in the Jötunn set because it wasn't even a mage item.

"So what's left?"

"I gotta run DL and UW a couple times each," I said. "Then I'll figure out what this set does."

"If you need help..." She didn't have to finish the sentence. I already knew what she was offering. I smile and nodded.

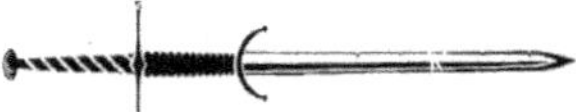

With my war effort done for the day, I returned to my room. I was dead tired and needed sleep since I was constantly tired these days. It came from little sleep and over working myself. It wasn't that I wasn't giving myself enough time to sleep; it was just that sleep was proving difficult. I lay down upon my bed and drifted off.

I found myself standing in a room. Internally, I sighed. Falling asleep was never the issue. What was proving difficult was staying asleep. Whenever I drifted off I was assaulted by the same dream. I was in a room, the details of which were becoming slightly clearer with each dream, but I was never alone in the room. Instead, I found myself joined by the same person, time after time: Steelion.

I stared into my friend's eyes and felt nothing but guilt. It was painful to stare at the face of my friend, of the man I ki---.

"Dead," Steelion said. "Kill."

I snapped awake. This was why I couldn't sleep.

With my war efforts completed for the day and sleep an impossibility, it was time to check in on my other duties, my Reaper Responsibilities. Since I --- since Steelion and my encounter with Galen Crowley, people had been calling me the Reaper. I hated the title and I hated the responsibilities that had somehow accompanied it.

The Enclave was a people but we had no justice system. We had few laws, preventing murder and assault, but we had no way to uphold them. The Enclave was but a week old, it hadn't had any real crimes but they were coming, it was only a matter of time. People were horrible. In place of crime, we had something almost as bad: trolls.

Trolls were dicks. They were people who sowed discord online. Did they do it for a cause or to fight some good fight? Nope. Most times they did it to be assholes. In Pre-Glitch, they would prank players, trick them into areas or dungeons that would get them killed. In Pre-Glitch, it was more annoying than anything; you die, you respawn and you walk away. Since the Glitch they were doing the same, only this time it was more dangerous and permanent.

I was the solution, albeit a temporary one, to the troll problem. People viewed me as a k---. People viewed me a man who would lay down the permanent solution when it was needed. It meant I walked with an air of intimidation.

I walked into the Sheriff's office. With the lack of real crime, the Sheriff Department was mainly there to support, aid and rescue PCs in need. It started as Bearcules tried to help those in need, to make amends for his wrongs. He helped trapped or lost PCs and eventually they started labeling him with the lawman's title. I hated it, he tried to kill me, but there was little I could do. Luckily, I didn't have to deal with him.

I walked towards the familiar female Elf and flashed

her one of my charming smiles. "Hey, Gorgeous; what's cookin' good lookin'?"

Her name was Footkneebra - a name she chose by staring at her foot and making her way upwards - and despite being an Elf, she looked nothing like them. She had the same thin and lithe form as Elves, but her skin was red, she had a pair of small horns and a pointed tail that swooshed back and forth behind her. Footkneebra was a succubus.

In VCO's fifth expansion, *Sound of The Cuprric Echo*, Aspumer was being plagued by a demonic vanguard. They were looking to crawl up from Hell and claimed the mortal realm as their own. Their first attack was a demonic virus that existed as sound. The noise turned the Errosites feral while transforming the unlucky Elves and Damphir who heard it into succubi and incubi. According to lore, those who could free themselves from the demonic hold returned to their faction, transformed and empowered by a new magical source.

In game terms, the Succubi and Incubi were VCO's second heroic class. They were part rogue and part mage, except where the mage blew shit up, the succubi would strength allies and weaken foes. They were buffers and debuffers, the boon and bane to each battle.

"Mr. Rake," Footkneebra said with a sultry smile. "What brings you here? Looking for some ERPing fun or you here all for work?"

The Succubi class transformed Elves, an already lithe creature, into the incarnation of sultry desire. They dripped pure sexuality and lust and those that played the race, knew exactly how to exploit it.

"I'm here for work," I gave her body a once over and flirted back, "for now."

"Promises, promises." She escorted me back to one of the three desks. "Let's see what I've got for you."

I looked around. Bearcules was nowhere to be seen and I let out a small sigh of relief. I wasn't ready to deal with him. The door opened behind me and a bald Dwarf with a monstrous beard walked in. "Hey, Rake. Sup?"

He was Deputy Ddaaxx. He was a hunter and the final member in the Enclave Sheriff Department. There were only three of them; it was all they needed for now. I gave Ddaaxx a nod.

"Where's the Boss-Bear?" Footkneebra asked.

"He's still out at Hermi Pass," he replied. "He's in cat-form looking for clues; told me to head back here and to start looking at leads."

I tried to look like I wasn't curious but I have a horrible poker face. Footkneebra saw my expression and started to explain. "There was an attack at Hermi Pass earlier. A sniper took out three PCs and injured a couple more. Boss-Bear is investigating beside Mystylz."

"Is this an attack?" I asked.

"That's what the pair is trying to find out. Is this Brotherhood? Is this PC? Is it something new?" I opened my mouth to speak but Footkneebra shook her head. "Nope; you're not getting involved. This is a joint Military-Sheriff operation. You're neither, remember? Besides, we already have enough people on it for now."

"I never get my way," I jested with a faux pout. Footkneebra rolled her eyes as she handed me a piece of paper.

"We have some reports on trolls that could use a visitation," she explained. "We've done what we can but they just scoff at us. Perhaps a visit from the Reaper will change their mind."

I gave her a nod and read over the list. I sighed as I recognized one of the two names: Jhaara.

Chapter 03

"I will kill your dicks!" - Trishka Novak (Bulletstorm)

Scarrow stood atop the hill, a bow in his hand and an arrow notched. He looked down at the valley below and watched a party of lowbies as they tried to creep past a group of goblins. The tiny menaces were never overly difficult but they did move in groups. They knew how to swarm and how to flank. In short, if they swarmed you, you were fucked.

Scarrow looked back at the warrior that stood behind him. Jhaara just smirked as she edged him on. "It'll be funny, I promise."

"Are you sure?" Scarrow asked. He didn't show emotion, he was firm.

"We aggro the 'nobs, watch as they swarm the lowbies and then we ride in as big damn heroes and take their gold as a reward; simple."

"And they're holding?" Scarrow asked.

"We're not monsters; we're opportunist." Jhaara said with a smirk. "We don't do things willy-nilly."

All of this happened without them knowing I was there. But as my Lucky Dagger suddenly planted itself in the ground at their feet, both became instantly aware that someone was watching. They both spun around and saw me. I stood in a tree, my dagger rematerializing in my hand. Jhaara scowled at me. I snapped the dagger into my glove. I leapt from the tree and gracefully landed on the ground.

"It's been a couple weeks, Jhaara," I said as I approached.

"Fuck off, Lowbie," she snapped. "This doesn't have anything to do with you."

I eyed the hunter. "Who's the replacement?"

"What do you want?" she snapped.

"What happened to Boomzile?"

"He got all patriotic," she spat. "The idiot joined up with Slashlore's army. He's military now." That shocked me. I didn't expect a troll to enlist.

"Who is this guy?" Scarrow asked.

"He's Rake. He used to be Stov," she explained, "but you'd know him as the Reaper."

Scarrow solid face cracked. It started with a twitch in his eyes and it grew into a subtle look of fear. I hated the look my new name drew. Scarrow lowered his bow. He eyed me while shooting inquisitive glances at Jhaara.

"This has to stop, Jhaara," I said sternly. "You're hurting people."

"And why do you care, Reaper? You got some Batman fetish you're trying to live out? If I meow, hiss and try to scratch you, will you let me go?"

Maybe if she was dressed like Michelle Pfeiffer.

"Please, Jhaara." I begged. "This has to stop. There has to be something better you can be doing with your time then hurting people."

"What are you going to do? Kill me like you killed Steelion?" Her words cut deep and she knew it. I felt a part of me die. Steelion: I ki---

"You're the one who killed Steelion?" Scarrow said in disbelief. He turned to Jhaara. "I ain't fighting him."

The warrior scowled. I eyed her hands as it dropped to her belt. "Jhaara, don't."

"Or what? What will happen if I drew my blade? Will you kill me? Will you cut me down? Will I just be another notch on the Reaper's belt? Another dead warrior lying by Rake's feet?"

She never gave me the chance to answer. She simply drew her blade and struck. My blades jumped to my hands and Whaitiri Edge moved to quickly deflect her longsword. As a jolt of electricity ran through her body, Splinter's Bite slashed at her leg. Jhaara pivoted and struck again, only to once again meet up with Whaitiri Edge. She attacked with strike after strike, causing no damage save for the jolt after jolt that ran from my blade and through her body. I stayed on the defensive, moving faster then she could. I didn't dodge her attacks, instead I blocked with my Edge. Every jolt that ran through her body slowed her down, each electric sting munching away at her stamina.

Eventually, I saw the opening I wanted. I parried her attack with Splinter's Bite and twisted the blade, ripping her sword from her grip and pitching it across the ground. I pulled Whaitiri Edge against her side and watched as she winced in pain. She crumbled to the ground as I kicked at her leg wound. I stood over her and sheathed my blades then I drew a small pouch from my belt and dropped it on her. The pouch, which was no bigger than a coin pouch, transformed into a tangled mess of thorny vines and stems. I watched as the tangle grew into a small rose patch.

"This is a Rose Trap," I explained. "If you move, even an inch, the thorns will tear into you. It won't ever be enough to kill you, but it will be painful AF. It'll vanish in an hour or two."

I looked at Scarrow. "At this moment you have two choices. 1: cut her free and continue this life. 2: Walk away, now.

"One of those options will involve frequent meetings with me. We'll fight over and over and every time I'll win. It'll be some comic book shit. But one day things will change. One day you'll go too far and someone will die. Then I'll have no choice but to be the Reaper you've heard about. On that day you will witness the Reaper first hand."

I walked away.

"And you just walked away?" Scova said with a grin.

"That is so freaking Batman."

"I'm the *God Damn* Batman," I said in my best Bale voice. I sat on a couch, drinking a beer in Scova's house. Technically it wasn't her house, it was Lady Adelaide's Havenhold house, but these days Scova was basically living there.

"So what's next, Dork Knight?" Scova asked. She leaned back in her chair and my eyes fell upon the Cat's Eye Pendent that hung from her neck. It was a magical item that increased range of sight while providing night vision. It wasn't a rare item but it was pretty, with the pendent having the green iris and the black pupil.

I shrugged, "Loot runs and research."

"Where the hell do you find time for either?" The mage asked. "Tialla has you running strike after strike while playing Batman? Dude, are you even sleeping anymore?"

"I am the night," I Bale'd. "The Dark Knight needs no sleep."

"I'm serious," she declared.

"He is a Whisper," Lade Adelaide said suddenly as she walked into the room. "Give those who live amongst the shadows the credit they deserve, Little Flame." I stood up to bow, she was a lady of noble birth, but she waved me away.

"Don't defend him, Ade," Scova protested.

"Shadow walkers need less sleep then most, they exist in a level that most other do not. So do not bother a Whisper about trivial matters such as sleep." Lady Adelaide sat across from me and took a good look at my face. "Holy shit, you need sleep."

"Why don't people just assume I'm always right?" Scova mocked.

"That is a highly dangerous precedent to set, Little Flame."

"Yeah, like *Baby-Groot-With-Explosives* dangerous," I laughed.

"Rake," Adelaide began, looking at me once more. "Why do you avoid sleep? What is it that troubles you about slumber? Is it dreams?"

"Kinda," I said. "Falling asleep isn't hard but when I do I see his face."

"Steelion's?" Scova asked. I nodded.

"The hours before sleep are no easier. Those moments when you lie on the bed, you stare at the ceiling and you are left with nothing but your memories, your conscience and your guilt."

"It's a time when all that accompanies you are the cerebral remnants of your past deeds." Adelaide frowned.

"When does it go away?"

"It doesn't," she admitted. "You simply become numb to the feeling. Some take comfort in the knowledge that the horrors they do are for a greater cause."

"Is that what you believe?"

Adelaide simply shook her head. "Many Whispers believe in the cause my father has lain before them. It is why they willingly joined. I had no such choice."

A child forced into her Father's lifestyle. It was painful. For a moment I forgot what Adelaide really was, I forgot that she was a NPC. Then it all came crashing back. What would happen to Adelaide when we escaped VCO? What would happen after the game's unavoidable shut-down?

"Every soldier, spy and Whisper has to discover their own reason for what they do." Adelaide put her hand atop of Scova. I frowned. What would happen to Scova when Adelaide was deleted?

I stood inside a room. The details were much clearer than before. It was a large room built with grey, ash covered stones. The rest was a blur. Steelion stood before me and once again I painfully stared into his eyes.

"Dead," Steelion said. "Kill."

I awoke and sat in my bed. Seconds later there was knocking at my door. I sat up and mumbled to myself.

"You better be a James Earl Jones sounding MF if you are rapping at my chamber door," I said loudly. I pulled it opened and saw the familiar form of Tialla.

"Quoth the Raven, 'Nevermore.'"

"What up, General Lady?" I muttered as I let her into my room. I had only been sleeping in my pants so I walked to my bed for my shirt.

"The President needs you," she said quickly. "The Enclave government has been requested to speak with the Havenhold's ruling body."

"You don't make a big speech about how we're our own people without pissing off the Queen," I laughed. I pulled on my shirt. "So why does Pressy want me?"

"Tomorrow the Queen wishes to negotiate a treaty between the Enclave and the descendants," she explained. "We think it'll help both parties. Slashlore wants to benefit from their legal system and military."

I eyed Tialla suspiciously. She saw my look and kept talking.

"It'll probably mean taxes on the PCs but we'll figure that out as well."

"What aren't you telling me?" I asked. "What are you hiding?"

"The Witch Queen requested you." Tialla nervously rubbed the back of her neck. "She requested Rake by name."

Chapter 04

"Video games are the quintessential social texts of our present cultural moment." - Steven E. Jones

I've always liked Seraphim Castle. It was the glimmering bastion for the Descendant's of the Eternals. It stood firm, jetting into the heavens with pristine stone work, its spiraling towers and its wing-like walls that stretched outwards. From a distance the castle almost looked like an angel, down on one knee with its head lowered as it held a sword. The castle looked as if at a moment's notice, the angel would awaken, rise and defend its people. As we approached the bastion, I looked up and once again admired it.

Slashlore wore formal clothing while Tialla was dressed in an elegant blue gown with golden trims. I was dressed in nice-ish clothes. I didn't have formal gear; Stov did but Rake did not, I had nicer looking armour. We were stopped at the door by a guard before being escorted in by Havenhold's Chancellor. Slashlore, Tialla and I were brought into a large chamber with a massive table and dozens of chairs.

On one side there was the three of us, on the other was the Witch Queen, her Chancellor and the commander of her army. In between both parties were Lord Dorian Bullmourn and his daughter Lady Adelaide Bullmourn, the ruling faction of the Whispers. The Whispers were an ally with both the descendants and the Enclave so they were a neutral third party that could help with the proceedings. We all performed quick greetings and got down to our political talks.

Political talks are hella boring.

I sat, more or less, silently until we broke for lunch. I watched as people talked and I hated every moment of it. It was boring, tedious and filled with meaningless double talk. My morning basically went like so:

Queen: We would like to thank the Enclave and the Whispers for being here.

President: We thank you for having us.

Lord: We thank you as well.

President: We would like to show that we recognize the steps you've taken to meet us.

Queen: We have recognized that you have recognized.

President: We would also like to recognize the contributions the Whispers will make and thank them for that.

Lord: We recognize your thanks and pass along the thanks to the Queen for having us as well.

Queen: We have recognized your thanks.

Lord: We have recognized that you have recognized our thanks.

President: We have recognized that the Whispers have recognized that the Queen has recognized the thanks.

Queen: We have recognized that the Enclave has recognized that the Whispers have recognized that we have recognized the thanks and we thank them for that.

President: We recognize that thanks.

Lord: I propose that we all go out back and shoot ourselves in the head?

Queen: I recognize that proposal!

President: Off we go then, shall we bring tea?

Lord: I recognize the desire for tea.

I may have stopped paying attention and replaced what really happen with what I wanted to happen. When we broke for lunch, I was ready to smash my head against a brick wall and not stop until I gave myself another concussion. Hopefully this one would either kill me or at least rob me of my memories of this.

"That went very well," Slashlore said as we walked out.

"I know," Tialla agreed excitedly. "I didn't expect them to give us the tea."

I blinked. "Tea?

The pair looked at me in surprise. "T...as in Tango; Project: Tango. We *literally* just went over this in the meeting," Slashlore explained. I blinked dumbly. "The Enclave now has the right to have its own armed forces within Havenhold's wall. We act as our own entity but we can be drafted into any Havenhold conflicts. It was a powerful item in our agenda."

"I mean it did require a large portion of our tax budget to go to the Crown but we're okay with that." Tialla laughed, "I thought we were basically going around back and shooting ourselves in the head with that option."

I had to start paying attention more.

I sat outside, eating alone in the courtyard. In the distance I could see Tialla talk with Mystylz. They were hovering over a couple folders, talking quickly. Slashlore was talking to some Gnome named Ladytramp. She was helping Slashlore run the Enclave, his Chief of Staff. I sat alone, eating and watching the sky.

I watched as dozens of PCs crossed the sky on their flying mounts and I felt jealous. I missed flying, crossing the sky atop my winged steed as the wind blew through my hair. I was land bound, forced to ride atop a horse. Flying mounts needed level 60. Flying wasn't an item like my blade, it was a skill and those still held fast to their level dependency. I was so close. I couldn't wait to take to the sky, to fly around atop my mounts. I had several to choose from. Flying mounts, while useless in PVP tournaments, were a player's one chance to needlessly show-off. If you were seen riding into a battleground on an armoured winged three-headed dragon, you made an impact. Professional players *loved* making an impact.

My favourite mounts were my Hellforged Kite, Chained Infernal and Thundering Cloud Serpent. However, none were as iconic as my Corrupted Warbat. It was an *exceptionally* rare mount that was - according to official VCO statistics - only used by 1.9% of players.

It used to be that when people thought of Stov, they thought of him on his Kite or his Cloud Serpent. That all changed when I got the Warbat. Now the image was that of Stov flying into battle on the back of a giant winged bat, held aloft by giant leathery wings with glowing red veins.

I missed that mount.

"What about the sky holds your attention, Mr. Rake?" I looked up at the voice and found the Witch Queen standing over me. I scrambled to my feet but she waved me to a halt. I looked past the Queen and spotted the woman who stood several paces behind her. She was stoic and silent and carried no weapons. I didn't need to ask who she was, I already knew. She was Gine, the queen's bodyguard. Gine simply nodded at me as the Queen took a seat. The Queen was dressed in an elegant royal blue dress, a gown not fit for ground sitting but she sat none the less. She looked up at the sky, curious as to what I was looking at.

"I'm looking at those who fly," I explained. "I used to be able to fly among them but I no longer can. I'll be able to join them again, soon, but I miss it."

She nodded. "I never had the stomach for flight. It's why I prefer to teleport."

"Bleh," I said with a chuckle. "I can't do that, 'porting makes me ill."

She smiled. We sat in silence, staring up at the sky. Eventually she looked at me. "How goes your research?"

"Very slowly, your Highness," I admitted. "I've been

kind of side-tracked lately but there is so much to research."

"What specifically are you looking for?"

I pulled my leather-bound journal from my bag and opened it up to the sketches I'd done on the series of runes. I handed her the book. She smiled at its use and glanced at them.

"Those are runes that showed up on the moon the night of the Gli-- of the first attack," I explained. "I believe they have a connection to the changes that have happened. I want to find more about them but I can find diddly."

"I am not familiar with these," she admitted. Her face scrunched as she examined them. I smirked. I couldn't help but marvel at how even while undergoing an undignified scrunch, her face still looked regal. "They are very old but do look like they are from the illusionary school. The ridges and cross lines are a dead giveaway. I'm surprised your mages didn't know that."

I blinked in surprise. Magic was broken into numerous schools such as evocation, conjuration, aberration and so forth. Mages got to know them very well. However, PC mages had few, if any, illusionary and necromancy spells at their disposal. They weren't put in the game for PCs. They were limited for NPCs and villains. No wonder Scova and I didn't know them.

The Queen stood up and once more looked to the sky. "I always pondered why your kind favours such fearsome and vicious mounts. I never saw the need to boast with such horror. To me nothing seemed more amazing then a mage riding a Hellforged Kite across the sky."

Then she turned and walked away, once more leaving me stunned.

Chapter 05

"Stay a while, and listen!" - Deckard Cain (Diablo)

"This is what I know of your people," Queen Arcona said. "You come from another world, live in bodies that aren't your own and normally you travel to and from these two worlds but now you are trapped here."

"That is an over simplification," Slashlore defended, "but, basically, yeah."

"Since the event you refer to as the Glitch, the natives of this world can be killed but will return to life shortly after. Your people, however, cannot. If you die, you stay dead. So if this is the case, then why do you fight the Brotherhood? Why do you fight at all when there are those who cannot perish beside you?"

"In all honesty, your Highness," Slashlore said carefully. "We are stronger and more powerful than your kind. Some of the threats are beyond what you can handle. And besides, we aren't that easy to kill, we just don't get back up afterwards."

The Queen sat silently as she took it all in. She looked at each of us, one at a time. She was studying us but it seemed, especially as she looked into my eyes, that she was studying me *more*.

"Perhaps we should continue the negotiations," The chancellor suggested. "We do have much to talk about, like the regulations of your people living amongst ours.

"There already exists some trepidation from our people about their inability to differentiate themselves from your kind. We have devised a proposal that will require your people to wear an insignia to highlight your difference."

"No," Tialla snapped. "This is a hard no."

"This is not an unreasonable request," The Chancellor defended. "It would only be an armband."

"Fuck that. I'm not allowing them to visibly mark us as different," she snapped, the anger in her voice quickly growing. "Are we seriously going to let them treat us like the Nazis treated my family? I'm not letting Hitler here do that."

"Tialla, pull back on Goodwin's law." Slashlore turned to the Queen, "In our world there was a very hateful man who marked an entire religion in a similar fashion. It turned out poorly and although it was many decades ago, it is still a very difficult memory for my kind. While I believe you have no ill will with this decision, I must insist against this ruling."

"Your kind is vastly different than ours when it comes to skill and power," the Chancellor said. "Do you expect us to send our guards into a situation with your kind without knowing who they are up against? Not every ruler would allow a militant people to live within their borders. We are allowing a superior force to live amongst us with no way to enforce our laws."

"I agree that this is an important issue," Slashlore said. "We can provide you a copy of registry of our kind that we are currently working on. As for your rules and laws, we will enforce our own kind."

"Absolutely not," the Chancellor snapped. He went to argue more but the Queen silenced him by simply raising her hand.

"If you live amongst us," she began, "I require that you abide by our laws. I will not agree to a militarized force that operates within my city that is policed by its own forces. That is, as you called it, a hard no. However, my forces are ill-equipped to deal with dissuading any incidents involving yours.

"Perhaps a compromise; your kind will not be required to wear markings. Your Sheriff Department will continue to police your kind but they will do so under the jurisdiction and oversight of the city guards."

Tialla scribbled on a notepad and slid it over to Slashlore. He gave it a quick read and nodded. Our President turned back to the Queen. "I *tentatively* agree with those terms. Now let's discuss funding for the Sheriff."

At that moment I was so bored that I wanted nothing more than to shoot myself.

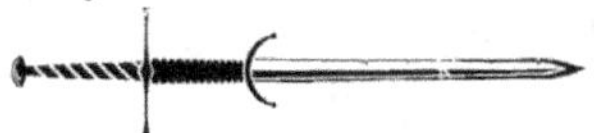

Footkneebra smiled as I walked into her building. I gave her a smirk and sauntered over. "You're back."

"From outer space," I said. "I just walked in here with this stupid look on my face."

"Ddaxx!" she called out. The Dwarf looked up. "I told you to change that stupid lock. I told you to make Rake give back his key because I knew that he'd be back to bother me."

Ddaaxx glared at the both of us. "Some of us have actual work to do."

Footkneebra and I burst out laughing.

"What do you want, Rake?" Footkneebra asked.

"Anything you need me to do?"

She shook her head. "The Reaper business is quiet."

"How goes that attack investigation going?" I asked as I eyed the folder that lay on her desk.

"Well it's--"

"It's none of his business," Ddaaxx interrupted. "It's police business only."

"So it wasn't an attack," I deduced. "Wait, does that mean we have a killer on the loose?"

The two deputies nervously looked at each other. Their looks told me more than any words could. "This isn't your job, Rake, it's ours. Let us do our job."

"Besides," Footkneebra added, "you look horrible. Go home and get some sleep."

"Yes, Mom," I mocked, and then proved her right by yawning. "You're right. I'm tired anyways. I'll just head home and get some shut eye."

I lied. I headed directly to Hermi Pass.

Hermi Pass was the main path that stood between Havenhold and Hammer Forge. It was used by literally hundreds of NPCs and PCs a day. I walked along the path and stared into the woods. Pausing at the crime scene, now unmarked and unguarded, I stared into the trees. The only reason I knew that where I stood was in fact the actual crime scene was from the rumours that spread through Havenhold. With enough work one could take rumours, weed out the false and be left with a pretty accurate truth. Yet as I opened the folder I'd stolen from Footkneebra's desk, I was left with one thought.

Deciphering rumours felt like a lot of work.

I read over the case file. The sniper hid in the forest and took out several PCs in the process. He killed them with red-fletched arrows. I walked into the dense trees and moved through the trees, following Ddaaxx's notes to the sniper's perch.

I didn't know why I was doing this; I wasn't law enforcement and I wasn't military. Was I doing this simply to avoid sleep? The answer was probably yes.

I stopped at a tree, marked with a couple small flags and turned around. I stared through the trees and looked at the pass. I stood there amazed. That shot was not an easy one. Dozens of trees stood between him and his target and had his shot been off by a mere inch would have put the arrow into a tree instead of someone's neck.

I raised my arms and held an imaginary bow in my hands. I notched a pretend arrow and aimed down the trees. This sniper not only made an impossible shot but he did it twice in less than twenty seconds and then made a third one against a moving target. I whistled to myself. This archer was good. He was damn good.

I looked at the tree and ran my fingers over the five lines. The sniper had carved an equilateral triangle with three acute triangles in its interior. The case file had it a little more than the bored carvings of a man waiting for it. I, however, disagreed with that assumption. I didn't think it was random, I thought it was a symbol.

I flipped through the case file and landed on the victims. I frowned as I saw a familiar name. The Elven mage that was killed was Boomzile.

With nothing else to see, I mounted my steed and rode back to Havenhold. My brown horse and I travelled, watching daylight vanish. Hermi Pass was always a scenic route path. Every time I passed through it I always found my eyes focused not on the road but on the scenery that surrounded it.

A rustle in the trees caught my gaze. I snapped my head over and squinted as I tried to see through the darkness. Was it the sniper? I pulled my horse to a halt and dismounted. Activating my stealth, I crept towards the trees and I entered the forest while moving slowly. The mysterious movers became clearer, the closer I got. They were a handful of men dressed in light armour, onyx black, and wore half-masks.

The Nohorian Brotherhood.

They were only five minutes away from Havenhold but why? I stayed still and spied upon them. They weren't warriors who wore full-plate and carried massive swords and gigantic shields. They were rogues and assassins who moved silently, had bows, light blades and deadly daggers. They weren't here to invade Havenhold, they were here to assassinate someone.

Chapter 06

"Video gamers are joy seekers." - Pascaline Lorentz

    I quickly PMed Tialla but got no response. I cursed and stared back at the group, doing the math. There were twenty of them and one of me. I couldn't take the odds, not even remotely. I needed help. I popped open my PMs and started typing.

Rake: 911 - 911 - 911
Rake: 911 - 911 - 911
Rake: 911 - 911 - 911
Scova: Jesus-Spam, WTF?
Rake: Brotherhood is going to attack. I need help - NOW!
Scova: Did you msg Tialla?
Rake: Yes, of course I did. No answer.
Rake: Look I need help, like NOW. Where are you?
Scova: I'm at home. Where are you?
Rake: I'm near Havehold on Hermi Pass. I'll send you my location. Get here ASAP.
Scova: Out the door.

    I sent her my coordinates then looked back to the Brotherhood gaggle. Who were they here to assassinate? Was it the Queen? Did the Brotherhood suddenly get the balls to go after the Witch Queen?

    I silently hid amongst the trees and the shadows. I watched and I waited. Each minute painfully ticked by as

I watched the Brotherhood prepare. After half an hour had passed, I found myself getting anxious. Where the hell was Scova? I glanced at my clock and found that only a few minutes had passed. Damn it.

The more I watched the Brotherhood group, the more I realized what I was in for. The attack group wasn't entirelycomposed of assassins and rogues as I once thought; they were accompanied by a Brotherhood mage. I watched the caster as he prepared himself. He was readying spells and wands. In a perfect scenario, I would target the mage first. A mage could single-handedly alter a battlefield for better or worse. When I was Stov, I could move an enemy where I wanted, how I wanted and when I wanted. In one raid I threw up a series of ice walls that forced several mobs into a choke point. They were cut down and a tough battle became infinitely easier. We set a VCO record that day for fastest run. Our record was eventually beaten but never without using my technique; Stoving they called it. Mages were dangerous and the Brotherhood mage needed to be taken out.

The other members all stood up and the mage began to cast. I recognized it as a portal spell. They were going to 'port into the city and attack whoever their target was. I snapped my Lucky Dagger into my hand and crept a little closer. Where was Scova? I cursed. I didn't have time to wait, I had to act and hope I could hold out until she arrived. With a flick of my wrist my dagger departed my hand and flew, diving into the mage's arm. His incantations turned into a scream. The mage flicked his wrist, drew a red-jeweled wand and fired a tongue of flame in my direction.

I was already gone.

A good sniper, or so *Enemy at the Gates* told me, would shoot and then change positions. This meant that it was harder for the bad guys to pinpoint the shooter. So after I threw my dagger into his arm, I bolted for another tree. My Lucky Dagger would rematerialize in my hand regardless of where I was. When the familiar weight of the blade returned to fingers, I was already three trees over. I pivoted out from behind my new tree and fired the dagger once more. It dove into the mage's leg, pulling a scream once again. I bolted for another tree. This time they saw me running. A rogue drew a bow and fired at me. I dove into a roll, the arrow passing over my head, and came up behind another tree.

"Spread out," the mage snapped. "Find him."

I activated my ring and blinked into the branch of a tree several feet away. The dagger returned to my hand and I fired it a third time. This time the blade never reached the mage, instead it simply bounced off the arcane shield he had summoned. The mage snapped its eyes at me and aimed it wand in my direction. I blinked again, this time appearing beside the mage. I kicked at his knee, forcing his leg to buckle, grabbed his wand-hand and pushed it upward. The tongue of flame, meant for me, shot upwards and illuminated the night sky. I twisted the arm and turned my body as I rolled the mage over my hip and threw him to the dirt. The Brotherhood rogues and assassins turned towards the sudden light and spotted me. They charged and I cursed. I could blink away but I'd never outrun all of them.

A flurry of fiery bolts rained from the sky and dove into the chest of several rogues. They went flying backwards and bounced off of the dirt. Two figures fell from the sky. One was a familiar fiery form and the second was a graceful blur. Scova smirked, her hair ablaze, as she drew her katana, Keshim's Fang. Lady Adelaide didn't profess the same joy for battle, her face was firm and dutiful. She was all business. I slid in beside the duo and drew both my blades.

"Having fun without us?" Scova asked.

"You were the first person I called," I lied. She scoffed.

"I'm the first you called who *answered*."

"Now is not the time for banter," Lade Adelaide reminded us. "Is the mage slain?"

"No."

"I'll deal with the mage then," she instructed. "You two deal with these....riff raff."

"I love it when she gets all bossy," Scova said with a grin. For a second I froze. Was that TMI? I stole a quick glance at the pair. An image of an Adelaide-Domme/Scova-Sub relationship flashed through my mind and brought a small but indecent smile upon my face. At that moment I decided that it was not TMI, in fact perhaps I needed to know more. Scova glanced at me. "Get your head in the game, Captain Lecherous."

"Right," I smirked. "I'll take the riff,"

"And I'll take the raff."

Scova tapped out a spell and the ground around her started to warm up. I could feel the heat rising up from the dirt. In the simplest terms, she had just consecrated the ground with fire. If any enemy came with a couple feet of her, they would receive fire damage. It was a great area control spell. I had a similar spell as Stov, the difference being that my ice spells slowed while her fire spells burned.

The Brotherhood descended on us and we were there to meet them. Whaitiri Edge leapt to meet the defense square as I blocked an assassin's longsword. I moved Splinter's Bite to the attack circle and stabbed the assassin. My blade dug into his gut.

Scova slashed at a Brotherhood's leg, Keshim's Fang cutting deep and implanted a spell within his leg. The fire mage kicked him backwards, then raised her left hand and tapped out another spell. A fiery bolt erupted from each of her fingers and shot into the chest of a third assassin. Seconds later, deep inside the leg of the second assassin, a fireball erupted.

Adelaide joined the fray moments later. Her ninjatō were faster than my blades and Scova's combined. She was quick, she was deadly and she was accurate. She never wasted a slash or needed more than one. I could find myself in a strike and parry duel with an opponent but Adelaide would never lower herself to that level. When Lady Adelaide struck, she left bodies in her wake.

I pulled Splinter's Bite from a Brotherhood neck and

watched as the body fell to the ground. I pivoted as a Brotherhood rogue approached me. He held a dagger in each hand, both were large and jagged, clearly a fantasy exaggeration. They had razor-sharp edged red-stained steel and a curved blade. His blades were quick and fast as they lunged and slashed at me. Whaitiri Edge moved quickly, slapping away the daggers. I'd thrust with Splinter's Bite but he rogue's daggers were faster than mine.

I cursed. Since being trapped in Rake, I'd been training to be a better fencer. I had learned how to deal with sword and board, two handed swords and speedy single blades. My weakness, however, lay in the dual blade. When I faced another dual wielder I would struggle. I had trouble dealing with two attacks and two defenders. My strength in defense came from Whaitiri Edge. Against a foe like the Brotherhood rogue, I was forced to use my dominate hand to block as well.

The rogue's blade moved faster than I could and they slashed against my legs. Both daggers cut across my left thigh. First I felt the stinging cold of one dagger then a nauseating feeling from the second. I retreated a couple steps but found my move sluggish. I glared at the rogue. He'd slowed me with the enchantment on one dagger and poisoned me with the enchantment on the other.

The rogue never gave me a chance to recover as he struck again but this time I was able to defend. Splinter's Bite and Whaitiri Edge moved quickly. The pair slapped away the daggers and gave me a brief opening. I activated the magic in my boots, turned my feet into stone and kicked forward. My foot collided with the rogue's chest and sent him flying backwards. I deactivated the stone, activated the boots' speed and tried to dash forward. I made it only a step before a wave of nausea overcame me and I dropped to my knees. I wanted to throw up but I fought to keep it down. A dagger stabbed into my shoulder and I screamed in pain. Panicking, I activated Feore Shell. My body became an impassible mist and shot me two feet forward. The dagger was no longer in my neck but the pain was still there. I quickly activated the Second Wind spell of my Third Eye headband and felt the healing spell deal with my wounds.

"You could really hurt someone with those," I mocked. "I'd be careful with them."

The rogue turned to me. He needlessly spun the daggers on his hands as he approached me. I rolled my eyes and fought a second wave of nausea. The Second Wind had healed my wounds but it did nothing to combat the slow and the poison.

I pushed past the nausea and took to the offensive. Splinter's Bite opened with a shadow strike and Whaitiri Edge followed with a saber slash. With each strike I added points to my combo meter. Level 58 had added new moves to my arsenal - like gloom blade - and I wasn't about to ignore them. Gloom blade covered my blades in a hint of dark energy, added more damage and did additional damage over time (or DoT as the cool kids call it) for the next 13 seconds. I blinked behind the rogue and let my blackened blade slash down across its back. I moved to run Splinter's Bite through the rogue's back but he spun and caught me by surprise with a foot to my face. I fell to the ground and lost the battle against nausea. I threw up on the grass.

Throwing up is horrible but it does have a lone benefit. Nobody - and I mean nobody - wants to stand next to a vomiting dude. It's gross and most time people tend to worry about their clothes. So as the rogue stepped away from me in disgust, I was granted a moment's reprieve. I glanced at my combo meter and smiled when I found it full.

"The thing about daggers is that they're dangerous. They can really hurt someone. Hell, if you're not careful," I said as I snapped my Lucky Dagger to my hand. I activated my new finisher, Between the Eyes, and tossed the weapon. It flew through the air and landed directly in the rogue's left eye. "You might even poke someone's eye out with one."

The words Level 59 floated above my head as I crawled to my feet. I held up my hand as my dagger returned to my hand. I looked around the battlefield and found the remainder dead. Scova and Adelaide stood to the side watching me.

"How Batman was that?" Scova said. "Seriously, that one-liner was super Caruso. I feel like you should be putting on a pair of shades as The Who plays in the background."

"None of you felt the need to help?" Both shook their heads. I sighed and then, for a change of pace, threw up once more. "Antidote?"

We went through the Brotherhood's belonging. Scova handed me a note, I read it over and handed it back. The Brotherhood weren't trying to assassinate the Witch Queen. Their primary and secondary targets were Slashlore and Tialla.

"Tialla has to know about this," I said, "and so does Slashlore."

We returned to the Enclave's capital building quickly and showed the pair. Slashlore looked surprisingly pleased. "This is good news."

"Okay, what?" Scova asked, confused.

"They are getting desperate," Lade Adelaide explained. "They are resorting to smaller attacks in hopes that they will prove more successful than their invasion did."

"You need protection," I insisted.

"I'll be fine," Slashlore defended. My eyes moved towards Tialla. She just shrugged.

"So what now?"

"Now," he said with a smile. "Now we continue our attacks."

"What if they Michael Fassbender you?" I asked. "Nothing is true; everything is permitted."

"Law of Inverse Ninjutsu," Scova said. "$NP=(NT/NN)+NN$."

"What?"

"NP is the total power of all ninjas, taking into account the Law.

NT is the total power of all ninjas, disregarding the Law.

NN is the total number of ninjas.

If NN=NT, then the effectiveness of ninja squads remains constant.

If NN>NT, then the effectiveness of ninja squads decreases.

If NN<NT, then the effectiveness of ninja squads increases.

NP is always less than NT."

We all just stood there, stunned to silence. I tried to open my mouth twice but nothing came out. I knew Scova was the math girl for puzzles but that was something else entirely. The silence came to an end when Lady Adelaide leaned in and kissed the mage on her cheek.

"Whoot, math got me a kiss. Suck it everybody else."

I stood inside a room. The details were much clearer than before. It was a large room built with grey, ash covered stones. Racks of weapons lined the walls. The rest was a blur. Steelion stood before me and once again I painfully stared into his eyes.

"Dead," Steelion said. "Kill Everyone."

Answering my door in nothing but pants was becoming a habit and not one I was enjoying. It was the middle of the night, I was awake - of course - and there was a woman standing on the other side. I was hoping it was Tialla but I wasn't disappointed when it turned out to be Footkneebra.

"You know I had a dream that started like this," I mumbled.

"I bet you have," she said with a wicked smirk. "But you're gonna have to put those thoughts aside for now. I'm here on official business, official sheriff's business."

I rolled my eyes as I invited her in. I walked to my

desk and grabbed the case file then handed it to her. "You could have come during the morn."

For a moment she looked stunned at the file. A h*ow did he get this?* look crossed her face. She shook it off. "I'm not here for this. We will talk about this later but I'm here for something different."

I raised a quizzical eyebrow.

"There's been another murder," she said. "I've been ordered to bring you in."

Chapter 07

"Oh, hi. So, how are you holding up? BECAUSE I'M A POTATO!"
- GLaDOS (Portal 2)

I stood atop the gates of Havenhold and looked down at the entrance below. Any person who wanted to enter the city did so by passing through these gates. Even those with flying mounts passed through the gates - albeit the upper parts of them. Footkneebra flew me up her atop her two-seater mount. I looked at her, confused; I had no clue why I was here.

"So....."

"Look down," a new voice asked. I cringed at the sound of it. "Look at the speed of the flyers. How hard would it be to kill someone coming in on one of those things?"

I turned around to see Bearcules approach me. My lips tightened and I clenched my hand until my knuckles were white. The Sheriff, when not in Bear form, was a tall elf with long flowing green hair tied into a ponytail.

"How fast does a flying mount --" He never finished his question.

My fist flew out as I punched Bearcules across his jaw. The Elf fell over, completely surprised by my attack. I grabbed the druid by his tunic and punched him again. I dragged him across the gate-top and hung his head over the edge. The gate-top was forty feet in the air.

"You tried to kill me!" I yelled. Ddaaxx and Foot-kneebra moved to stop me but the closer they got, the more I pushed the druid over the edge. "You fucking tried to kill me, you were going to hand me over to Steelion and now you are our fucking sheriff. How is that okay?"

"I'm trying to make amends," he gasped. "I'm trying to seek justice."

"You want justice? Justice would be me letting you fall for what you've done." I was livid. In a mere week everybody had forgiven him for his attempted murder. In a mere week everybody named him a sheriff. Now, two weeks later, everybody had forgotten about it, everybody except me. "Give me one good reason why I shouldn't throw you off the edge?"

Bearcules opened his mouth a couple times but nothing came out. I shook my head at him. "I'm not you." I said as I pulled him back to safety. "Now tell me why I'm here."

The two deputies looked at the sheriff for a hint as of what to do next. Bearcules just shook his head and climbed to his feet. "The sniper struck again approximately an hour ago. He sat atop the gate and killed three more PCs. He shot them off of their mounts mid-flight."

"What does this have to do with me?"

"You were one of the last people to see one of the three victims." Suddenly I was interested. Who did I know? Then I got worried. Who did I know that was dead? Names ran through my head. Scova? Was Scova dead? "The woman's name was Jhaara."

I froze. The troll was dead?

"Last I saw her, she was stuck in a Rose Trap," I explained. "That was -- a day ago? Maybe two."

"You don't know?"

"Days blend together when you don't sleep," I said. "I haven't seen her since. You need to look at her new partner. His name is Scarrow. He's a hunter..." my voice trailed off. I had my first suspect.

To paraphrase Douglas Adams:

Aspumer is big. You just won't believe how vastly, hugely, mind-bogglingly big it is. I mean, you may think it's a long way down the road to the chemist's, but that's just pea-nuts to VCO.

Finding someone in VCO who happens to be in your friends list is hard. Finding someone who isn't is damn near impossible. There were apps a player could install but I never used them. They seemed creepy and a little too close to stalk-ing. Luckily, as the case may be, I knew someone who was both creepy and lived a little too close to stalking.

The Gnome's name was Danak and I found him in a house deep in Old Hold. Danak was an unusual type. He was squirmy and weird. He had the type of attitude that most found off-putting.

"What do you want, Stov?" Danak was abrupt with his words. The Gnome didn't like talking and he didn't like people. Danak was the type of person who used VCO to hide from the world. For him, VCO was easy when it was just a game. Now that it was real, it was too much for him to handle.

"How goes, Squirrely Dan?"

"Squirrel isn't the insult you think it is," Danak de-fended. "Squirrel Girl is one of the only people to defeat Doc-tor Doom and Thanos."

"Doctor Doom is now Iron Man," I laughed, "and Thanos was beaten by a lucky thievery dice roll."

"What do you want, Stov?" Darak said with a smile.

"I'm looking for someone."

"You know the deal?" he said.

Danak was the type to get easily bored. He liked hav-ing something to tease his brain, even for a brief moment. Danak was smart - hella smart - so any puzzle or riddle I gave him literally took him only a brief moment.

"Alright, Edward," I said, using the Bat-Villain's real name. "I have one for you.

"A driver has car trouble in the countryside. He looks out at the nearby clearing and sees a hiker in the distance, by a stream, enjoying nature. The driver tries to start his car, and it backfires. He looks at the clearing again. The hiker is dead. What happened?"

Danak thought for a second before allowing a small smiled to creep across his lips. "Who do you need to find?"

Scarrow slept soundly in his home, deep within the Dwarven halls of Hammer Forge. I took great pleasure in disturbing that sleep. I kicked open the door to his apartment and stormed into his bedroom. I grabbed Scarrow, pulled him from his bed and dragged him out into the streets of Hammer Forge. Ddaaxx stood outside, stunned by my actions.

"So...." he stammered. "We just kick open doors now? I'm pretty sure that's breaking and entering. This is how police law works."

"Aspumer doesn't have those laws," I snarled. "We can legally do just about whatever we want to a suspect."

My snarl was for show. I wanted to scare Scarrow. I wanted to unleash the full power of the Reaper. The public feared me and I wanted to play that up. I turned and glared at Scarrow; a second snarl slipping past my lips.

"Two days ago we talk and I gave you a choice. One of those choices was going to involve seeing me again. Here I am." I shook my head. "I said you'd go too far, I said someone would die and someone did." I put my foot on his chest and pressed down. "You called upon the wrath of the Reaper now beware my fury."

"I....didn't....do....anything," Scarrow gasped. "Who...died?"

"You killed your partner," I said in my best Bale-Batman accent. "You killed Jhaara!"

"No.....I...." I removed my foot from Scarrow's chest. He coughed as he fought for air. "Jhaara's dead?"

"She and two others were killed a couple hours ago," Ddaaxx said. "They were shot off of their flying mount as they entered Havenhold."

"Holy shit," Scarrow said. "That's a difficult shot."

I grabbed the archer by the shirt, hoisted him up and slammed him against the wall. "I've been asking around.

You're damn good with a bow; you could have made that shot."

"So...a bunch of us could have."

"So prove to me you didn't."

Scarrow looked to Ddaaxx but the deputy just shook his head. "If you're looking to me too be the good-cop, than you're looking at the wrong person."

"After you showed up the other day," Scarrow said quickly, "I walked away. I called it quits. Jhaara tracked me down and asked me to reconsider but I told her no. I haven't seen her since."

"Why the change of heart?" Ddaaxx asked.

"I didn't want to deal with the Reaper," he said quickly. "And a friend of mine was convincing me to enlist. He said an archer of my caliber would be needed soon. He said the Enclave was about to be pushed into a bigger war and everybody with even a hint of skill was going to be riding high when that happened."

I looked at Ddaaxx. He gave me the same confused look that I was currently wearing. The war wasn't about to explode. The war was winding down. We were winning. We had almost wiped out the Brotherhood.

"Who told you that? Who told you to enlist?"

"Commander Santiago," he said. "The man is on a recruiting warpath."

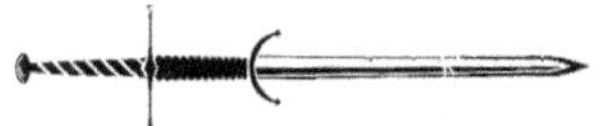

Ddaaxx and I walked the streets of Hammer Forge. Day was coming up and we were trying to piece together everything that was happening. "What do you know about Santiago?"

"He's a Beta," he said. "He's been playing since the closed beta test. He's been a huntard the entire time. Ddaaxx is my alt but for Santiago its bow or nothing.

"He has a reputation of being a great shot. I think he did archery in RL. He always loves teaching hunters to shoot better. I used to go to him before I found the joy that was the crossbow. We haven't really hung out since then."

"What was he like though?"

Ddaaxx shrugged. "He was one of those nutjobs types; like part Trump supporter part anti-government. He always talking about how Obama did this or Bush did that. Mostly, though, he was all talk. Back home I can tell the difference between the dangerous ones and the harmless ones. Hell, I have a list by my desk at the Sheriff's office in RL."

He froze in his footsteps and his eyes went wide. I looked at him with a raised eyebrow. We both know he broke The Rule. The question was what did we do about it now?

"Did you...." I asked.

"Shit," he replied.

"So..."

"In for a penny, in for a pound," he sheepishly said.

"You're a Sheriff in RL?" I carefully asked.

"No," he said. "I'm a deputy there and a deputy here."

"If you have actual police experience then why are you not our Sheriff instead of the bear?"

"It was mentioned," he explained, "but people trusted the Bear. He was a public name. I wasn't. So I'm working my ass off for someone who doesn't know shit about police work except for what he's seen on TV."

I shook my head.

"I mean he's not that bad at it," he continued. "He just needs a push in the right direction. That's my main goal. To make sure we can all look ourselves in the mirror afterwards."

"So what do you think about Scarrow?"

"I don't like him for it. We searched his apartment and found nothing. He doesn't have any motive for it either,"

"He didn't have an alibi either," I said. Ddaaxx nodded. I thought for a second before I asked Ddaaxx a follow-up question. "So what do you think about Santiago?'

Ddaaxx shrugged. "Things don't add up. We need to look into him."

I looked at the sky. The sun was coming up. "So what would you do now?"

"We would stake him out," Ddaaxx explained, "until we had enough evidence to get a search warrant. Then we'd search his apartment and go from there."

"That's a lot of work for a search warrant," I said.

"It's the law."

"Not here, it isn't."

Chapter 08

Video games are well positioned to be a spectator sport - Rob Pardo

The three of them sat together. They were huddled over maps and papers as Santiago and Mystylz debriefed Tialla of the previous day's raids. The hunter spoke of his men's attacks and what discoveries they'd found.

"With each strike we find more weapons and more supplies," he said. "They are getting strong and stronger. We need to push harder, Ma'am. We need to increase our attacks. We need to strike them so hard that they won't be able to get back up again."

"You're like a broken record, Commander," Tialla said. "I know what you want. I know what you think is needed but we need to also look at what is possible."

"That big speech had dozens of volunteers," he argued. "Each of them was ready to fight the Brotherhood."

"But they are *just* volunteers. Their support is only as good as their attention span." Tialla shook her head. "What you're suggesting is a campaign that would need a large standing army. We don't have that and I don't foresee us ever having that."

"It's what we need to survive," Santiago said. "We will beat the Brotherhood, that is inevitable, but they aren't alone. VCO is filled with bad after bad. There *will* be another threat after this one. We have to make sure we can handle and survive the next threat and the threat after that.

"I'm looking at the long game. We might be here

a while and Aspumer isn't a friendly world. What happens when the Dragons return or the Orcs attack? We need to build an army and we need to stake our claim in this world or we'll just be run over."

"Be mindful of the future but not at the expense of the moment," Tialla quoted (I smiled as I heard that). "Your long game isn't wrong but it is impossible right now. We don't have the man power."

"As it stands," Mystsylz said, "with our current army numbers I predict that we would be struggling against the Brotherhood. Our success is due to these volunteers."

Tialla and Mystsylz were doing me a favour. I PMed her as asked her to run the morning debrief long. It gave Ddaaxx and me a chance to search Santiago's home. The search left us with more questions than answers. We needed to talk to the hunter face-to-face but we weren't coming alone.

Santiago saw me and Footkneebra before we entered the room. I don't know how but he saw us enter from the left door and Ddaaxx and Bearcule enter from the right. His body tensed and he gaze became erratic. Suddenly he stood up and swiftly drew blades from his belt. Two daggers flew at the left door and another pair rocketed to the right. Footkneebra dove behind the wall and I, on instinct, activated my rogue escape.

As a result of my power leveling, I'd gained a bunch of new abilities. One of which was my rogue escape. It was an acrobatic dodge that allowed me to dodge an attack. With limited room my body had no choice but to back-flip. Like some *Matrix* style wire-work, I back-flipped into the hall, the daggers passing by my face.

It's a weird feeling when VCO automatically moved my body. Whether it was to dodge or to finish a combo, I always felt uneasy when it happened. I wasn't uneasy in a sense I was ill or nauseated. I was uneasy in an *I have control issues* way.

Back on my feet, I willed my boots to life and burst foreword with magical speed. I dove for Santiago and tackled him to the ground. The pair of us smashed against the floor and slid into the wall. A pair of blows slammed into my stomach and I groan. Santiago, somehow a UFC-skilled ground fighter, climbed back to his feet. He turned around as he heard the roaring charge of a bear. Bearcules, in his grizzled form, stood on his hind legs as he swiped at the hunter. Santiago fought back. He didn't fight like a VCO monk. Instead he fought like Jason Bourne. It wasn't dramatic or pretty fighting; it was dark, cheap and dirty. This wasn't VCO fighting. This was RL skill.

I scrambled to my feet and took a look around. Footkneebra was back on her feet, looking for an opening, while Ddaaxx still lay on the floor, a dagger in his back. Across the room I saw Tialla and Mystylz, then pointed towards Ddaaxx. Tialla's gaze followed, saw the wounded deputy and nodded. She bolted in his direction.

A blast of crimson energy slammed into Santiago. Footkneebra was trying debuff the hunter by lowering his defense. She slammed a second crimson bolt against his hide, this one meant to damage him. She fired a third but as Santiago grabbed Bearcules by his arms and twisted, the magic slammed against the sheriff instead. The bear roared in pain and the hunter kicked out the sheriff's legs. He twisted the bear's body and tossed Bearcules to the ground. He drew a fifth dagger and readied a throw. He never got the chance.

I bolted forward and switched the enchantment in my boots. My foot turned to stone and I slammed it into Santiago's side. He flew across the room and slammed into the wall. I thought he was down but the hunter turned out to be resilient. He flipped to his feet and lashed out. His fist snapped across my face and his leg lashed out at my knee. Before I could blink his left hands was gripping my head and his right hand pressed his sixth dagger to my throat.

"Where do you keep all those daggers?" I asked.

"What the hell is going on?" he yelled.

"We need to talk to you, Santiago," Bearcules said as he shifted out of bear. "We need to ask you about the sniper killings and about some of the things we found in your room."

"You searched my room?" he spat. His eyes narrowed as his mind raced.

"We found red-fletched arrows that match our killer," Bearcules explained slowly. "And your tattoo matches the symbols at the two crime-scenes. We also found attack plans for the Enclave army."

From my trapped position I could see Footkneebra and Bearcules both moving slowly. Neither tried to draw a weapon or cast a spell. They just waited and watched as Bearcules continued to talk.

"Our army is a joke," Santiago said. He was stalling. I could hear it in his voice. His mind was racing to figure out what was going on and he needed a few seconds more to piece it together.

"Why did you do it?" Bearcules asked. "Why did you kill those PCs? What does it have to do with the army?"

"Were you trying to make it look like a Brotherhood attack?" Footkneebra asked. She paused as realization cross her face. "You were hoping that PC deaths would trigger fear. You wanted people afraid so you could push the military agenda."

"That's some Sheppard level bullshit, *Modern Warfare 2*," I mocked. Santiago pressed the blade tighter against my neck. I decided there and then to shut up.

"We want to talk," Bearcules said. "Let Rake go and let us talk."

"What's the point," Santiago spat. "You've made up your mind."

"Let Rake go."

"Fuck y--" Santiago never finished his words. The familiar sound of a crossbow filled the room as a crossbow bolt suddenly appeared between Santiago's eyes. Both of us tumbled to the ground. I felt pain in my neck and the moistness of blood on my fingers. Breathing became difficult until I felt Tialla's touch. Magic flowed through my body and the wounds knitted together.

I sat up and looked over at Santiago. Mystylz knelt by

the hunter, a golden glow fading from his fingers. He looked at me with a crestfallen gaze and shook his head. Santiago was dead.

I was never one to make light of death, my mother would literally slap the stupid out of me for doing so, but as I spent the afternoon in negotiations I wanted little more then to take Santiago's place. Slashlore and the Chancellor bickered back and forth, rambling on and on about gold and cost. I sat there, zoned out. God, I hated negotiations.

"I am saddened that we've reached an impasse," Lord Bullmourn said. "Both parties have achieved so much at these discussions. We cannot allow thing to break down now.

"There are two issues at hand for which we disagree on. The first is housing and where the cost will come from. The second is the treatment of the children from your world who are now in the bodies of adults."

"What you ask," Slashlore said directly to the Queen, "goes against what we believe as a people."

"I ask simply that your children behave as such while they are here,"

VCO was a game played by people of all ages. Regardless of the player's age, all characters looked like adults. Even before the Glitch it was impossible to know who was a minor. Now, the only way to determine someone's age would be to ask them and that broke The Rule.

The Rule - unwritten as it was - stated that nobody asked about their lives before The Glitch. We were all stuck in VCO and nobody wanted to be reminded of that by constantly being asked about their former lives. We were here, we were stuck, there was no sense dwelling on it what was when we were trying to fix what is.

"If I may," the Lord interrupted. "I am reminded of the negotiations between our Queen's grandfather and the Dwarven King. We learned that there is truth beneath truth. Your Highness, what is the truth beneath words? What is the meaning you are trying to convey?"

"Before Havenhold was formed," the Queen explained, "there were several smaller kingdoms. They fought amongst each other. As the war drew on several kingdoms found their numbers dwindling. They resorted to forcing children into combat. When the war ended and the first bricks of Havenhold were lain upon the ground, the first decree was no longer would a child participate in combat.

"Your Enclave is a military body. You are more powerful and better armed than us and already you have seen combat. In fact before our negotiations, the only infrastructure your people had setup was for your war effort. My worry is that with your military body our first decree will no longer be upheld."

"Perhaps," Tialla added, "we could add an amendment to our structure. We can formulate a method to make sure your first decree is upheld. We will ask age but nothing else."

"I could accept that," the Queen said, "under the circumstance that if any child approaches your government seeking aid that it is provided."

"This simply leaves us with one final issue," Lord Bullmourn said, "Housing and payment."

"You ask too much of our taxes," Slashlore said abruptly. "Between the military costs, resources, payments to the Whispers and food, our taxes are all but spoken for. We cannot stretch our coin any further."

Both sides continued their debate and once again I found myself not caring. I knew it was rude but to be honest, I didn't care. I didn't have a mind for economy, city structure or governmental policies. I wasn't Sora, this wasn't *No Game No Life* and I never played the *Civilization* games. I just stared at Adelaide and her father as the pair tried to play mediator.

Both Dorian and Adelaide were dressed in formal clothes. Adelaide wore a stunning emerald dress with several shades of green with gold trimming. The Cat's Eye Pendent that hung from her neck matched her dress perfectly. A smile crossed my lips. Scova liked liked Lady Adelaide. I'd never seen her give a magic item away, to damn near anybody, ever. Not even to me and I'm her BFF.

I sat up straight in my chair.

"Holy shit!" The room went quiet at my outburst. Everybody looked at me.

"Excuse me," the Chancellor said sternly, "but these outburst are not allowed in---"

"Shut up, Toadsworth," I snapped, instantly feeling bad about my comment. Toadsworth wasn't the Chancellor. The Chancellor was from *Super Mario RPG*. Toadsworth wasn't introduced until *Super Mario Sunshine*. However, Toadsworth was meant to replace both the Chancellor and Toad Minister so I was okay with the joke. I looked at Adelaide and pointed. "Where did you get that? The pendant, where did you get the pendant?"

"It was given to me by my...." Adelaide carefully eyed her father as she searched for the proper words. "It was given to me by a good friend and a faithful companion. It was a cherished gift that--"

"Scova," I interrupted, "was it Scova?"

"Ms. Scova did bless me with this gift, yes."

"Does it work? Can you see better?"

"Yes, I can even see at night," she said hesitantly, unsure of my questioning. "Why do you ask?"

I looked around a stunned and silenced room. My eyes fell upon the face of the Queen. A smile crept on her face and she nodded, as if to edge me forward. I looked back to Slashlore and Tialla.

"We'll farm for you," I said slowly. I was trying to choose my words as I said them I needed this proposal to sound perfect. One wrong word and my intent could be mistaken. One wrong word and negotiations could break down or even worse, I could be forced to sit though even more of them. "Your guards and your army wield crappy weapons, like basic gear. We have access to much better weapons and armour and items. We can get them for you and give them to you.

"I'm not saying we have to go orange picking for them but we can harvest greens and blues like nobody's business. We can arm them in a way they have never had access to. It's never been an option because Pre-Glitch, giving a non-quest item to a NPC wasn't possible. Adelaide is living proof that now it is."

"That could work," Tialla said slowly. She eyed Slashlore and he nodded. The pair looked at the Queen and the Chancellor.

"This idea could work," the Queen said.

Oh, thank god. If I had to spend one minute more in negotiations I was going to---

"Now let us discuss the numbers of weapons we will be requiring," the Chancellor said.

It was then I wanted to stab Toadsworth in his mushroom skull.

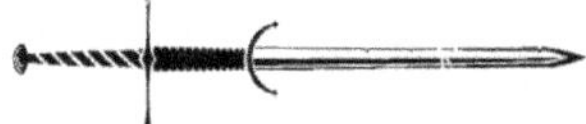

It was late afternoon when I entered Tialla's office. She waved me over and offered me a seat. She opened her desk, pulled free two glasses and a bottle of Dwarven Ale. She poured a finger for each. She slid me a glass.

"Good word back there," she said as we each raised our glasses. We tapped them against each other and then quickly brought our respective glasses to our lips. I took a sip. I am no stranger to drinking but Dwarven Ale isn't a thing in RL. So when it hit my mouth I ended up hacking and coughing like a 16 year-old who just got offered his Dad's scotch for the first time.

Tialla smirked.

"I'm sorry," I said, "about Santiago."

She shook her head. "Mystylz is going over all of the files in his room. We're going to piece together everything he had but to be honest, I didn't see this coming. I always knew he had issues with the government but I needed his leadership skills and military knowledge. I mean he was drummed out of the marines but he still had troops."

"He told you that?" I asked. Tialla shook her head. "Then how the hell did you know all that?"

"I figured it out by what he said. I've been around enough military boys to tell the difference between Jarheads, Squids, Flyboys and Ground Pounders. I knew he was a Marine. The way he spoke of it showed he was out and not by choice, I've heard that speech enough times to pin it down. The scary part, he had to get drunk to tell me enough to pin this part down, is that he leads a small anti-government militia."

"Seriously, who the hell are you?" I laughed. "WTF do you do in RL?"

Her face tightened. "I never expected you to break The Rule."

"I'm not," I quickly defended. "I'm just thinking out loud. You're a woman of mystery and I love a good puzzle."

"Speak for yourself, Rake." She took another sip. "You tackle mysteries and puzzles like nobody's business, you leap head first into battle and you want to save the world. Just thinking out loud here but WTF do you do in RL, Mr. Rake?"

She was going to be hella disappointed when she found out I stocked shelves.

"So I asked you here to talk about something." Tailla became squirmy in her chair and she avoided eye contact. "I've seen the way you look at me. I know what we've been through and I wanted to talk to you about your feelings and mine."

Oh shit, this was never good.

"I like you, Rake." Whoa, I did not see that coming. I was expecting a we're perfect as friends speech not I like you. "I like you a lot but I'm married."

Shit.

"I have a husband in RL. I'm not sure if we're getting out but I can't give up hope, not yet. I don't know how long we will be here but....."

Silence; how does someone respond to something

like that? How was I supposed to react? I did what any guy would do and I nodded, shrugged and guyed it off.

Guy it off: to play cool and pretend like the words and/or event that just occurred was no big deal when in reality it was soul crushing.

"Nah, that's cool. Yeah, I get it." Yep, that's me. I'm guying it off like a pro."

We chatted for a few more minutes, finished our drinks and then I excused myself. I left her office and spotted Mystylz talking to a hunter. It took me a second before I recognized the hunter as Hizzous.

"Mr. Rake," Mystylz said. "How goes your evening?"

"Been better," I muttered.

"What are you up to now?'

"I'm going to get a group together and run UW," I said. "You wanna join?"

"I'm sorry but I'm busy."

"I'll join you," Hizzous said. I looked at the hunter. He was level 87, a dog's breath away from max level. It was a far cry from the newbie I found a couple weeks ago.

"You sure?" I asked. "Even at max, UW is no easy dungeon. You might get hurt."

"Sure I'm sure. I owe you one, remember?" I nodded. He smiled. "Besides, the only reason anybody feels pain is because they allow it."

Chapter 09

After all, it could only cost you your life, and you got that for free
- Sailor (Earthbound)

VCO's first expansion, *The Ashen Downpour* (TAD), involved the Crypt Walker's march across Aspumer. In his campaign to destroy the living, the Crypt Walker allied himself with the cannibalistic trolls - transforming them into Skin Feasters -, took control of an alchemist sect - forcing them to become plaguemancers - and controlled the Nohorian Brotherhood. Yet his worst plan involved harnessing the souls of the previously deceased and transforming them into arcane bombs. The bomb would explode, cause massive damage and the soul was forever destroyed, no longer allowed to rest in peace in the great afterlife.

In the *Under Way* raid, the party would enter the Crypt Walker's forge and descend downward until they reached the membrane that separated the realm of the dead from the living realm. They faced undead hordes, horrific monstrosities and even faced off against Jhen'ta Mornif, the Forge Master. UW was an end game prep instance for TAD. The loot a player found would leave them properly geared for the *Assault on Death's Keep* raid, the final attack on the Crypt Walker.

My party of five was replaying UW with the hopes of find the Eye of Cocijo, a magical jeweled amulet that was etched with the Kahail symbol. I was running UW with an even party.

Skith; Son of Zook - TANK (Revenant: lvl 100)
Hizzous - Range DPS (Hunter: lvl 87)
Monta - Healer (Monk: lvl 100)
Cornerhook - Buff/DPS (Incubus: lvl 99)
Rake - Melee DPS (Rogue: lvl 58)

UW had five bosses in normal mode and six in heroic mode. Each high level dungeon had a harder difficulty called heroic mode. The increase difficulty came with tougher mobs and more bosses but it rewarded the players with better loot. The Eye of Cocijo was only available in heroic.

We fell the first three bosses with little struggle. The first was an ogre guard named Glutkob. The second was a four-armed giant skeleton named Chop Master. The third was a trio of goblins ninjas named Stuey, Phuey and Quey. Even at its heroic mode, UW was still only a level 80 instance. With our party's advance level this instance shouldn't have been a challenge but since the Glitch, level mattered less and less. Even the lowest level dungeons were suddenly proving difficult and heroic even more so.

We stood outside the forge and stared inside. A decaying stench rolled across the air as dead bodies hung from the walls, in various stages of intact. Workers would rip limbs from the bodies and sew them onto the aberration that they were currently creating. Further back, the sound of chanting could be faintly heard. This work floor of UV looked like something out of *Silent Hill* sans Pyramid Head. Stov had run UW dozens of times so I knew that in order to clear this section we'd have to tear through several forge workers, the accompanying necromancers, a large handful of undead and the foreman Hexilian.

"Let's gooooo already," Cornerhook said in an exasperated tone. I rolled my eyes. Cornerhook and Monta were people Hizzous knew. He called them up to help us on this run. He apparently had a tank he knew but when she didn't answer I gave Skith a ring. I didn't know either of Hizzous' crew but I instantly figured out that Cornerhook was one of those players who liked to rush through an instance as fast as possible. He hated slowing down for any reason. Cornerhook walked around the corner without waiting for an answer from the rest of us and raised his hands. Two blasts of crimson energy shot outward and crashed into the nearest forge worker. They screamed in pain, signaling the others. Dozens of skeletons ran towards us as the foremen scrambled to grab weapons. In the back we could hear the shuffle of casters as they entered the forge's work floor.

Cornerhook tapped out another pair of spells. My blades suddenly gained a crimson glow, adding a demonic DOT effect to them, while Monta gain a boost to attack speed. I glanced at Skith and received a nod. Our tank stormed the room first, his glaive held firmly in both hands. Skith's un-orc rested on the Gnome's belt, unsummoned and trapped within its statue. Skith didn't need his undead brute; instead he relied on his magic and his strength. Sickly green energy flew from his fingers. The magic caused a burst of threat and drew aggro from the mobs, sending them in his directions. Skith swung his glaive hard, cutting down the first skeleton he came across.

Monta and I charged in. My blades danced as I knocked away the flimsy swords and slashed at the bone legs. Monta's fist moved quickly as she struck, each punch collided against bone until the bones broke and skeletons crumbled to the ground.

Montra was not the type of healer to simply stand back and heal afar. Instead she built her character to be a front line healer. Each attack she landed healed each party member for 3% of the damage caused. Montra still had her big heal spells like traditional healers but the majority of her damage came from her melee strikes. From the corner of my eye, I saw as Montra's spin kick collided with the skull of a skeleton. The blow separated the head from the remainder of its body and sent it flying across the room like a soccer ball. The headless skeleton stumbled away, moving across the work floor, desperately searching for his head.

A series of arrows flew past the skeletons and collided with the forge workers. One screamed and fell over. I marveled at Hizzous's skill. In the few short weeks, he had become an expert with that bow. Each shot was quick and deadly accurate. It only took a few moments for us to strike down the skeletons and kill the forge workers but the fight wasn't over. The necromancers walked into the room, each wearing dark robes and held large staves. They waved their hands and we watched as the fallen forge workers rose again, only this time as zombies.

Skith ran into the undead horde and once again drew aggro. Montra and Cornerhook assisted with the mobs. Her fist and his spells knocked down skeleton after skeleton. The undead would keep rising as long as the necromancers continued their spell. It was the job of Hizzous and me to break that spell.

I activated my boots and dashed through the horde. With the assistance of a blink, I emerged on the other side. With both blades at the ready, I descended on the first caster and quickly ran my steel through him. Hizzous dropped another with a pair of arrows. There were eight necromancers, but we only needed to drop four to end the spell. I activated my boots again and kicked at the other with my stone foot. I heard the bones in his chest snap as I sent him flying across the room. Another arrow crossed the room and found itself a new home in the chest of the fourth caster. With four gone, the spell ended. The remaining four quickly blinked away. I wanted to smile but I didn't. I knew what was next.

Boss #4: Foreman Hexilian: Part One.

Hexilian was a corrupted Elf Mage that now acted as the foreman of the Crypt Walker's forge. With his empty eye sockets, he glared at us as he walked into the room with a sickly green glow emanating from each one instead of eyes. His ailing hand, which held a small wooden rod, rose as necromantic words slipped past his lips. A wave of sickly green energy rippled through the room and pitched each of us against a wall.

Tactic: Just get to him.

Some battles used techniques like tanking, crowd control or AOEs to win. The Hexilian fight used none of those. The necromancer would cast spell after spell to knock us back, stalling us while he armed a soul bomb. If we didn't get to him in time, the bomb would detonate and killing us all in the process.

I bolted forward and activated the speed in my boots. The first shockwave came at me at waist height and I leapt over it. I dove into a roll as the second wave, travelling chest high, passed overhead. I expected the third to be waist high, much like the first, but as I leapt I realized my mistake and was pitched back. I slammed into the wall and fell to the ground, only to find myself tangled up in one of the bodies that had fallen from the wall. A loud girlish scream was heard and to this day I do not know who it came from. Reports say it was me, but that couldn't possibly be true. Those reports were not to be trusted. Hizzous and Cornerhook both tried to fire from a distance but a small barrier prevented their range attack from reaching Hexilian.

It was Skith who finally reached the Foreman. He used Montra and I as human shields, hiding behind each of us as the shockwaves came, then when the monk and I were tossed back, he only had a small dash before he reached the boss. Skith's first strike stopped the shockwaves, his second cut the mage down at the legs and his third sent the mage skipping across the floor.

The mage, eventually, climbed to his feet and retreated to the back wall. He opened an arcane gate and watched as several undead marched into the room. I grumbled as I climbed out of yet *another* dead body, wondering once more where that mysterious girlish scream had originated from, and readied myself for the next part of the battle.

Boss #4: Foreman Hexilian: Part Two.

Hexilian was a foreman. This meant he had control over all of his troops. For most foremen, their control ended when the lives of their subordinates came to an end but not for Hexilian. The necromancer raised his hand as his fingers danced in the air. The room filled with a sickly green hue. Every corpse in the room, from the bodies that hung along the wall to the he corpses we'd fell earlier, began to stir. As the necromatic magic filled their bodies, they rose to their feet - those that had them - and lumbered towards us.

Much like the earlier fight, the undead mobs adds wouldn't stop attacking until we killed the necromancer. Every ninety seconds Hexilian would cast another spell and re-animated any undead that wasn't moving.

Tactic: Crowd Control.

Crowd Control meant that there were more adds then a tank could realistically handle. It was the DPS' job to thin the herd to something reasonable while other DPS attacked the boss. For this battle Skith would be tanking as many adds as possible while Montra, Cornerhook and I kept the overflow off of him. We did this by killing, stunning or rooting them; anything to keep them from attacking.

"Ready?" I asked.

Montra nodded as she eyed the battlefield. The monk was meticulous. She was playing the battle in her head before she actually fought it. I was never one for sports but my Dad often spoke of a pitcher named Roy "Doc" Halladay. My old man was obsessed with the pitcher and he wasn't even a *Blue Jays* fan. My Dad told me stories how the other players weren't allowed to bug Doc Halladay in the hours before a game. Doc would just sit there, quietly, picturing the game he was about to throw. He visualised each batter he was about to face and each pitch he would throw, one after another. Only after he'd done this in his mind would he step out onto the field and throw for real. Watching Montra, staring out over the battlefield, reminded me of Doc Halladay. She was visualizing each punch and every kick she was about the throw before she actually threw them.

"Jebus," Cornerhook groaned. "Can you be any slower?"

I glared at the incubus. It only took the monk a couple

moments before she said she was ready. I eyed my blades, my steel still giving off a crimson glow, and took in a deep breath. I glanced at the monk and nodded back.

"We may not have the biggest stature or be blessed with the strength of giants," Skith said, "but we have strength unlike any other, strength of will and heart and in that, we will never be bested by any race."

I glanced at the smiling gnome. He shrugged. "It is a quote from Toshel Gearrigger, King of the Gnomes. It seemed fitting in our time of trial." Skith grabbed the idol from his belt and tossed it on the ground. In a beam of bright light his Unorc materialized in the battlefield. Skith leapt onto the back of his summon and rode it into battle. "No gear ticks alone!"

I always found RPers to be way too weird for my liking but damn if I didn't always want *that* one on my side.

We charged after our tank, Montra going to the right of Skith as I took to the left. My blades danced quickly, leaving a crimson trail in the air that dissipated seconds later, as I cut through the undead horde. Unlike Garruil, Montra's fist and feet didn't move in a blur. Unlike Punchocalypse, Montra's fist weren't devastating weapons. Montra's punches were precise and impactful. No punch was wasted and every attack she selected was chosen for its efficiency. She didn't want a punch that could only fell one skeleton when a punch could fell one while sending two more toppling to the ground. Cornerhook stood behind, his crimson spells weren't directed at the enemy but on us. With each enchantment he cast, we became faster, stronger and did more damage. Hizzous fired from the rear. His arrows passed over the battle and collided with Hexilian. The necromancer's health bar would drop with each arrow but only by minor slivers.

It only took a minute for Montra and I to cut through our respected numbers. Much like the Battle of Crypt Walker's Keep, I didn't need to fell each zombie or skeleton on my own. The crimson enchantment on my blades meant with each strike I would infect the add with a DOT effect. I could weave through the horde, propelled by the speed in my boots, slashing each of them and then, as I moved onto the next foe, the first would succumb to the ongoing damage and eventually drop.

When the numbers dropped, I dashed towards the necromancer. Hexilian saw me coming and tried to blast me with a spell, but I dove into a roll as the blast moved past my head. I pulled myself to my feet and raised Whaitiri Edge to meet the defense square. My steel blocked the necromatic rod as Splinter's Bite lunged forward. It fed on the necromancer's side and filled the combo meter. I pivoted behind the boss and dragged both blades across his back, using a fully powered cross slash to remove a chunk - much bigger then a single arrow could - off of his health bar. A pair of crimson blasts collided against the mage's skull as an arrow dove into his shoulder. Montra casted a pair of healings spells on Skith. She only had thirty seconds to replenish the tank's HP before the process began again.

The clock ticked zero and Hexilian's rod began to glow. All the fallen undead were reanimated and the clock reset. With a replenished horde, we began the process anew. We would cut through the undead masses, arrive on the other side, attack the boss and watch as he reanimated his minions once again. We went through the process four times before Hexilian finally fell. It was a crimson blast to his skull that finally did him in. With the necromancer dead, only two bosses remained.

Chapter 10

Psychos will always be psychos; they don't need video games to help them – Scott Ramsoomair

Boss #5: Scull Northwing and Muller Fox

Scull and Muller were both members of the Nohorian Brotherhood. Scull was a dual-wielding woman and Muller was a sword and board fighter. Alone, each of the fighters was above average in difficulty but together they were *insanely* difficult. In regular UW, they were the dungeon's final bosses, a well earned title.

They were the perfect pair of fighters. When one had weaknesses, the other had strengths; when one moved left, the other moved right. In lore terms, they were two random Brotherhood members who were assigned to work with one another. As their time together grew, so did their skill and their trust of each other. They become a powerful pair, unstoppable my most means. Yet through that time, they also developed feelings for each other and began a relationship. Using power-ful magic, they each removed their own hearts and implanted it into the chest of their partner. So strong was the spell, and the blessing of their love, that if one had fallen the other could bring them back from the dead.

In game terms: this battle came with a crap load of blocked attacks and unless both were killed within fifteen sec-onds of each other, they would be resurrected at 50% health. The boss was difficult as hell but when you completed it you had an amazing sense of accomplishment. The feeling I felt the first time I beat it was like the first time I killed The End in *Metal Gear Solid 3: Snake Eater*. It was a nearly two hour sniper battle that caused me to swear, to curse and to get mad but when I finally beat him, when I finally put that bullet through his head, I felt on top of the world; I felt unbeatable. Of course then I turned the corner and tripped on a landmine. Unbeatable doesn't last long in *Metal Gear Solid 3*.

As we turned the corner, I prepared to face them again. I had never fought them as Rake and I was eager to have my skills tested against the pair. As I eyed the empty room, I planned how the fight would go.

Tactic: -----

Empty room, why was there an empty room? I blinked in surprise as I stared again. They weren't there. There existed only a chest in the center of the room. Where the hell were the bosses? Pre-Glitch I would call *this* a glitch but now, I didn't know what to say. It was like the boss abandoned their post. Was that possible? It made sense in a way; Scull and Muller were Brotherhood members. They were probably on the run or getting ready to launch some last ditch attack on us.

But could a boss just simply up and leave their dungeon? Wasn't this the plot of *Wreck-It Ralph*?

Since the Glitch, I'd run dungeons over and over, some of them multiple times. Each time I did, the dungeons were the same. The bosses respawned and they dropped loot from the same treasure table. For whatever reason, while the NPCs in Aspumer were becoming real the ones *within* a dungeon were not, up until now.

I carefully walked to the chest and opened it slowly. I stared at the loot inside. The boss was gone and they simply left all of their loot behind. I glanced at the others and just got shrugs in return. I handed out the loot.

"Can we rest for a moment?" Montra asked. Cornerhook let out a long sigh in protest but agreed. Montra materialized some food and started to enjoy her snack. For a few moments we all sat quietly, either checking our weapons or having a small bite to eat. Cornerhook was the first to break the silence.

"Did you hear what happened to Jhaara?" I raised an eyebrow. "She'd dead. She was killed by that crazy Santiago."

Montra nodded and lowered her head. I looked at the incubus. "How did you know Jhaara?"

"We used to troll together," he explained with an apathetic shrug. "We used to pick on lowbies together."

"I did the same," Montra said. I gave her a surprised eyebrow. "I like pulling pranks on newbies but then we learned of the death consequences and I stopped."

"I didn't; I still wanted to troll but I wasn't going to get anybody killed." Cornerhook laughed to himself. "I found this lowbie huntard - never bothered to learn his name - travelling in a kobold cave. I stuck him in a Rose Trap and dragged him deep into the cave. He was outnumbered and had to wait, in the dark, for four hours for the kobolds to fall asleep before he could escape." The incubus laughed loudly.

"Did you do that?" I asked Montra. The monk shook her head.

"I was never *that* mean," she defended. "I'd do things like slap a slow-debuffs on player as they were trying to complete a time sensitive quest. It was harmless but annoying stuff."

"There is no honour in such actions," Skith said sternly.

"Fucking trolls," Hizzous frowned.

"Don't be a hater. Trolling is nothing more than something to pass the time," the incubus defended. "We have to do something in this world for entertainment."

With the food eaten and our gear ready, we marched onto the final boss. We cut down the few mobs that stood between it and us with little effort. I walked beside Montra and called upon the age old magic of small talk.

"So...." I began (good start), "How do you know Hizzous?"

"I don't really," she replied. "He messaged me a couple days ago to thank me. He said we'd partied together after the Glitch. I didn't remember him but that wasn't odd. I don't remember most people I pug with. He wanted to party together again, so I said sure." She shrugged. "What about you?"

"We were both level one when the Glitch hit. We partied for a bit."

"You're noob?" she asked in disbelief.

"Worse," I explained. "I'm epic stuck in a bank-alt."

She laughed for five full minutes.

I was growing tired of that reaction.

The last boss of UW was hard. It was the heroic only boss and was one of the most difficult five-man bosses at the time. I remember the struggle I had beating it for the first time. I watched dozens of youtube videos before I figured out the best and quickly solution to best this boss.

Boss #6: Jhen'ta Mornif, the Forge Master.

In lore, Jhen'ta Mornif was a Dwarf who had died nearly 800 year prior to Vanilla VCO. He was legendary blacksmith and genius with a forge and had created two of VCO's legendary weapons. His soul was ripped from the afterlife by the Crypt Walker and forced into a new body, forever trapped to do the Crypt Walker's bidding.

In game terms, he was a mutant Dwarf with vein-riddled arms, bulbous legs and glowing green eyes. He held an axe in one hand and a hammer in the other. He carried on his shoulder a symbiotic lizard - that looked like a new-born xenomorph from *Aliens* - which spat acid at anybody that got close.

Tactic: Tank and Spank.

Jhen'ta's weapons were no mundane items. They were powerful, enchanted up the wazoo and each blow hit like a truck. He had more HP then he knew what to do with, a powerful defense and even did minor bursts of damage simply by being close to an enemy.

Skith, mounted atop his un-orc, charged in. He let out a thunderous yell and drew the Dwarf's aggro. Jhen'ta swung with his hammer and slammed it against the un-orc. The brute stumbled backward, let out a hollow roar and barrelled forward once more.

Before the inclusion of the succubus/incubus, the Jhen'ta battle was considerably harder. A healer had to work overtime to keep the tank's health up as the DPS were called upon to slap a staggering amount of damage onto the Dwarf. Now we could lay more debuffs on him to tip the scale in our favour. It still wasn't an easy battle but it wasn't *pull your hair out Homer* Style hard.

Hizzous and Cornerhook stood back; one fired arrows as the other casted blast after blast of crimson energy. Montra and I swarmed Jhen'ta, the monk from the right and I from the left. Whaitiri Edge sparked with anticipation as I felt the longing for flesh emanating from Splinter' Bite. My blades, bathed in a crimson glow once more, cut fast and hard. I started with a saber slash with Splinter's Bite and quickly followed with a Whiatiri Edge shadow strike. My blades were quick and cut deep, the crimson enchantment adding an extra DOT to the mix, but their combined impact on Jhen'ta's health bar was almost invisible. Montra's strikes were fast. Unlike the last battle, she favoured multiple hits versus devastating ones. We needed the extra healing and she was more than happy to sacrifice her DPS in order to keep us alive.

Jhen'ta launched a whirlwind attack. It was a move that caused him to spin like The Flash and knock down everybody at once. I tried to block but caught the hammer to the face and I flew backwards, skipping off the dungeon floor. The un-orc took an axe to the chest and doubled over. Montra, somehow, pulled a Johnny Cage and dropped to the ground as she did the splits. She fired a punch into Jhen'ta's nuts and every guy in that room felt it. Of all the stuns in VCO, that was my least favourite.

Cornerhook quickly tapped his fingers as he casted spell after spells. The first volley were debuffs. They slowed Jhen'ta and lowered his attack and defense albeit for only a few seconds. The second wave was entirely buffs. They increased our damage, our armour and our attack speed. In between those, he pummelled Jhen'ta with blast of raw incubus energy.

I activated the speed in my boots and shot forward. Combined with the speed boost granted to me by Cornerhook's spells, I was a blur. My blades moved faster than they ever had before. I called upon my dark energy and stabbed my gloom blade into Jhen'ta's back. I added another DOT onto the boss but still his health bar barely budged.

Jhen'ta roared and turned to Montra. I cursed. He had an ability to single out a player and for two seconds focus all of his attacks on that one person. It wasn't a rare boss ability in VCO but it wasn't common either. At most, I'd colour the symbol silver. For ten long and agonizing seconds, Jhen'ta slammed our healer with as many attacks as he could muster and for the Dwarf wielding two weapons and carrying an acid spitting xenomorph on his back, that was a lot of attacks.

Montra rolled out of the battle, panting for air. She looked bloodied and bruised. Jhen'ta had done a number on her and her health bar was showing. Somewhere, an annoying Zelda beep was going off to warn Monta that she only had half a heart left.

As she casted a few spells, the rest of us continued our onslaught. We pilled DOT after DOT onto the Dwarf, each class using their own, but still his health bar barely moved. Jhen'ta spun around and did a double-tap on me. It was a move where he slammed his hammer into my chest then went for my neck with the axe. The hammer hit my chest like a mule's kick and I doubled over. The blow knocked the wind from my lungs and I gasped for air, desperate for the O2 that I am so addicted to. I looked up and saw the axe descending for my neck. I tried to dodge but found myself unable to move. In Pre-Glitch time, Jhen'ta's double-tap would be a massive damage but Post-Glitch chances were it would kill me. Left with no choice, I activated my Feore Shell. My body became an impassible mist and shot me two feet backwards. Jhen'ta's axe passed by harmlessly.

The battle continued as my blades fought to deflect the Dwarf's attacks. I felt the sting of his steel and the burn of the xenomorph's acidic spit. The worst part of the xenomorph's attack wasn't the acidic burn or the smell of burning flesh. The worst part was the fact that somebody just spat on you. I mean who does that? It's disgusting. I mean, it could be worse. Google the *Made This for You* achievement from *South Park: The Stick of Truth.*

Jhen'ta roared and turned towards me. I cursed once more. For the next ten long and agonizing seconds, I was going to be playing the role of Jhen'ta's bitch. I could try and block or parry but for a boss combo like this one, there was no way to stop the animation. I just had to sit there and watch my ass get handed to me. His hammer slammed into me, his axe slashed across my body and the xenomorph spat acid at me. I did my best to block but his weapons were too swift. Blow after blow clobbered me as my health bar fell drastically.

Then I saw it.

It was a small hitch in Jhen'ta's right arm. It was a small gap on which to strike, an opening I could exploit. I sliced with Splinter's Bite. The blow caused to Jhen'ta's strike to miss. I stabbed at his gut with Whaitiri Edge and watched as he dropped to one knee.

C - C - C - Combo Breaker!

I could hear the words echoing in my head. I had just used a cancel to interrupt Jhen'ta's combo. Cancels - the act of breaking out of a current animation with another move - weren't in VCO Pre-Glitch but suddenly they were. This was big news. I wondered who else knew about this. I activated my boots, spun and fired a back-kick with my stone feet into the Dwarf's chest. Jhen'ta flew backwards. He crashed onto the ground and I noticed the word VULNERABLE glowing over his head.

"Hit him," I yelled. "Hit him hard and fast."

One Paradigm Shift to *Commando* and we're hitting the Stagger Jhen'ta with everything we had. I started with a saber slash, moved into a shadow strike, added another DOT with gloom blade and, when my combo meter was full, I used a fully powered cross slash. Skith attacked with a series of powerful strikes and Montra pummelled the Dwarf with a flurry of blows. Hizzous and Cornerhook blasted from afar. It was a devastating attack that encompassed eighty or more hits. His health bar drastically dropped with each hit. Minutes later, with a glaive to the skull, Jhen'ta fell and the battle ended.

ULTRAAAA COMBOOOO!!

Mike Willette's words echoed throughout the world of VCO so everybody could hear the utter pwnage that we'd just laid on the boss (not really but I *totally* wish his voice had). The Dwarf fell to the ground, stone dead. The xenomorph leapt off his back and tried to scamper away but Montra blocked its escape. I watched as she knelt down before it and began to whisper softly.

"What are you doing?" Cornerhook asked, disgusted.

"I'm trying to tame it," Montra explained. "I have the Animal Friendship trait."

I watched in silence as she pulled food from her pocket. She offered it to the creature. The xenomorph sniffed it hesitantly before allowing itself to eat. Seconds later a small glow surrounded the *thing* and it crawled onto her back.

"Why did you take Animal Friendship?" I asked. Nobody took that trait.

"I'm an Asher," she said. "I gotta collect all'em pets."

That I could understand. VCO had small pets whose importance ranged from not at all to adds small bonuses. There was a small group of players who tried to collect them all like some damn 90's anime.

I walked over to the fallen Dwarf and looted the corpse. I ignored everything save for the Eye of Cocijo. It was a magical jeweled amulet that was etched with the Kahail symbol. It added magical bonuses to my armour and had the bonus ability to summon lightning from above. The bolts would strike near me like some AOE burst and damage those nearby.

"Hey, Cornerhook," Hizzous suddenly asked, "did you ever find out the name of that hunter you left in the kobold cave?"

"No," the incubus replied. "Why?"

"It was me."

I heard the sound of an arrow diving into flesh and spun around. Cornerhook stood, stunned, with a red-fletched arrow in his throat. I whipped my head towards Hizzous. The hunter stood there with another red-fletched arrow notched in his bow and this one was aimed at me.

Chapter 11

Maaaaaaaaaio? – Luigi (Luigi's Mansion)

Cornerhook dropped to the floor. I could hear him desperately try to breathe but as blood filled his lungs a gurgling sound filled the air. Skith, Montra and I stood stunned, none of us sure of what to do next.

"Dude," I said slowly.

"Shut up," Hizzous snapped. "He deserved what he got and if any of you try to help him you'll get the same."

My mind raced as I tried to figure out what to do. Was Santiago innocent or were they working together? Snipers rarely worked alone, even the crazy ones had backup. John Allen Muhammad and Lee Boyd Malvo proved that in DC.

"Talk to me," I said. "Why did you kill him?"

I was stalling - I'm *always* stalling. So much of my VCO life was spent stalling that people had started calling me Joseph Stalling. Okay, nobody actually did that but you get the point.

"He deserved it," Hizzous snapped. "He's a troll and trolls deserve everything they get."

It suddenly started to make sense. The killings weren't random. Hizzous was killing trolls. The other victims were to cover up the true targets. He killed two to cover up the Boomzile murder and two more to cover up Jhaara's death. Now he'd just killed Cornerhook and there were three witnesses.

"I hate trolls," I began, "but killing them seems excessive. Trolls are dicks but murder, seriously? They were pranks."

"Ever since the Glitch I've fought against these trolls. They kite mobs towards us and try to get us killed. They slow me when I'm running for my life, they attack me during the night and they trap me in a cave. Cornerhook said it was four hours but he was wrong. It was closer to eight. Eight long hours I spent stuck in that kobold cave. I was out leveled, outnumber and a single wrong step would get me killed. That's not a prank, that's torture." He shook his head. "For three weeks I have fought to stay alive, fought against the NPCs, the monsters and the other players. For three weeks I have lived in hell. Now it's my turn to finally get even."

"So what now?" I asked, eying both Montra and Skith. "You have three witnesses. What's your exit strategy?"

"Montra's a troll who deserves the same punishment. Skith wasn't supposed to be here but people have always died because they were in the wrong place at the wrong time," Hizzous said. He looked at me. "You, Mr. Rake, are the worse of the bunch. You'll die alongside the rest."

"Well shit," I said, "if we're all gonna die anyways..."

Skith and I charged the hunter as Montra bolted for Cornerhook. Hizzous was fast. He fired an arrow into Skith's leg, fired a second at Montra and a third at me. Montra cart wheeled out of the way and I activated my ring for the second time that day. I blinked behind Hizzous. I thought I had him but he spun and swung with his bow. The bow's upper limb slammed against my forehead and sent me tumbling to the floor.

Shit, he was really fast.

I drew both blades and struck again. Most times, fighting a hunter at close range was pure victory but Hizzous was quickly proving to be different from most hunters. He moved quickly, using his bow as a melee weapon. He fought like Oliver Queen and for some reason, I suddenly felt like I failed this city. He moved from defense to offense with little hesitation. He'd easily block my steel only to kick at me, knock me back, nock an arrow and fire it at me. I didn't have enough time to dodge and suddenly found an arrow in my shoulder. He drew another pair of arrows and fired them behind him. One dove into Skith's gut while Montra snatched the second arrow from the air and tossed it aside. She bolted at the serial killer, dodging the pair of arrows he fired until she got close. Hizzous swung with his bow but she blocked it with her arms. He swung again and Montra flipped over the weapon. She lashed out with her foot, an attack he easily blocked with his bow. She fired a pair of punches and forced him backwards. Watching them fight was like watching Hawkeye taking on Black Panther in *Captain America: Civil War.*

I ripped the arrow from my chest, winced like wuss, grabbed my blades and climbed back to my feet. I ran into battle and struck with my swords. Hizzous put himself between the two of us and willed the magic in his bow to activate. The range weapon morphed into a double-bladed sword and suddenly our battle became an Obi-Wan/Darth Maul/Qui-Gon three-way. He spun quickly, both blades snapping at each of us as he held both of us at bay. As the battle raged, I expected Hizzous' attacks to slow but they didn't. Like some Zul'jin wanna-be, the more he fought, the faster he got. A glow from his bracers caught my eye but so did his foot. A spin kick sent me backwards. A twist of his wrist brought both blades down across Montra's chest.

Both of us fell to the ground. Hizzous stood over me, the double-bladed sword aimed at my throat. He smiled. "The best part of this is I'll just blame it on a dungeon wipe."

The roar of an undead brute filled the room as the unorc charged Hizzous. The brute slammed the hunter against the wall. I scrambled to my feet, blood dripping down from the cut by my eye. I glanced at Skith. He lay on the ground but he had still saved us. I glanced at Hizzous and found that he'd rooted the brute with a hunter's ability and was bolting for the door. I snapped my Lucky Dagger to my hand and tossed it at him. Hizzous snapped the sword back into a bow, drew an arrow as he pivoted towards me, notched it and fired, knocking my dagger from the air with a single, well placed shot.

"I'll see you around, Rake," he sneered, "but you won't see me."

"You shoot like a girl, Katniss," I yelled.

"Hey," Montra cried in protest. I ran over to her to help but she was already healing herself with a spell.

"You okay?"

"Yeah," she said. "Cornerhook's dead though. I tried earlier to save him but it wasn't possible." We moved to Skith. I pulled the arrows from his body as Montra casted another heal spell. Moments later, the Gnome was back on his feet.

"I mean not to speak ill of your allies, Mr. Rake," Skith began, "but I believe that, somehow, Mr. Hizzous and I got off on the wrong foot."

I burst through the door of the Sheriff's office and marched towards Bearcules. The druid jumped to his feet at my entrance and glared at me. For a moment he didn't know if my arrival was good news, bad or the fight he'd been expecting.

"Santiago was innocent," I said. "Hizzous is the killer."

I quickly explained and Bearcules listened without interrupting. Only when I was finished did he ask his questions. I answered what I could and shrugged off the rest.

"We have to hunt him down," he growled. "Stay here where it's safe."

"Are you fucking kidding me?" I cried out.

"This is *my* job. Let me and my deputies handle it."

"He's out to kill me. He's targeting me *directly*. I'm coming with you."

"So am I," Montra said as she grabbed a bow and a quiver off of the wall.

"Monk's can't use bows," I said.

"No, but I did archery in RL," she said.

Bearcules looked at each of us individually before rolling his eyes. "Fine but first we have to find him."

"I know just the guy."

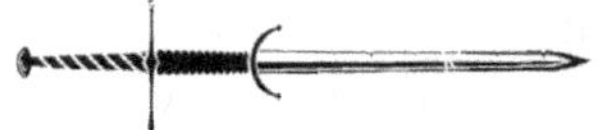

"You know the rules," Danak said. I sighed.

"Two girls ate dinner together. They both ordered iced tea. One girl drank them very fast and drank five of them in the time it took the other to drink one. The girl who drank one died while the other survived. All of the drinks were poisoned. What happened?"

Danak thought for a second before allowing a small smiled to creep across his lips. "Who do you need to find?"

In VCO lore, Denmorne Hill was the birthplace of the Fenririan Rebellion. Eons before Vörissa's fall, the Fenririan were an offshoot of the Elven race. The animalistic Elves were viewed as a lower class of people and made up most of their soldier caste. As their numbers grew and their *curse* grew greater, the *pure* Elves got worried and tried to exterminate the abominations by method of controlled breeding, sterilization and even euthanasia. Their goal was to lower the numbers without losing the soldier caste that had proven so victorious during the First Human-Orc War. After their initial defeat, the Orcs prepared for a second war but this time they proved smarter than before. Under the guise of negotiations, Orc Warchief Roushin found the ear of a Fenririan named Falnium. The two chatted of the poor conditions that both the Fenririans and the Orcs were forced to live by. Both races were forced to disarm and have territorial concessions, all by Human and Elven enforcement. Roushin spoke of the Coalition he wanted to form, a government where all were equal and there were no second class citizens. He planted a bug in Falnium's ear, one that never went away.

When the Second Human-Orc War began, the Elves leapt to the aid of their human allies. Once again, they sent their soldier caste, made almost entirely of Fenririans, into war. Roushin, a slyer Warchief then his predecessor, leaked fake intel about a crucial Orc stronghold, albeit one that would be nearly impossible to take. The Elves, knowing that this attack would suffer astronomical losses, sent their Fenririan caste. Seeing they were being sent on a suicide mission, with no back-up from the Elves, Humans or Dwarves, Falnium refused his orders and lay down their weapons. No longer content to have abominations in their presence, especially ones that were no longer loyal, the Elves tried to wipe out the Fenririans. The *abominations* fought to stay alive but they were out skilled, outnumbered and were pushed back to Denmorne Hill. The Fenririan held the hill for two weeks. With each day they lost more men and women as the Elven numbers grew. On the dawn of the fifteenth day, Roushin arrived with the Orc army. They descended upon the Elves and the two armies claimed a decisive victory. On that day, on that hill, the Fenririan Rebellion was born and the seeds that would eventually grow into the Coalition of the Damned were planted.

Decades had passed since the Second War and heroes like Roushin and Falnium had either passed away or were no longer fighting age. Even the Elven government, the *Old Guard*, had been replaced by younger and more liberal acting Elves. The military bases that once stood upon that hill had long since been torn down. All that stood now atop the hill, with the help of Fenririan druids, was a magical forest of strong, thick trees. It was a beautiful hill and a beautiful forest. Sadly, for any archer who sat atop of it, the hill was also a sniper's paradise.

"You sure he's still here?" Bearcules asked. I glanced at the Elf and nodded.

"Darak says he hasn't moved." Hizzous sat atop Denmorne Hill, hidden from view. I didn't doubt that he could see us and I knew that the moment any of us stepped onto that hill that we'd become a target. He could pick us off and kill us before we even knew where he was. I glanced at Footkneebra. "Ladies first?"

She rolled her eyes.

"I'll go first," Bearcules ordered. "Footkneebra: try

to keep our armour up. Montra: Try and keep us alive. Everybody remember, stick to the trees, call out your shots and, for fuck's sake, do not die."

Bearcules stepped onto the hills and bolted for the first tree. His hand had a purplish glow as he readied a spell. Druids had the ability to blast with spells. Bearcules didn't spec into a blaster but he still had access to the spells.

I snapped my Lucky Dagger to my hand and bolted for another tree, using the thick trunk as cover. One by one, we each did the same. Each of us would move for a tree while looking for any sign of Hizzous. I glanced at Ddaaxx. He scanned the horizon with his crossbow as Montra did the same with her bow. I glance at my ring. I only had one remaining blink for the day. I had to use it sparingly.

I peeped out from behind the tree and looked for the sniper. He was nowhere to be seen so I bolted up the hill for another tree. An arrow slammed into me and sent me falling backwards. Montra, Bearcules and Ddaaxx all fired at the shooter's location. As my rolling fall slid to a halt, I scrambled behind another tree. My breathing was heavy. I was alive, thanks to the arcane shield that Footkneebra had casted up us.

I looked upwards. Hizzous wasn't in the same place anymore. He was moving. It was Sniper 101. First you shoot, then you move positions. In a forest like this, Hizzous had dozens of places to hide.

I moved back up the hill, going from tree to tree. From the corner of my eyes, I spotted something. It was movement. I glanced over, just in time to see a form moving from one tree to another.

"Contact!" I yelled as I threw my dagger. Montra, Ddaxx and Bearcules turned towards the direction I was pointing at and each fired. Hizzous didn't run, he simply popped out of his cover and fired. His first arrow knocked my dagger from the air and his second knocked Ddaaxx's bolt off course. He sidestepped Montra's arrow and fired a third shot. This arrow dove into Bearcules' shoulder and canceled the druid's spell. Hizzous ducked behind his tree. I activated my Third

Eye headband and used its Sight Beyond Sight power. If Hizzous tried to stealth away from that tree, I was going to see it. We had him now. Bearcules and I circled around the tree from either side but as we got there we noticed that Hizzous was gone. How? There was nowhere he could have run that we wouldn't have seen, especially not with my enhanced sight.

"He's beh---," Ddaaxx's warning transformed into a cry of pain as two arrows slammed into his back. I spun around and saw Hizzous behind us. He was near the bottom of the hill shooting upwards at us. Montra spun and fired an arrow but Hizzous knocked it out of the sky with an arrow of his own. The sniper quickly notched another arrow and let it fly, only this one dove directly into Ddaaxx's head.
Hizzous had just killed Ddaaxx.

The world seemed to slow as my mind raced. How did he get behind me? How could a hunter sneak up on a rogue? How would I have done it? It was a stupid question because I was a treasure hunter. I wouldn't use regular methods. I would.....

He had a Blink Ring, just like me. The items weren't rare; they were silver symbol at best. Many players had them. I looked around as I tried to figure out where he'd blink to next. I knew the range of a blink and I knew the speed. He was going to Tracer away and he expected me to Widowmaker him but I wasn't. I was going to Symmetra him and place a trap.

I spotted the small branch high atop a tree, at the edge of his range. It would put him high above us and give him the best chance of a kill shot. I looked back at Hizzous just as Montra fired a second arrow and Bearcules casted another blast spell. I had to time my plan perfectly or it would be a waste. As the spell and arrow got close, Hizzous vanished. I quickly pivoted toward the branch and fired my dagger. I prayed I was right.

Hizzous materialized on the branch only to see my dagger coming at him. He didn't have room to move or dodge and he didn't have time to plan a course, he just blinked. I knew the script for an emergency blink so I knew where he was going to end up. I blinked there first.

Play of the Game: Rake

Hizzous materialized several feet away only to see me materialize a second later, right above him. My foot smashed against his face and sent us both tumbling to the ground. I rolled to my feet, drawing both of my blades in the process. Hizzous scrambled to his feet with only enough time to raise his bow in order to block Splinter's Bite. He pushed me back and struck but Whiatiri Edge moved to the defense square and knocked his weapon aside. An attack square formed and Splinter's Bite dove towards it. Hizzous tried to block the blow but wasn't fast enough. My steel dove past his bow and fed upon the hunter's shoulder. Hizzous back-pedalled a few paces, his bow morphing into the double-bladed sword.

"I've been looking forwards to this fight," he told me, "but I wanted you to see the others die first."

"God damn it, Kagome," I mocked. "What the fuck did I ever do to you?"

"You're Rake the Reaper, the Enclave champion and defender of the weak." I hadn't heard that title before. "You help those in need but where were you when I needed you? I asked for your help, I begged you, but my letters and PMs always went unanswered."

Flashes of me hiding in the library, danced before my eyes. I had received his letter and dozens like it but I had ignored them all.

"You helped me before and I needed your help again. I messaged you twice while I was stuck in the kobold cave but all of my messages went unanswered. I figured that Rake had forsaken me."

"I wasn't helping anybody back then," I said. "I'm still...I'm trying to do my best."

"You only helped your friends," he spat. "Well, those you haven't already killed."

Steelion.

"The champion of the people but only when it suits

him." Hizzous lashed out at me. I readied my Edge for the moment the defense circle appeared but it never came. I frantically stepped to the side as the blade tore through my shoulder. Hizzous struck once more but again, no defense circle came. This time, however, my arm knew what to do. It moved on its own, clumsily blocking the double-bladed sword with my Whaitiri Edge. Muscle memory was kicking in but it wasn't going to be enough. Hizzous sneered. I glanced at his bracer. They were magic and somehow they were messing with my attack and defense targets.

"Having trouble?" he asked as his blades struck over and over. "I knew I wasn't good enough to beat you on my own, what hunter could best a rogue, but my Mistress taught me what I needed to know. She taught me how to beat you."

My steel moved, getting faster as I learned to operate without the circles and squares. I blocked each strike, initially using both blades to deflect a single strike but moving back to blocking with one weapon as my skill grew. Then, he hit me with a combo. It was one of those moves when a player started the combo and the VCO system finished by moving your body for you. Hizzous hit me with three slashes and a flying butterfly kick that snapped his feet across my face.

Hyper Combo!

I crashed against the ground and winced in pain, crawling to my feet. I needed to hold him off; I needed to know more about this Mistress of his. I willed every inch of magic into my body and activate my ultimate skill. In that moment I became a Power Ranger and called upon the source of my power.

It's Morphin' Time: Joseph Stalling!

"Ha, Legolas got a Mistress. Is it Evangeline Lilly in a black leather corset with thigh high boots and a riding crop?" That was actually a hot image. I shook the fantasy off and pushed forward. I needed him angry and talking. "Did she put your little dude in a chastity cage?"

"I gave up *everything* that I was to survive here and I was still losing," Hizzous roared. "Then she found me. She taught me to fight, she taught me to survive and she taught me the truth of this world."

"She taught you to kill?"

"She taught me that the only reason anybody feels pain is because they allow it," he spat. "I promised that I would never feel pain again."

"Sorry to disappoint then," Bearcules roared. He charged on all four towards the hunter, the druid wearing a grizzled look on his face (because he was a bear -- get it? High five! Anybody?), and pounced. He knocked the hunter back but Hizzous quickly recovered. He rolled to his feet - his sword back to being a bow - and notched a pair of arrows. They weren't red-fletched like before, instead they were green tipped. He fired both into Bearcules' hide and drew a yellow-tipped arrow. He notched it, fired the yellow-tipped arrow at me and then drew a red-tipped arrow and fired it at Montra, who was charging up the hill. He drew a purple-tipped arrow and fired at Footkneebra but missed. The arrow dove into the ground a few feet before her.

Each of us reacted at once. Montra snatched the red-tipped from the air, I deflected the yellow-tipped with Whaitiri Edge, Footkneebra simply stepped over hers as she climbed the hill and Bearcules simply ignored the two green-tipped arrows that stuck out from his body. It would take more than two arrows to stop a charging bear. Sadly all four of us had made mistakes.

The red-tipped arrow exploded in Montra's hand and pitched the monk into the air like a surprised Loki. Bearcules's found his body slowing as the poison in the green-tipped arrows quickly moved through his body, the purple-tipped arrow sprouted vines that rooted Footkneebra and I found myself absorbing a jolt of electricity from the yellow-tip arrows. Somebody decided to arm Speedy with trick arrows instead of heroin.

For a moment I felt stronger and faster but, like last time, I suddenly felt an unbearable pain as every inch of my body was being electrocuted. I fell to the ground, screaming.

I stabbed the blade into the dirt and let out a sigh of relief as the pain dissipated. I looked up and saw Hizzous fired a third green-tipped arrow into Bearcules. The hunter looked at me and smirked. His bow shifted back into the double-bladed sword. The bracers on his wrist glowed as he attacked again.

I struggled to parry and block as his attacks got faster. He had me struggling on defense that I couldn't even think about switching to offense. I needed an opening, I needed to turn this around. Hizzous' blades moved as he wound up for another five-hit combo. The first two slashes cut across my chest and I prepared for the next three blows. Then I saw it. It was a hitch in his swing. My mind raced back to the Dwarf boss we'd fought earlier. I had a chance for a cancel, I had a chance to turn the tides of this battle. I stabbed at the hitch with Whaitiri Edge.

C - C - C - Combo Breaker!

I body checked Hizzous and sent him crashing to the ground. I activated my boots and kicked with my stone feet. The blow sent him crashing into the nearest tree, his sword dropping from his hands. I switched back to my speed and shot forward. I expected him to go for his sword but he didn't. He drew a red-fletched arrow and stabbed at my arm. The move caught me off-guard and I dropped Splinter's Bite. He kicked at my other arm and, like a bad action film, knocked Whaitiri Edge from my hand, the blade landing *just* outside of my grip.

Hizzous dove for me and knocked me to the ground. I'm not a MMA star. That fact alone explained why my ground game and my grapple game are sub-par, but as we rolled around the ground I was proud to admit that I got a couple nice shots to his body. I think I hit him in his cockles but to be honest, I have no clue where the cockles are. I think they're near the colon or something.

We separated and scrambled to our feet. He dashed at me again but this time I was ready for him. I snapped my Lucky Dagger to my hand and tossed it at his knee. The blade dug deep and Hizzous crashed to the dirt. He tried to climb back to his feet but I grabbed him. Moments later my left hand was gripping his head and my right hand pressed my Lucky Dagger to his throat.

"Kill me," he spat. "Kill me like you killed Steelion."

"I'm not going to kill you," I said.

"Then I guess that proves that we really aren't friends." He knew how to cut me deep.

"This isn't you. Your Mistress manipulated you," I said. "We can help you. Tell me who your Mistress is."

"Hush now, Reaper. If you speak then you'll miss the whispered secrets," he laughed. "My Mistress freed me. She made me strong."

"Let me help you," I begged. "Let me save you."

"You had your chance to save me, Rake. You missed it. Maybe if you had found me instead of her, this wouldn't have happened but now we'll never know." He smirked, "you missed your chance."

"I can still save you," I begged again.

"All of this is the product of your failure, Reaper," he hissed. "And so is this--"

Hizzous jerked his head quickly and forced the blade to cut open his throat. I cried out as the hunter fell to the ground, bleeding. I looked down the hill. Bearcules was still suffering from poison and Montra was busy trying to rez Ddaaxx. I knelt beside the hunter and whispered. "I'm sorry."

Then I watch Hizzous die.

Chapter 12

Video games are the quintessential social texts of our present cultural moment – Steven E. Jones

We stood before President Slashlore and his cabinet and I explained what had happened. I told Slashlore and Tialla of the error we'd made. I told them how Hizzous knew that Santiago would be the perfect fall guy and set him up. I told Garruil and Adelaide how I thought his Mistress was the same Brotherhood spy amongst the Whispers and finally I told everybody about how he died.

They asked their questions, they debated over this and that, as politicians do, but mostly they just listened. When it was over they dismissed me and I was standing outside the Enclave capital building as I stared up at the evening stars. Night had finally fallen during my explanation and for some reason; I found the stars to be soothing.

The door opened behind me and I turned to see Tialla standing in the doorway. Neither of us spoke, we just stared at each other. I needed support but in a way that Tialla couldn't offer. So without a word, I turned away and vanished into the night.

Footkneebra exited the Sherrif's office and found me waiting for her. She smirked and, with a seductive walk, approached me. "Hell of a night, eh?"

"One of the worst kind," I replied. "We should get a drink or something and blow off some steam and see where the evening goes."

She cocked her head and gave me a smirk. "If that's

what you're up for, we should just skip the drink. I could use some NSA bump and grind fun." I smiled and motioned for her to follow me but she grabbed my shoulder. I quizzically raised my eyebrow.

"I have something to tell you first. In RL---" she drew a hesitant breath. "In RL I'm legally a guy. I'm in the middle of transitioning and VCO's been part of my process but I'm still technically a guy."

I paused. I didn't expect *that* curveball but the more I thought about it then the more I wondered if there were others who used VR games as a tool during the transitioning process? I knew there were a lot of players who played both male and female characters in game like these, so it made me wonder how many players were stuck in the wrong sex since the Glitch?

"Thanks for telling me," I said softly. "I have one question. What do you identify as?"

"A woman," she replied.

"Then I don't see any problem on my side."

She leaned in and kissed me. "Good. Now let's go have some fun."

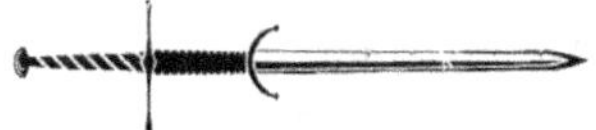

I stood inside a room. The details were much clearer than before. It was a large room built with grey, ash covered stones. Racks of weapons lined the walls. This was a castle, a castle I kind of recognized. Steelion stood before me and once again I painfully stared into his eyes.

"Dead," Steelion said. "You'll...Kill Everyone..."

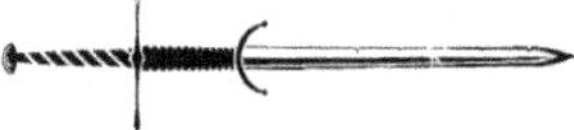

I woke with a start, my body covered in sweat. I looked beside me and saw the naked form of Footkneebra asleep beside me. I climbed out of bed and tried to catch my breath. I was so done with these dreams.

I threw on some clothes and exited my room. I made my way through the library until I got outside. Once again I found myself looking at the stars. I missed flying. I couldn't fly until I hit Level 60 and.....

I glanced at my character screen and saw that I'd leveled up during my dungeon run earlier. I just hadn't noticed it with everything that happened. I bolted to the nearest flight trainer and slapped down a crap ton of gold. Twenty minutes later, I was high in the sky once more. I rode my Hellforged Kite as I swooped in and out of the clouds. I felt the wind rushing past my hair and I, for the first time in a *very* long time, felt calm.

I landed gracefully on the library roof. I expected to be alone but found The Witch Queen waiting for me. I bowed to her and she simply nodded back. With the formalities out of way she stepped forward and handed me a book. I glanced at the cover. *Delusionary Illusion: Manifesting Reality through Belief* by Lthena Oakenhide.

"That symbol has been bugging me," she said. "I knew I'd seen something like it before. You'll want to read through this. It may help you."

"Thank you, your Highness," I said. I paused for a moment. "May I ask you a question?"

"Go ahead."

"Why did you want me at the negotiations?"

She smiled at me. "Since the event that trapped your kind here, I have noticed a pattern. Things seem to revolve around you. You fought Steelion and brought an end to the gangs. You bested Crowley and ended the attack on Havenhold and you stopped the sick individual who was killing your kind. This change isn't something we can ignore and you seem at the center of it.

"There are many questions I have about your kind and the event. Who triggered the event and for what purpose? Why are you here? Why did the event make your kind so emotionally unstable? I want answers, Mr. Rake, and I think you are the key to finding them all out."

I stood there as she stepped away from me. She waved her fingers and she opened a portal. "I don't mean to put the weight of your world and mine on your shoulders, Mr. Rake, but I am not a woman who ignores a pattern. One instance is nothing, two is a coincidence..."

"And three is a pattern," I finished. She nodded.

"Goodnight, Mr. Rake," she said before stepping through the portal and vanishing.

I stood there, silent and unmoving, as I thought about what she just told me. I was the key to getting out of here? I was the key to things? What little sleep I was getting was probably going to dry up now. Being the saviour sounded like a job that had crappy hours.

Epilogue

Jerril entered the room to find Garruil sitting at her desk. She was reading over the magical note that Rake had found in his raid of the Brotherhood. He coughed silently to get her attention.

"I already knew of your presence, Jerril," she scolded. "Your stealth needs work. What do you want of me?"

"Your hound has been slain," he reported.

"I know," she said, "and Rake still lives."

She closed the book and pushed away from her desk. She had hoped that Hizzous would remove Rake but that was Plan A. She still had other plans at her disposal. However, her campaign against Rake would have to come to a pause.

With other forces, mainly the Queen, involving themselves into the Master's plans, her attention was being pulled away. She was worried that they were getting too close.

"Jerril."

"Yes, M'lady?"

"Contact my opposite number on the right side," she ordered. "Tell them they will have to hasten the time table."

"Yes, M'lady."

"In the meantime prepare our information channels. We need to plant information for Lady Adelaide and the Enclave." She turned around and smiled at her underling. "It's time we sacrifice the Nohorian Brotherhood, they no longer have a use in our plans."

Vörissa's Catalyst
ONLINE
PATCH 1.04
IN ANOTHER CASTLE
LARRY GENT

Chapter 01

**"What is a man? A miserable little pile of secrets." - Dracula (Castleva-
nia: Symphony of the Night)**

If you could be one of the Avengers, which one would
you be? Everybody knows who they would like to be. For me,
it's either Hawkeye or Captain America, but that is unlikely
who I am suited to be.

The thought, among others, occurred to me as my
feet raced across the forest floor of the snow-covered forest.
Slashlore led the Enclave army against the final stronghold
of the Nohorian Brotherhood. We were running through the
snow, like the Avengers, in the battle that would hopefully be
the Nohorian Brotherhood's last stand. If everything went as
planned, by the end of the day the Brotherhood would be no
more. This was our *Age of Ultron* moment and our *Avengers
Assemble* cry.

President Slashlore led the way, using his paladin
abilities to magically throw his shield. He stood as our icon of
strength and guidance. He was, without a doubt, the Captain
America of the group.

Tialla controlled the battle with her abilities, ordering
us to and fro as she used her shadowy tendrils to grapple and
toss the unlucky Brotherhood members who got before her.
She was our Iron Man.

Punchocalypse called on destruction like it was a bolt
of lightning. He would send Brotherhood member flying, destroy watchtowers with ease and doing it all while looking
suave and confident. He was our Thor, son of Odin.

Montra's moves were swift and deadly. Every strike was precise and efficient. Never was a punch or a kick wasted. She moved in ways others couldn't and performed feats other thought impossible. She was our Black Widow.

Scova rode atop her mount, firing spells from her hand. Her fiery blasts were exact, felling people with an amazing accuracy. She never missed and used the smallest of spells to cause the greatest of damage. She was our Hawkeye.

Skith, son of Zook, atop his Un-Orc, was the unstoppable force barrelling through the battlefield. Enemy blows bounced off their hides as he tore through their forces. Men fell from single cuts of his glaive. The gnome was our Hulk.

As we ripped through the snow-covered forest, I found myself realizing that rarely was a person the Avenger they thought they were. I wasn't Hawkeye or Captain America, my shitty aim and lack of helicopter grappling skills were proof of that. I wasn't even any of the second-tier Avengers like War Machine or the Falcon. I wasn't even Ant-Man. I was, at best, Daredevil and I wasn't even the good Charlie Cox one.

Slashlore and Tialla had laid the plan out before us. Our goal was to reach the Brotherhood's Stronghold, breach its walls and destroy the final strands of their organization. We'd do that by tearing them down, one mob after another, and destroying their resources, one watchtower at a time.

Tialla assigned us to groups of five and placed us across the field. Each party was assigned to one of five raid groups. Each raid group would attack from a different point and push inwards. We would overwhelm the Brotherhood and tear them down. This was our do-or-die moment. We could end the Brotherhood here. The Brotherhood invaded Havenhold, they launched attacks on the PC - targeting parties and solos in the wild- and they even tried to assassinate Slashlore. The more desperate they became, the more brazen their actions. What would the Brotherhood do when they had nothing left to lose?

With my blades at the ready, I ran alongside my party.

We descended on the nearest Brotherhood watchtower and unleashed hell upon the mob. I activated the speed in my boots and shot forward. Reaching the mob first, my blades started dancing. Like a practiced waltz, my blades moved to meet the defense squares and attack circles. Whaitiri Edge slapped aside a Brotherhood spear as Splinter's Edge dove into the nearest chest. Music played as I danced, I started with a châiné turn as my blades deflected and parried any steel that approached and ended my turn with a feather finish. My dance was beautiful, or so I thought.

With each block Whaitiri Edge sent a jolt of electricity through the attacker's weapon and up into their body. The jolts had been getting stronger. They used to be akin to a small bee sting, now they were closer to the zap a child would get when they jam a fork into an electrical socket. It wasn't enough to drop any of the Brotherhood but it was enough to stagger their step.

"No gear ticks alone!" With a cry of battle, my own personal Hulk - a three foot two inch tall gnome who weighed 43 and 1/2 pounds - plowed into the mob. Riding high atop his Un-Orc, the pair sent the unlucky Brotherhood grunts flying. The Un-Orc roared and Skith struck with his glaive. Blasts of necrotic energy flowed through the mobs. Like greedy boney hands, they gripped the life force of the mobs and started to drain them of their health.

A trio of sickly green darts soared inwards. The warlock spell ripped through the chest of the unsuspecting Brotherhood guards. Fleyming - a woman I still didn't completely trust - raised her hand as she tapped out another spell. A blast of green flame ignited a grunt and caused him to scream in pain. She flicked her hand to the left and the burning man flew sideways.

Scova, the burning typhoon of chaos, descended from above. With a single, deadly accurate blast of flame, the watchtower ignited in flame. In two seconds the tower became a burning beacon akin to the Warning Beacon of Gondor. I didn't know who our Hawkeye was trying to signal but I sure as hell didn't expect the Rohirrim to come to our aid. Her feet touched the ground, flames rippling outwards, and she gripped her katana with both hands. Keshim's Fang swiftly cut through the Brotherhood, the steel ripping through their skin with little resistance.

With each strike of Montra's fists and feet, healing rippled through the party. The Brotherhood members fought back against us, cutting into us but Montra kept us going. When they struck us, our Black Widow made it so we could strike back. She was the one who kept us together.

Rake: Tower 34 down.
Tialla: Move to the waypoint. I'm regrouping Juno Raid.

Tialla. Was it possible to miss someone that you were actively avoiding? I missed hanging out with her and I missed talking to her but after her truth bomb I needed space. I wasn't ready to cut her out of my second life but I needed time to readjust my feelings.

Rake: Anything wrong?
Tialla: Yes and No. *Gold Raid* and *Sword Raid* are taking some losses but mostly the Brotherhood are providing little in the way of a challenge.
Tialla: I'm having all Raids wrangle in their parties. Then we're going to push towards Zareed Bastion.

Zareed Bastion was a daunting castle that resided deep within Glacial Woods. In lore, it was the home of Enchantress Icial Zareed. She was a mage who had an affinity for ice magic, a desire for eternal life and a tendency to commit human sacrifices. When the Crypt Walker rose, she allied herself with him. He instantly killed her and resurrected her as a lich. Her magic power increase tenfold and a winter's curse spread across the forest. The woods were encased in eternal snow and ice, forever cold and never melting.

In game terms, the Enchantlich (as she was called by the players) was the boss of the 25-man raid called *Zareed's Curse*. She was tough, hid in a castle protected by an army of ghosts and specters and she wasn't afraid to unleash a flurry of glacial spells. Luckily, we didn't have to fight her. Zareed Bastion, much like the Crypt Walker's Keep, was void of the undead and their ruler. The castle was instead held by the Nohorian Brotherhood.

My party came to a halt at the waypoint. We weren't the first of *Juno Raid* to reach it but we were far from the last. Each of the five raids was made from twenty parties. The Enclave army was five hundred PCs strong. If the *Guinness Book of World Records* still existed, this would be listed as the largest coordinated player mission.

Tialla was leading *Juno Raid* while coordinating the battle with Slashlore. Her eyes fell upon me as I approached but she quickly looked away. "All five raids are nearly ready. We'll make our final push against the Bastion."

I listened intently. I tried to push my feelings aside and focus on the plan but Stov's way of thinking still resided in me. A mage examined everything; he thought about every angle and tried to predict the outcome; in short, we over thought everything.

"--then Rake's party will lower the gates."

I blinked. Oh shit, what did I just miss? Tialla looked at me.

"You good with that, Rake?"

"Uh...yeah, sure."

Of all the castles in VCO, none were as scary as the Crypt Walker's Keep. The second scariest castle was the Warchief's Hold in the Orc Capital. When it came to scary castles, Zareed Bastion didn't make the top five. It didn't even make the top ten. It was daunting with its ice covered stone and the eerie echo but in a world that had the monopoly on *All Time Scariest Castles*, Zareed Bastion just came up short. What it was, however, was effective. It had walls that were long, thick and hard (don't giggle, you're an adult). The walls climbed up and seemed to endlessly echo upwards. Archers stood atop the wall and fired downwards, like Zeus tossing lightning bolts from the heavens. Titanic spires stood on the corner of each wall, unscalable by normal means and it was my job, somehow, to scale it.

Omaha Raid attacked from the north, *Gold Raid* came in from the south, *Utah Raid* and *Sword Raid* attacked from the west, assaulting the main gates directly, which left *Juno Raid* to assault the rear gate from the east.

The five of us in my party dodged arrows as we bolted across the battlefield like the unlucky bridge-carrying fools in a Brandon Sanderson book. I heard the gargled cry of Fleyming from behind me. I spun around to see the warlock lying on the ground, a pair of arrows in her chest. I turned around and tried to bolt to her rescue her. I wasn't about to let Fleyming, regardless of what I thought about her, die in the middle of the battlefield, alone. I started towards her but Tialla waved me off. She ordered two tanks and a monk to retrieve her. I breathed a sigh of relief and turned back to Scova.

"Well?"

"She'll be here," the mage quickly replied. I looked up the walls and watched as volley after volley of arrows rained down. I glanced back at Scova.

"Are you sure?"

"She'll be here."

"Well she's late."

"She's *not* late. You're just impatient." I looked back up. I opened my mouth to speak but Scova waved me off. "Yes, okay. Now she's late."

"I'm *not* late, Little Flame." I turned around as Lady Adelaide stepped from the shadows. "Both of you require lessons in patience." Scova quickly kissed the ninja on the cheek.

"So you have our entrance?" I asked. Adelaide didn't speak. She just pointed up as five ropes dropped down from the wall. "How did you...never mind. Let's go."

Each of us grabbed a rope and started climbing. It was the job of Adelaide and the Whispers to find us a way in. Then her team and mine would attack until we found a way to open the gate. As we scaled the wall, doing our best *Batman '66* impression, we used the spires as cover. The last thing we wanted was for archers to see us and open fire. We needed to stay hidden.

"Hey! They're climbing up the wall!"

Crap.

I looked to my left and saw one of the Brotherhood members leaning out of a spire's window. He was pointing at me and screaming. I snapped my Lucky Blade to my fingers and whipped it at him. My dagger dove into his head and, like a bad movie, he fell out the window screaming.

I called him Wilhelm.

I heard the sound of more men rushing to the spire's windows. They knew we were here and that meant we'd be fish in a barrel unless I did something. I tightened my grip on the rope and braced my legs. "Climb faster."

"What are you going to do?"

"Something stupid I saw in a movie," I said. "Something stupid I saw in a *Three Musketeers* movie." I pushed sideways off the wall and ran horizontally. Activating the speed in my boots I allowed the magic to propel me sideways. The hope was that I looked like some wire-fighting kung-fu fencer but the truth was I probably looked like those guys in a Youtube video seconds before it turned to an Epic Fail.

I pushed off the wall and let go of the rope as the archers took shots at me. Diving down the wall, I waited for my opening. I had one shot at this move. The results were either going to be legendary or splat. There was no in between.

I waited until I was lined up with the window then activated my ring. Blinking into the room, I found myself completely surrounded by Brotherhood soldiers. For a second nobody moved. Each of us was as surprised as the next at what I had just done, mainly because none of us expected it to work.

"So which one of you fellers wants to ask me for a dance?" Sarcasm: how I love thee.

My blades leapt to my hands and I struck. Splinter's Bite went right as Whaitiri Edge went left. Both blades dove into flesh then quickly retracted as they moved to deflect the Brotherhood's attacks. My blades danced from front to back and side to side as they deflected the weapons of the four Brotherhood goons that assaulted me in the room. I switched the magic in my boots from speed to stone. In a small room, speed wasn't going to do me any good. I slammed my foot into the goon behind me and sent him flying, then pivoted in the room and ran both blades through the chest of a second. I jumped into the air and pushed off the wall. It made me spin in midair and I pulled my stone-covered foot across the face of the third goon. His body went limp and crumpled to the ground. My blades twisted as Whaitiri Edge slapped aside steel while Splinter's Bite dove in to feast on the final foe in the room.

I switched my boots back to speed and bolted up the stairs. I had to regroup with my party. I found them waiting at the top of the stairs, high atop the wall. Adelaide looked at me and gave me a small smirk. "You're late."

"You're impatient," I retorted.

"Perhaps my training hasn't been as effective as you'd hoped," Adelaide said. Ever since my battle with Hizzous, I realized that I needed to improve my fencing. I turned to Adelaide for training. "I should increase the intensity." I winced at that. Adelaide was a monster of a teacher.

"What's the sitch?" I asked. Call me; beep me if you wanna reach me.

"We have only a few moments before more Brotherhood come looking to see why this corner isn't shooting," Scova said. "So we need to get out of here, fast."

"My gnomish eyes lack the strength of the elves," Skith said, "but I see the rear gate. The release mechanism is heavily guarded."

"So is the front one," Montra pointed. "Which do we go for?"

"We can't hit either directly, not the way they're guarded," I explained. "We need a distraction."

"What do you have in mind," Lady Adelaide asked. I smirked and glanced at Scova.

The clear blue sky tried to hold its own as clouds assaulted it. The clouds weren't white or grey, they were a combination of red and orange, like they were aflame. They began to cyclone, eventually causing four tornadoes to touch down in Zareed Bastion's courtyard. The tornadoes weren't made of wind or dirt; they were made from fire and flame. Fiery spirals of death ripped through the Brotherhood's forces. Brotherhood mobs scurried away.

I looked at The Burning Typhoon. A massive grin rested on her face. I shook my head. There was going to be no living with her. I bolted across the wall and headed towards the main gate. Like a phoenix, Scova leapt off of the gate and dove downwards. Her cloak wrapped around her and morphed her into a fiery ball. She dive-bombed the diminished numbers guarding the gate and erupted in flames.

Skith and I dove down afterwards. I blinked to the floor but Skith didn't. He straight up did the superhero landing. Somewhere, in RL, Ryan Reynolds was commenting on how bad that was for Skith's knees. Montra and Adelaide quickly repelled down. Montra and Skith both grabbed a small statue from their belt. Each summoned a creature; Skith re-summoned his Un-Orc while Montra materialized a small xenomorph looking creature known as a Hive Lizard. Skith climbed atop his creature and Montra allowed hers to climb atop her. Both PCs braced themselves as the Brotherhood charged them.

Montra and Skith couldn't be more opposite of each other. Skith was about brute strength and devastating blows. He would sweep through a mob and send them flying. Montra, on the other hand, was strategic and precise. She didn't use her own strength to fight, she waited for the Brotherhood to attack then she'd use their strength against them. She would twist one goon into another, strike down another and cause three more to topple over each other; all the while her Hive Lizard spat acid at any foe who came close.

Adelaide and I attacked quickly as we cut through the unfortunate few who stood against us. My blades moved quickly, dancing from one defense square to another. It was my job to cover Scova as she lowered the gate. I would die before I let someone touch her and from the look on her face, Adelaide felt the same way.

Blades, spears and axes came at us but none reached Scova. Whaitiri Edge slapped aside any steel that got close while Splinter's Bite fed upon any flesh in range. The Brotherhood were unrelenting but we were unmoving.

Relief came when the gate lowered and Slashlore's booming voice led the charge. President Paladin led *Utah Raid* and *Sword Raid* as they stormed the front gate.

Slashlore was a born leader. He cared about the people and they cared about him. When he led us into battle, we felt honoured to follow. He was the type of leader who didn't spout catchy rhetoric line *Make Aspumer Great Again*. He was the type who actually made it better.

"For the Enclave!" He cheered, his axe held high in the air. Slashlore led the charge with a damn smile on his face. He was enjoying himself. This was his Aragorn moment. I just hoped it didn't turn into a Boromir moment.

"Sword Raid: open the rear gate and let *Juno Raid* in. *Utah Raid*: We hold this gate until *Omaha* and *Gold* get here." Slashlore was barking orders across the /3 LocalDefense channel. He glanced at me. "Your party sticks with me."

We nodded. I preferred fighting alongside Slashlore but it was no longer possible. He was the president. He fought with the Enclave Army and I wasn't a part of their numbers. I was a volunteer adventurer. We filled the lesser parties as they took the glory. I preferred it that way. As the Reaper, I had received too much glory for my liking.

The fight was almost non-existent. With the main gate lowered and the Enclave army storming in, the Brotherhood retreated inwards. They ran inside the castle and hid. The few left outside quickly fell by the Enclave's might.

Medieval warfare is so different from high fantasy warfare. Film, TV and even video games always have a difficult time showing the difference. Fights, like in *Game of Thrones, Fire Emblem, Lord of the Rings: Two Towers* and *The Hobbit: Battle of Five Armies*, are played out with swords, shield, spears, bows and arrows. It's a lot of smacking, stabbing, blocking and thumping. It works for those movies and shows because they don't have much in the way of magic. VCO, on the other hand, has a great deal of magic. War changes when you insert magic into the mix. The battle is no longer simply thumps and stabs, it becomes so much more. VCO magic allowed for acidic arrows, balls of fire and meteors that rained down from the sky. Magic made it so a dire bear could fight beside a human wielding a pair flaming great swords. Items allowed for valkyrs, zombie orcs, gryphons and other fantastical beasts to be summoned as allies. No screen, big, small or personal, has ever properly shown the chaos that was a high-fantasy fight.

So when we fought, we fight with a level of chaos that the Brotherhood couldn't even comprehend. When they were simply NPCs, they were coded to react primarily to mundane attacks: weapons and spells. Ever since the Glitch, NPCs were becoming real; no longer were they restricted to their AI programming. Now, they thought and acted on their own. They were learning and they were adapting. However, the pure chaos that a PC could bring to the battlefield was hard to predict.

With each member we felled, they lost more ground. We'd face off against their numbers, kill them, take control of another section of the castle and push the Brotherhood further inwards. We continued this until we had cleared the entirety of the castle save for the throne room.

Slashlore smashed open the glacial doors, the ice

splintering as it flew everywhere. Our paladin stood stoically in the doorway. He looked like a damn movie star standing the way he did, holy light billowing off of him. He marched into the throne room, his shield held at the ready.

The Enchantlich's throne room was vastly different then most I had seen. It wasn't built with gold and didn't have jeweled adornments on the wall. It wasn't constructed to impress. Instead, it was built to intimidate, with frozen corpses hanging from the wall and bones littered across the room.

One hundred Brotherhood members stood in the room, waiting. Each held sword or spear and each stood between us and the mages in the rear. The mages were busy casting a spell. It looked to be a large portal spell, much like before.

"This is your one and only chance," Slashlore declared in a booming voice. "Surrender now or be wiped out." The Brotherhood members didn't speak. They lowered their stance and readied themselves for a fight. Slashlore scowled. "Fine, but you won't live long enough to regret this."

"You haven't been paying attention," a female voice said suddenly. "If you kill us, we come back."

"However, if we kill you," a male voice added, "then you stay dead."

A pair of warriors pushed their way through the crowd. I scowled as my eyes fell upon them. I recognized them instantly. They were Scull Northwing and Muller Fox, the missing bosses from the UW dungeon.

"I guess that leaves us with one option," Scull cooed.

"We'll have to kill you all." Fox finished.

Chapter 02

"Games are transforming the brains of people who play them in largely positive ways." - Jane McGonigal

Nohorian Brotherhood Final Boss: Scull Northwing and Muller Fox

Scull and Muller were both Brotherhood lifers. Each of them joined at a young age and spent most of their adult lives as a part of the organization. Eventually they were paired up and they proved to be the perfect match. Their skills grew together as did their feeling for each other. Aside for a year-long sabbatical, they never worked apart from each other. They could overcome more as a pair then most others could as a party of five.

In game terms, they were the bosses of regular version of the UW instance. It was a tough boss back in the day and still proved difficult for anybody trying to grind to max. Scull was a dual-wielder like me. Muller was a sword and board fighter like Slashlore. Alone they were easy as crap. Together they were damn near impossible.

Then there was the kicker.

In VCO lore, Muller and Scull grew so in love with each other that they preformed a ritual. Using powerful magic, they each removed their own hearts and implanted it into the chest of their partner. They had switched hearts. The spell, combined with the blessing of their love, was so strong that either of them fell in battle, the other could resurrect them. This meant that unless both were killed within fifteen seconds of each other, they would both be resurrected at 50% max health.

Slashlore and Stov had run UW dozens of times and it was never an easy fight. I'd seen the pair drop him with a devastating combo. Slashlore and I have had some bad dungeon runs. Some of the worst were against these two. So when they stepped out of the masses, he froze.

"He's speechless," Muller laughed. Scull took a couple of sultry, hip-waggling step forward.

"The big, bad Enclave boss can't back up his boasts," Scull teased. "So what happens now? Does he slink away? Does he hide? Does he give up?"

"Neither," Muller finished. "He simply stands there and freezes."

"This is your one and only chance," Scull mocked. "Surrender now or be wiped out."

"W...w...we will never surrender," Slashlore declared. Someone once said that courage wasn't the absence of fear. It was the ability to be afraid and to overcome it. "We will never give in. We will fight until the very end."

The pair stood by each other, each wearing a wicked grin. Muller was the first to talk. "Fine; we will go up against your best and we will still find you lacking."

"Screw this." A warrior named Walton, one of Slashlore's military PCs, charged the pair with a rogue and monk following. The trio attacked. Walton struck with a flaming greatsword, the rogue struck with a pair of purple glowing axes and the monk struck with her spear. Each of the attacks were perfect and would have fell a lesser foe. Muller and Scull were far from lesser foes. Scull drew two scimitars. They danced quickly as they deflected the axes. She knocked the weapons aside and then pivoted to her right. Muller stepped in with his shield held high. The flaming blade bounced off of his guard. Muller's longsword fought off the axes as Scull's scimitars slapped aside the spear.

The pair moved in perfect harmony. When one moved left, the other covered the right. When one took offense, the other took defense. Where one had weaknesses, the other had strengths. It was a well coordinated dance that ripped through the three fighters. It only took twenty-seconds for the trio to fall.

They lay on the ground, injured and dying. Scull walked over to Walton and stared down at the warrior. She flashed Slashlore an evil smirk as she pulled her scimitar across his neck, separating the head from the body. Slarelore scowled.

"What else do you have, Slashlore?" she mocked.

Rake: We need to take them down.
Scova: We've done it before, we can do it again.
Scova: What's the plan?

Phase One:
Scova tapped out a pair of spells. The first caused flames to emerge from her feet. The second added a crimson glow to her blade. Scova and I had fought beside each other for a long while. We did it both when I was Stov and in the many hours I had logged as Rake. We knew how the other moved and we knew how the other fought.

I activated the speed in my boots and bolted forward. I moved Splinter's Bite towards the attack circle but my steel bounced harmlessly off of Muller's shield. He quickly pivoted away as Scull stepped forward. Her dual scimitars struck quickly. Defense circles popped up and I tried to meet them. Strike after strike bounced off of Whaitiri Edge. The speed of my blades matched that of Scull's (or she was taking it easy on me) and I held on until I saw an opening. Splinter's Bite dove for the attack circle that formed but the pair quickly shifted. My steel bounced off of the warrior's shield.

I shifted and Scova dove in. Her fiery hair burned brightly as Keshim's Fang angrily struck. Her billowing boots heated the ground around her to unbearable levels. Foes took small amounts of fire damage simply by being near her. Keshim's Fang dove for the warrior but met the shield time and time again. Muller struck back. He bashed Scova with his shield and stumbled her. He moved quickly as he struck twice with his longsword. The first came down across her chest and the second aimed for her neck. The second strike never made it.

Switch.

She pivoted to her right and I pivoted left. Whaitiri Edge moved to the defense square as I blocked the blow. My blades moved quickly as I struck over and over, looking for a chance to land the blow. My attack speed was faster than his block speed. I saw an opening and dove for it. My blade gained a hint of dark energy as my gloom blade dove for his flesh. It never made it. He pivoted and a pair of scimitars blocked the blow. The dark energy flowed into Scull, infecting her with a DOT. Muller moved to Scova, looking to finish what he started. He never got the chance.

Switch

The blade bounced off of Montra's bracers. She pushed the steel aside and struck with her fist. With each strike, regardless of if they landed or not, she healed us. Scova's wounds knotted together. From the rear she tapped another spell, one that would raise her attack speed.

Steel met steels as Scull and I faced each other. Neither of us could land a strike on the other. My combo meter had long since filled but I didn't dare risk using it. This battle was going to end on the first mistake. I had to have my finisher fully armed for when that inevitable error arose.

Switch

Scova leapt at Muller, her enhanced attacks striking harder and moving faster. Beads of sweat rolled down his cheeks as the heat started to take its toll. He needed out. The pair pivoted and I suddenly found myself facing the warrior.

Switch

Muller's arm stung at the power behind the glaive as it bounced off of his shield. Skith was an ungodly strong little gnome. One of these days I was going to have to examine his items. That, however, meant I had to put up with the RPing.

Switch

Montra did a Wonder Woman impression as she deflected the flurry of scimitar strikes from Scull. The R.A. Salvatore homage was fast but the monk was faster. Montra didn't try to attack; she just defended and allowed her Hive Lizard to spit acid.

I paused to catch my breath. I glanced at Slashlore and saw him busily working. He had figured out my plan and was ready to add more to the mix. We were going to overwhelm the pair with fighters and styles. But we had to be careful. If we did this wrong, we'd be tripping over our own feet.

Switch

Scull crossed her blades as she tried to block the explosive punch from the legendary Punchocalypse. The blow would have sent a lesser foe flying but Scull only slid back a few inches. The pair pivoted and the dwarf found himself trying to dodge a longsword strike. The steel tip ripped across his arm but Punchocalypse paid it no mind. He punched again and again, using his trademark strength, but Muller didn't give ground. The warrior struck back.

The pair shifted and faced each other. They tapped their bracers and watched as they glowed. I was waiting for this. Much like the JRPGs that defined the genre, VCO bosses often had secondary forms or tactics. In some cases a boss would pull a Freeza and transform into something stronger. The Crypt Walker had more forms than Zeromux. The second thing bosses did was shift their tactics. They would change how they fought. Muller and Scull took this option. With the activation of their bracers, they became faster, stronger and drastically tougher.

Phase Two:

Muller kicked at Punchocalypse and sent him flying backwards. Scull struck with a flurry of attacks that were Barry Allen fast. Skith couldn't keep up and fell back, his body riddled with slashes and wounds. Scova and I knew this was coming and we were ready to adapt.

Double Switch

Scova and I assaulted Scull as Montra and Punchocalypse laid the royal smack down upon Muller. Scova and I danced together, our blades diving in and out in harmony as we attacked. Montra and Punchocalypse were like fire and ice. She would use to speed to keep Muller off-guard as Punchocalypse would strike with a bone-rattling blow. The pair pivoted and suddenly Team Monk was struggling to stay afloat as Team Awesome (my team FTW) suddenly couldn't land a blow past Muller's amazing defense.

Double Switch

Team Monk vanished as Team Panzer jumped in. Skith and Slashlore used their defense to box Scull in. Her blows were still Max Mercury Fast but they weren't getting past the combined Panzer Power of two career Tanks. Her blows fell upon high defense and sturdy shields. Slashlore consecrated the ground beneath him, assaulting Scull for simply being near him.

Double Switch

Scova vanished and Punchocalypse stepped in. He attacked with his trademark power punches as I looked for an opening. His punches kept the Muller's shield busy as Splinter's Bite dove around it. It touched flesh when it could and hungrily feasted but the warrior's health rarely seem to drop. He struck back. Each blow from his longsword rattled my bones. His enhanced strength meant every blow felt like a kiss from Optimus Prime when he was in full on truck mode. When I staggered back, Punchocalypse stepped in. He'd go punch for punch and still beg for more. That, however, wasn't the weirdest part. As he took a devastating amount of damage, Punchocalypse's face never wavered. He'd stand there smiling. Worse yet, he was singing as he fought. The damned fool was singing *Eye of the Tiger* as he fought and he didn't miss a single word.

The pair pivoted and it was speed on speed. Our swiftness wasn't enough as Scull's Bart Allen speed ripped through our armour and skin. Meanwhile, on the other side of the fight, Muller was in a strength battle against Team Panzer and the tanks were coming up short. With simple pushes, Skith and Slashlore went skidding backwards.

Double Switch

Skith and I stepped out as Scova and Montra dashed in. Montra and Slashlore fought side by side as they tried to overwhelm Muller. The monk's punches were carefully chosen, looking for blows that would slow or stagger him while Slashlore used every holy spell he had to amplify his strength.

Scova and Punchocalypse was a combination made in a Michael Bay film. Both were destructive forces that, with their combined power, could split the earth if they wanted to --- or were bored. Yet in close combat, they were limited. They still found a way. Balls of fire erupted from within Scull's leg as the monk's punches sent her closer to the grave. Scull never backed down. She just got faster. Her Wally West speed took massive chunks off of the health bars of Punchocalypse and Scova but neither fell.

I looked to my right and saw Tialla standing where Slashlore once stood. She was taking command while our President of the Enclave (POTE) fought. She'd ordered twelve healers to front. She assigned two healers per fighter. That meant I now had two healers whose sole responsibility was to keep me alive. Behind that she had several succubi and incubi. Their jobs were to bane them and boon us. Tialla held the archers and mages back. Pre-Glitch: the archer and mages would never accidentally hit allies in a close combat. It wasn't possible. Post-Glitch: friendly fire was a very real issue.

To my left there was the Brotherhood army. They weren't attacking. They were watching and cheering as their leaders fought. I glanced back at Tialla and sent her a PM.

Rake: What do we do when the duo fall?
Tialla: I have that covered.

She motioned to the Enlcave army. Behind the healers and the succubi/incubi were a gaggle of tanks, rogues and shamans ready to move. Beside them were mages, armed and ready to cast. If the Brotherhood attacked when the bosses fell, we'd be ready.

I looked back to the battle. The pair had pivoted once again. Scull's Jessie Chambers speed was now facing Montra and Slashlore. The monk forwent the blows meant to slow, it wouldn't affect the speedster enough to matter. Instead, she once again played Wonder Woman. She deflected the blows as Slashlore attacked with everything he had. It was a clever ploy. Slashlore was the usual tank. Their ploy kept Scull off-guard.

Scova and Punchocalypse struggled with the warrior. Punchocalypse's blows were enough to crack most walls but against the defensive power of Muller, they were coming up short. Scova tried to add any spell she could but his shield proved difficult to get around.

Double Switch

Punchocalypse retreated and Skith took his place. With a gnomish cry, his glaive came in hard and fast. The cleaver-tied-to-a-stick added a reach element to the battle. Scova would strike with Keshim's Fang then sidestep as the range glaive swung in. It kept Muller on the defensive, forcing his sword to act as a second shield instead of a weapon.

Slashlore stepped back as I stepped in. Montra would punch and kick then step aside. I would lunge in with a flurry of strikes only to quickly step aside when I was done. Back and forth we went, using our speed and our mobility to keep her at bay.

Muller and Scull were out numbered but they still gave us no ground. One would think that numbers would make the game but it didn't. Even as they fought, as Scull stabbed me with one scimitar and slashed me with another, I respected the duo. They were, despite their low level, one of the most skill-demanding foes in all of VCO. Logically I knew that they were built and coded simply as bosses but deep down I felt sorry for them. They were more than just a farming hurdle. They were great characters. They had depth, they had a back-story filled with love and tragedy and they still had mystery behind them. Before the Glitch, fans cried out to for their return but were denied. According to lore, they were dead. But now, as NPCs became real, was killing them simply the answer? Would they respawn in the dungeon they somehow abandoned? Or would they be free?

A blade ran through my shoulder, teaching me to not let my mind wander in a battle, and I stepped back as Montra moved forward. Her heals, added to those of Tialla's gaggle of healers, would have me stitched up in seconds but during that time I watched. Scull was fast, she was accurate and she loved her three hit combo. The majority of her blows came from her stringing together a series of three-hit combos. I needed to interrupt that. I needed to use a cancel. I hadn't told many people about the cancel feature I'd discovered. I wasn't sure if it was real or just a fluke but now seemed like the time to test it.

I stepped in and struck. Whaitiri Edge moved to block a series of her strikes. I needed to keep her busy as I awaited her combo. All I needed was an opening. I looked around but since openings were scarce there were none to be found. Did that stop the Reaper? Nah, I simply said. If I can't find an opening, I'll make one instead.

I slowed my left blade and flashed an opening to her. I prayed she'd take it. Even if she did take it, timing the strike would be hard. Her Jay Garrick speed made it difficult to time anything properly but I had to try. Scull took the bait. She moved to strike the opening and into a three-hit combo. I sped up my left blade and brought Whaitiri Edge up. The steel caught her and I twisted my blade. Her arm buckled, her legs stumbled and Splinter's Bite dove into her gut. Splinter's Bite had fed on both in the battle but only through scratches. It was like being insanely thirsty and getting only a sip of water. So when Splinter's Bite dove into her gut, the blade fed and fed hard. Scull screamed and lashed with her foot. She forced me back and tried to escape but her body didn't respond. Gone was her Jenni Ognats speed. She was staggered and we *finally* had the opening we needed. I dashed in, emptied my combo meter and poured every point I had into my cross slash. Both blades struck in an X formation. Her health bar dropped. Montra stepped in and unleashed a flurry of blows. The stagger didn't last long but the damage was done. She had her Thaddeus Thawne speed back but there was a hitch in her legs. She couldn't pivot out and she was stuck. We pushed onwards, hitting her with everything. With each strike she slowed and weakened. The pain was getting to her. It was growing exponentially until she couldn't even keep her blades raised. I dove in and stabbed her through the neck. Scull fell, succumbing to the slow lightning. Her speed was gone and her race was over. At the end of every race was the Black Flash, the death speedster who took us all.

The result was instantaneous. Muller let out a roar of anger. Rage overflowed him. He tossed Scova and Skith back into the air and ran over to his fallen mate. His face was red, his rage was overflowing and the battle had just gotten harder.

Phase Three:

15 seconds

We had fifteen seconds to kill Muller or the spell that bound them both together would resurrect Scull. We had fifteen second to lay a massive amount of damage or this fight would drag on. The only problem was Muller was now tougher than fuck.

14

We charged Muller, each of us at once and struck. Slashlore and I got there first: two swords and one axe. Muller blocked the swords with his shield, slapped aside the axe with his sword and then struck back. A shield bash sent me flying - literally flying - into the air while a slash from his sword sent Slashlore spinning to the ground.

13

Montra and Scova hit next. The monk attacked from behind, her fist and acid spit slamming into his back. Each blow knocked off a sliver of health but not enough. Scova leapt in. Her crimson glowing blade - an incubi gift - infected the raging warrior with a DOT.

12

Muller fired a kick into Scova's gut. She doubled over in pain. Muller slammed his shield into her skull and dropped her to the ground. He spun around and struck the monk with his sword. Montra blocked the blade but the strength behind it sent her flying. His strength had multiplied. It was at a *Over 9000* level and we were highly outmatched.

11

"Die Bitch!" Punchocalypse yelled as his powerful fist slammed against Muller's shield. The warrior didn't flinch not even when Punchocalypse's next punch slammed against the warrior's chest, denting the armour.

10

Muller struck back, catching the monk on the chin with the side of his shield. For a heartbeat, Punchocalypse was stunned. Then Muller's blade dove into Punchocalypse's chest and out the other side. Punchocalypse fell to his knees. Muller withdrew the blade and raised it in the air as he prepared to separate the monk's head from his body.

9

Slashlore scrambled to his feet and tossed his shield. He didn't aim at the warrior, he aimed at the monk. The shield collided with Punchocalypse and sent the monk skipping across the floor. Muller's blade cut through the air that Punchocalypse once stood in.

8

Skith fell from above, using his glaive as a pole vault, and slammed his weapon into the warrior's back. Muller's barbaric scream got louder as he stood over his fallen mate. Over and over Skith stabbed, each strike putting the glaive deeper into the warrior's back and robbing the health bar of even more HP.

7

Muller dropped his sword and grabbed the gnome from his back. Like a mumbling Bane, he slammed Skith across his knee and the horrifying sound of cracking filled the room. Muller tossed the limp gnome aside and retrieved his sword.

6

"Fire!" Tialla cried. Spells and arrows fired through the room, each aimed at the warrior. With nobody surrounding him, friendly fire wasn't a problem. That simply left the Ripley Option: nuke 'em from orbit.

5

Muller knocked aside the arrows with his sword and used his shield to block as much of the spell damage as possible. Warlock blast, mage fire, shadowy sears and incubi rays all rained down, each taking a toll on Muller's HP.

4

I scrambled to my feet and snapped my Lucky Dagger to my fingers. I let the blade fly and dove it deep in Muller's leg. He glared at me and I scrambled to find my steel.

3

A fiery blast emerged from Scova's right hand. The searing ray burnt his flesh and slowed his step. With her left she tapped a second spell. Fiery darts flew across the room and collided with his skull. Muller spun and flung his longsword. It dove into Scova's chest and pinned her to the wall, her spells silenced.

2

Montra charged the warrior with a Liu Kang style flying dragon kick. The blow sent him toppling to the ground. Montra straddled the warrior MMA-style and pummeled him in the face with a flurry of punches.

1

Muller struck with his shield and caught Montra in the back of her skull. She toppled off of him. He grabbed her with his free hand and with his considerable strength, whipped her across the room. She bounced off the wall like a tennis ball and fell to the floor.

0

Muller stood up and called back his sword. It magically removed itself from Scova's chest - causing the mage to fall to the ground - and returned to his hand. He held it high, a sinister look on his face and spoke. "We shall not be parted. Rise my ----"

A shadowy tendril reached up from the ground. It dove through the front of his armour - entering through Punchocalypse's dent - and emerged from the back. The final sliver of HP vanished from his health bar and Muller fell to the floor. With his last ounce of strength Muller reached not for a weapon or a potion. He reached for his wife. With his last breath he took her hand into his and whispered a final declaration of love.

The pair died as they lived: hand in hand and together.

Chapter 03

"Remember that one time during the fight when it looked like you might actually win? No? Me neither." - Spider-man (Marvel vs. Capcom 3: Fate of Two Worlds)

The next hour was a blur. It was a flurry of spells, onslaught and concern. When Scull and Muller fell, the Brotherhood charged. They didn't last long. Tialla's preparation had a wave of spells followed by melee brawlers. They ripped through the Brotherhood.

As the slaughter was occurring, healers rushed the fallen Enclave. Their first concerns were Scova and Punchocalypse. The pair had taken the most devastating damage and they were the closest to death. Next on the list were Skith and Montra. She was barely moving, stumbling when she did and he wasn't moving at all. Slashlore and I were the lowest concern. We were both beat to shit and could barely move but we would survive.

I crawled to the nearest wall and sat with my back against it. I was exhausted and in a great deal of pain but I was alive and that was all that was important. I glanced at Scova. Lady Adelaide knelt by her side, holding the mage's hand as tears rolled down the Lady's cheeks. The healers were frantically working to make sure Scova survived. As I stared at the pair I found myself jealous. They were happy together. Having someone like that would make being stuck in VCO easier to deal with. I wanted that.

I glanced at Tialla.

I just couldn't have that.

When the healers finally reached me, I was going in and out of consciousness. I felt the warm glow of a holy spell. The warm light rolled over me and stitched my wounds together. I opened my eyes and found a gnome priest - whose name I didn't know - checking my vitals. I smiled at him and gave him thanks.

I wanted to go home and sleep for the next week but I couldn't. I wasn't allowed to. We had just ended the Enclave-Nohorian Brotherhood war and people wanted to celebrate. That night Havenhold was transformed. No longer was it the capital for the Descendants of the Eternals. We were Zion and Morpheus had just told us to get jiggy with it. The war was over and we had won. Despite the Brotherhood's best attempts, we were still here!

Music filled the streets and booze flowed more plentiful than water. NPCs - attracted by the music and free booze - joined in. Decadence and hedonism was the order of the night. Everybody danced, drank, partied and nearly nobody went to bed alone.

The war had made heroes, icons for PCs and NPCs to look up to. Those, like the Unbeatable Slashlore and Montra Ripley, had dozens flocking to them. They had their pick of the litter and in Skith's case, he picked a couple times.

I was the Reaper, I had a few men and women who wanted to share my bed. Yet none of them were who I wanted. Shit. I had to move on. She was married. She had chosen to spend her life with somebody else long before she had even met me. I had to respect that.

I stumbled down the street, not sure which one, with a beer in my hand. I spotted Montra, leaning up against a wall with a glass of wine in her hand while flirting with two men. She spotted me and waved me over. She leaned in and tipsily hugged me. I didn't judge because I wasn't standing any taller than her. "Hey, Reaper. It's good to see you up and about."

"It's hard to keep a good man down," I said.

"Even harder to keep a wicked one down," she added with a grin. We tapped glasses. "How you feeling?"

I shrugged. The smile faded away as she tried to find the right words. "You don't have any lasting effects do you?"

"No, why? What's wrong?"

"I've got a concussion," she sheepishly admitted. "I've had them before and I know what they feel like."

"I got one during the Glitch," I admitted. She sighed in relief. "VR makes them even worse. Have you heard how Skith's doing?"

"He's having trouble walking," she said. "But he's healing. Doc says he'll be walking normal in no time." I went to speak my sympathies but she never gave me the chance. "The little bugger is using the sympathy card atop of the hero card. There is a damn line-up outside his door."

I silently congratulated the gnome. That was a hell of a way to make the best out of a bad situation.

One of the two guys that was flaunting over Montra stepped back and tried to excuse himself. He gave me the standard *I've been outclassed by you* look. He thought I was trying to pick-up Montra. I glanced at her and found her giving me the same contemplative look I was giving her. We were both deciding if we were interested in hooking up with the other. I wouldn't say no to some horizontal grappling with the monk, nor would I ever be ashamed of it, but without a word we both came up with the same response: not tonight. Tonight we were heroes and celebrities. We wanted to live like big shots and enjoy the hedonism and decadence.

Montra wrapped an arm around the fleeing guy and pulled him close. She backed into the second suitor, seductively grinding between the two. I paused for a second and smiled as I momentarily watched. There was something undeniably sexy about a confident woman who knew what she wanted. Tonight was a definitely a no for me but I'd be damned if I didn't try for a yes at a later date.

I made my way back to the Presidential balcony of the *Aspen Ale* bar. The building was packed. PCs danced on the table in various stages of undress. I leaned on the balcony and looked down over them. A hand delicately touched my shoulder. I turned around to see Garruil standing behind me. She handed me a jug of Dwarven ale. I smiled at the Whisper agent and nodded in thanks.

"Your kind knows how to revel," she said amazed. "I was a spy who hides as a librarian. I don't have parties like this."

"You should have been in Chicago when the *Cubs* won," I said. She looked at me with confusion. I chuckled. "We have sports teams in my world. Local teams you can cheer for in season long tournaments. One team hadn't won a championship in 108 years."

"They were that bad?"

"They were cursed for insulting a goat." She laughed but stopped when she saw the expression on my face.

"You're serious?"

"In 1945 a man named William Sianis brought his goat to a stadium to see the championship game. People start complaining about the animal's odor. They asked him to remove the goat because it stunk. Sianis declared 'You are going to lose this World Series and you are never going to win another World Series again. You are never going to win a World Series again because you insulted my goat.' It's called it the Curse of the Billy Goat."

"Was this Sianis a warlock or mage?" Garruil asked.

"He owned a bar," I laughed. "2016 comes along and the Cubs win the World Series and break the curse. The party in that city makes this one look tiny."

She shook her head in disbelief. "You miss home, don't you?" I nodded. "So now that the Brotherhood is gone, you'll be going home?"

"As soon as we can find a way."

"Once we go through the Brotherhood's notes, you should find the way to break this curse. They were the cause of it all."

"No, they weren't." Garruil looked at me surprised.

"The Brotherhood was just the cannon fodder. They had no motive for trapping us here and we didn't find the spark."

"So what does that mean?"

"When this war started, the Brotherhood's numbers were bigger than ever before. They had more mages, weapons and resources. They even had a dragon - albeit a small one - at their side. They desperately wanted Havenhold. I think they traded the Spark for power and resources."

Garruil stood silent. "Where do you look now?"

I shrugged. I honestly didn't know. I was running out of leads. All I had left was the rune. "I'm going to investigate a mage named Lthena Oakenhide. It's a thin lead - like razor thin - but it's the only connection I got."

I had my copy of *Delusionary Illusion: Manifesting Reality through Belief* sitting back in the room. With the war coming to its apex, I hadn't had the chance to give a read. It was also a really big book with no pictures of hot women or dancing bears. It was going to be a long, dry read.

"Well, worry not about this tonight," Garruil said. "Tonight, you party like your *Cubs* have become victorious once again. Your kind seems good at celebrating victory."

"You should see what happen when our teams lose," I laughed.

I stood inside a room. The details were much clearer than before. It was a large room built with grey, ash covered stones. Racks of weapons lined the walls. I finally recognized the room. This was the throne room of the Crypt Walker's Keep. Steelion stood before me and once again I painfully stared into his eyes.

"Dead," Steelion said. "Rake...Stop....Killing Every-one."

I shot up in bed, sweat pouring down my face. My chest heaved as I breathed heavily. I cursed quietly. Steelion.

The memory stung. The guilt was overwhelming. Stop killing everyone. I know the words were just my psyche lashing out but damn if those words didn't sting. Steelion and Hizzous: they were my victims. They were the people I'd ki---. I still couldn't say the word. I still could barely think it.

I looked at the girl asleep in my bed. She was a PC named.....named.....oh crap. I tapped on her profile to remember her name: Lucifa. She was a max level swashbuckler rogue. I let my still-drunken mind retreat into the past. I met her walking from one bar to another. I was drunk and she was star-struck. I flirted, she wiggled her hips and I decided to show her my room. I don't think she got to actually see too much of my room save for the pillows and the bed. Such was the case in a drunken party.

I lay back down in bed and looked up at the ceiling. I sighed. Was I ever going to get a good night's sleep?

"186, 187 188." Adelaide counted loudly with each of my kicks. She had me kicking a boxing bag. I groaned, the hangover taking a toll on me. Hangovers and exercise did not mix, especially when I didn't have any Gatorade. My body needed electrolytes and it was making that need well known.

"This is a stupid plan," I complained. "Seriously, why are we doing this?"

"You came to me for help," Adelaide reminded me. When my attack circles and defense square didn't show up during my battle with Hizzous, an effect of his bracers, I had struggled to keep up. I had been relying on VCO's combat system far too much. I needed to build up my own skills and I asked Adelaide to help me. She agreed and put me on a training regiment.

"That was my last *brilliant* idea," I said with a groan. "But I mean why are we doing this *today*? We ended the war. Doesn't that warrant a morning off?"

"Ha," Scova laughed. "You're hungover."

"You're not?" I asked in disbelief. Scova trained

beside me. Her kicks were faster and stronger than mine. I would have used that as motivation to improve but two factors stopped me. One: Adelaide had been training her longer then me and two: I was *really, really* hungover.

"God yes," she admitted. "I'm just used to these morning events."

"You have to learn to control your body," Adelaide said. "To do that you must control your mind."

"Our Mind controls our body. Our bodies control our enemies," I recited from Netflix. If I was going to be Daredevil, I was going to recite his lines. "Our enemies control jack shit by the time we're done with them."

"Crudely put," Adelaide admitted, "but well said."

"The Devil of Hell's Kitchen," Scova laughed.

"If this is your weakest," Adelaide said. "Then we will strengthen that. Once your weakest has become stronger, so too will the rest of our body. Now stop talking. You still owe me 112 more kicks."

I struggled with the remaining, nearly throwing up twice (I didn't though!). My foot had barely left the bag for the final kick when Adelaide came at me with her sword. I struggled to parry the speedy blow with Whaitiri Edge. She was a fast attacker, faster than I was. I tried my best to keep up, moving my steel to deflect hers but even with two blades versus her one, it was not an easy task. I had to figure out where the attack was going before it even got to me. We had started with wooden swords. I expected her to go easy on me to start, she didn't. I left the first day covered in bruises. The second day, I left with even more. It was about a week before I realized a startling truth: She had been going easy on me. When we'd switched to real swords, she wanted my skill to be based on my weapon, and the bruises stopped. The cuts, however, were a brand new epidemic.

Since her tutelage, my fencing style hadn't changed but it had evolved. My left was no longer simply for defence. Now I could use it as the weapon it was meant to be. I wasn't fully ambidextrous, I was far from being Darth Maul or Drizzt, but I now had two weapons instead of one and a very sharp shield. Yet the biggest addition to my fencing wasn't the blade work, it was my footwork.

In the basement of her house, Adelaide had a grid painted on the floor. It was an eight by eight grid, like a chessboard, but instead of two colours there were four. The four center squares were red. The twelve squares that surrounded them were blue. The third ring, made of twenty squares, was green and the remaining twenty-two squares were white. They were called the Rings of D'artillion.

Aspumer had five minor deities, each one representing a point in a five-point star, and one major god that represented the star's center. One of the points was for Apeus, the god of magic, intelligence, trickery and charisma. Many rogues and mages worshiped Apeus and revered him, Just as many of Aspumer's womanizers and con artists did the same. Unlike other gods, Apeus didn't have paladins, at least not in the traditional sense. He had scoundrels and arcane tricksters. The best and most devoted were a part of an order called the Azure Assembly. The order was created by a man called Ogier D'artillion.

In VCO lore, D'artillion was once a violent fencer who was bound to Helus, the god of death and balance. His parents sold his free-will to the death god in order to extend their own lives. Helus trained the child in the ways of murder until he was a teenager. Then he sent the child on missions. D'artillion was known as a Death Merchant, a killer who worked to restore the Eternal Balance that Helus maintained. After years of service, he'd seen too much and pulled a Poe. D'artillion wanted out. He asked Helus to be released. The death god didn't want to lose his Merchant, good help was hard to find, but he also knew that as an adult, D'artillion's free will was once again his own. No longer would he be bound by his parents' deal. Helus presented him with an impossible task. If he completed it, he would earn his freedom.

D'artillion set out on his quest. For eight years he worked, trying to complete the impossible quest. During which he had to become cleverer, trickier and even resorted to the learning of magic. After eight long years, D'artillion earned his freedom. On that day, he discovered who he really was and that Helus was not his patron god. There had been another looking out for him, Apeus. D'artillion dedicated his life to him from then on. He died an old man, a century passed by, Vörissa fell and still he was spoken of. He was Apeus' favourite and the example of what one could achieve.

D'artillion was famous for a fencing style known as the Parca style. It was a fencing style that had emphasis on its footwork. D'artillion was often seen nearly dancing as he fought. This was the style that Adelaide was teaching me.

Everyday Adelaide made me dance across her grid, moving from colour to colour. It was to teach me how to properly move as I fought. She started me in the white ring. The goal was to get me to the red ring. I was currently in the green ring. Fighting in these rings taught me how to move and how to fight in tight quarters.

Adelaide's blade bounced off of Whaitiri Edge. I twisted the blade and tried to toss it from her hand but the Lady was fast. She withdrew her blade, stepped around me and struck again. Strike after strike came from the ninja and I struggled to deflect each one. Fighting Adelaide wasn't a struggle to gain the offensive; it was a struggle to simply not get hit.

"You're not moving," she snapped. "Move along the green. You have to flow with each step or your moves will be nothing but wasted energy." That was the risk of the Parca style. Excessive moving could unnecessarily tire the swordsmen but if done correctly, the fencer became a dancing dervish of death.

I moved my blades to deflect Adelaide's but I was too slow. Her steel dove in and slapped me with the blunt edge. The ninja spun around and struck again, this time at my legs. My leg buckled. She lashed out with a forward kick aimed directly at my chest and quickly put me on my ass, sliding across the floor.

I still didn't vomit (despite my chest's best wishes).

"You suck at this," Scova laughed. I looked over at her and scowled.

"You went through this?"

"Nope," she laughed. "I'm a mage. I don't do this ninja thing. My style is different. More spells and less dancing. You do the Kevin Bacon thing; I'll stick to actual fencing."

"Little Flame!" Adelaide snapped. Scova glanced at her partner and saw the irritated look in her eyes. "I believe you have your morning kicks to do."

"Yes, Mistress," Scova joking replied. She looked at me. "I love it when she gets all bossy."

Chapter 04

"It's a whole new world every time you start." - Jennifer Hale

I lay on my bed and stared at the ceiling. Every inch of my body hurt, Adelaide had that effect, but I knew that if I didn't move then the pain wouldn't surface. It wasn't a great plan, it was a stopgap at best, but it was the only one I had. A knock at my door challenged the long-term viability of my plan and instantly made me curse.

"Come in," I winced. I lifted my head and glanced at the door, rolling my eyes as Scova entered. "Tell your masochist of a Bae to leave me alone. I'm all but dead."

"All butt," Scova giggled. I wanted to roll my eyes but I giggled instead. We were adults. "She's a tough one. You should see what she does to me when we're alone."

"Anytime you want to invite me in, I'll definitely watch what you two do alone." Scova smacked my chest. I winced. "What are you here for?"

Scova shrugged. "I was bored. When I'm bored in VCO, I normally do one of two things."

"You seduce females for ERP," I said as I sat up.

"Aside from that," she laughed. "I treasure hunt. I came to talk to you about your cache."

I stood up and walked to my desk. Opening the drawer, I pulled out my notes and handed them to her. "I've got it all but one item and guess what, I'm screwed."

"See that's why you need *my* help." She looked over my notes, flipping through the numbers and the writing. She tapped the final page and let out a low whistle. "*Dragon's*

Legacy, you have to run DL? Dude, you're fucked."

"Yeah," I said as I ran my hand through my hair. *Dragon's Legacy* was an end-game dungeon from *Scalebound Scism*. The dungeon's story took place during the Dragon War. It started with freeing a large dragon from it captors and ended with the party riding and fighting on the dragon's back. It was a fun dungeon Pre-Glitch but nobody had done it Post-Glitch. The dungeon had a mechanic where the party had to keep balance on the back of the dragon. If, between the parties and the enemies who leapt on, the dragon became too heavy on any one side it would roll in midair and toss everybody from its back. The dungeon had a forty percent death ratio because the balance was so hard to keep. Pre-Glitch, I would have run the dungeon over and over with party members. We would revive if we died - when we died - and go again. But with a forty percent death ratio, nobody was running DL these days.

"So what are you options?" Scova asked. "We can run DL."

"Not happening," I said. "We'll never find people."

"Then we buy the item."

"I thought of that," I said, shaking my head. "I don't even know *which* item it is."

"How did you figure out which items were part of the set in the first place?"

"I'd run the dungeon over and over," I explained. "Then I would examine each item until I found the one with the Kahail symbol on it."

"That's not going to work," she said as she rolled her eyes. She looked at the list of items. "There has to be more to it. I mean it's Casper. He's not going to just leave it to something as simple as *had a symbol on it*. There has to be more to it."

Scova looked at each of the items. The Whaitiri Edge, the Meging Cord and the Eye of Cocijo. To her there was no link; there was no connection. "These all seem random."

"I know. I've looked into the items as much as possible but there is nothing about them. The only thing I know is that Meging Cord kinda sounds like Megingjörð."

"That's a Thor thing, right?"

"The Megingjörð was the belt of Thor. It doubles his already prodigious strength,"

"Random," she laughed. "Did I ever tell you that I am so jealous of Thor?"

"Why?"

"He gets to hang out with Kat Dennings and bang Natalie Portman." Scova waggled her eyebrows in a ridiculous manner. I laughed. "I mean if I had my chance, I'd steal them away from the lightning god faster than zap."

It was a bad pun. I opened my mouth to groan but paused. Scova looked at me quizzically. "What?"

"Lightning," I said slowly. My brain was piecing things together. "Thor was a lightning god."

"Thor is a lightning god," Scova corrected. I rolled my eyes at her.

"My blade has this lightning side effect. If I block with it, it send a small jolt into the attacker." I held my hand to my chin. "It's lightning based."

"That's a coincidence," Scova scolded. "You need more."

I wracked my brain. What else was there? There had to be a hint. There had to be a clue. This was a Casper Cache. They were meant to be to found. They weren't meant to be found easily but they were meant to be found. Lightning, I needed lightning. I needed an idea; I needed a jolt of inspiration. A jolt....

"The blade absorbs lightning. When we fought Galen Crowley, he zapped me with lightning. My blade absorbed it and for a moment I felt stronger."

"For a moment?"

"Then it hurt like a bitch," I laughed. "But after getting the Eye, I got zapped again. The same thing happened but the moment lasted longer."

"One is data, two is a coincidence and three is a pattern," Scova declared. "We have a lightning pattern. So what do the Eye and the Edge have to do with lightning?"

"No clue," I said with a smirk. "But I know who probably does."

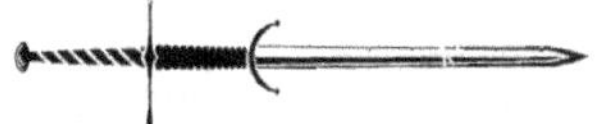

Tialla looked up from her desk with wide and surprised eyes. She eyed me carefully as she struggled to find the right words to say. After a moment of nothing, she simply said my name.

"Rake."

"Hey," I replied. Scova's eyes moved back and forward between Tialla and me. She didn't say anything but she was hella curious.

"It's good to see you," she said slowly. I nodded. Her mouth began to form the word the words I and miss but no sound emerged. "What can I do for you?"

"I'm....I mean--"

"We're looking for Mystylz," Scova said quickly. "Is the Dwarf around?"

The four of us stood over a large table. Mystylz looked at the notes as I laid them out on the table. Each of my notes was a brief write up on the items I'd found.

"So these are the item I found," I began. "The Whaitiri Edge - Lightning sword -, the Eye of Cocijo - burst lightning attack - and the Meging Cord - gives me Might Strike. The mark etched on each of them belongs to Kahail.

"Kahail is a mage who is obsessed with lightning. He believed that each man held lightning within them. He put his personal current in all the items he forged. Because of this we believe there is a recurring lightning theme.

"I know the Meging Cord sounds like Megingjörð - you told me that. You told me that's a Thor thing. So I have to ask, how did you know that?"

"That wasn't in the Marvel films," Scova added. "Trust me; I watched those over and over."

"Hemsworth fan?" Mystylz asked.

"Not even a little," she laughed. "It's more jealously

than worship."

"I studied," Mystylz answered. "This is what I went to school for. It's what I studied for the last twenty-five years." Mystylz was suddenly a lot older than I originally thought.

"I want you to see if any of these other items have some Thor connection."

"Not in the least," Mystylz said with a shake of her head. "Whaitiri is a female goddess from the Māori mythology. She's a thunder goddess. Cocijo is a lightning deity of the Zapotec civilization of southern Mexico."

"Cocijo, Whaitiri and Thor," I began. "They're all thunder gods. So chances are the next one will also be named after a thunder god." I materialized my brown journal and placed it on the table. I tapped it twice and activated my second add-on. The journal glowed and flipped open. This was my wiki-journal. It gave me a link to the VCO wiki. I flipped to the page on *Dragon's Legacy*. I thumbed down the list and looked at DL's loot list for the final boss. I spun the journal around and showed Mystylz the list. She looked it over.

    Blackened Icicle: Dagger (Off Hand)
    Diçian's Hide: Shield
    Scyonna's Tongue: Sword (Off-Hand)
    Raid End: Bracers (Leather)
    Executioner's Hood: Helm (Leather)
    Lady's Oath: Ring
    Empress' Promise: Belt (cloth)
    Grinning Skull: Boots (Plate)
    Dragon Tooth: Necklace
    Frost-touch: Gloves (Plate)

Mystylz carefully read the list. One by one she shook her head. After a while she pushed the journal back and shook her head once more. "None of these names ring a bell."

"Not even Diçian or Scyonna?" Scova asked but Mystylz just shook her head. "Shit."

"Well that was a bust," Scova said. I rolled my eyes.

Scova was so helpful sometimes.

"Perhaps you need another look," Tialla said. She had been quiet the entire time. Her words seemed hesitant. "You have an amulet, an off-hand sword and belt. We know the dagger, the shield, the sword, the necklace and the belt are out."

"That's a good point," I said. "That leaves Frost Touch, Lady's Oath, Raid End and the Executioner's Hood."

Scova made a coo of excitement. I looked at her and saw her bouncing on her feet. "The other three are associated with thunder gods, right?" Mystylz nodded. "Then I know what it is. It's the bracers; it's the Raid End bracers."

I blinked. If Scova was expecting me to get it, I wasn't. She sighed. "Say the name over and over."

"Raid End, Raid End, Raid End," I said it faster and faster until the words blended together. "Raid End, Raidend, Raidend."

"This is taking too long," Scova sighed. "It stands for Raiden, the Thunder God."

"I'm not familiar with that deity," Mystylz said slowly.

"That's because it's not a real one. It's from a video game," I said, suddenly catching up. "He's the God of Thunder and Protector of Earth Realm. It's from the *Mortal Kombat* series."

"Clever," Tialla said. "Now that you have the item, what happens next?"

"Now we wait," Scova said. "Nobody's running DL so we have to wait until someone sells it."

"I have a better idea," I said suddenly. "I've run DL dozens of times as Stov. I have that very item in Stov's collection."

"What good is that? You can't get to Stov," Tialla asked.

"If the item was in Stov's possession, yeah I'd be screwed. But it isn't, the item is in Stov's bank."

"Again....what good is that?"

I materialized and apple and tossed to Scova. The

mage caught the fruit and glanced at it. She gazed in my direction for a moment, reading me. Seconds later she smiled and took a bite.

"I need the reason. And don't say money. Why do this?" Scova asked.

"Cause yesterday I walked out of the joint after losing four years of my life and you're cold-decking *Teen Beat* cover boys," I quoted. "Because the house always wins. Play long enough, you never change the stakes. The house takes you. Unless, when that perfect hand comes along, you bet and you bet big, then you take the house."

"You've been practicing this speech, haven't you?" Scova asked.

"Little bit. Did I rush it? Felt I rushed it," I replied.

"No, it was good, I liked it. The Teen Beat thing was harsh," Scova ended with a smirk.

The mage and I smiled at each other. Mystylz just looked confused. Tialla nodded in approval.

"Did I miss something?" Mystylz asked.

"They're quoting *Ocean's Eleven*," she explained. "They want to plan a heist."

"I want to plan *the* heist," I corrected. "I want to rob Havenhold's bank!"

Chapter 05

"Do a barrel roll." - Pepper (Star Fox)

"You want to rob a video game bank?" Tialla said. "That's not even possible."

"I think it might be," I said slowly. "Look at the changes since the Glitch. Food is real, magic is real and pain is real. I think that what used to be just 1s and 0s is now brick and mortar. Everything has to go somewhere,"

"We just have to find where," Scova said. Her mind was already racing. "Are we doing this *Leverage* style or *Ocean's Eleven* style?"

"A little bit of Column A, a little bit of Column B."

"Then we need a rogue, a hitter, a con--"

"We'll need a brain, a greaser--"

"We'll need connections and minions." Scova's mind was a buzz.

"I'm going to stop you right there," Tialla said. We looked at her. "This goes against our deal with Havenhold. We agreed to abide by their laws. Theft is against their laws."
"Technically I'm robbing myself, so it's not really theft."

"The NPCs don't see it that way," Tialla explained. "They understand that we're using bodies that aren't our own but they haven't gotten to the *we have multiple bodies* part yet."

Tialla walked out of the room and into her office. She returned a few moments later with an envelope that she dropped onto the table.

"If you do this, you'll have to deal with whatever law

Havenhold sends after you plus Bearcules. You may be innocent but that will be an after-the-fact detail in their eyes." She pushed the envelope towards me. "If you're doing this, start with him."

I picked up the envelope and opened it up. It was marked 23 and was obviously a part of a set. I opened it up. "What is this?"

"We keep files on PCs who might be potential issues to the Enclave. He's one of them."

I read the file. "The psychic, you want me to recruit the psychic?"

"He knows everybody - NPC and PC - and if anybody can help pull off this heist, it's him."

The samurai's name was Shuteye and he had people convinced he was psychic. I'd heard about him through the grapevine, word had started spreading a couple weeks after The Glitch. Shuteye had, somehow, become a link between Aspumer and home. He was able to communicate with people back home. PCs were coming to him, handing over their gold just for the chance to get a message home. They were being scammed. My own beliefs aside, I couldn't help but be impressed. The Glitch was filled with confusion and wonderment and Shuteye was cashing in on it. People went from living in a mundane world to being in one where there were hundreds of swords and literal sorcery. Why couldn't there be psychics as well? The possibilities were endless and nobody knew that better the Shuteye.

I opened the door to his office and quietly entered. I moved through the house with my rogue stealth until I came upon his study. He had the room decorated like feudal study. It was barren with kneeling cushions and a small table. He knelt on one side of the table as a female mage knelt on the other.

"What can I do for you?" Shuteye said softly.

"I'm looking to contact my husband," the mage said

whispered. "His name is Steve. I'm worried about him being all alone."

Shuteye nodded and took her hands into his own. Her hands were held palms up, his thumbs making small circles on her wrists. He took deep breath. "Let us reach out to Steve. We'll both have to close our eyes." She shut hers but his stayed opened. "Now focus on Steve, picture him in your mind."

"I sense Steve but contact is difficult. I need you to focus. I'm sensing," he took a pause, a dramatic pause. "I sense another soul around him. Someone close; someone he cares for. Someone he's confiding in."

"Judy," she said with a burst of anger. "That bitch. She couldn't wait to get her claws into him."

"Yes, Judy. I sense her. She came to comfort your husband. They have gotten very close."

"That fucking bitch! She's had eyes for him for years. I'm gone for a few months and she pounces. We have a daughter, god damn it."

"He was lonely. He loves you so very much he's just lost without you."

"That fucking asshole. He's not the only one who can cheat," she mumbled.

"Wait, I sense another who wants to speak to you. She's young."

"That would be Crystal, our daughter. She's only two."

"I sense her as well. Her presence is strong; let me link her to you," he said. "Do you feel that flutter in your heart? Do you feel that burst of happiness and love?"

"Yes."

"That's Crystal. She misses you, she misses her mommy and she loves you. She's young and doesn't know how to say it but as much as she wants you home, she just wants you safe and happy." Shuteye took another deep breath. He shifted his hands slightly so her finger was lightly touching his wrist. "Can you feel that? Can you feel her heartbeat? It's flowing through you. Crystal wants her Mommy back and she's sending you her love. With each beat of her heart she sends you strength. Open yourself up; take your daughter's love into you. Ba-bump, ba-bump."

"I can feel it," tears rolled down her cheek. "I feel her."

"Focus not on Steve," he said, watching her face. "Focus on Crystal. Focus on getting back to her, focusing on staying healthy and remember, she wants her Mommy to be happy. Do what it takes to stay happy and safe."

The pair ended their conversation. The mage stood up and hugged the samurai. I rolled my eyes. He was good, he was *so* good that they hugged him and thanked him as they forked over large amounts of gold. I waited for the mage to leave before I allowed myself to be seen. He looked at me with a start.

"You're the Reaper," he said, reaching for his katana. Samurai was a warrior build that allowed players to focus on a specific weapon.

"I'm not here for trouble," I said. I nodded to the door. "How many of those do you do a day?"

"I tend to do three to five a day," he said cautiously.

"How do they not know that you're scamming them?" I asked with a laugh. "I mean, it's in your damn name."

Shut Eye was a lingo term in the world of stage magicians, illusionists, and mentalists. It stood for a performer who becomes so adept at the illusion of mind reading that they believe that they possess psychic powers.

Shuteye relaxed. "It makes them feel better and I earn some coin. It's not like anybody is getting hurt."

"What about Ms. Mage's marriage?"

"She came here looking for an excuse to cheat," Shuteye explained. "I read that off of her almost instantly. She was going to cheat anyways. What I did was give her a way to cheat and not feel like shit about it. I also made her feel happy by reminding her about her daughter." I nodded. Shuteye narrowed his eyes. "If you're not looking for a fight and since you obviously aren't here for a connection, what are you here for?"

"I'm pulling a job and I need your help."

"What's the job?"

"We're robbing the Havenhold bank."

"Well, count me interested," Shuteye said with a smirk.

Shuteye and I stood in Havenhold Square and stared at the bank. We watched the traffic, studied the guards and talked. Before the Glitch a PC would enter any bank, touch one of three lock-boxes and they would gain access to their stash. It didn't matter which lock-box in which bank (as long as it was a part of your faction) you always had access to your stash. Millions of PCs would touch the same lock-boxes and gain access their own specific stashes. The process still existed now but the question was how? A PC would walk in, place their hand on the lock-box and moments later it would open with that player's stash.

"So the lock-boxes are fueled by magic," I said. "Most of our PC abilities, like our attack squares and communications, are now magic in this world and it's been proven that it's magic that can be countered.

"What we need to do is find a way to get into the bank and redirect the lock-boxes' magic. That way, instead of opening up Rake's or Shuteye's stashes, we can open up *anybody's* and get what we want from them."

I looked at the samurai. He scratched his chin in silence. It took a moment before he spoke. "Okay, that *might* be possible but there are some issues. We'd have to deal with the bank guards. They're not going to just let you cast a spell on the lock-boxes."

"So we come in like a real bank heist then," I said. "We lock down the bank, wear ski-masks and the like."

"Then you have the city guard getting involved. Not to mention we there is a legion of people who pay $15 a month just to be a hero. One of them is going to pull a McClane and get involved," he explained. "This is all on the assumption that we can manipulate the lock-boxes. The first thing we need is to find a lock-box and study it. We'll need to study the magic on it and see if any of this is possible."

"It is," I said. I thought for a moment. "I have a mage who can help but chances are we'll need a couple hours. Where will we find a lock-box that we can hold for that long?"

"How do you feel about the desert?"

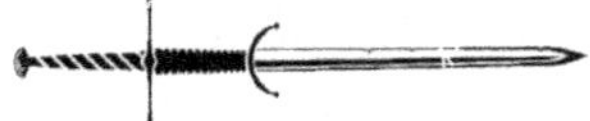

Aspumer was a wide and varied world. Much like our world, different areas had different climates. The desert portion was in the south-east. The Vizallan Desert was filled with a couple oases. The one belonging to the Descendants of the Eternals was called Ouani. It was a rarely used town in a rarely used area. The Vizallan Desert was a level 45 - 50 area and not an easy one. It was long, difficult and not very pretty to look at. The area boasted little on the surface except for miles of endless dunes. With Casper being who he was, there was lots that took place beneath the surface - like *Dune*-esq sandworms and brown dragons - but they took a lot of effort to get to.

The three of us stepped out of the portal and immediately I dropped to my knees with nausea. Shuteye looked at me and raised an eyebrow. Scova explained my portal intolerance but the samurai just laughed. I was beginning to think that this con man was a jerk.

"The plan, if Rake can stand," he began as I gave Shuteye the middle finger. "Is that tonight we storm their bank and lock it down. Scova will study the magic while Barfolomew and I deal with the few guards here."

Ouani had one lock-box within its oasis walls. It only had one bank teller and two guards that looked after it. This, compared to a regular city's bank guard rotation of thirty-four, made our job easier.

"We're only going to get one-shot at this," Shuteye continued. "What we do here will set off some major bells and alarms. We won't be able to come back. Chances are we may never be allowed to set foot in Ouani again."

"I'm fine with that," I groaned. "I hate this place."

Ouani looked like what one would expect from an oasis. There were palm trees, green grass and ponds of fresh water. What looked different were the large stone walls and building built from bones of a colossal sized dragon. In VCO lore, Ouani was one of the great wurms. Long before the age of PCs and the Vampire Insurrection, eons before the era of man and the gnome arrival, before the birth of Elves and Dwarves, there was there were the great elementals. Tasked by Torrina, the goddess of nature, they riddled the land with nature. Vizallan was the aspect of earth and nature. She took the form of a massive tree and walked around like a Tolkien-esq Ent. She covered the land with green and life and she prized no area more than her vast forest. It held trees that grew high into the sky and vines that reached across the globe.

Ouani was an aspect of wind and storms. He took the form of a colossal dragon. He loathed Vizallan and lashed out at her creations. He called upon the power of the great magic storms and laid waste to the great redwoods and watched as the forest burned. Vizallan was furious. She fought back and the two went to war. The battle was costly. It robbed the great forest of all life, forever leaving it a desert. It also cost Ouani his life. His dragon avatar died and Ouani was forever cast from the material realm. With his dying breath, Ouani saw the error of his hatred. He breathed what little life he could into the sand, creating the two oases. His bones survived the test of time, standing true for an eternity. When explorers moved to the Vizallan Desert, the Descendent forces found the bones and built from it the oasis base. It never grew to be a vibrant city but for the few desert dwellers, it was home.

We waited for nightfall before the three of us moved towards the bank. Ouani's bank was a small hut. It had two guards and a vault. Inside the vault was the lock-box. I was familiar with the bank, the oasis and the desert. I had spent a massive amount of time there as Stov, hunting every inch of sand for treasure and walked away with a mint in RL money. It was worth every moment but it was far from fun. It was work, through and through.

Havenhold at night was still a busy city. Much like New York, Havenhold never slept Ouani was vastly different. When the day went to rest, so too did the desert dwellers. Ouani was quiet and still. We swiftly moved through the town and stopped at the bank. Each of us pulled on a mask before we entered the bank hut.

The guards spotted us and went for their blades. Scova and I dashed for the guards with steel in our hands. We didn't kill the guards, we didn't want them respawning, instead we knocked them out and tied them up. Shuteye grabbed the teller. He dragged her to the vault and forced her to open it.

"Watch it," I snapped. Shuteye glared at me. He eased the grip on the teller's neck. The teller put in the combination and pulled on the vault door lever. The large steel door opened and Scova ran inside. I glanced back at Shuteye. "Tie her up."

I followed Scova. She was kneeling by the lock-box, frantically tapping away spells. Nostalgia swept over me as I watched her work. I recognized some of the spells she tapped and I missed them. It had been so long since I had the might of the arcane power at my fingertips. I missed it. I longed for the ability to call upon magic, to reshape the world and to force the universe to reveal its secrets to me. No, I was lying to myself. It wasn't the magic. A mage was the master of their domain and that, more than the magic, was what I missed. A good mage could change a battle; a great mage could stop a battle by turning away an army. Give a mage time to prepare and he was unbeatable. A rogue, no matter how good he was, could never reach that level of power.

Shuteye watched the guards and the door. I paced between vault and the lobby as seconds turned to minutes and minutes turned to hours. One by one Scova had us enter the room. She studied the lock-box as we summoned our stashes. I waited in the lobby as she studied Shuteye's. It was well over two hours when Scova was done. She stepped out from the vault. Her face was hidden beneath her mask but I hoped she was smiling. She waved her hand and summoned another portal.

"Time to go," she said. I groaned, not again.

Adelaide stared at me in wonder as I lay on the ground. I fought the urge to vomit. My battle against nausea seemed like a never ending one. I hated portals.

"Does he always act like that?" Shuteye asked from the table. Scova nodded.

"Every. Single. Time."

"Glorious."

As the nausea dissipated, I found the strength to lift myself from the floor. I climbed into a chair and took a glass of water. I sipped deep. The water helped calm my stomach. I looked up at Scova and forced a roguish smirk upon my face.

"So, what did you find?" I asked.

"I have good news and I have bad news," Scova began. "Bad news: our plan is screwed."

"Little Flame?" Adelaide hesitantly asked as she entered the room. "What are you doing?"

Scova looked at me. I nodded to her. The mage quickly filled the Whisper in. The Lady's expression went from stern to shock. "What in the Six Gods are you doing?"

"We're---"

"You're going after the Onyx Vault! Do you know what that means? Do you know the level of stupidity required to even *fathom* something that dangerous?"

"Ade---"

"Don't you *Ade* me. This is not some simple heist," she snapped. "This is the Onyx Vault. This isn't simple. If you go after them then you run afoul of the Black Bankers."

"I'm lost," I interrupted. "What's going on?"

"All of the Enclave's banks belong to the Onyx Vault," Adelaide snapped. "They are an organization that lends gold to kingdoms, funds wars and overthrows emperors. They have their own army made from fanatics and loyalists. None are more feared than the Black Bankers. Their infamy is renowned. If you challenge the Vault, you challenge them."

"So all of our lock-boxes are being magically transported from the Onyx Vault?" Shuteye asked. Scova nodded. "So what's the big deal? We're bypassing them anyways."

"We're not," Scova interjected. "That's the bad news. Our original plan is screwed.

"The boxes work on a rune system. Each one is labeled with seven arcane runes. These seven runes are connected to each toon. It's like a phone number. There are enough combinations to cover each and every toon in the game.

"The Black Vault is filled with millions of boxes, one for each toon. When Shuteye touches a lock-box, the magic instantly reads his specific combination of seven runes. Then it searches the Black Vault for the box that has the matching combination. It transports the lock-box to his location and Bob's your uncle.

"The plan was to change a lock-box so when Shuteye touched it, instead of reading his rune combination it would read Rake's or mine or whomever's we decided. The problem is that the magic that connects the runes together is strong. I'm talking epically strong, legendarily strong. This is a whole new level of strong. We can't mess with a lock-box. It's out. They may not be tamper proof but they are beyond what you or I could do." She glanced at me. "Even in your arcane hayday, it was still well beyond the like of even you."

"So what's the good news?" I asked.

"The good news is that the system isn't fool proof," Scova explained. "Fact: there is no way to break the chain between the lock-box and the runes. However, hypothetically, we could change where the chain ends up. We could put on temporary runes on another box and grab that one instead.

"For example, we find Rake's box and replace his

rune combination with Shuteyes, and make them glow brighter. That way, when Shuteye touches a lock-box, he gets Rake's stash instead of his own."

"But in order to do that," I began.

"We'd have to be *inside* the Onyx Vault," Scova finished.

Silence. Neither of us spoke for a while. We just sat there, staring at each other. The room seemed to fade away as did Adelaide and Shuteye. It was just Scova and I. We just stared at each other, talking without speech and communicating without sound or movement. We just stared and said nothing.

Was it worth it? This wasn't for our survival, this wasn't for a war and this wasn't for our escape. This was for our selfish need. This was for a Casper Cache. The answer was simple. We should just call it and walk away. And yet.......

"What do the Whispers know?" she asked quickly.

"Not enough," I responded just as swiftly. Our comments went back and forth, our speech gaining speed with each response.

"It's dangerous," she said.

"Very dangerous."

"Our crew's not big enough."

"So, we'll get more."

"They'll need motivation."

"So we get them a payout."

"We'll be crossing the lines into thieves."

"Only if we get caught."

"If we pull this off---"

"*When* we pull this off---"

"Some will think us heroes."

I smirked. "Hero ain't on my resume."

We both stood up and clapped hands. A large wicked smirk crossed on both of our faces. We had made our minds and while it wasn't the smartest or the best decision, it was the one we both eagerly wanted to make. The room and its occupants slid back into our realm of notice. I glanced at Adelaide.

"I'm going to need access to any knowledge the Whispers have on the Vault."

"This is insane, Rake," Lady Adelaide scolded.

"We're going to need resources, crew, another rogue and a hacker," Scova said.

"I know some people," Shuteye said.

"We'll need to keep the law and these Black Bankers off of our backs," I said.

"I...." Adelaide sighed. "I can slow them down but they will get to you and when they do, it will not be an easy fight."

"We'll need a hitter," Scova added.

"There is nobody better than who I have in mind," I smirked.

"I need you to know," Adelaide began, "that if -- that when you get in trouble, I cannot come after you. The Vault is beyond even our reach. If you get taken, I cannot come rescue you."

"Ade, I understand...." Scova's words trailed off as she noticed Adelaide's eyes moving between Scova and I. Scova narrowed her gaze. "Wait, exactly who are you warning, me or Rake?"

Adelaide turned and left the room.

Chapter 06

"For me, inventing video games was just one successful thing i had done among many others." - Ralph Baer

Walking through Old Hold was always an interesting stroll. Old Hold was made up of older buildings. They were as well kept as the remainder of Havenhold but the styles of buildings were vastly different. The buildings were constructed in a time when architecture was different and the time put into each was far greater. Havenhold used to be entirely filled with buildings such as these but most were lost in the various wars before and after VCO's launch.

Before the Glitch, the sector was rarely used. It was a residential area that had little use in the game. Yet since the Glitch, Old Hold had become a busier sector as many PCs had moved there. Each building was being used as housing; even the buildings that were once little more than decorations before the Glitch, were now fully fleshed out homes.

I moved through the sector and headed towards the far corner. Through the grapevine I had learned of an area of Old Hold nicknamed the Nicodemus. Not much was known about it. It was a corner of Old Hold that was filled with a random gathering of PCs and was watched over by PC guards. They stopped any who tried to gain entrance and turned them away. Some thought it was a cult; others thought it as a crime family. While I was curious about them, it was out of my jurisdiction and I wasn't looking for a fight. I was, however, looking for Punchocalypse and he had taken up residence in Nicodemus.

I saw the two PCs on guard duty as I approached. There was a warrior and rogue. They both stepped into my path as I approached. Neither seemed well equipped or well geared. The rogue looked me up and down as the warrior spoke.

"He plows early." I shook my head. I had no clue what this meant but I assumed it was a code phrase. The warrior repeated himself. "He plows early."

"I don't know your codes," I said. "I'm looking for someone inside."

"Then PM him," the warrior snapped.

"He's not answering."

"Then take the hint," the warrior scoffed.

"I'm looking for Punchocalypse," I snapped. "You need to find him and tell him that the Reaper is looking for him."

The rogue's body tensed as he took a step back. The two guards looked at each other. I hated using my title but sometimes it opened doors that were jammed shut. The warrior eventually succumbed and stepped back. I watched as he quickly PMd. Five minutes passed by before I saw Punchocalypse walking towards us. The monk didn't walk with his normal cockiness or bravado. He looked lackluster and dull, like a brass statue that had lost it shine.

Punchocalypse met me at the edge. He looked at me and frowned. "What do you want, Rake?"

"I need your help."

"Not interested."

"We need to talk," I said. He reluctantly sighed and escorted me in. We silently walked down the street. I looked around at the PCs as we walked. The average gear level of each player was low. They were wearing mismatched armour and had weak weapons. From my best guess, the few strong users in this cult were giving the weaker ones their leftover equipment. Punchocalypse brought me into a house and moved up the stairs. We entered a small room. I looked around, it reminded me of the room that Stov used to have. I took a chair.

"What's up?"

"Something big is going down," I said slowly. "We'll be going up against a couple big bads. It's not going to be easy so I need a hitter."

"No."

"But you're the best hitter there is. I don't know if you realize this but you have some of the highest DPS that I've ever seen in this game."

"No, I'm done," Punchocalypse snapped. "I'm done risking my life. I almost died last time. I got stabbed in the chest and almost lost my head. This was all fun and games before but I can't do this."

I didn't know what to say. He was a frontline fighter who was damn good but even the greatest could succumb from self-doubt. I assumed that nearly dying had that effect on people. I'd gotten close to death, I'd even kil---, but I'd never almost died. I didn't know how he was feeling. I could only guess, I could only grasp at straws.

"I'm done fighting and I'm done being the adventurer. I want out of this game. I miss RL, I miss my family and I..." His voice trailed off. "I just want to go home."

"Every soldier----"

"Don't give me that," Punchocalypse snapped. "I know the drill. Add one part flashback, two parts nightmares and two parts emotional confusion and you get some PTSD shit. I'm a crazy soldier suffering his crazy soldier shit."

"You're not crazy." I took a deep breath. "You don't have to fight. You don't have to do anything that you don't want to. I know that it's been tough. We've all been suffering and we're all lost in it. I don't think we've had time to realize that some are suffering more than others.

"But you have to realize that you are not crazy. You and I are both adults on the frontline. There are thousands of soldiers in RL who are going through the exact same thing that you are. It's norm---"

"I'm fifteen."

"What?" I nearly choked on my words.

"I'm only fifteen year old," he began. "I'm a teenage boy in high school. I played VCO after school and I was good at it. I was a min-maxer who just liked punching things. I didn't ask to be in a war and I didn't ask to be a soldier. I just wanted to play a fucking video game."

"But Tialla's age requirement?"

"I lied."

We sat in silence. I did not see that coming. I knew that there were minors in VCO, minors who were stuck in the game like the rest of us but of all the people I didn't expect Punchocalypse. I hummed and hawed as I searched for something to say but nothing emerged. Shit. What the hell was I supposed to say to this? I looked around.

"Shit, I have to get you out of this cult," I said. "The last place a minor needs to be is in some freaky cult."

"Cult?" Punchocalypse said confused. "What the hell are you talking about?"

"Nicodemus," I said. "People have been calling it a cult."

Punchocalypse laughed. "I started playing VCO with a bunch of classmates. From them I met more people in the same age group as me. We didn't form a guild, each of us was in one guild or another, instead we're essentially a clan or a secret society. The guy - kid - who started the society called us Nicodemus. We were the rats and the mice scurrying beneath the sight of men.

"When the Glitch happened, we decided to band together. We looked out for each other, we live near each other and we supported each other." He shook his head. "We don't want to be treated differently. We just want to help make decisions and aid in getting us home. So, we hide what we are and we fight the cause."

"I've seen you with girls," I cautiously asked. "Are you..."

"I only hook-up with people I know are my age, my real age," Punchocalypse said. He looked at me. "I want to help you but...."

"I know." I shook my head. "I shouldn't even be doing this. I mean you---"

"Don't," Punchocalypse snapped. "Don't treat me differently."

"If you ever need anything from me, and I mean anything, you just ask," I promised. Punchpcalypse opened his mouth to argue but I spoke before he had the chance to say anything further. "I'm not doing this because you're a kid or anything. I'm doing this because I owe you. You've helped me a dozen times over, so if you need me then I'll be there."

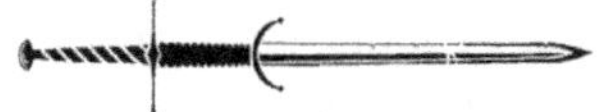

I strolled through the Havenhold streets, running late for a meeting with Scova and Shuteye. I was walking through the industrial quarter when a voice called out for me. Coming to a pause and turning around, I smiled as I saw the familiar succubi face of Footkneebra. I scowled when I saw the Elven face of her partner.

"Rake," Sheriff Bearcules said, "I would like a word."

"Well you just got six, so I'll be on my way."

"Cute," the bear-druid said. "This is official so how about you slow your role and behave."

"Sheriff," Footkneebra scolded.

"So I get a visit from one of the crown's judicators. Turns out three PCs broke into a bank and held the workers hostage. They didn't take anything but they spent a couple hours studying the lock-boxes. One of the NPC guards reported an azure blade with a red-velvet grip. That weapon sounds an awful lot like your Whaitiri Edge to me."

"I'm not the only one with that blade, Sheriff," I said calmly.

"You kinda are," he said. "That blade is so rare that fewer than few have it. You're one of the few."

"What are you accusing me of?" I asked. I faked a disbelieving laugh. "You think that I'm a bank robber? Wow."

"Well, am I wrong?"

"This is rich," I mocked. "First you get to play Sheriff with no experience to back that up. Then you realize that playing cops and robbers sucks unless you have a bad guy so you start making one up. Do you want me to wear a mask and a black and white striped shirt?"

"You little shit," Bearcules spat.

"Enough!" Footkneebra put herself between the druid and me. She glared at Bearcules before glancing at me. "Rake, if you're tangled up in something you need to let us know. We know that the bank robbers were casing the joint for something bigger and so do the Black Bankers. These PCs need to deal with us before the Bankers get to them."

"Thanks for the warning, Foot, but seeing how I'm innocent, I'll take my chances."

"You're late." Scova spoke to me as I entered a warehouse. I gave her an apology and looked around. The warehouse was built by the crown to store food and grain but somehow it found itself under Whisper ownership. "Something wrong?"

"How the hell did we get this?" I asked. "You know what? I don't want to know. Is our team here?"

"Shuteye and Adelaide are upstairs with them."

"Then let's go,"

"Wait," I paused at the stairs and glanced at the mage. "You....this team is...."

"That bad?"

"That bad."

I climbed the stairs and entered the room. The first face my eyes fell upon was that of Montra. She nodded and smiled. Then my gaze went from left to right and every face I fell upon went from bad to worse.

There was Snookie and Pauly D - the guidos. Shocking as they were, the biggest surprise was yet to come. As my eyes reached the far right, I stared in disbelief at a pirate captain with two scimitars, a wide brimmed hat and a glowing red eye. I was staring at Captain Airmo Hau, the legendary pirate. Snookie and Pauly D - real names Anize and Noran - nervously stood before me. I could see both fear and anticipation in their eyes. Hau, however, stood like he didn't care if he was there or not.

I snapped my head around and glared at Shuteye. "What the *actual* fuck?"

"What we want to do," Shuteye said quickly, "requires their skill sets. Noran is a bomb ass hacker and Anize is one of the stealthiest rogues I've ever found. Montra is a hitter and she's good."

"And Hau?"

"You want to break into the vault," Hau said. "I have a plan to get inside, I have a plan to get us out and I have the crew to pull this off. If you don't want my resources and skills, then walk."

"You're a pirate," I said. "You will betray us."

"I see my reputation precedes me," Hau smirked.

I glanced back at Shuteye and Scova. "We need him."

"But….pirate," I protested.

"We *really* need him."

I sighed. "Welcome aboard."

"This isn't going to make sense to all of you," I said glancing at Hau and Adelaide, "but we all have alts. We all have gear that we need access to. To do that, we need to rob a bank. You're here because apparently you're the best of the best with honours, sir. This isn't going to be an easy heist but it will be a profitable one. That, I promise."

"I'm going to play devil's advocate," Montra said. "I don't have an alt. What's in it for me?"

"Stov, Steelion, TeenyGoku, RocknCola, Kella and DaxterDrake," I explained. "These six were some of the biggest treasure hunters and pro-gamers. They weren't logged in during the Glitch or they are no longer with us. These six, plus ten lesser ones, make up the biggest collection of gold and magical items on our side of VCO. We split up the loot, sell what we don't need and live like kings."

I let the words hang in the air. A couple moments later, Montra spoke. "Okay, that works for me."

"Good, now we have a lot of work to do. We'll be scouting, planning, putting people where we need them and all of this is before we even set foot into the Vault."

Scova stood up and began to talk. She explained the plan to the group. Hau listened without speaking a word. Anize listened while picking her jaw up off the floor while Noran started asking questions. He asked about the runes and their connection to the players. She replied and the two began a dialogue. A lot of what they discussed was very mathematical, very technical and way over my head. But his words seemed to energize her and her responses seemed to excite him.

"There is one more thing I have to mention," I interrupted. "The law is already onto us. Bearcules is already asking questions. This means the judicators and the Black Bankers are already aware of us. We have to be quick, we have to be quiet and, most importantly, we have to be careful."

I let my final words hang in the air. If they wanted out this was the chance. Nobody moved. I let out a sigh of relief. "Okay, let's get to work."

Chapter 07

"Requiescat in pace." - Ezio Auditore da Firenze (Assassin's Creed 2)

The Black Vault was located a short hop from Diamondfax. It had a small town - Kimonish - that surrounded the massive building but mostly it consisted of a large barracks, a couple stores and little else. The Vault's major nearby city was Diamondfax. Before the Glitch I had spent very little time in Kimonish. I did some quests, I had some fun and I moved on. There were better areas out there to quest. For some reason, Kimonish was always underused. I often suspected that there was more to the town, hidden in a way that only Casper could, but I had yet to find it.

Nearly three days had passed as I kept watch on the city. I had found an abandoned apartment and I had made it my base of operations. From there, I watched the Vault. I watched who entered, who exited and where they went.

Hau had a list of Vault employees. It included what they did for the company and what access they had. I didn't know how he got the intel but in truth I didn't ask either. My job was the find out as much as I could about the key employees.

"Hey." I turned around to see Anize enter the apartment. I shook my head and looked back at the street below. "Any news?"

"Not yet." A stakeout wasn't a one person job. It was made up of multiple shifts that you shared with at least one partner. My stakeout partner was Anize and I was *far* from pleased about it.

"Can we talk?" she said as she sat beside me. I shrugged. Anize squirmed as she tried to find the proper words.

"You want me to be nicer to you and forgive you?" I suggested.

"No, fuck that," she defended quickly. "My husband and I tried to take you out, twice. You can treat us however the hell you want." She shook her head. "We ain't asking for your forgiveness either. We just want a chance to prove ourselves."

"That's um....."

"Not what you were expecting?" I chuckled as I nodded. "I figured. You had every right to kill us after the second attempt on your life but you didn't. We fucked up and you let us walk. I'm grateful."

"I'm not the bad guy. I'm not a kil---" the words trailed off.

"I was there," she explained with her thick Jersey accent. "I saw what he made you do. I'm....I'm sorry. Steelion went off the deep end and a bunch of us decided to follow."

"He was still a friend," I mumbled.

"I know. He didn't deserve that and neither did you." She looked out the window. "They say everybody's emotions are messed up. If you get mad, you get *really* mad. If you get sad, you get *really* sad. I heard that a couple days ago a shaman named Reit go so down that he took his own life."

Reit; shit. He was one of the guys who messaged me but I never got back to. I hung my head. Was that another name added to my list?

"My point is each of us is carrying some emotion with us, some emotion we can't let go of. For my man and me, it is love; our love for each other is amplified to a dangerous level. If one of us gets hurt, the other freaks out. In the first couple days we'd freak out if we were apart for too long." She shrugged. "What emotion are you carrying?"

Guilt; I was carrying guilt.

I stood inside a room. The details were much clearer than before. It was a large room built with grey, ash covered stones. Racks of weapons lined the walls. I finally recognized the room. This was the throne room of the Crypt Walker's Keep. Steelion stood before me and once again I painfully stared into his eyes.

"Dead," Steelion said. "Rake...Stop....Killing Everyone."

I jolted awake. I looked over and saw Anize staring back at me. She was sitting by the window, watching the street below. My TV-esq nightmare wake up routine had momentarily grabbed her attention.

"You okay?" she asked. I nodded. "Since you're up, look at this."

I climbed to my feet and walked to the window. She pointed to the street below. I watched as a Vault guard walked along the streets. He weaved his way through the street as he headed for the Vault. "That is Tsa Rikkiam. He is a key-holder."

"Where can his key get us?"

"According to the pirate?" Anize laughed. "According to Hau, it will get us the stocks."

"So Hau can get us into the building and that key will get us into the stocks." I glanced at our notes. "That's steps 1 and 3."

"How Underpants Gnomes is that?" she said with a laugh.

"So we still have to get past the inner checkpoints." Anize nodded. I just shrugged. "We'll worry about that later I guess. So tell me about Mr. Rikkiam."

The sound of cheering accompanied the smell of sweat and blood. I stood in the crowd, watching as a PC paladin and a PC warrior slugged it out in the middle of an underground ring. Hidden amongst the slums of Diamondfax was *Vixen Ring*. It was an underground MMA ring that was run by an NPC crime lord. Her name was Jiwi and she was the Dwarf Queen of Crime. She ran drugs, weapons and illegal substances but what she truly enjoyed was watching what she called the *Idiot Others* beating the crap out of one another. She paid good gold for fighters and made even more with each fight. NPCs poured in by the dozens and cheered at every fight. They paid in hard earned gold and walked away happy. There was a large number of NPCs who still didn't know what to think of the Enclave but they did enjoy watching them beat the shit out of each other.

"You sure you can do this?" I asked. "You took a hell of a hit in the last fight."

"My head's fine," Montra assured me. "I've been better and I've been wors. What I am now, however, is ready to fight."

"You don't have to---"

"Rake, shut the hell up." Montra smirked as she spoke, "It's my job to fight. It's your job to track Tsa and get that key."

We both stepped to our left as the warrior from the ring flew past us. We glanced back to see a paladin stand victorious. Montra looked back at me. She winked. "I'm up next."

The announcer climbed into the ring and congratulated the paladin. He spent the next couple seconds mocking the bested warrior before calling upon the next.

"Let's keep the carnage rolling," the announcer said in Bruce Campbell-esq voice. "Our next fighter is as stunning as she is beautiful. She'll bend you over as much as you want to do the same to her: Montra."

"Did you write that?" Montra snickered.

"No." I said with an faux innocent look. She shot daggers at me with her eyes. I quickly caved. "Okay, maybe."

"Just get the key," Montra said with a smirk. She moved through the crowd and climbed into the ring. The announcer introduced a rogue called Früitninja. The pair stepped into the ring. The announcer mocked the pair for a couple moments before hitting the bell. Montra and Früitninja circled each other slowly. A bare knuckle fight between a rogue and a monk should have been one-sided but the moment the rogue attacked I realized I was wrong. Früitninja's strikes were surprisingly fast. Montra's arms moved as she struggled to block them. No wonder his odds were 2:1 to win while hers were 6:1.

I would have loved to watch Monta fight, I would have loved to watch Montra do anything, but I had a job to do. I climbed to a higher level and glanced down. My eyes fell upon Anize on one-side of audience and Noran on the other. I cast my gaze across the audience until it fell upon Tsa.

Rake: I have eyes on him.

From our observations - let's call it what it truly was: stalking - we knew that Tsa was one of the many who were uncertain about the Enclave and the PCs. He enjoyed watching them fight and he enjoyed gambling on it.

I directed the guidos through the crowd and watched Tsa. People flocked around him and handed him drinks without charge. This favouritism could be from his success as a gambler but truth was he wasn't *that* good. This meant his royal treatment must have come from his position. Anize theorized that he and the Vault were funding the Vixen or they were working with them.

Our stalking had told us Tsa was methodical, observant and highly intelligent. He saw everybody and remembered everything. It made sense why the Vault entrusted him with the key.

Noran: I'm in position.
Anize: Ready to strike.

Noran and Anize moved towards our target. The guidos were the perfect team. They trusted each other completely and knew what the other was going to do without speaking. If anybody was going to pull off a lift from a highly observant, paranoid guard it was those two.

Noran struck first. He bumped into Tsa and knocked his drink to the floor. Tsa looked down, disgusted and angry. He snapped his head up and narrowed his eyes. He didn't look at Noran, instead he looked around, scanning and memorizing every face around him. Tsa was smart and paranoid. Somebody bumped into him and the first thing he suspected was it was a diversion. He was looking to see if anybody else was sneaking up on him.

In truth there was but he couldn't find Anize. Shuteye said she was the best at being stealthy and at that moment she was proving it. Nobody could see her except for those in her party like Noran and I. I watched as she brushed past Tsa and grabbed the key from his pocket. Her lift was amazing. It wasn't VCO skill; it was real life pick pocketing. Anize was a legit quick hand. She moved through the crowds and up the stairs. I fished out small box. It was made with clay so I could make a key mold and eventually copy the key. Anize handed me the key. I put it in the mold and pressed down.

"You are...." I began. I wanted to ask who she was in RL but I didn't. I wasn't about to break The Rule. "You are doing well. That was smooth AF."

"Thanks." She smiled at me. We both glanced to the ring. Früitninja had Montra on the ropes. Our monk was fast and meticulous but the rogue was hella fast. He was building up combo points at an incredible speed and attacking with fully powered finishers. I had to marvel at his technique. Yet as I watched Montra, I couldn't help but notice the calm in her eyes. She wasn't out, not by a long shot. "Did you put any money down?"

"I have 5k on our girl." I admitted. "You?"

"Nah," she revealed. "I don't gamble in things I don't participate in. Card games: sure. Fights: nope."

"Never do card trick in front of you poker buddies," I

laughed. "I saw that lift. I'm not playing cards with you."

"That's good," she said with a sarcastic smirk. "I'm actually *really* terrible at poker."

"Hustler," I jokingly accused.

"Hush now," she jested back. "My husband didn't know I posed in that magazine."

I rolled my eyes and opened the molder. I withdrew the key and handed it to her. "Get it back to Tsa."

She nodded and vanished. I was a rogue; I knew how to be stealthy but damn if she didn't outshine me in every possible way. She made her way back to Tsa. Noran reached the guard first. He handed the Vault worker a replacement drink and several apologies. Tsa still cautiously eyed the man but accepted it. As the two men talked, Anize slipped the key back to its original location, slinked away and made her way to the club's exit. Noran disengaged with Tsa, vanished in the mob and eventually did the same as his wife. I looked back at the ring just in time to see Montra's spinning foot send Früitninja against the mat, hard. Everybody waited for the rogue to get back up but he didn't. Monta won and I had to go collect my winning.

Montra and I exited the club. We walked through the streets of Diamondfax, talking about the fight.

"I swore he had you," I laughed.

"For a while I thought he did," Montra revealed. She shook her head. "He was good, very good. We should look him up."

"I think we've got enough rogues as it is."

"We'll need a replacement after I kill you for that opening."

"I don't know what you're talking about," I joked. She pushed me up against a build's wall.

"You want to bend me over do you?" I did. I really did and she knew that. There was some physical interested between the two of us. There wasn't anything romantic but neither of us seemed against the bump and grind. "I'm a little worked up after that fight. Who knows what will happen?"

She leaned in and kissed me. It was passionate and damn if she didn't taste nice. It was a combination of blood, sweat and an orange she ate afterwards. I don't know why that specific combo set me ablaze but it did. I wanted her but I knew I shouldn't, not while we were working.

"We're...on a job," I said, instantly hating myself. "We should save this for our victory celebration."

"You're the guy," she groaned as she reluctantly pulled her lips away. "Aren't you supposed to be all *slave to your emotions*?"

"I'm a piss-poor example of a guy," I laughed. "The Man Union has tried to revoke my membership card a couple times."

"I can see why. I can't wait to see what they'll do when I report this incident to them." She made tsk tsk sounds. "Turning down a Ronda Rousey style woman who is throwing herself at you: expulsion!"

Our laughter was interrupted by the sound of a man loudly clearing his throat. We turned our heads to see a pair of men dressed in black clothes standing by us. They each wore a high quality tunic but from the lack of slack in the material told me that they wore chainmail beneath their clothes. Weapons hung from their belts.

"I'm normally not one to interrupt the amorous pairing of two such as yourselves but I need a word." One of the men was tall with plenty of muscles while the other was lean. Tallboy carried a longsword on his belt while Matchstick had a pair of handaxes on his belt. Matchstick stepped forward. "I would like to talk to you about you recent activities, Mr. Rake."

"And who the hell are you?" I asked. I had a guess but I prayed I was wrong.

"We are known as Black Bankers," Matchstick explained, "but I've often loathed that moniker. I prefer to think of myself as a solution supervisor."

I hate being right.

"Either way," he continued, "I need you to come with us."

"I'd prefer not to," I said quickly. "I have plans. You see we have to get home quickly. I...um.....left my cat...in the oven?"

Montra had been standing firm. Her body was in battle-mode and her mind was planning every punch she was about to throw. Yet as my lame-ass excuse reached her ears she turned to me with a confused look of disbelief. She silently mouthed the words *left your cat in the oven*? I just shrugged. She shook her head and turned back. We watched as Tallboy drew his longsword and Matchstick spun a hand axe in each hand.

"I'm afraid we're going to have to insist," Matchstick said calmly.

Damn it, my cat was going to have to wait.

Chapter 08

"If I had three hours on a Friday night, I'm not our partying. I'm probably playing video games." - Felicia Day

Montra dashed forward and planted her foot directly into Matchstick's chest. The banker stumbled backwards. He was in awe of her speed and precision. Montra followed up with a Mark-Dacascos-Eric-Draven style butterfly kick. As Matchstick struggled to dodge, I snapped my Lucky Dagger to my hand and flung it at Tallboy. He slapped the dagger away with his longsword but the damage was already done. In the few seconds he spent focused on my projectile, I had drawn both my blades, activated the speed in my boots and rocketed forward. I attacked with a spinning attack, slicing first with Whaitiri Edge, then Splinter's Bite and once more with Whaitiri before I thrust deep with my longsteel. Tallboy blocked what he could but Splinter's Bite still feasted upon his flesh or so I thought. My blade connected with his armour.

Tallboy was faster than I expected. He recovered and began his counter-attack in just a few seconds. He held his blade one-handed, using a style that reminded me of Steelion. His speed was remarkable and normally I'd be struggling to keep up. Yet as the battle progressed, my blades were moving on their own. This wasn't VCO's combo system, this was muscle memory. I was moving my blades without thinking. When a defense square popped up, Whaitiri Edge was already there.

Adelaide's training was proving *very* effective.

Montra's body twisted and turned as she avoided the

flurry of dual axes. Matchstick was fast but somehow Montra saw each attack before it hit. He was telegraphing his attacks. She struck back, her fist moving Bruce Lee fast. Each blow should have been enough to fell the banker but somehow he withstood it. She tossed her own body into the air and wrapped her legs around Matchstick's neck. Montra twisted her body and, in Black Widow style takedown, rolled to her feet as she tossed the banker to the floor. Montra was a revved up monk who had just been turned down for sex and Matchstick was the idiot who decided to pick a fight with her. I was just the moron who turned her down for sex.

Not to be outdone, I activated my boots and spun my now-stone foot towards Tallboy's face. The kick should have put Tallboy's nose into the back of his skull but my foot came to an abrupt halt. Tallboy held my ankle in one hand. He was holding my entire body into the air with one hand. He smirked and I crapped myself. Tallboy was much stronger than I expected.

Oh shit, they were toying with us.

I suddenly took on the role of Loki as Tallboy slammed me back and forth into the ground as he did his best Hulk impression. Eventually the banker took mercy on me and released my body, letting me fall to the ground. I winced in pain, I whimpered in pain and I cried in pain.

From the corner of my eye I saw Montra. She was frantically moving as she tried to survive Matchstick's onslaught. His speed had increased and she was suffering. Her arms and legs were covered in cuts and blood was pouring out from a cut to the chest. We were outmatched and outclassed. We were boned. It was time to Ghost like Swayze before we *became* a ghost like Swayze.

I scrambled to my feet, turned my boots back to speed and bolted towards Monta. We stood back to back and waited. Matchstick and Tallboy both charged us and I activated my Eye of Cocijo. A bolt of lightning cracked down from above and crashed into the ground before me. It sent the two Bankers flying backwards. The blast wasn't meant to deal massive damage; it was mainly a push move. It was meant to put distance between the PC and his foes.

"Run," I yelled.

Montra and I took off. We ran down the street, moving as fast as our feet could take us. We took a corner with a slide. The Bankers were following behind us and they were gaining. They were *freaking* fast.

"Door." Montra moved to the nearest building and kicked open the door. We both ducked inside the building and bolted up the stairs. Montra paused as she reached the top and hid. She waited for the Bankers to get close. As Matchstick reached the top, Montra leapt from her cover and struck. Her foot caught a surprised Matchstick in the jaw and sent him barrelling back down the stairs Wet Bandit style.

We bolted across the building floor and leapt out the window. We landed on the ledge of the next building. I nearly crapped myself but Montra seemed at ease. She moved quickly, parkouring her way across the various roofs and ledges in Diamondfax while I struggled to keep up. I was a good rogue but I was never going to get my invite to the Assassin Order.

"What have you guys been?" Scova asked as we entered the warehouse.

"Black Bankers," I said with a stern response. She raised an eyebrow at me.

"Bankers showed up and attacked us. We had to ditch them before we headed back here," Montra answered. "They're tough and they totally ruined the mood."

"I warned you of them," Adelaide said. "I'm just happy you both survived."

"They are definitely going to be a problem," I said. "We need a plan to deal with them."

"That's not our only problem," Scova said. "I think your succubus friend has been camped out all night."

"Great," I mumbled. "If Footkneebra's watching us then that means Bearcules is closing in on us."

"Is there any good news?" Anize asked.

"We got the key," I said.

"Noran and I cracked the code," Scova added. "Each PC has an alpha-numeric code associated with it. The runes act as a replacement cypher. It took a while to crack, especially with actual hacking not being a possibility, but we found things out."

"Do I want to know?" I asked hesitantly.

"I'm about to go full on math here," Scova warned. "So unless you want me giddy, excited and wet like Niagra Falls just say pass."

"Do I get a say in this?" Adelaide asked with a wicked smirk. I rolled my eyes, not from disgust but from jealousy.

"So what do we do?" Montra asked. "We have all this progress but we still can't get past our second security hurdle and now both forms of law have their eyes on us."

"I'm just going to say what we're all thinking: it might be time to think about bailing," Noran said. "I mean if the law descends then what? Do we go down together?"

"If the law descends then it's every man for himself," Shuteye declared.

"I ain't walking away," Hau said. "I know when a job goes belly up but we're not there yet. This be the biggest score for me crew and I. We ain't giving that up."

"I ain't givin' up either," Anize said. She reached for her husband's hand and took a hold of it. "We're both staying."

"That's great and all," Adelaide said sternly. "But that does little to aid us with our second of the three hurdles."

"Hurdle one is entry into the building," I began.

"That one is taken care of." Hau explained. "One of the building guards works for me. He's a crew member that I inserted into the organization a while ago. He's from where most of our intelligence came from."

"You inserted him into the Vault?" Adelaide asked.

"I have been interested in hitting the Vault for a long

time." Hau looked at Lady Whisper and gave her a cocky pirate smirk. "Besides, I have people everywhere."

"Hurdle two is getting past four check-points in the building," I continued, "and hurdle three is gaining access to the inner vault itself."

"And we have the key to do that," Noran said. "So our main problem is getting past those checkpoints."

"Each checkpoint is manned and guarded. They are enchanted to dispel illusion," Shuteye explained. "So we can't just illusion us. Also, the number of people actually allowed inside the inner vault is few."

"Can we just skip them and Ethan Hunt our way into the Vault?" Noran asked.

"Ethan Hunt?" Hau asked.

"It's from *Mission: Impossible*. It's a mov--- never mind. Ethan Hunt climbed through the air-vents and lowered himself down into the Vault."

"No. They are protected against that very specific attempt."

"See this is what happens when designers are geeks. They make safes that can't be broken into movie-style," I laughed.

"So we need to disguise ourselves without magic?" Montra asked. I nodded. Montra tilted her head as she thought. "I *might* have a solution. We'll need some supplies though."

I moved through Havenhold's evening streets. My bag was filled with the various fruits, dyes and paints that Montra had requested. Her list was weird and oddly specific. It took some effort but I found everything she was looking for.

"Rake!" The voice called out. I turned around and saw Footkneebra approaching me. I gave her a nod. "I need a word."

"If this is work related then tell your boss to go f---"

"Shut up and listen," she snapped. "I'm risking my job telling you this so just give me a freaking moment." She shook her head as she formed the words. "I know you're robbing the bank. Somebody just ratted you out."

"What?" I spat. "What are you talking about?"

"You know the psychic in Old Hold?" I feigned ignorance. "I'm doing you a favour. At least respect me enough to see past the badge for a second."

"Sorry. Yeah I know him."

"He walked into our station and demanded to speak to Bearcules. He started talking about the bank heist and told us how it was going belly up," she said. "He told us how they were going to switch lockboxes."

"So what does this have to do with me?" I asked.

"He named his crew. He named each and every one of you."

"Let me guess, he said I'm working with Scova, Montra and Adelaide. They are some of my best friends. Anybody could come up with that story and name us three. It's not a big stretch."

"He said you're working with Hau." I froze. "I knew it. When he said that name I knew it had to be real. There is no way he'd think that I'd believe that name unless it was real and the look on your face just proved it."

"So what happens now that Shuteye has turned evidence?" I asked.

"Walk away from the plan and come in to the station," she said. "You don't have to go down for this." I stood there for a moment, uncertain as to what to do next.

"Let me think about this, okay?" She nodded. I walked away and vanished into the night.

Chapter 09

"Get over here." - Scorpion (Mortal Kombat)

"I often think your kind may be insane," Hau said. I looked at him and raised an eyebrow. We were walking through the streets of Kimonish. From a glance it seemed like we were only traveling the streets on an evening stroll, in reality we were keeping watch for the guidos. The rogues were breaking into a Vault barracks to steal several vault uniforms. I was paired with the pirate for lookout duty.

"Insane is a strong word," I replied. "What got you to that conclusion?"

"Your kind speaks of other worlds. You speak of other bodies and other faces," he explained. "I've talked to monks who speak of other states of consciousness but none like that.

"You kind flock to me. It seems that you all fear me and adore me at once. I have several of your kind on my crew. They volunteered to be a part of it. They...." His voice trailed off. This was a side I'd never seen of the legendary pirate captain. He wasn't all suave and swagger, he was thoughtful and contemplative. "I've accepted that you are from another world. I've accepted the impact you've had on the world since your so called *Glitch* but I feel that whatever magic event trapped you here, it had messed with your minds. None of you seem right in the head."

He wasn't wrong. Although it had lessened since the Glitch, the emotions of the PCs were still erratic. Mad was still very mad and sad was still very sad.

Noran: We're in.

I relayed the message to Hau. We stopped at a corner and paused. We acted like we were simply talking but again it was only a feint. Our eyes scanned the streets. We watched as NPCs walked along the streets, living their lives.

Noran: We got the uniforms.
Rake: You're clear. Moving to rendezvous point.

Hau and I turned the corner and started moving once more. We were meeting at a small park only a couple blocks away. We didn't want to be seen together near the barracks but we didn't want to be too far away that we couldn't run back to help in the guidos got in trouble. As we approached the park I came to a halt. Standing before me was the familiar frame of Tallboy. I spun around and saw Matchstick standing behind us.

Rake: Black Bankers: Scatter

"Mr. Rake," Matchstick began. "We never had our discussion from before. It's sad that Ms. Montra isn't here but I will suffice with Captain Airmo Hau."

"I ain't in the talking mood, Agent Smith," I said as my hands lowered to my belt. The Banker's hands did the same to his belt. "So do me a favour and GTFO."

"I worry that I am crossing the line into pushy," Matchstick mocked. "But again, I must insist you both come with me."

"We ain't going with you, savvy?" Hau smirked. He drew his scimitars. "But you are more than welcome to try."

"Then try I will."

Matchstick drew his hand axes and dashed forward. My blades leapt to my hand and I pivoted to my right. Hau met axe with scimitar as the pair began to duel. My steels met Tallboy's familiar longsword.

"Hey honey, how you been?" I said to Tallboy with a mocking wink. I shifted back and let Whaitiri Edge block the next longsteel strike. Splinter's Edge dove in, moving before the attack circle even appeared, but it never reach skin. The blade was a blur as it knocked aside my sword. In our last fight the pair started off slow and then got faster, DBZ style. This time they weren't pulling punches. This time they were going all out. Tallboy's blade moved faster than before. It was a blur of steel and I was trying not to get hit. My tactic in battle had obviously changed. I knew how strong Tallboy was and how fast he could be. Using my stone kick was out and my speed being my advantage was no longer a winning solution. I had to fight carefully, skillfully and smartly if I wanted to survive.

From behind I could see the match-up of Hau Vs. Matchstick. Hau was one of the best dual-blade fencers in all of VCO. He was better than most NPCs and blew past any PC when it came to skill. Yet despite the difference in skill, somehow Matchstick held his own. Was it skill? Was it magic? What made the Black Bankers tougher than anybody?

A battle-cry came from above us. I looked up to see the diving form of Noran crash down on Tallboy. His Ezio style air assassination didn't kill Tallboy, that man was surprisingly tough, but it didn't leave him as a crumpled mess. Matchstick suddenly froze, a stunned effect from a rogue's sap attack, as Anize shimmered into view.

"We gotta jet," she said. She grabbed a round item from her belt and tossed it at the ground. A billow of thick smoke filled the air. By the time it had dissipated the four of us had vanished.

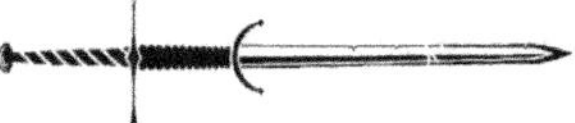

"I warned you," Adelaide said. "They will not stop. You are not the first to attempt such a heist. There have been others. The Black Bankers travelled from one corner of Aspumer to the next, hunting them down. They tore through governments and families and even crossed faction lines in order to bring those responsible to *their* form of justice. Whoever steals from them, they will find."

"We haven't even wronged them - yet - and they won't leave us alone," I said.

"Well it will only get worse when you do."

"How do they keep finding us?" I asked. "They *always* know where we are and when we enter their town."

"It's called the Teller Network," Shuteye said as he entered the room. I glanced at him with a quizzical look. "Bank spies are called Tellers. They are scattered around and they listen to everything and report it all. They have eyes everywhere."

"Can we break it?" Scova asked.

"Ha!" Shuteye shook his head. "I can't even figure out who's in the damned network."

"The Whispers may have a name or two but not enough to break the network," Adelaide said. She walked over to Scova. She leaned down and kissed the mage on the forehead. "You can still walk away, Little Flame."

"You know I can't, Ade."

"I know. My girlfriend could never walk away from such an....endeavour." She kissed the mage again, this time on her lips. "Then I will come with you two. I cannot allow myself to lose both my disciple and the woman I love in one day." Scova and I burst out in smirks. Adelaide looked back and forth in confusion. "What? What did I miss?"

"We were wondering how long until you volunteered to be a part of the entry team."

"We're two nights before. I didn't expect it to take this long. I was beginning to get worr---" Scova's words suddenly stopped. A look of surprise crossed her face. "What did you just say?"

"She said that she's join---"

"Rake, shut the hell up." Scova loudly snapped. She stood up and looked at Adelaide. "What did you say? Did you just say the *woman I love*?"

Anize and Noran entered the room, the pair investigating the sudden yelling. Anize opened her mouth to speak but Shuteye stopped her with a shake of his head.

"Yes, Little Flame," Adelaide said with a nod. "You are the woman I love."

"I...um....since when?" Scova was flustered. I don't think I had ever seen her flustered.

"Does it matter?" Adelaide smiled. "Scova - Ms. Cobie Palimo - I love you."

"I love you too, Lady Adelaide." A tear ran down Scova's cheek. The pair kissed several times. It started tenderly but grew exponentially with each kiss. Anize let out a small coo and held her husband's hand.

Montra entered the warehouse, a new Elf following behind her. She paused and looked at the kissing pair. She looked at the guidos and found them looking all romantic. She rolled her eyes and approached me. She lightly punched my shoulder. "Really? They get sex but I don't? Way to drop the ball on that one, Rake."

"Actually, I didn't. I kept my balls to myself." I laughed. She punched my shoulder again, only this time harder. I rubbed my sore shoulder and tried to move the group away from what was quickly about to become a group watching of two people boinking. "Who's the dude?"

Scova and Adelaide pulled apart from one another. Scova was blushing hard; her skin was red as her armour and hair. Adelaide, however, looked composed. That woman never blushed it seemed.

"This is Locke," she explained. I looked at the Revenant Elf and nodded. "He's our solution to the second hurdle. We have detailed pictures of the people we need to be right?"

"Yeah, right here." I tapped my wiki-journal.

"Well Locke will make us look like them."

"We can't use magic," I reminded her.

"We won't need to. We'll use face makeup and masks," she laughed. "We're going to Ethan Hunt this bitch."

"Okay," Anize said, "but how the hell are we going to do that? We don't exactly have a face-make machine."

"We do now." Montra turned around and pointed to Locke. "Let me introduce you to my RL friend. This is Locke and he was once a finalist in *Face Off*."

"The Nik Cage film?" I asked.

"The makeup show," Noran said excitedly. He paused for a second. "Did you do the one with the VCO character contest?" Locke nodded. "Shit, can you really do this then?"

"I don't have my show tools but I'll make do." Locke didn't speak with many inflections or variances in pitch. He was a very monotoned speaker. He was quiet man who always had an aura of solution about him. Whatever the problem, he could solve it.

"You know this is our most insane idea yet," I said. "What are the chances we can actually make this work?"

"Our chances are better than if we do this with no mask or makeup." Montra pointed the pile of supplies on the back table. "Is that everything I asked for?"

Locke walked over and looked at all the fruits, the paint and the dyes. He moved through the clay and inspected the tools and brushes. He nodded slowly. "I think this will work."

"Okay then...." I didn't know what to do. Maybe Hau was right. Maybe we were insane. "So what do you need us to do?"

I walked through Old Hold until I reached Nicodemus. Two PCs approached me. I nodded at the guards. The first spoke. "He plows early."

"I'm looking for Punchocalypse," I said. "You need to find him and tell him that the Reaper has an offer for him and all of Nicodemus."

Chapter 10

"It feels like there is something for everyone in video games."
– Rich Moore

My face itched and it was hell. I don't know why people bothered to waterboard terrorists when you could just put clay, mold and paint on their faces. After five minutes of wearing it I was spilling all of my guts. I told Locke when the allies would be landing on Normandy Beach and all the details of the Manhattan Project. I am not to be trusted with secrets if there is paint on my face.

Locke was a genius. There is no getting around it. Using the clay he built face masks, using the fruits he created paints and adhesive to stick it to our skin and using the dyes and paint he decorated the mask. It took days but we went from PC to NPC. We looked nothing like our actual selves and more like those we were trying to impersonate. Our face masks and stolen uniforms transformed Adelaide, Scova and I into three members of Vault security.

"These aren't perfect," Locke warned. "With RL equipment, I could make it *perfect*. It would be art. If they spend any real time staring at you they will see through it. Be quick and don't let them stare."

"I owe you big, Locke," Montra said.

"Get me that share you promised and we're good."

I looked away from the window and stared at my team. Each of us stood in various stages of dress. Montra and the Guidos were dressed for battle, armed with the best ar- mour and weapons they could muster. Hau and his goons were dressed in black, ready for a raid. Shuteye was dressed normally. He was our all-seeing eye in the sky.

"We all know what we're about to face," I said calmly. "Any final questions or thoughts before we go?"

Silence.

"All Right, ramblers," I said in my best Tarantino. "Let's get ramblin'."

The reach of the Black Vault was massive. It never ceased to impress, and scare, me with how far they could reach. Why would Casper and Co. build such a horrifying entity into the world of Aspumer? Was the Vault a statement, a horrifying allegory of the financial system? To me it felt like more. It felt like some future evil, some final menace that was to try and tear the two factions apart and for some reason that scared me more than The Crypt Walker. Yet as wide as their net was, it wasn't without weak links.

Shuteye: Seed is planted. Expect incoming.

Shuteye's message came across the /p chat. Every PC member of our party could see it. The team was spread out, some of us in Kimonish while others stayed in Diamondfax, but we could still talk.

I walked the streets of Kimonish, occasionally glancing upwards to the low roofs. From the corner of my eye I could spot Noran and Montra. Azine was nowhere to be seen but that wasn't surprising. That woman was the Queen of the Unseen.

Scova nudged me with her elbow and nodded to the street-corner a few blocks away. I followed her gaze until my eyes fell upon the familiar visage of Matchstick and Tallboy. The Black Bankers, looking menacing as always, were not heading towards us. They were heading towards Noran and Montra.

How did you make sure the Bankers weren't around

when you tried to rob the bank? You provided another target for them. Using the intel Adelaide had provided, Shuteye was able to *leak* a tip that Montra and Noran were in Kimonish. The Bankers climbed to the roof and cornered the monk and rogue.

The hardest thing to do was to watch my friends fight a battle they could not win. Their job was to drag the fight out, to keep the Bankers busy. Every urge in my body wanted to run over and help them, to stop them from needlessly risking their lives but I didn't. I suppressed the urge and kept walking. They were doing their job, I had to do mine.

I took a final look before we turned the corner. Montra was holding back Tallboy while Noran struggled with Matchstick. I looked away. If they got into trouble Anize was there to pull them out but still I couldn't help but worry.

Adelaide silently put her hand on my shoulder. I looked at her - or at least the face that was covering hers - and frowned. She understood. She didn't speak, she simply nodded but I still knew that she understood.

We walked to the Vault door and a guard approached us. His badge said Helmhorn and he carried a clipboard with him. He asked for our names. We quickly gave them. He looked at his file. "I'm not seeing your names on here. You're not scheduled today."

"Looking to get some overtime in," I said quickly.

He glared at me. "Why isn't this in my notes? Is it approved?"

"Of course."

"By who?" Shit. This wasn't Hau's contact. Our access through the front door was gone. What options did we have left? Aside from breaking in, there weren't any. My hand dropped to my belt and slowly moved to my sword.

"Whoa, whoa, whoa," a second voice said. I looked up to see a second guard, named Jigni, approach. He handed the first guard a piece of paper. "You didn't get the updated list."

Helmhorn glanced at the list and eventually nodded. "Sorry. Come on in."

I didn't know what to expect the Vault to look like but I definitely did not expect it to look like a call center. The floor was filled with endless cubicles. It was three partial walls that separated one desk from the next, endlessly replicating as far as the eye could see. There were offices along the walls and second floor balconies that looked over the work floor. I expected something violent and scary, like conniving devils and armed warriors. What I got was the perfect illustration of endless hopelessness and adulthood.

Scova: We're in. Tell the pirate he is a go.

In the case of an attack on the Black Vault, security would take up position across the building with select few being assigned to guard the door to the inner vault. It was the only time people could amass by the inner vault door without raising suspicion. Now that Adelaide, Scova and I were in the building we just had to wait for someone stupid enough to attack the building.

That was where Hau came in.

The pirate rode down from Diamondfax with an army of pirates behind him. Each wore a simple mask to cover their faces. They rode into Kimonish upon midnight steeds with torches in their hands. They razed the village like Vikings, setting fire to the buildings while robbing them of their goods. Then, like a torrent of death and destruction, they turned towards the Black Vault.

The alarm was ear piercingly loud. It echoed through the entire building and every worker leapt to their feet. Security scrambled through the building, running as fast as they could. Adelaide stood tall and started taking charge.

"Security: on me!" They huddled around her, not

questioning her authority. In a crisis, people listened to the loudest person who had a plan. It didn't matter if the plan was good or if the person was the proper rank, people just listened. Adelaide moved through the building, assigning guards to each checkpoint. By the time we reached the inner vault door, there was only the three of us. I glanced back and saw Hau's pirate crew fighting with Vault security. Vault Security was well trained and fought better than most of Havenhold's guards. Scova took our repli-key and inserted it into the door. The building gave a shudder as we turned the key. We looked at each other cautiously. We didn't expect that to happen but we couldn't turn back now. We pulled open the door and stepped into the inner vault.

The inner vault was surprising. The room used some TARDIS-level *bigger on the inside* physics. It dug down into the ground and went on for what seemed like miles. There were several spires, each with hundreds of rows of black boxes on the outside. Each spire reminded me of the computers from *Rogue One*. I was here to find my Death Star plans. I just didn't want to die like --- well everybody. I especially didn't want to die like Alan Tudyk. Forget Sandra B; if anybody knows that space is dangerous it is Mr. Tudyk.

Scova: We're in.

"You know what we're looking for," Scova said, moving from the /p chat to out loud with us. Our mage was taking charge. "Let's get looking."

Each of us took a spire and started climbing down it. We searched the boxes until we found the ones we were looking for. The searching process could have taken hours but luckily the spires were laid out like a library. Whatever these runes were, they seemed to work more efficiently than the Dewey Decimal system.

Adelaide was the first to find a desired lockbox. Scova blinked towards her and started casting her spell. She wasn't rewriting the runes that were already on the box, she was putting a temporary set above it, one that would burn brighter and catch the attention of the transfer spell. It was like when Roadrunner was speeding down the highway. He's suppose to turn left but Wile E. Coyote puts up a detour sign and the bird turns right instead.

    Scova: The first batch is done.
    Shuteye: Hau is retreating. The PCs on his crew are moving to the bank as we speak.

    Hau's pirates were about to open their lockboxes and find new gear in them. They were going to empty it, close their lockboxes and wait for Scova to assign their rune combination to another box. Then they would restart the whole process. I had some concerns about putting our loot into the hands of pirates but there was little choice.

    I looked at Scova. We were making good time. Nothing was going wrong and everything was going according to plan. So, according to our luck, this would be the moment when our plan turned upside down. The building gave a shudder as the inner vault door opened. I glanced back as saw Matchstick and Tallboy enter. I sighed. I *really* hated being right.

    "Keep working!" I snapped my Lucky Dagger to my hand and whipped it at Matchstick's face. The Black Banker dove into a roll, my dagger passing above him, and returned to his feet with both handaxes in his hands. My dagger returned to my hand and I fired it again, this time at Tallboy. He simply knocked the dagger aside with his longsword, Aragorn style. The two made for the nearest spire and started climbing.

    I took a small run and leapt off of my spire, blinking mid-jump and reappeared near Tallboy. I dropped kicked him off of the spire and watched him fall. He crashed into a ledge a few yards down. I glanced upwards at Matchstick. I snapped my Lucky Dagger into my hands and fired it again. This time it dove into Matchstick's leg.

    I climbed atop of a row of lockboxes and watched as

Matchstick did the same. I drew my blade and held them at the ready. My feet were carefully placed, each lockbox giving only 18 inches^2 of sturdy foot space. Each lockbox also had a 12 inch gap between the next. This was far from ideal fencing condition but damn if it didn't look cool.

I didn't activate the speed in my boots, it would be more harm than good, nor could I activate my Feore Shell. Becoming impassible mist was always helpful but being rocketed forward a few feet was very dangerous. Even my blink ring had to be used carefully and sparingly or I could find myself falling down a seemingly bottomless pit.

Matchstick struck quickly, his axe lashing for my gut. Whaitiri Edge deftly blocked the blade as I carefully stepped backwards. My footing was slow and clumsy but I couldn't make a mistake, not here. Splinter's Bite lunged forward, hungrily desiring flesh, but the blade was slapped aside. Back and forth we fought, slashing and parrying. The battle was slower and less flashy then my normal duels but this was proving a benefit for me. I had theorized that no PC could take on a Black Banker, especially in a one-on-one duel. They were coded to not loose. They were meant to strike fear in the players. It was world building: Create an unbeatable foe, tell the PCs very little about them and then watch the rumours and speculations grow. Mysteries would flow, players would try and their reputation would eventually swell. If they were unbeatable in a standard fight, then a clever PC had to even the battlefield. Black Bankers were faster and stronger than us, they were the Agents to our Freed Humans. The only way I stood a chance against Agent Jones and Agent Brown was to find somewhere that their speed and power were useless. Speed was a bane with poor footing and strength was just going to put him off balance more than he already was.

Shuteye: First wave empty.
Scova: Starting on the second.

Scova leapt to another box and began her spell all

over again. Tallboy began to climb towards her but Adelaide wasn't going to allow the Banker to lay a finger on her Scova. The ninja leapt from box to box until she reached the banker. Her ninjatō was fast and her feet were swift. Speed would be my downfall but for Adelaide, for a ninja, she was fine. She'd spent her career learning how to move quickly with very little footing. Give a ninja a tree or a branch and she would transform from a noble Lady to Yu Shu Lien.

The more I attacked Matchstick with my blades the more I was thankful for Adelaide's tutelage. My attack squares were all but useless in this fight. Rogues were acrobatic and mobile and our attacks circles represented that. A rogue combo could place me without footing. I fought to ignore them and relied upon the teachings I had used. Each stab and each thrust pushed Matchstick back. The banker was slower then I expected and I didn't know why until I saw him with a limp. My dagger attack had slowed him down.

I shuffled forward and slashed with both blades, Whaitiri first followed by Splinter's Bite. I expected Matchstick to step back but instead he stepped forward. His axes knocked aside my blades and his daring startled me. For a brief moment I panicked and I slid back. My foot slid off of the box and I fell. I desperately grabbed for a ledge. I snapped my blades into my glove and summoned my dagger. If I dropped my dagger, it would come back. If I dropped my blades, they were potentially gone forever. I hung by the box and frantically tried to pull myself up. Matchstick walked over to me a stared down with a villainous smirk. He kicked at my face but I didn't let go. He kicked again and I heard a sickening crack. I felt blood drip down across my face. Every inch of my body said *let go and protect your face* but I ignored it. He stared down me like Darth Maul. I was Obi-Wan Kenobi and there wasn't a lightsaber in sight that could help me. There was, however, an eye.

I willed the magic into my Eye of Cocijo and activated the lightning. A burst appeared from nowhere and struck the amulet. A ripple of lightning surged outwards and pushed everybody in a small radius backwards. Matchstick stumbled backwards, allowing me the freedom to pull myself back up. I activated the stone in my boots and fired a kick directly into The Banker's body. It was risky, putting myself off balance, but it also could prove invaluable. The kick collided with his chest and sent Matchstick flying off of the spire. He flew across the hole and crashed into a far spire. He climbed to his feet, glared at me.

Scova: Second Wave done.
Shuteye: We're emptying it now.

Matchstick pushed off of the far spire and leapt toward me. His eyes were wide and angry, his body was filled with murderous rage and he let out a blood curdling scream. I arched my arm back, took aim and fired with my Lucky Dagger. The problem with jumping wasn't the danger of not making the leapt; the real problem was that during the jump you were vulnerable. I'm not big on the math but if a man leaping at 10.1 meters per second to the right and a dagger is being thrown at him at 40.2 Meters per Second, how long will he have to react before the dagger ends up between his eyes? The answer: not long enough.

His body slammed against the side of my spire and bounced off. With my dagger in his head, he fell down into the hole, down past the miles of lockboxes and deep into the core of the vault. Two seconds later my Lucky Dagger returned to me; Matchstick did not.

I looked over to see a surprised Scova, a shocked Adelaide and a stunned Tallboy all staring at me. Tallboy was afraid. He disengaged from Adelaide and bolted for the door. He wasn't running; he was getting reinforcements. I panted heavily. Blood dripped down from my nose and onto my lips. I could taste it and I was not thrilled at that fact. I spat it out and did my best to wipe the blood away.

Shuteye: Wave Two is emptied. Ready for Final

Wave.

I moved my way towards Scova and Adelaide's spire. The mage was busy at work casting her spell once again. Adelaide came over to me and looked at me. "Your mask is ruined."

"Thanks," I muttered. "You're so caring."

"I worry not if you are okay or not," she said sternly. "You are a Whisper and more importantly you're my apprentice. Neither would have been true if I had to ask something trivial as *are you okay?*"

"I love you too, Mom," I laughed.

"Wave Three is ready," Scova said. She didn't message it this time, she said it out loud. "I'm starting Wave Four."

Wave Four were the lockboxes for the Alts belonging to Scova, Shuteye, Anize, Noran, Montra, Steelion and me. Scova worked quickly. For several moments Adelaide and I waited. We watched as Scova worked and waited for the inevitable building shudder. It came several minutes later. The door opened and Tallboy, followed by three other Blank Bankers and two dozen vault security, charged into the inner vault. I drew both my blades and readied myself. Adelaide stood beside me, her ninjatō held firmly in her hand. Vault security rushed the spires and started climbing towards us. They were like a swarm of evil ninjas. They were the hand and I was Daredevil. It was time to fight like a blind guy.

"Here we go," I said in my best Charles Martinet.

"You PCs talk too much," Adelaide said with a sigh.

"You've never complained about my tongue work before," Scova called out.

"Focus!" We both yelled at her.

Security reached our level. They were armed with swords and axes. We were armed with the high ground, the combat reflexes feat and several attacks of opportunity. I kicked and slashed at any who came close to me. The goal wasn't to kill them, just to stall them. If they got knocked off the edge, then so be it. Fighting security was easy compared to the Bankers. They were slower and weaker. Adelaide's blade was a blur as she cut down one guard and moved to next. She ran alongside the spire walls and seemingly vanished, only to reappear seconds later, behind her target.

Scova: Wave Three is done.

"Good," I yelled as my blades danced. "Get us the hell out of here." I glanced down and saw the four Bankers starting to climb towards us. "Like right fucking now."

It was impossible to teleport *into* the Vault but there were no spells to stop someone from teleporting out. Scova's hands worked quickly as he tapped out a new spells. Second later, a burning portal appeared. "Portal's up; let's jet."

Adelaide was the first through the portal and Scova was next. I was last. I leapt through, action-film style, and emerged on the other side. We were safely back in Havenhold. I sighed in relief, dropped to my knees and did the one thing that felt right at that moment: I violently vomited.

I hate portals.

"We've got a problem," Shuteye yelled as he ran up to us. Montra and the Guidos followed behind him. "Hau isn't at the rendezvous point. He's taken all of the loot."

I shook my head. He was screwing us. I called it. He was screwing us and he was screwing us hard.

I hate pirates

Chapter 11

"Fus-ro-dah!" – Dragonborn (The Elder Scrolls V: Skyrim)

"So what's the plan?" Noran asked. I stood up and pulled the blood stained mask off of my face. Scova and Adelaide did the same. We tossed them aside. "We're not letting him run are we?"

"God no," I snapped.

"How much loot did you get?" Adelaide asked.

"Fourteen chests worth," Shuteye replied quickly. Adelaide did quick calculation in her head.

"He'll need three horse-drawn wagons, minimum." She looked up to the sky as she pondered, her eyes following the dozens of random PCs flying above them. "We cannot allow him to reach the docks. His numbers are small on land but Hau runs these docks."

"So how do we find him?" Montra asked.

Adelaide pointed to the flying mounts. "We fly."

I sailed through the skies above Havenhold atop my Hellforge Kite. My eyes scanned the world below. I scanned for the wagons. Hau was stealing our gear. This was a nearly perfect heist. The last thing I needed was Hau getting away with the loot before we got to him.

Anize: I have eyes on him.

She sent up coordinates and I steered my kite towards

him. Scova wyvern pulled alongside me. In the distance we could see the Anize's gryphon, Noran's magic carpet, Shut-eye's Pegasus and Montra atop a floating cloud.

Montra had a nimbus cloud? No freaking way! I was hella jealous now.

"So what's the plan?" Anize asked. She looked at me but I was no longer there. "Where the hell did Rake go?"

I'd leapt off my kite. I dove for the wagons. With a loud thud, and a pain across my entire body, I slammed onto the rear wagon. The driver turned around and gave a look of shock as he eyes fell upon me.

"Hi. Are you my Uber?" I yelled. "I ordered a wagon under the name Rake? Maybe Rake the Great?"

Each wagon had three pirates plus the driver. The three pirates scrambled towards me. I moved forward to greet them, drawing my blade as I did.

"Wait, wait, wait," I begged. The three pirates froze for a moment. "How cool is this? We're fighting atop a wag-on. How Clint is this?"

The pirates attacked. Whaitiri Edge snapped to life as it intercepted the flurry of blades. Assisted by Splinter's Bite, my steel knocked aside the pirate's attacks. I kicked one pirate off of the wagon and ran my steel through a second. The third suddenly froze as a hidden Anize came into view behind it. We both looked at the driver. He didn't say anything. He just released the reins and dove off the side.

"You drive," I ordered. "I'm going after the second wagon."

I activated my ring and blinked atop the second wag-on. A loud thud shook the wagon as my trusty samurai stood beside me. Shuteye drew his katana and lunged. He slashed quickly. Pillars of fire exploded in the street ahead of us. I glanced up and saw Scova casting from above. Her fiery blast would be seen by everybody. It was not going to go unnoticed by the judicators, guards and the Sheriff Department.

Just like I wanted.

As Shuteye finished the four pirates on the second

cart, I glanced up at the lead wagon. Hau stop atop of it, smirking at me. His blades weren't drawn, instead he held only a single pistol leveled at me.

Fuck.

Guns were introduced in VCO's second expansion *The Hellforge Assembly*. They were primitive firearms. The new addition never really took off popularity wise and because of such they were never expanded on afterwards. This meant that any gun in VCO was weak, four expansions ago weak. They were not something you had to worry about.

That was Pre-Glitch.

Post-Glitch a gun was a whole new threat. They hurt, they were deadly and they were a dick move. Hau shifted his aim and fired at Shuteye. The samurai never saw it coming. The bullet slammed into his shoulder and pitched him off the side. Shuteye crashed onto the street. The wagons sped away.

"What the hell?" I spat. "Where is the honour amongst thieves?"

"The Coalition of the Damned is at war with one another. Their desire for quality steel is sky high," Hau laughed. "I'm just the pirate who will sell them the weapons they so desire and make more gold then I ever humanly thought possible."

"You money grubbing......"

"Pirate?" Hau offered. He smirked and suddenly took the air. With a powerful leap, Hau departed the lead wagon and descended upon the middle one. I dove for the reins. The horses were running on pure instinct and fear. How they hadn't crashed yet was beyond me.

Hau kicked me from behind. I fell forward and landed between the two horses. With each hand I held onto a different horse and stared at the street rapidly moving beneath me, only inches from my face. I pulled myself up and glanced behind me. Hau had both of his scimitars our and he was beckoning me to fight.

"I am curious, Reaper," he taunted. "Why does your kind fear you so?"

I climbed back to the wagon and attacked. Splinter's Bite lunged forward but was slapped aside by pirate steel. My blades danced, lunging and slashing, striking at flesh and feeding on life but my steel had little effect. Hau's speed wasn't greater than mine but his skill was. He knew where I would strike before I did. His scimitars were always right where they needed to be to deflect or block my attacks. They few that snuck past did so barely and with little real damage.

A thud rocked the wagon and a foot lashed at Hau's skull. The pirate dodged the kick and pivoted, gracefully moving atop the wagon. He stared at the monk that had decided to join the fray.

"Need a hand?" Montra asked. "You look like you need a hand."

"I'm going easy on him," I defended. I smirked at Montra. "You know, now that the job is over...."

Montra laughed and shot forward. Her fist lashed out as my blades swiftly struck but neither did damage. Hau's scimitars seemed to move independently of each other. Hau's left blade twisted and spun as his deflected and parried attacks from both of my steel while his right blade assaulted and blocked Montra's melee onslaught. We were attacking with everything we had and Hau was barely breaking a sweat. At the moment I realized a very important fact.

Captain Airmo Hau was Drizzt AF.

The wagon ran over a loose stone and the entire wagon violently rocked. Hau took that moment of confusion and attacked. His right blade cut across Montra' right arm as his foot kicked her hard. She pitched backward and bounced off the cart. Hau pivoted towards me and quickly lashed with his blades. One scimitar slashed at my wrist as the other dove into my gut. I froze as steel pierced my flesh and dropped to my knees. It was possible, so I had read, to stab someone in a manner that didn't hurt. Hau didn't know that method or if he did, he chose not to use it.

Hau kicked my blades off of the wagon and smirked at me. "I have faced the Reaper and have been left wanting.

Your kind is pathetic." He grabbed my chest and hung me off of the edge of the wagon, my face mere inches from the fast-moving wagon wheel. "Any last words before I end your life?"

"Something does comes to mind," I spat. "Mighty Strike!"

Mighty Strike was powerful melee hit that I got twice a day from the Meging Cord. It was a dumb warrior move that had little benefit for a rogue but I had found a use. I snapped my finger and summoned my Lucky Dagger. The weapon glowed as my belt's magic flowed through it. I stabbed at wheel. With the power of the belt, the wheel instantly broke and sent wooden splinters flying in every direction. The wagon slammed down on its axel and the horses suddenly got spooked by the flying debris. The horses sharply turned and the wagon couldn't keep up. The entire wagon pitched over on its side. The loot went flying, Hau went flying and so did I. I got pitched at a wall but seconds before I hit it, I activated my Feore Shell. Hitting the wall at this speed was deadly on its own, hitting a wall at this speed while chests full of loot flew alongside me was just asking to have my already diminishing luck tested. My body became impassible and I rocketed forward several feet. I reassembled on the other side of the wall. I was in incredible pain but I was still alive.

I scrambled to my feet and limped around the wall. I saw the first wagon ride off towards the docks and the third wagon, somehow driven by Hau, following behind it. The pirate spotted me in the distance and nodded. Captain Hau rode away, laughing as he gave us the finger.

I hate that guy.

Yet despite the pain, the stabbings and the betrayal, I couldn't be happier.

Chapter 12

"Video games are a huge, incredibly popular, world-transforming medium." - Austin Grossman

"Stop your lying," Matchstick yelled at me. "We know you broke into the vault."

I sat in a judicator interrogation room alongside Montra, Scova, Anize, Noran and Shuteye. On the other side of the room were Bearcules, Footkneebra, several Royal Judicators as well as Adelaide, Tallboy and Matchstick. After our beats in the streets, with Lady Scova on fireballs, Five-0 came running. They scooped us up, threw us in a cell and had spent the last two days grilling us. When the arrest came Adelaide was nowhere to be seen but this was planned. She resurfaced hours later, dressed as a full noble woman and spoke in our defense.

"They have said many times," Adelaide yelled, "they had nothing to do with this robbery."

"They broke in, we know this," Matchstick yelled.

"Really? I have not heard of one report of any of these six individuals stepping foot in your vault. No one has reported seeing them in your vault." Adelaide shook her head. "Someone broke into your vault but it was not these six. We'd have told you who it was."

"You lying bit--"

"I am a noble woman," Adelaide firmly reminded. Her voice was firm, strong and commanding and I swore I could hear Scova getting wet at the sound of it. "You will watch what you say to me or I will have the insolent tongue cut from your commoner mouth. Do you understand me?"

"Yes, M'Lady." When dealing with Lady Adelaide, Mistress of the Whispers, it was easy to forget that she was also a woman of noble birth but as she spoke and took charge, it was quickly coming back to me. "I simply question, M'Lady, their reason for their appearances with the Pirate Captain, Airmo Hau."

"Sheriff Bearcules," Adelaide asked. "What is Rake's role within the Enclave?"

"He is the Reaper," Bearcules reluctantly said. "The Reaper is combination of a spymaster and a champion. He defends our kind when needed."

"Would investigating the potential theft of Enclave supplies and then attempting to protect and retrieve them fall under the duties of a spymaster and a champion?"

Bearcules reluctantly nodded.

"But he did neither," Matchstick said. "The theft still happened."

I silently stared at Matchstick. It was weird looking at a man that I had killed not two days ago. I was curious to know what he'd remembered since his respawning but now *really* didn't seem like the time to ask.

"Rake and his crew retrieved a third of the stolen goods," Adelaide added. "I will not allow him to be punished for not completing his job. Failure is not a criminal action. If it were, we would be looking at you for failing to stop the theft from your vault."

Scova leaned towards me and whispered. "I'm going to jump her bones so hard when I get out of here."
I elbowed her.

"The Black Bankers will not stop until we have caught who is responsible."

"We have told you who is responsible: Airmo Hau. Then I suggested you pursue him and not," she pointed to me then Scova, "my batman and my mate."

I'm Batman!

Matchstick stood silently a moment before turning and storming out of the room. Bearcules stepped forward. He glanced at Shuteye for a moment before turning towards me. He placed a small box on the table. It was a portable bank. They were rare.

"Open it," Bearcules said sternly. I shrugged and placed my hand upon the box. The portable bank glowed as the magic read the rune combination that was coded to my body and searched for the accompanying lockbox deep within the vault. None of the six had had a chance to open our lockboxes since our heist. We were arrested almost immediately. This would be my first time accessing and opening my lockbox. A loud clicking sound filled the room and it opened the portable bank. Bearcules looked inside. He inspected each item and found only Rake's gear. There wasn't Steelion's gear or Stov's gear. There was only Rake's stuff.

"What the hell?" he muttered. "Where is Stov's gear? Shuteye told me what you were doing? Where is it?"

"My batman has said this over and over, Sheriff," Adelaide defended. "They did not rob the Vault."

Bearcules closed the bank and pushed it before Scova. One by one he made each of us open our banks and one by one he found no gear aside from that of our characters. Scova only had Scova's, Anize only had Anize's and Montra only had Montra's. He glared at me when it was all over.

"I was getting close so you gave me an inside man," Bearcules deduced. "If I had an inside man proving my theory, then I would stop investigating and prepare for the arrest. You played me."

"That's impossible," I spoke. "Because assuming what you said was true, Deputy Ddaaxx would have warned you against that." Bearcules glared at me, anger and embarrassment crossing his face. I shrugged. "That kid always seems to know what he's talking about."

"Next time...."

"Next time what?" I challenged. "I'm an innocent man, what are you going to do? Are you going to try and kill me, again?"

Bearcules stormed out of the room. Footkneebra gave

me a look. She shook her head and followed her boss. Adelaide looked at the judicators and crossed her arms. "May they leave now?"

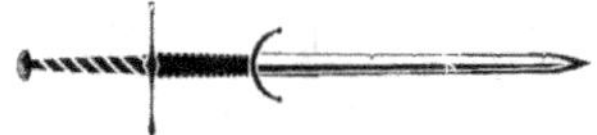

We pushed opened the warehouse door and entered our former headquarters. I walked straight to the booze. I poured seven drinks and handed them out, one by one. We each raised our glasses and, for the first time since the arrest, we smiled.

"I cannot believe that went according to plan," Shuteye laughed.

"When was me getting *stabbed* a part of the plan?" I asked.

"We may have forgotten to tell you about that part," Anize said.

"Of course, the guidos just happen to forget to let me know that I'm getting stabbed," I shook my head and took a sip of booze. "This is the library all over again."

The two guidos stiffened for a moment. They looked away nervously. I smirked. "There were so many places this could have gone wrong. You guys gave it your all and put your lives on the line. You proved who you really are and that you really wanted to make amends. As of right now, considered our history forgiven."

They looked at each other and smiled. It was like a weight had been lifted from their shoulders. I continued talking. "I owe each of you a favour. Just, please, no threesomes. That is still a little weird for me."

We laughed.

The warehouse door opened and six PCs entered. Each was carrying a large chest. They carried it upstairs and placed them on the floor. I looked at the familiar face of Punchocalypse.

"Here is your loot," he said with a grin. I thanked him. "So I'm confused. You guys went through all of that just for your alt's gear?"

I walked to my chest and opened it up. I stared at Stov's gear and gold and a shudder of excitement ran down my back. I dug through until I found a set of bracers, the Raid End Bracer, and I slipped them on. I now had the full set. I just had to figure out how to activate it.

"We needed our gear," Scova began, "but if we robbed the bank, the Black Bankers would never stop hunting us down. We needed a scapegoat."

"That's why you had Captain Hau?"

"I asked for him specifically," I explained. "Then I acted shocked when he showed up."

"So why the big, noisy fight in the streets?" Punchocalypse asked.

"The goal of this all was to have our theft go unnoticed," Scova explained. "We couldn't break into the bank without throwing up flags, so we needed a bigger heist to catch everybody's attention. So we stole more than we needed, knowing that Hau would double-cross us and rob us blind."

"Dirty pirates," Shuteye cursed.

"But if he robbed us without people knowing, then the Black Bankers would never go after him. So we made our wagon-fight big, bright, explosive and noisy. We wanted everybody's attention on Hau," Scova smiled. "We knew we'd get arrested so we couldn't have the gear on us. That's why we sent it to you, Punchocalypse, and the rest of your Nicodemus cult."

Punchocalypse looked at me. I didn't correct Scova. I knew how to keep a secret.

"I guessed Bearcules would search our banks, so when we were putting on a new rune combination on the lockboxes, we used yours instead of ours. That way when Bearcules searched our banks, everything seemed normal."

"That damned Bear druid," Anize laughed. "He almost ruined everything. He got real close, real quickly. We weren't planning on sending Shuteye in as an informant but we had to adapt."

Shuteye held up his glass. "To Bearcules."

We laughed and drank. As the party continued, I brought Punchocalypse outside the room. I hushed my voice as I talked. "What did you do with the seventh box?"

"You mean Steelion's gear?" I nodded. Punchocalypse frowned. "I have it back in Nicodemus, like you asked."

"Good," I took a sip. "Keep it."

"What?"

"You're doing a good thing with Nicodemus, you just need gear and gold," I said. "Use Steelion's bank to gear yourself and the rest of Nicodemus."

"You sure?"

"Steelion and I may have had a rocky end but he was a good guy. If the roles had been reversed, he would have done the same with my gear. Use his loot, protect you and yours and if you need anything else, don't be afraid to holler."

Punchocalypse smiled and offered his hand. I took it and firmly shook.

I took one look at the book and yawned. *Delusionary Illusion: Manifesting Reality through Belief* was a massive book and I was nowhere near in the mood to crack it tonight. I tossed it in the chest. I closed my new chest, locking it with an enchanted padlock and pushed it beneath my bed. I was dead tired, I was sore and I was more than a little drunk. I was not in a reading mood.

"Hello, Rake." I spun around at the sudden voice. I saw Garruil standing in my room. "Did I startle you?"

"WTF, girl?" I said between gasp for air. My chest was beating quickly. I shook my head. "Do you sneak into men's room often?"

"I'm sorry, Mr. Rake," She stepped forward. I narrowed my eyes. Something was different. She was walking in a fashion so unlike her. She didn't seem innocent and she didn't seem timid. She seemed cold. "I needed to talk to you and it was quite urgent."

"What's wrong?"

"Have you started to read *Delusionary Illusion* yet?" she asked. I shook my head. "What do you know of its author Lthena Oakenhide?"

"Nothing yet, why?"

"The Nohorian Brotherhood were answering to a Master," Garruil explained. "This is also the same master that the traitor within the Whisper is answering too."

"Okay that makes sense. Wait, how do you know that?" I asked.

"The truth is they are not obeying a master," she continued, ignoring my question. "They are obeying a mistress. Now this mistress would like to remain hidden until she decides to reveal herself. This is a relatively simple task as she is well hidden. However there is always the chance that someone will discover who she is by stumbling across her research."

"Her research?" I looked at my chest. "You mean that book you were asking about?"

Garruil sighed. "She wrote that long before she started formulating this plan of hers. Such is the irony of history. She complained that nobody read her work and now she trying to make sure nobody ever does."

"Wait, so this mistress, the one who caused the Glitch and manipulated the Brotherhood, is named Lthena Oakenhide?"

"That was her old name. My mistress goes by something different now," Garruil explained. "For the record, she's not responsible for the Glitch, as you call it, but she isn't innocent of it either. It's complicated."

"And that would make you----"

"The traitor within the Whispers," Garruil finished. I bolted towards her, my blade leaping to my hands. My steel lashed out. It would have been a deadly attack if it weren't for the fact that a) she knew I was coming and b) I was drunk.

Garruil hands were their usual blur as she struck. She fired several punches, before grabbing me by the arm and spinning me down to my knees. She drew a dagger and pressed it against my throat. "It's time to die, Mr. Rake." She jammed the dagger deep into my neck. She leaned in and whispered into my ear. "It's time to die in the same manner that Steelion did."

She pulled the dagger free and watched me fall to the ground. She stood over me and watched as I bled out. Darkness overcame me as death took hold. I was dying and Garruil had just killed me. I tried to move, I tried to activate my magical items but nothing worked. I was dying and there was nothing I could do.

No, please. I needed help. I needed someone to save me. I looked to the door. Someone would burst through that door and save me. They always showed up at the last moment. I just had to hold out until the count of five. If I could hold out to five then everything would be okay.

1
2
3
4
Why couldn't you let me get to five?

Epilogue

They stood around his grave. They had never dug a grave for a PC before but this was special. Slashlore looked at the tombstone and read the inscription.

Rake
Friend, Warrior, Hero

"I..." the paladin's voice trailed off. His friend was dead and he didn't know what to say. He looked around at the gathering. Nearly ten dozen had showed up but only a few mattered. Slashlore saw Scova, crying into Adelaide's chest. He saw Punchocalypse and Skith, neither moving nor emoting. He saw the guidos, Bearcules, Footkneebra, Ddaaxx, Montra and Shuteye, just to name a few. He also saw Tialla and Queen Theresa Archona, both crying quietly to themselves.

They were all looking to him, to their president, to say something. But what could he say? What could he say that would be worth the life and achievements of Rake? There were few others within the Enclave who had done what he had. Rake was the Reaper, he was their saviour and he was the only PC to ever slay a Black Banker - although everybody seemed very hush-hush on that achievement. What words could sum up Rake? He couldn't think of any but he had to at least try.

Slashlore stood at the podium and stared at the masses that had joined them for the funeral. The paladin opened his mouth and took in a deep breath. He had to try. He had to say something.

A suddenly cry caught his attention. He looked across the masses and saw nearly everybody, including the grieving and crying, glancing up towards the sky. Slashlore looked up. He stared in confusion until he saw it. Falling, from the grey covered skies, was ash. The Ashen Downpour had begun once more. That meant only one thing and it wasn't good.

The Crypt Walker was returning.

Vörissa's Catalyst
ONLINE
PATCH 1.05
SILENT PROTAGONIST
LARRY GENT

Prologue

Fear was a powerful enemy. It seemed to vanish, it seemed to lessen but fear was never defeated. Fear always found a way to return, bigger and stronger than before. This was a fact she couldn't avoid. Fear ruled her life before, now it *was* her life.

Her name was Ziena, a Fenririan monk. She was hiding in a deep forest, dark and foreboding. It was the type of woods that she'd seen in every horror film, where every tree emanated death and fear. She was terrified. She glanced over at the Orc starting a small fire. He was a warrior named Geist and he was her husband. Geist started a small fire. Ziena looked over at her husband and frowned. "Is the fire a good idea?"

A horrific howl echoed through the forest. Ziena shivered in fear. For days on end they had been running for their lives. They had been fleeing from the horrors that hunted them. They were the prey and they were quickly tiring of it.

"Tyger, tyger, burning bright in the forests of the night. What immortal hand or eye could frame thy fearful symmetry?"

"You're doing poetry now?" She asked.

"It's a poem by William Blake," Geist explained. "It questions how a God that made such beauty can also make such evil and horrors."

"Like *him*?" she asked. Geist nodded. "So why bring

this up now?"

"It seemed relevant," Geist said with a shrug. "The fire may not be the smartest thing but we need it. We need sleep and he isn't the only thing out there. This will keep them away."

"What about *him*?" she asked. "Won't this help him locate us faster?"

"Not if we keep the flame small." Geist took his wife in his arms and pulled her close. Ziena melted. She knew it wasn't very feminist of her but in her husband's arms, his strong Orc arms, she felt safe and she felt protected. She knew he was just as afraid as she was but at that moment he wouldn't show it. He'd get his chance to be afraid and seek comfort from her but right now he had to focus on comforting her.

He smiled at her before kissing her gently on her forehead. "We will be okay, Daisy, I promise."

She smiled at the pet name he had for her. "Thanks, Donald."

Another howl echoed through the woods. Geist's grip tightened as fear ran through them both. Fear was no longer simply a part of their lives, fear was their lives.

Chapter 01

"...." – Gordan Freeman (Half-Life)

I'm dead and spoiler alert: it sucks. Garruil stabbed me through the neck and watched me bleed to death. She stood over me with an evil grin and watched as the last drops of life escape from my body. I had never been that scared, ever. I didn't know what to expect next but of all the possibilities, me waking back up was not one of them. The last thing I remembered was dying in my bedroom. The next thing that happened was me waking up, alone, in some forest. I sat up and instantly my hand went to my neck. Feeling for the wound, I surprisingly found none. There was only a small scar where the wound once was.

What the fuck?

I looked around. I was alone in a forest. Trees echoed endlessly, making a forest that could only be described as creepy AF. The forest looked like the type you would see in a kid's cartoon. Our animated hero would come to a fork in the road. On the left was a bright, sunny path decorated with rainbows and flowers. On the right there was a dark, scary forest with dead trees, black clouds and evil owls.

I hate owls.

To clarify, I don't *really* hate owls, I just hate that their speech isn't skippable when I accidently tell them that I don't understand.

I climbed to my feet and narrowed my eyes. The forest looked odd. The colours weren't vibrant; they were lifeless and dull. The more I stared, the more I realized that it wasn't just the forest, everything looked odd. Everything seemed to exist in a paler hue, as if a faint fog had rolled across the land.

Where the fuck was I?

I ran my hands over my face. It wasn't Devon's; I was still wearing Rake's face. I waved opened my menu. It looked the same except both my map and my clock were gone. The logout button was still missing. I wasn't dead; I was still in VCO, but this didn't look like the game. I've travelled from one side of Aspumer to the other and I had never seen anything like this before. I took a deep breath in. What was going on? What happened? Why wasn't I dead?

I tried to stay calm and reached for the side of my head, touching behind my ear. Every immersion gear had an automatic exit button. If you tapped behind your ear, where your ear met your skull, the gear would instantly - and safely - log you out. Nothing happened. I pressed it again. Nothing happened. I didn't expect it to work - actually I didn't know what to expect - but it was worth a shot.

If I was still in VCO, then I could still talk to my friends. I could message Scova and warn her and Adelaide about Garruil, warning warning them all. Opening my social tab I found every name greyed out. Communication wasn't possible. I sighed; it was another long shot that didn't pay out. It made sense, dead men tell no tales and I was dead. I guess that made me the silent protagonist.

I looked around at the small clearing I'd awoken in. I couldn't stay here. I needed answers and I needed somewhere to rest my head but I wasn't going to find either staying here. I sighed. I needed to get moving,

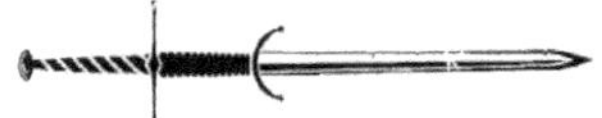

I didn't know where I was going; I simply choose a direction and kept on walking. Seconds turned to minutes, minutes turned to hours and hours somehow turned back into seconds. Without a clock or a sun, I had no way to judge time. I just put one foot in front of the other and kept walking.

The haunting forest was alive with sounds. I heard the menacing screech of bats, the startling clicks of insects and the unsettling cries of owls. I hate owls. But of all the noises, none scared me more than the horrific howls. It was dark and hollow, echoing throughout the ever-still air. The echoes were faint which meant that this howler was far off. I didn't know what could make such a sound but I was in no rush for a face-to-face.

After several hours, or what I assumed to be hours, I found my stomach grumbling. I grabbed a sandwich from my bag and materialized it in my hand, then took a seat by the nearest tree and started to eat. As I silenced the grumbling beast, my mind started to wander. Where was I? VCO lore never spoke much of the underworld. We saw glimpses of it in various instances but they were hell-like dimensions of tortured souls. That was nothing like the realm I found myself in. This world, this Pale Forest, was vastly different. It had stale air that never moved, it had no sun or sky and it felt hollow. Aspumer felt alive. You could walk across the plains and see birds in the sky and field mice dashing through the grass. Here, I saw none of that. The Pale Forest was still.

No, I couldn't focus on *where I was* at the moment. I had no way to solve that right now. The bigger question was *where was I going*? I didn't have any markers and I didn't have any references, I didn't know where I was and I had no clue if I was even heading in the right direction. Were there actual locations in the Pale Forest or was I essentially walking in an endless circle in some digital purgatory? I hoped this wasn't the latter because the only way I was going to survive purgatory would be if I found my Benny. Even a Winchester couldn't survive purgatory without a Benny.

I took my last bite and wiped the crumbs from my hands. Standing up, I looked in the direction I had been heading. What were my choices? Did I keep on walking the path or did I change directions? I looked in various directions but nothing stood out. I sighed once more; I had been doing that a lot since I'd gotten here. If I was in for a penny, then I was in for a pound. I turned back toward the path I began upon and started walking.

The urge for sleep came next. I found my body tiring and my eyes beginning to droop. My strides became smaller and my speed drastically dropped. I was nearly falling asleep upon the very feet that moved me forward. Finding a large tree, I came to a halt. I snapped my Lucky Dagger to my hand and carved my intended direction into its bark. Without any markers or landmarks, it would have been impossible, come slumber's end, to figure out from which direction I had come from and in which direction I was heading towards. My bark carving would point me in the right direction. I sat on the still forest floor, leaned against the tree and allowed sleep to overtake me. I didn't dream, I just slept. The horrifying sounds persisted through my sleep. It didn't make for a restful snooze.

The sky never changed and the world never altered. I had no way to gauge what a day was. So I marked them by my sleeps. I'd begin the *day* by waking up, eating from what few rations I had in my bag and then I would walk until there was no strength left in my legs. Then I found a tree, marked my direction and slept. When I awoke, I began the process all over. I kept track of the *days* by notches I left in my journal. For three *days* the process continued uninterrupted. On the fourth *day* the fog arrived and everything changed.

The fog rolled in from behind. At first all I noticed was a hiss, like water escaping from a radiator, but then the fog rolled in. It was a thick grey fog that hid all from view, save for the trees immediately in front of me. The fog was menacing and unnatural. With each step I took within it, I found myself expecting Pyramid Head to emerge. I moved to the nearest tree and once again I carved my direction into its bark. I didn't want to get turned around in the fog.

The hiss came to an abrupt halt and for a moment the Pale Forest was silent. Then the growls began. They were sharp and close and I could hear the sound of the beast's tongue lashing against its own fangs. I crouched down and tried to hide. The beasts numbered, by my best estimation, at least four and they sounded close. A scraping sound filled the air, like steel was being pulled over dirt and rocks as it was being dragged across the forest floor.

Then it stopped.

The fog dissipated and the still grey of the Pale Forest returned. I looked for my carving but found dozens of other trees now bore claw marks in their bark that hadn't been there before. The creatures were toying with me, stalking me as I walked. They had been close enough to scratch at the very tree I stood by but still they chose not to strike. What were they and why did they toy with me?

On *day* six the fog returned.

Like before, it started with the hiss before the terrifying grey fog covered the trees and land. The low growls and scraping steel filled the air once more. The sounds lasted longer and the beasts got closer but when the fog vanished, so too did the sounds. When my vision returned, the beasts were nowhere to be seen. Their only proof that I was not succumbing to madness were the claws marks that decorated the trees around me.

On *day* eight things changed once more. On *day* eight, the creatures decided to attack.

Chapter 02

"...." – Red, (Pokémon Gold/Silver)

The first attack came in the form of a slash across my back. The creature growled into my ear then tore its four claws down my back. I didn't scream and I didn't cry out but the strength behind the blow sent me flying forward. I crashed into the ground and twitched in agony. The pain was unbearable. I rolled over and tried to spot my attacker but it was nowhere to be seen. This fogling was fast, strong and toying with me. I climbed to my feet and drew both of my blades, holding them before me. They were ready to deflect any attacks but there was nothing to defend against. I circled slowly, searching for my attacker but I saw nothing.

Another set of claws slashed across my back. I spun around and slashed with Splinter's Bite but my steel hit nothing as it passed through the fog. A low growl filled my ears and a third set of claws slashed my back. I dropped to one knee, overcome by the pain. My body wanted to give up and die but I chose to ignore it. I dove forward and rolled away, pulling myself to my feet and snapped my blades around.

For the first time my eyes fell upon the creature. It was a humanoid beast with monstrous fangs, pale decrepit skin and long skeletal limbs with baleful claws. Each of the creature's wrists were bound in shackles. The steel restraints each had a broken chain attached to it, one that dragged behind them as they walked. I had seen these creatures before but not in a long time.

These were Nethall.

I lunged forward and let my blades dance. Splinter's Bite dove forward as my blade tried to feed upon the rotting flesh. The Nethall slapped aside my blade with a vicious swipe but Splinter didn't dance alone. Whaitiri Edge slashed thrice, each swifter than the last but still my steel never connected with Nethall flesh. I never saw the beast move but when my blade struck, they were never there.

I struggled to stay alive for as long as I could. The Nethall's claws were as fast as the creatures were, moving with speeds faster than I could track. Twice more the claws slashed across my skin, yet as the creature prepared for a third, it suddenly stopped and vanished. Moments later the fog vanished with it. I had survived the fog but just barely.

Nethall. They were Nosferatu spawns. They were horrific creatures that were a part of the Vampiric Army. It had been almost fifteen years since I'd laid eyes on the Nosferatu, the Nethall and the Vampires. They hadn't been seen since VCO's beta.

Before VCO's retail launch, Casper's company launched the VCO beta. The beta was used to test server strength and reliability. Betas were common in the video game world but instead of releasing a portion of the main game, they instead released a small stand-alone game. Size wise, it was a sliver of the full-release and took place ten years prior to vanilla VCO.

Lore wise, the game dealt with the Vampiric Armies that roamed across the world. They'd been assaulting the living for nearly a century until the heroes of the beta stormed Aspumer and assaulted the undead armies. The vampiric forces were slaughtered, staked and slain by thousands of orcs and humans.

In game terms, the beta had a level 30 cap, had only two playable races - humans and orcs - and had a limited number of enemy sprites. The creatures were limited to the Vampire Nobles, the thralls, the Nosferatu, the Dhamphir, the Nethalls and the dozens of other minor minions associated with its army. After the beta's conclusion, most of the Vampiric army was never seen from again. Some resurfaced during the *Ashen Downpour*, a few of the Noble Vampires made appearances during quests and instances and the Dhamphir found freedom and joined the Coalition but the Nethalls were never seen from again. Their race was completely wiped out. No player had laid eyes upon the Nethall since the beta. I was not happy to be the one to break that streak.

The next *day* the fog returned, as did the Nethall. They attacked like before, striking from the fog. Their claws would tear into my back or sides and dig into my skin. My body would spin and my blades would clumsily dance as they tried to deflect the attacks but never once did they deflect the attacks. Never once did my steel feast on the rotting flesh. I started to panic and activated my Feore Shell. My body became an impassable mist. I should have shot forward two feet but instead my mist-body merged with the fog. The fog tried to disperse my body throughout the fog. Pain unlike anything I had ever felt tore through every inch of me as my body was literally being torn apart. I tried to focus my thoughts, to keep myself together, but the pain assaulted my concentration. I tried to ignore the pain and willed my body together. My form reassembled and I dropped to the ground, whole once more. The pain still remained but I was left with one undeniable thought.

I was *never* trying that again.

On *day* fourteen things changed once more. In the distance I spotted a light. For two weeks I had seen nothing but trees, forest, fog and the Nethall. It was like an endless echo. This light, however, was a speck of hope. I hated to admit it, even to myself, but the Infinite Forest had robbed me of hope. The blue ring had long since left me but with the sight of light, it returned.

All will be well.

Ever the Paranoid Peter, I crept towards the light. What if this was a trap? What if the creatures that had been toying with me had decided to create a more intricate trap? What if I was dealing with some sort of afterlife Jigsaw? That thought terrified me more than anything.

As I got closer, the fog rolled in and the sound of combat filled the skies. I pushed through the trees and peered at the campfire. There I saw a small circle devoid of fog with a fire at the center and two PC fighting for their lives.

The first was an Orc. He was a large green beast with muscles upon muscles. Wearing a leather kilt and a harness across his chest, he looked like Planet Hulk's version of the incredible Marvel character. He held a greatsword and swung it powerfully.

The second was a Fenririan woman. She was a wolf-woman who stood upright and had fur across her body. From her robes and armour, she was clearly a monk but unlike Montra or Punchocalypse, she didn't fight unarmed. She fought with a quarterstaff. Her weapon spun quickly before snapping outwards like a serpent.

The pair fought against the Nethalls but I didn't leap to their aid. Instead, I watched and waited. I was watching how the Nethall fought. It was a different experience to witness from the outside of the battle and it gave me a whole new perspective. The Nethall seemed to circle-strafe around the PC, using the mist as cover, then they would attack from behind. I waited until the Orc turned his back. Then, just as the Nethall emerged from the mist, I struck. Leaping from my cover, I tackled the beast to the ground. I snapped Splinter's Bite to my hand and stabbed it deep into the creature's shoulder. It screeched and started to flail about. I stabbed Whaitiri Edge into its other shoulder and properly pinned the undead beast to the ground. Screaming, I slammed my first into its face. Over and over, I struck the undead beast. Each punch was for a moment of pain and anxiety they had gifted me. Each punch was payback for all of the torture and suffering that they cast upon me. Each punch was me succumbing to the pure anger and rage that had resided in me. With a final scream, I snapped my Lucky Dagger to my hand and thrust it deep into the creature's skull, ending it for good.

I sat on the creature, my legs still straddling it, as I fought to regain my breath. Moments passed and I did nothing but breathe. With each exhale the rage diminished and with each inhale my calm returned. Eventually all that was left was the calm.

I looked behind me and saw that the Nethall had retreated and the fog had dissipated. All that remained was the campfire, the dead corpse and two frightened PCs, each pointing a weapon in my direction. They were scared of me and, to be honest, I didn't blame them.

"You know this is the first time I've spoken in two whole weeks," I said suddenly with a relieved look on my face. "Not speaking: it's a new experience for me and to be honest, I do not care for it."

Chapter 03

"...." – Chrono, (Chrono Trigger)

"Who the fuck are you?" The Orc asked.

"I'm Rake," I replied. I expected a reaction to my name but I got none. "I'm the Reaper."

No reaction. Every PC in the Descendents knew of me. Then it hit me, they weren't part of the Descendents, they were an Orc and a Fenririan. They belonged to the Coalition of the Damned.

"My main's Stov," I revealed. The Fenririan's eyes went wide in surprise.

"You're the legendary mage? But why are you in a rogue's body?"

"This is my bank-alt."

The pair laughed for five full minutes.

I was growing tired of that reaction.

"Shit," the Orc said suddenly. "If Stov died then what chance do any of us have?"

"I don't know about the PCs up there," she said, pointing to the sky, "but I think our odds just increased down here." She stepped forward and offered her paw. "I'm Ziena and this is my husband Geist."

"Pleasure," I took the paw and fought the urge to say *shake*. "Where are you guys headed?"

"We're heading to what we called west," Geist said. "We've been feeling a draw in that direction. We think there is something there." He pointed in the direction from which I had just come and I died a little inside.

"I hate to say it but there is nothing in that direction. I just came from there."

"And you were heading east?" I nodded. "Shit."

"Well fuck your instincts," Ziena laughed at Geist. "So now what?"

"Well if *west* and *east* are out. That leaves only *north* and *south*," I began. "The only issue is which one do we choose."

"We ask Professor Batty," Geist said proudly. Ziena groaned loudly as she shook her head.

"Who is that?" I asked, eyeing both of them.

"He is the charlatan who created Flipism." I blinked in confusion. Geist continued to explain. "Flipism says that all decisions should be made with a literal flip of the coin."

"And this is a scientific belief?" I asked.

"No, it's from a fucking Disney comic book," Ziena snapped. "My husband has a thing for those silly comic books."

"Like *X-Men* and the *Avengers*?" I asked.

"I wish. Those comics are at least cool," Ziena said. "My husband prefers the likes of Disney Comics and Harvey Comics. He chooses comics like *Casper the Friendly Ghost, Wendy the Good Little Witch, Ritchie Rich, Mickey Mouse* and *Donald Duck*. My husband is obsessed with them."

"I like what I like. Don't geek-shame me," Geist defended. He looked back at me. "Flipism was an idea created by Carl Banks in June of 1952. It was a philosophy introduced in a Donald Duck cartoon called *Flip Decisions*. A grifter tells Donald about Flipism and convinces him to spend money on membership into the *Great Society of Flippists*."

"And things go well for Donald?"

"Not at all; hilarity ensues and Donald's day sucks ass."

"Then why the hell would we use Flipism as our decision method?" I asked.

"Well, you have any better ideas?" Geist asked. He

pulled out a coin and with a giant smirk on his face he flipped the coin upwards.

The three of us walked north.

"How did you die?" Geist asked. Ziena snapped at her husband but I waved her off.

"I trusted the wrong NPC," I admitted aloud for the first time. "She killed me; put a knife through my neck."

"Shit," Geist whistled.

"What about you guys?"

"We're bodyguards," Ziena admitted. "We were killed protecting our Warchief from an assassination."

"And that needs an explanation," I laughed.

"After the Glitch, we all realized that we were not going to survive on our own. We had to unite and fight as one," Ziena began. "The only problem was that nobody could agree on who should lead. This started a civil war of sorts between the Coalition PCs.

"The most powerful and popular choices for leaders came from the largest guilds or gangs but there were dozens trying to be warchief. One by one, each was crushed, swallowed or forced to withdraw by the bigger candidates. Before we died there were only four that remained. We were following a woman named Idracab. She was an Orc woman who knew what she was talking about. She was strong, smart and she knew war, like really knew it. The woman had a lot of support."

"The only problem was that she was a woman," Geist said. "Some even called her *Warchief Make me a Sandwich*. We believed in her so much that we even became her bodyguards. We were hella good at it as well."

"We died protecting her when another wannabe Warchief tried to assassinate her." Ziena said. "They sent an Orcish Arcane Assassin called Rozé to take her out. We stopped her but died in the process."

"Our Warchief escaped and that's what matters," Geist said proudly. His face dropped for a moment. "I hope she's still alive, though. It's been weeks since we died. I don't know what's happened since then."

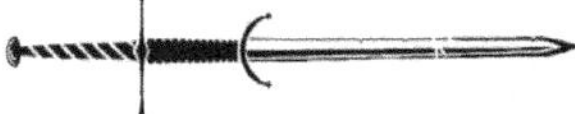

The next *day* the fog returned. It appeared with its usual hiss before the terrifying grey consumed the forest. The Nethall emerged but with three of us it was easier to protect ourselves. Back to back to back we fought. We covered our vulnerable sides and worked as a team. Geist's massive blade swung hard as Ziena's serpent staff struck in threes. My blades danced, knocking aside the claws as I tried to keep them away. The Nethall quickly retreated, realizing that their attack would have no effect, and we bathed in our victory. We knew it wouldn't last but a win's a win.

On the sixteenth *day* they tried again. They summoned the fog and attacked with greater numbers but our defense held firm. At times it wavered and we feared being overrun but in the end they retreated before our defense crumbled. Again we bathed in victory.

On the seventeenth *day* the Nethall returned again. They summoned with them the hissing fog which swallowed the forest save for a small fogless circle with us at the center. It was like the campfire but without the flame. I glanced at my two companions but found them suddenly on the ground, paralyzed with fear.

"What's wrong?" I yelled, my blades working harder to keep me alive. "It's just the Nethall. We've got this."

"This is something different," Geist snapped. "This is worse."

I looked back at Geist and instantly regretted it. A Nethall pounced on me, its long skeletal limbs quickly pinning me to ground. I could see the decrepit skin fall off its body and flake upon me. The Nethall screeched as its fangs dripped with black ichor. I wanted to vomit. I activated my ring and blinked away, landing a few feet away, free of the creature's grip. I stepped in and swung at a surprised Nethall. The creature was trying to figure out where I had vanished to. Splinter's Bite carved through its neck and separated the head from the body. I spun around as two more appeared.

"I need your help," I yelled. "Whatever it is, we'll face it together. We're three now."

"You can't fight against the Fog Lord," Geist yelled back. He held his wife closer. "We tried. He...he...."

Fuck. Fuck. Fuck. I activated the stone in my boots and fired a backwards kick. The boots sent the vamp flying backwards. I quickly switched to the boots' speed and dashed forward. My blades slashed quickly as I felled another. Adelaide's training pivoted me to the next vamp but its baleful claws tore across my side. I dropped to the ground, rolled away and pulled myself back to my feet. I retreated toward a tree and placed my back to the trunk. Glancing at the pair I found that they hadn't moved.

What was the Fog Lord? What was so bad about him that he had broken a max-level warrior and monk? What had broken their spirit so much that it had left them as little more than mush?

An arrow emerged from the fog and slammed into my shoulder. I screamed as the arrow pinned me to the three. What the fuck? I glanced at the arrow and swore again. The arrow - the red-fletched arrow - was distinctive. I raised Whaitiri Edge and quickly deflected a second arrow. I shook my head. It couldn't be, could it?

Splinter's Bite snapped the arrow and I pulled myself off of the projectile (FYI: That hurt like a bitch). I bolted toward the arrow's origin and raised my short steel to deflect a third missile. I blinked forward, expecting to land atop my attacker, but found no one there when I landed. My attacker also had a Blink Ring. I quickly blinked again and attacked with my blades as I landed. My steel connected with the lower limb of the Fog Lord's bow. A boot kicked me back as the Fog Lord spun, twisting his weapon above him. His bow magically changed into a double-bladed sword. The Fog Lord quickly shifted the direction of his spin and struck with one side of his sword and quickly followed with the second. Splinter's Bite parried the first side as Whaitiri Edge blocked the second. The

Fog Lord smirked as he glared at me. My eyes went wide as I stared at the face that I recognized.

"Hello, Rake," he hissed.

"Hizzous?" I asked in disbelief.

Chapter 04

"...." – The Rookie, (Ghostbusters: The Video Game)

I backed away and stared in disbelief. His hair was dishevelled, his skin was pale and his body was sickly and thin but none of those features were as frightening as his eyes. Hizzous' eyes were wide and bloodshot. They were chaotic, mad and constantly convulsing. They were devoid of sanity. He paced with a twitch of his neck and disheartening smirk. He looked like a man who had seen the face of the Old Gods and lost his sanity along the way. He looked like a damn Cthulhu cultist.

"H...how are you still alive?" I stammered.

"Alive? Who is alive?" He cackled. "Life is pain, pain is life and I feel neither pain nor life." He let out a wicked laugh that sent shivers down my spine. He stepped forward and spun his blade. I leapt back, dodging the blade.

"But how? I...I..." I still couldn't finish that thought.

"You Rake'd me." He laughed. "You *Steelion*'d me."

"Where are we?"

"Welcome to the land where the dead walk and the creatures of yester-patch now exist. This is a land of the for-gotten and discarded. This is the land of the dead, Rake. Wel-come to hell."

It was impossible. VCO didn't have a land of the dead and it didn't have a hell. It wasn't in the game. When you died in the game you simply blinked back after a respawn period.

"This land is filled with everybody that you've ever

killed or let die," Hizzous said as he backed away. "Be careful where you step, Rake. Your history exists now only to haunt you." With his final words, the fog rolled in. It consumed him completely. Seconds later the fog dissipated and took Hizzous with it.

⸻

"Tell me about the Fog Lord," I began. "I need to know everything."

Geist shook his head. After much prodding, Ziena eventually spoke. She reluctantly told of their first meeting with Hizzous, with the Fog Lord.

"I don't know how long we had been here, in this world, but we had spent endless days fighting the *True Blood* rejects. They were vicious but never deadly. Then one day, the lord came. He wears the fog like a cloak, wields the Nethall like hunting dogs and strikes without being seen like The Boss. Not Big Boss, *The* Boss. He attacks but doesn't kill, what he does is much worse.

"The first time he attacked we thought we could take him. We had fought and beaten every monster here, what was one boss? We were wrong. We were no match for him. He used the vamps to steer us where he wanted us to go then filled us with arrows. After the first fight we both lay on the ground, each of us filled with arrows. We suffered and bled and...." Her words trailed off. Ziena bit her bottom lip as she suffered through the painful memories.

"We healed from his attacks and kept marching," Geist said, picking up from where his mate left off. "Then he'd restart the cycle. He'd send the fog, then he'd send the Nethall and eventually he'd attack. He'd riddle us with arrows and leave us to suffer. After each attack we spend longer and longer lying on the dirt, bleeding and feeling the unbearable pain flowing through our body. This attack, the one you fought, would have been our fourth."

"He's not an NPC," I corrected. "He's a player named Hizzous and I killed him."

"That's a person?" Geist asked in disbelief.

"He was a decent player whose mind broke after the Glitch. He got trolled pretty hard in the beginning and suffered through a lot. Then someone got a hold of him and took his broken mind and molded it into something worse. He's a serial killer now. Went on a rampage and took out a handful of PCs before I ended him."

"And he's only gotten worse since being here," Geist finished.

I shook my head in disbelief. If Hizzous was bad before, how bad had he gotten now?

Two *days* passed before the fog returned. It returned with its trademark hiss and brought with it a new wave of monstrous threats. The Nethall that attacked this time weren't the usual breed; they were new variations with their own challenges. The first were a gaggle of winged beasts the size of a large dog. They looked like a gargoyle with decaying flesh instead of a stone-hide. The second was a gigantic muscle-bound brute that reminded me of Solomon Grundy.

Grundy charged the three of us, roaring loudly as each step shook the ground. Goliath and his crew circled in the air as they swooped down to attack. I dove out of the way of Grundy's charge and rolled to my feet, drawing my blades as I did. Pivoting on the balls of my fee, I slashed with Splinter's Bite. My blade sliced through the gargoyle's flesh. The beast screeched and quickly climbed upwards. Geist attacked with his greatsword. His steel dared not to swing for the flying creatures; his speed was too slow for such a fast moving Nethall. Instead, the Orc swung for Grundy while Ziena backed him up.

Ziena's quarterstaff style was a controller technique. Its primary function wasn't to cause massive damage or to strike with a flurry of swift strikes. Her style was meant to control the battlefield. With a swing of her staff she could push the enemy away, pull them forward or force them left or right. Highly skilled controllers were able to command the battle by forcing when and where an opponent stood. She'd strike; you'd move and think you were safe. Only too late did you realize you were right where she wanted you to be. She'd give herself and her team the greatest advantage by forcing an enemy into poor placement. Ziena had been an early adopter of controller style, using the style and abilities back before it was an official build. She had spent countless hours practising it in 2s and 3s. She was very good at being a controller.

As her staff shot out, she forced Grundy to slow, robbing him of his speed. This opened the beast's side to a powerful swing from Geist. Grundy roared as the greatsword crashed into his side. He tried to stagger back but Ziena wouldn't let him. The wolf-girl sidestepped and struck again. She blocked Grundy's escape and forced him back towards Geist. The Orc was waiting and swung once more. The greatsteel's cut was devastating as large chunks of decrepit flesh fell off the Neth-all.

I ran my blade through another diving gargoyle and watched as Goliath crashed into the ground. I willed the speed in my boots to activate, charged at the next and took a running leap upwards. I twisted mid-air and pointed my body downwards. Turning my blades cut through Brooklyn's neck. I dove downward and slammed into Lexington, bringing him down with me. We both crashed into the ground. I snapped my dagger to my hand and stabbed through the stunned beast's next. Rolling to my feet, I glanced upwards. Hudson was circling in the air and preparing for a dive. I flipped to my feet and fired the dagger towards him but the creature turned way. The dagger instantly rematerialized in my hand. I fired again, this time taking greater time to aim, but once again Hudson dodged. The gargoyle was fast. Hudson tilted his wings and dove for me. I didn't move or try to dodge, I simply waited. This was going to require perfect timing. At the last possible second, mere inches away from him striking me, I blinked away. Hudson titled his wings and skimmed across the ground, inches away from the dirt, before tilting his wing again in an attempt to pull himself back up into the air. That's when Hudson saw me. I was in the air, falling from my blink, when our paths crossed. I knew when Hudson was high in the air he had full manoeuvrability but on a high-speed upward climb, he was little more than a floating brick. I fired the dagger down at him and watched as it tore through the undead beast's face and emerged out the other side. Hudson was dead. Sorry Disney, but *Gargoyles* had just been cancelled. With the air support down the fog began to dissipate, taking Grundy with it as he vanished. We were left there, three exhausted and injured warriors, wondering how many more fights like this we could endure.

Days upon *days* passed with nothing but endless walking and sporadic attacks. The three of us spoke very little. I wondered if my connection to the Fog Lord frightened them. We ate from whatever food we had in our packs at the time of death but our reserves were running low. Was this what happened to every PC that dies? Were they transported here, to this grey abyssal wasteland, where they starved? What happened next? What happened to the dead when they starved to death? Were they freed from the game or did they fall deeper?

I'd lost count of the days when the routine changed. In the distance I saw a light. It was different from the light that emanated from Zienna and Geist's campfire. This was a pillar of light continually pouring down from the sky and crashing in one spot. It was like the alien laser from *Independence Day* that destroyed the White House. Next we heard a blood curdling shriek that filled the air. It wasn't an attack shriek; it was a cry of terror.

"Incoming!" Geist yelled as he drew his blade and steadied his stance. Ziena pointed with her fur-covered paw. Dozens of Nethalls were running at them. "Oh fuck! We've gotta get out of here."

"And go where?" Zienna said as she drew her staff. "If this is it, then we go down fighting."

"If this be our end then I'm glad it's beside you, Babs."

"I don't regret anything, John." Zienna said with a smile. She scrunched up her face. "I mean the dog-girl thing made our virtual sex more *furry* then I expected."

"It's okay. Furry is my secret fetish," Geist joked.

"I'm suddenly glad that you're about to die," Zienna jested.

As weird as their goodbye was, I was jealous. I wasn't jealous of the furry sex (to each their own but STIs are bad enough without adding fleas into the mix) but I was jealous of having someone there in the last moments.

Tialla.

I drew my blades and stood beside them. Now was the moment of our death and I was not about to simply let it happen. Geist glanced to his wife. "For the Damned?" She nodded in reply.

"For the Damned!" both yelled.

"Greatness is Eternal!" I responded. We charged the stampeding horde. Zienna let out a wolf howl, Geist let out a roar and I quoted the wisest sidekick and cried out "Not in the Face!"

I reached the stampede first and struck with my blades. Splinter's Bite dove in, searching for flesh but it found none. Whaitiri Edge leapt to block the inevitable Nethall claw but none appeared. I slid to a halt. All around me the Nethall were running but not at me. They were running *past* me. What the *actual* fuck? I glanced at the other two and saw a similar scenario. The undead were avoiding us. I snapped my head towards the light and suddenly it was clear. The Nethall weren't charging at us. They were fleeing from the light.

"The light," I yelled. "We have to make for the light."

"Like hell," Geist yelled back. "If they scared the undead then what the fuck is it going to do to us?"

"You have any other suggestions?" Zienna asked. "Get your coin."

"Fuck my coin."

"We're going," I ordered. I carefully moved through the stampede and pushed my way across the wasteland as I made my way closer. The push felt like hours, even after the Nethall were all gone. The light was summoning great amount of magic and creating shockwaves that kept pushing us back. But we were not going to be stopped. I pushed on until I reached the apex.

The first thing we came across was a druid, she was a woman with glacial coloured hair done in one long braid. She wore green leather armour and carried a long wooden staff. Her face looked liked a human but in reality her face was pale and, while containing all the necessary characteristics, seemed featureless. She silently glanced in my direction. She didn't move; she just eyed me up and down. Eventually she gave me a nod of approval and ushered me forward.

Standing in the eye of a storm of magic and light was a Dwarven shaman. He sat cross-legged on the ground with a hammer and shield carefully placed before him. The shaman was deep in meditation and hovered inches above the ground. Magic swirled around him. The shaman suddenly opened his eyes and stared at me, his gaze digging deep into my soul.

"I have waited a long time for us to meet, Rake," The shaman said as he uncrossed his legs. He lowered the ground and snapped his fingers. His shield and hammer vanished, re-appearing in his hands a second later. "My name is Reit."

Chapter 05

"...." – Red Robe, (Journey)

Reit was a dwarf with blonde hair in a flat-top hair style that made him look like Guile from *Street Fighter*. He had a long Dwarven beard that formed three burley strands. He was dressed in epic level gear that was decorated in a motif that looked like lava ripping through the earth. On his chest was a white dog paw print. The gear didn't make me cringe. It was simply the name.

Reit. He was a PC that had messaged me for help but I never answered. Then he went and took his own life and I was to blame. I could have helped him. I could have saved him but I was too wrapped up in my own shit. Hizzous had warned me that this land was filled with those I let die.

Your history exists now only to haunt you.

"I...I..." Should I strike first? Should I try to talk my way out of it? The thoughts ran through my head. I drew my blades and held them aloft.

"I honestly didn't expect it to take this long," Reit said with a laugh. He attached his shield to his back and hung his hammer on his belt. He walked over and offered me a hand. I carefully sheathed my blades and reluctantly took it. We shook. "I also didn't expect it to be here."

"I...um...what?" I sounded like I owned a mall in *South Park*. This conversation was good but it wasn't cheese and sausage good.

"What are you doing here, anyways?" Reit asked. "I

mean, you're dead - duh. But how did Reaper die?"

Geist and Ziena suddenly came into view. Reit looked up and smiled. He waved with a thick Dwarven hand. "You brought friends, good idea. We'll need them for my plan."

"Stop, I'm confused. What the hell is going on?" I snapped. "What plan are you talking about?"

"Yo, Rake," Geist said carefully. "Who's the girl we just passed and who's this guy?"

"The druid's name is Scáthach and I'm Reit but you'd probably know me better as my real name," the shaman introduced. "I'm Casper Ramirez."

"Casper?" I asked, not even trying to hide my shock. "As in that Casper? Creator of VCO Casper?"

"Hi!" Reit kept waving his Dwarven hand, endlessly waving it as he watched us three stare in shock. "Are we past the introduction stage yet 'cause my hand is getting tired."

"You can't be Casper Ramierez," Ziena said. "Casper has two alts: Brucallas the Orc warrior and Valiarr the human paladin. How do we know you're not just some guy *saying* he's Casper Ramirez?"

"The name," Geist suddenly interjected. Ziena and I turned to look at him. Geist bounced on the balls of his feet like the excited kid on Youtube who just got a N64. "Oh my god, you are him. You are *the* Casper Ramirez."

"I know," Reit said with a smile. "I have the same reaction every morning."

"Care to bring the rest of the class up to speed?" I asked.

"It's all in the name. It's a brilliant riddle." Geist let a shiver run down his back. He looked at the two of us. "*Casper the Friendly Ghost* was created in 1939. Does anybody know by who?" We all gave him blank stares. I literally had no fucking clue about a ghost comic from the 40s. "It was created by Joe Oriolo and Seymour Reit."

Shit. I couldn't help but smile. Casper loved his riddles and he was hiding in one. Casper was hiding in a Casper Cache. Then it hit me. I was standing in front of the creator.

Casper was the god of VCO. He created the game to which I have given my life. He created the world in which I lived. I opened my mouth to speak but nothing came out. What did a person say when he came face to face with his creator?

I decided to punch him.

"What the fuck did you do to us?" I yelled. "Why did you trap us here?"

"This isn't my fault," Reit said as he climbed to his feet. He spat out a mouthful of blood. Gone was his jovial tone. A more serious one stood in its place. "I'm trying to figure out what the hell is going on just as much as you are. I'm trying to get us home."

"Then why are you here? Why did you commit suicide?" I snapped. Ziena and Geist stared at me in shock. "Reit tried to contact me and I ignored him. Then he killed himself." I trailed off.

"Why?" Geist asked.

"Because I needed to get here," Reit stressed. He shook his head as he carefully chose his words. "I want us all to get back to RL but we have to survive in order to do that. People who end up *here* are not surviving. I needed to save these people."

"What exactly is this place?" Ziena asked. "Are we even still in the game?"

"We are still in VCO. This is just the Grey Land; the land of the dead," Reit said. He looked around and sighed. "The problem is that I never put this into VCO and I have no clue who did."

I sat by the campfire as everybody around me was asleep. Scáthach slept like a cowboy, leaned up against a tree sleeping in an upright position with one eye open. Geist and Ziena lay side-by-side, cuddling as they slept. Reit sat beside me. Technically he wasn't asleep, he was meditating, but the outcome was still the same: it left me alone with my thoughts. I stared at the crackling fire as my mind raced. I was trapped in the world of the dead and I couldn't get out. But if I was being honest with myself, that wasn't what weighed heavily on me. I was used to having the odds against me. The more I watched the couple sleep the more I hated the fact that I was alone. Geist had Ziena, Adelaide had Scova and Tialla had her husband. I was alone. I sighed. Why does everything always feel worse at night?

"I have been watching you for a while now." I jumped in my seat and snapped my head around. Reit sat down beside me. He smiled that goofy smile of his. "I keep my eye on dozens of different players but you, Stov, has always been one of my favs. People love my Caches and you have unlocked some of the best ones. It's a shame you sell them off.

"I watched your raid the day your first activated the *Jötnar Set* and I got a notification the moment you ninja'd the Whaitiri Edge. I was excited to see what you'd do with it. It's a shame that now I never will."

"I completed the set," I replied, "but I haven't figured out what it does yet." Reit flashed me an eager smile. I looked at him expectantly but he revealed nothing. I rolled my eyes. "Tell me about the Grey Land. The lore junkie in me *needs* to know."

"The Grey Land is the space between the living and the dead. It is the infinite veil, the final challenge for those seeking the afterlife." He frowned as he poked the fire with a stick. "This was a new area I had built a couple years ago. It was going to be part of a storyline I was writing. It was going to be about the archons but I never went through with it. I scraped the patch because it wasn't....fun. I needed something better if players were going to die.

"Like any good writer or artist, I never deleted my work. I just stored it on one of our servers. Someone took my work and secretly installed it on the last patch, the Glitch Patch."

"Somebody is changing your world without you knowing it?"

"Sadly, yes," Reit admitted. "To be honest, it's not

the first time. There have been anomalies since the beginning. Things change and new assets appear. Someone is messing with my world and I don't know why."

"So why come here?" I asked. "How did you know there actually was a here?"

"I've been studying the world since the Glitch," Reit explained. "I've been studying the flows of magic and listening to the spirits. They speak of the new areas; the realm of light, the realm of death, the realm of nature, the realm of healing and the realm of fire. Each of these were places that I wrote but never implemented. Now they all exist within my game."

"The spirits talk to you?" Shamans were weird casters. They drew some of their magic from nature and the rest came from the spirits. Lore said they were powerful creatures long since passed that now gifted those with their strength, wisdom and magic. "Like as in for real?"

"It started shortly after the Glitch. Voices started to speak to me. I thought I was losing my mind." Reit said with a chuckle. "The loudest spirits were from here. I came here to figure out why and to free people.

"I've been using my magic pillar to fend off the Nethalls and to attract other players. It's how I found Scáthach." Reit pointed to the sleeping druid. "I met her a while ago. She's a changeling druid. I found her and she saved me. Now we work together."

Changelings were a Coalition race. They could change their appearance to partially mimic one of the other races. In their natural state, they were grey featureless humanoids. When they took the appearance of another, most looked like an unpolished copy. It was like when a Ditto took the form of any other Pokémon in the anime. There were some Changeling PCs that specialized in their disguise. Their imitations were practically flawless. Two years ago, in a 3v3 PVP tournament, a team call *Release the Hounds* added a Changeling rogue into their roster. During combat she would disguise herself as one of the opposing team and then attack, catching them off-guard. Release the Hounds made it to the semi-finals before losing to an opposing team's Hail Mary AOE spell.

"She doesn't speak much but she's a strong healer and a great partner," Reit said. The two of us stayed silent. "There is a way out of this realm but you won't like it. We will have to travel through the *Under Way* but from the *other* side."

Day came and the five of us packed up and kept moving. With Reit in the lead we knew the proper directions. Sadly, we had been *slightly* off in our choice of direction. With the correct path before us, we crossed the Grey Lands.

With a hiss the fog appeared and with it the Nethall emerged. No longer restrained, the undead attacked without hesitation. Their baleful claws tore at our flesh as gargoyles circled above. I drew both my blades and used my steel to deflect the attacks. Whaitiri Edge danced before me as its magical steel protected me while Splinter's Bite looked for a place to strike. Beside me the couple defended each other. Ziena used her staff to move the foe as Geist sliced them in two. Magic danced across our skin as Scáthach's spells kept us healed. While we dealt with the forces on the ground, Reit directed his attention to the sky. The shaman called forth the power of nature and molded it into his weapons. A bolt of lightning, a burst of fire and ball of bubbling lava; each was used to rip a gargoyle from the sky and send it plummeting towards the earth.

The ground suddenly quaked as a large creature took a massive stomp. The five of us looked over and spotted a bulbous giant stomping towards us. The creature stood ten feet tall, had an enormous gut and a chest that was covered with chain, each held together with a series of thick locks. Attached to its wrist was a large steel shackle with an eight foot chain that dragged behind it. It had glacial blue skin, hollow eyes and a roar that seemed too echoed endlessly. I stared in awe. I had absolutely no clue what this was. I had been from one end of VCO to the other and back and I had blasted each and every monster the game had with an ice spell or two but this, this was something new.

"W-T-F?" I called out.

"Paenido ," Reit muttered. "It just *had* to be the damn paenido."

"Care to share with the kids in the back?" Geist asked.

Reit held his shield aloft and tightly gripped his hammer. He frowned as he eyed the beast with a cautious gaze. "When I built this land for an expansion, I created the paenido. They were an undead creature that, in lore, would feast upon the wayward souls lost in the Grey Lands and add the consumed to their strength. In game terms, they would have replicated the PC's powers."

"Are you shitting me?" Ziena asked.

"If you die in Aspumer, you come here," Reit continued. "From here one of three things happens. 1) you starve to death, 2) you're slain by one monster or another or 3) you get consumed by these things."

I glanced at the beast and shuddered. I was not in the mood to be eaten.

The paenido shifted its leg and dragged the chain across the dirt. The chain was as thick as my arm. Reit steadied himself and each of us followed suit. With both blades before me, I carefully watched the beast move. It was big which meant it was slow and I could easily take out---

With blinding speed the beast snapped the chain across the battlefield. It collided with my side and sent me flying. I was pitched into the air and came down; hard. I skipped across the ground and for a moment I hoped I was dead. The pain was unbearable. Each and every bone in my body was screaming in shock and horror. How unbalanced was a creature that big that also had such speed?

"New rule," I winced. "Don't get hit."

I looked up and saw the paenido charging the remaining four. The ground no longer shook with each step but the brute moved with blinding speed. None of them could survive a charge attack. Scáthach grabbed Reit and pulled him away.

Ziena pole vaulted away as Geist dove to the side. The orc rolled behind the paenido and came up swinging. His great-steel sliced up the back of the beast's leg and caused it to buckle. Reit charged in, his hammer glowing bright red. He slammed the hammer into the beast's good leg and watched as the knee shattered. The beast tumbled forward. Reit swung again, his hammer this time colliding with the beast's skull. A satisfying crack filled the air as the beast crumpled to the ground. Ziena leapt forward and brought her staff down, across the beast's skull, in a powerful downwards strike. The neck snapped and the beast fell still.

"That wasn't so hard," Ziena said, catching her breath. "I mean aside from Rake, none of us got hurt."

"You guy suck," I muttered as I limped towards them. "How am I the only one who got-" An arcane blast slammed into my chest and sent me flying back into the air. Once again I crashed into the ground, hard. My chest burned from the blast. I looked up, confused and in pain, and allowed my eyes to fall upon the beast. The creature once thought dead - or re-dead - was now glowing with jade arcane energy. It climbed to one knee, as magic formed around it's outstretched arm, and let out a ferocious roar. The locks on its body glowed with a similar jade energy.

"Oh fuck," I groaned as I picked myself up one more time. "I fucking hate this place. It sucks. The service sucks, the food sucks and the waiter is hitting on my girl. This place is getting a bad review on Yelp: Zero stars!"

The paenido climbed back to both feet and let out an-other monstrous roar. I stared in wonder as a face began to take form on the surface of the locks; it was an Elven face that I recognized. It was Boomzile.

This land is filled with everybody that you've ever killed or let die.

The paenido must have consumed Boomzile after he died. It took the mage's magic and added it to its own. I cursed. This was bad, this was very bad. Mages did massive damage but were weak as shit. This beast was big, strong and had magic. This was very unfair. These paenido were OP AF.

"So....." I muttered. "Any thoughts, Reit?"

"Let's hit him, really hard," Reit suggested. I rolled my eyes. It was a terrible plan but, to be honest, I didn't have a better one. Flowers began to blossom around me as my wounds began to knit back together. I glanced at Scáthach and gave her a silent nod in thanks.

"Let's hit him," I repeated with a sigh, "really hard."

Reit summoned lava and fired it forth. The flaming ball tore through the sky and collided with beast's chest. The smell of burning flesh filled the air but I gave it no mind. With both blades at the ready and speed in my boots, I bolted forward. The paenido fired a trio of arcane darts in my direction. I dodged one, ducked under another and knocked the third one away with my blade.

Geist ran alongside me, his greatsteel held high and ready. I struck first, my blades diving in swiftly. Each attack sliced away a chunk of undead flesh. I quickly sidestepped and allowed the devastating strike of Geist's steel to come raining down. The paenido swung with its chain. I slid beneath the chain and slashed at its legs. Geist struck again, the greatsteel moving with enormous strength as it horizontally sliced across the beast's chest.

The paenido roared and let a burst of arcane energy explode from its chest. The shockwave pitched Geist and I back and away. It twisted its arm and danced its fingers as it summoned forth another spell. A ball of fire ripped from the paenido's palm and shot forward. It exploded and filled the air around us with billowing flames. The paenido dashed forward, charging through the flames and directly towards me. It slammed its fist into my chest and caused me to instantly double over. I hacked, coughed and I swore as I spat up blood.

The paenido tried to charge for the druid but Ziena didn't let it. Her staff's serpent strikes lashed out, stopping the beast's movements and forcing it back. Each strike did little to no damage but it did place the beast exactly where Reit wanted. Large stones ripped up from the ground and flew towards the undead. Each pummelled the beast with a ferocious amount of damage. A blast of solar energy shot past the group and burned through the paenido's flesh. I glanced at Scáthach. The druid had her staff pointed outwards with a stern look on her face. Solar energy began to circle around her once more as she readied for another attack. She stepped beside Reit, the shaman summoning more lava as he prepared for another spell of his own. Like a coordinated pair, the two fired as one. The beam of solar energy shot forward as the lava spiraled around it like a ripped-off version of the special beam cannon. The dual-spell ripped through the beast's chest and forced it to drop. The jade lock shattered and a glowing blue light evaporated from the body. Boomzile was free.

Not to be forgotten, the beast let out a final roar as it died. The dark necromantic energy that held the beast together released its hold and black electricity filled the air. It dove into Ziena and she screamed in agony. The dark bolt retracted, sucking a hint of her life-force back into its undead body. The paenido climbed back to its feet and began to swing the chain once more. A second bolt dove into Geist. Much like the first, it caused him great agony before retracting. With each victim of the black lighting, the paenido regained a little more strength. A third bolt fired at me. With little in the way of options left, I raised the Whaitiri Edge in defense.

I had dealt with electricity before and I knew what to expect. I would feel a momentary surge in strength and speed only for it to fade and be replaced with unbearable and unspeakable pain. As the bolt touched my blade I braced myself for the agony but it never came. Instead the world began to slow. I blinked in confusion. I could see the paenido's chain swinging toward me but it moved *hella* slow. It looked like trying to play a game on a computer that just couldn't handle it. It moved a single frame at a time. My body seemed to tingle with power. I took a step forward and suddenly found myself several paces forward. What was happening? What was going on? I glanced at Reit and saw a smirk on his face. He seemed eager to see what would happen. It was as if he *knew* what was going to happen, but how?

The Casper Cache.

I had collected the entirety of the Kahail set but I had no clue what it did. Hadn't found a way to activate it but perhaps this electricity had done just that. It made sense. Everything was based around electricity so the thought of a bolt triggering it was not far off. The only question left was what benefit it gave me. I knew only one way to find out. I bolted forward with incredible speed and allowed both blades to strike. Like a dance of death my blades moved, slicing and hacking away at the body with incredible speed. Suddenly the world returned to normal speed but I was still moving like a blur. I ducked beneath the paenido's chain and thrust my blade into its gut. I dodged the arcane blast and cut off its arm. I leapt over its decrepit body and thrust my Edge into the back of its skull. The creature froze and after a brief silent moment, fell to the ground, still once more.

"These paenidos may need some balancing tweaks," I said to Reit. "Either way, I fucking hate them."

Chapter 06

"...." – Chell, (Portal)

I stared at the campfire, the flickering flames were hypnotic. Once again I found myself the only one awake. I was once a mage but now I was a rogue. Both classes required me to think before I leapt. Thinking was my friend but here, alone by the fire, my thoughts were my greatest enemy. They assaulted me.

- Guilt
- Loneliness
- Homesickness
- Burden

I sighed. One after another I had to work through these thoughts. The first was guilt: nope, not dealing with that one. Fuck that, not tonight.

The second was Loneliness. I had friends in VCO. I had Scova and Adelaide. The pair would do anything for me - well not *anything*. Scova was very clear about that. Yet hanging out with those two always left me feeling like the third wheel. So where did that leave me? I didn't want to be alone but I didn't have anyone. Tialla: that path was closed. She was married which meant we could never be. I didn't want that drama damage. Theresa Archona: Did I have a chance with the Witch Queen? I mean she was a Queen but she was just an NPC. I caught myself the moment I thought it. Adelaide was an NPC but I didn't think of her as such. She was a person and so was the Queen. Theresa was a person who somehow remembered Stov. Should I tell her that I was or am Stov? Would she hate me for lying to her? Either way, I needed somebody. I didn't know how long I was going to be stuck in VCO but I couldn't do it alone. Loneliness was deadly.

Homesickness: I did not see that one coming; my life wasn't exciting or bold in the real world but it was mine. As I sat by the fire and stared at the flames I found myself - for the first time in a long time - thinking of home. I missed the real world. I didn't have many friends there and I didn't get along with a lot of my family but I did have my cousin. He was a geek like me but he fell more into music then gaming. He enjoyed a good Zelda and craved a solid FPS but he was never into VCO like I was. He had a toon - a few actually - but he wasn't a lifer like me. He was the one who'd drag me out of the game and into the real world. He dragged me to shows and clubs where he'd DJ. He introduced me to people and even hooked me up with chicks from time to time. I'd complain every time he dragged me out into RL but I missed it now.

Fuck. I really did miss it.

That left the burden. Thousands of people in the Enclave were counting on someone to find a way out and lots of them were looking at me. I was Stov. I was the legendary player. Thousands others were looking to me for protection. I was Reaper. I was their champion. Now all of these people before me were looking for a way out of Hell and back into the living. Each additional load I was forced to carry made the weight more and more unbearable. I sighed. It was too much for one man.

"Do you ever sleep?" I jumped again. I glared at Reit with an ice-cold stare. He flashed me a goofy smile as he sat down. The shaman's meditation was over. "Every night you stare endlessly at that fire. It makes me think that something dark has taken hold of you. I've learned that each person here is afflicted with extreme emotions. If you get mad you get *really* mad. If you get sad you get *really* sad. What emotion weighs on you?"

"I'd rather not...."

"I'm not going to drop this until you tell me."

I sighed. I guess I *was* dealing with this tonight. "Guilt: everyday, in every way possible, I feel guilty. I killed Steelion. I let others die like Boomizle and Santiago. I ignored cries for help from desperate players like Hizzous and...." I trailed off. I ignored Reit's cries for help, time and time again.

"My *suicide* was not your doing," Reit said. "I needed to get here. I needed to find a way to save anybody who is here. I messaged you 'cause I wanted your help."

"I'm tired of helping," I admitted. "I'm tired of being everything for everyone. I can't protect people and I can't save them. I always end up failing. People die and we're still stuck here. Worse still, I trusted the wrong person and had my only lead destroyed."

"Stop being the hero," Reit said. "Just be you. You need to realize that this isn't you talking, it's the guilt. Ever since the Glitch we've all be slaves to our emotions and I finally figured out why." I glanced at him in shock. He smiled. "The *Looking Glass* system that brings us into VCO doesn't allow us to dream. It's impossible to be in REM sleep while in the system. That was the reason the *Looking Glass* was *suppose* to boot you when you fell asleep. Dreams are meant to ground our mind and body and right now none of us are dreaming."

I sat quiet for a moment as I tried to process what I had just heard.

"You said you had a lead," Reit asked. "Care to share?"

"I had a book called *Delusionary Illusion: Manifesting Reality through Belief* by Lthena Oakenhide," I began to explain. "It was given to me by the Witch Queen. I told the wrong person about it and she killed me. Her name was Garruil and she was the traitor in the Whispers. She said that Lthena was the one manipulating the Brotherhood. She also said that Lthena, while not responsible for it, was not innocent of the Glitch. She is my lead as is that book but now I have neither."

"Lthena Oakenhide." Reit repeated the name over and over, searching his memory for it. "I don't know this name."

I pulled out my journal and opened it up. I activated my wiki add-on and watched as the book glowed. I searched the name Oakenhide and found one entry.

Name: Skaroll Oakenhide
Class: Spellblade
History: Skaroll was part of an ancient order of human spell-blessed warriors known as the Spellblades. They possessed the ability to cast spells while clad in mail armour. They were fast and honourable warriors who lived only to serve the Elves. During the great Elven Civil War, the Spellblades fought and were a major cause for the Dusk Elves' loss and their imprisonment in the shadow realm. During that battle, Skaroll was cursed by shadow magic and slain by a Dusk Elf. Unable to cross to the land of the dead, he remained on Aspumer as a ghost.

Skaroll spent centuries as a ghost unable to fight. Instead he strengthened his magic, becoming a powerful source of arcane might and knowledge. As an undead, Skaroll watched over his family. He encouraged them to become strong in the arcane ways and even to adopt those with magical potential. While the spellblades are no more and the name Oakenhide has all but vanished, the teaching of Skaroll still exist. He trains any who come to him and only the worthy and most skilled are rewarded with his knowledge. Fewer still are rewarded with the honour of carrying his surname.

"Why would you make a ghost-mage?" I asked.

"I thought it was cool," Reit laughed.

"But you make him a teacher and not use him as such in the game." Reit remained silent. He just smirked. My eyes went wide. "I could have trained under Oakenhide as Stov? I missed that? God damn it." Reit just laughed.

His face became more serious as he re-read the article. He frowned and shook his head. "If this Lthena has the Oakenhide name then she was definitely special but I never wrote her into VCO." He looked troubled. "I don't know who this character is but I'm going to find out. Skaroll Oakenide isn't the starting point of Lthena's history but it is a jumping point. I will search the lore and the world and the scripts until I find her. I will build a timeline."

With the handle of his hammer he drew in the dirt. He drew three horizontal lines, a couple squiggly lines and several vertical lines.

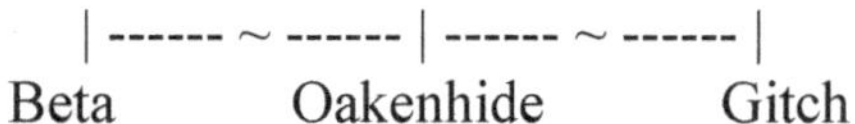

"Everything starts in the beta," Reit explained. "If Lthena's around now and making trouble than it's safe to assume that. Somewhere between the beta and the Glitch this Lthena met Oakenhide and trained with him. We now also know that she is a powerful mage because nobody has the name Oakenhide without being a powerful mage."

"Your timeline is pretty empty," I said sceptically.

"It is for now. The more we learn, the more it will grow and fill. The fuller it gets, the more ammo we have against her." Reit had an eager smile. "I haven't been this eager for a lore hunt in eons." I rolled my eyes but deep down I was also excited. I was on a treasure hunt with my hero.

Morning came but it brought with it no sun. It brought with it only the paler hue that existed across the Grey Land. We tore down camp and walked forward as Reit led the way. I walked with them, examining my equipment as I did. I had completed the *Kahail* set and somehow triggered its special ability. By absorbing lightning I would temporarily become faster and stronger. The Kahail set let me Billy Batson. It was a powerful ability that I had to learn how to use in combat. Was it possible to draw it out at will or did I have to wait until I fought a villain with a lightning attack?

One by one I looked over the set. It all started with Whaitiri Edge. The blade provided amazing defensive abilities with assaulting any attacker with small electrical stings. Next was the Meging Cord. It gave me a Might Strike. The Eye of Cocijo called down a bolt of electricity that acted as a burst attack. That left the Raid End bracers. The bracer's stats had increased when it joined the completed Kahail set. It also had the ability to grant its wearer a regeneration ability. I wasn't opposed to a healing ability but I already had one with my Third Eye headband. The bracers were an upgrade, but what really excited me was trying to see how they worked with my new Batson form. All I had to do was figure out how to activate my new form. I needed to figure out how to go Super Saiyan. Where was a dead Krillen when you needed him?

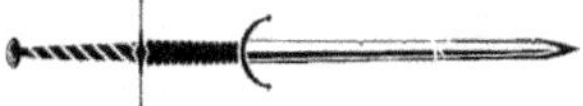

"There," Reit said with a point of his hammer. I followed his gaze across the Grey Lands to a large stone archway in the distance. It looked like a Stargate, half buried with only its top exposed. "That is the Corrax Gate. We can use that to cross from the Grey Lands into the Helruss realm."

"Helruss's realm?" Geist said, shocked and afraid. "You want to take us into the realm of the God of Death?"

"The Crypt Walker launched his initial invasion from those lands," Reit said. "If there is one way back to the land of the living, then it's from there."

"What of the Fog Lord?" Ziena asked.

"He will try and stop us," Reit said. He shook his head. "That boy is damaged....."

Geist glanced at his wife. They stared in silence before nodding. "We have no other option." Reit glanced at Scáthach. The druid didn't speak; she just nodded. That left me. Was I ready to face Hizzous once again? He was faster, he was stronger and he had new abilities. He was the perfect example of a reoccurring baddy.

"Let's do this."

A loud hiss filled the air as a thick fog rolled across the Grey Lands' rolling hills. On the top of the hill stood the Fog Lord as his legion of Nethall pooled around him. From afar I locked my eyes on Hizzous and scowled. He was bad when he had been killing people, he was worse when he was torturing them. Ziena slowly spun her staff as she steadied her breathing. Geist held his greatsteel with one hand and he slapped his chest with the other. With each smack he grunted louder and louder until his cry became a roar. Reit gripped his hammer tightly as he quietly mumbled. Magic swirled around him as he called on one spell after another.

The Fog Lord had sent his numbers towards us and he wasn't holding back. The legion charged forth. It was much like earlier, making our way to the glowing pillar, except this time there was no doubt to where they were going. They moved like a wave of death, bobbing and weaving as they rippled over the hills and down towards us. "Who do we fight for?" Geist yelled. Ziena and Geist cried out in unison. "For the Damned!"

"Why do we strive for greatness?" Reit asked. I smirked and replied in unison. "Greatness is Eternal!"

Like a cascading tsunami, they crashed down upon us. Reit was the first to strike, a rippling torrent of stone jetting up from the ground and impaling any in its path. Scáthach stood in behind, her staff held horizontally in both hands as her lips quickly moved. Magic energy, which glowed with a moonlight essence, swirled around her body as she prepared a spell. Reit shifted his stance and slashed the air with his hammer. A shockwave of lava ripped through the air and burned through the decrepit flesh. Reit dropped his hammer into the dirt and called upon his third spell. A stone elemental ripped its way up through the ground with a roar. Elementals were creatures born of the primary elements. A stone elemental looked like a stack of stones that had legs, arms and an insatiable urge to maim. It charged forward and swung with its massive stone arms. Each hit swept across the air and took three or more Nethall with it.

"The casters have had their fun," Geist roared. "Now it's our turn."

The Orc charged into battle and swung with his great-steel. He'd swing with both hands, his blade slicing through multiple beings at once, but then would release one hand off the hilt. With his free arm he formed a ball of glowing blue energy and fired it at close range. The blast detonated and took several unlucky undead with it. I gave him a jealous smirk. Geist had a blast ring. They were rare and they were powerful. I wanted it.

Ziena cart-wheeled into the mob and she started spinning her weapon. Her staff quickly snaked around, darting in and out with each strike. The staff began to gain a crimson glow and with each impact the weapon's crimson glow grew stronger and brighter.

With my boots on speed, I dashed forward, I took a flying leap and moved into a drop kick. I switched my boots to stone as they connected with the first Nethall. The blow caved in the beast's chest and sent it flying backwards. I flipped my boots back to speed, snapped out my Lucky Dagger and then tossed it at a charging undead. My blade dove into its neck but I didn't have time to watch. I recalled my dagger, snapped my swords back into my hand, spun around and lunged at the nearest foe. My blades would rip apart their necks and slice off their legs. My body twisted and pivoted as I danced across the battlefield. My blades moved together as I allowed both of my steel to feast on undead flesh. One after another, I would cut them down. I rolled back as Reit charged in. His shield held high as he defended against the dripping claws that slashed at his face. His hammer swung in, shattering the Nethall's neck with a satisfying crunch. The flames at his feet began to hungrily billow. Tongues lashed out, burning any foe nearby.

Ziena's staff made a loud crack as it shattered a Nethall leg. Her staff glowed bright red. She slapped her stick on the ground and watched a pillar of flame jetted up from the ground and a shockwave of fire rippled outwards. Many undead burned.

A red-tipped arrow tore across the sky and dove into my right shoulder. I screamed in pain and looked up. Hizzous stood atop the hill with his bow in his hands and a pair of arrows notched in his bow. He smirked as he drew back on the bow string and fired another pair of arrows in my direction. Hizzous had joined the fight.

I growled, raised Whaitiri Edge and I slapped away the two arrows. With a cry of pain I grabbed the one lodged in my shoulder and ripped it out. I kept my eyes locked on the sniper. I knew his beef was with me but he wasn't above hurting someone else. Hizzous' aim shifted and he fired another shot. This one was aimed right at our healer. I bolted across the battlefield, ignoring the undead between me and Scáthach, and I dove with my Edge extended. With a last second strike I knocked the red-tipped arrow away, but only just.

Scáthach glanced at me but didn't stop her chanting. She was casting something big and that arrow would have ruined everything. I rolled to my feet and looked around. At Hizzous's command the Nethall were moving towards me. No, not me; they were moving towards Scáthach.

"Reit!" I called. "What is she doing?"

"She's going big," he said. "She is going spirit bomb big."

"Shit," I said. "She's not doing the *actual* Spirit Bomb is she? That can't be in the game, can it?"

"Well....."

"Not the time," Ziena said. "If it's that big we need to protect her."

Reit nodded. He stood before the druid with his shield held high and his hammer swinging. Ziena's staff spun and struck as she pushed the undead back or to her left, directly into Geist's range. The Orc's greatsteel frantically sliced, dismembering any that Zeina sent his way; yet as many fell, more approached. They struck with their baleful claws and bit with their monstrous fangs. Their skeletal limbs were long and dexterous, sneaking past Reit's shield and weaselling around Ziena's staff as they slashed across our hides. Neth-all fangs dug deep into Geist's shoulder and a set of claws tore across my chest. Pain tore down my body but I pushed through it. I needed to ignore it. Reit lifted his shield as a pair of red-tipped arrows rained down. Both harmlessly bounced off of the shield.

Scáthach let out a cry. Her spell was ready. The magic that surrounded her shot upwards, into the sky. The Grey Land's sky filled with the eerie glow of magical moonlight. For the first time since coming to the Grey Lands, there was something other than grey. There was light; there was hope. The moonlight splintered, forming dozens of shards. They rained down onto the ground, each causing a great devastation upon impact. My jaw hit the ground as I watched the shards crashing. The druid spell was starfall and it was powerful AOE spell. It was never this powerful. Each crashing shard would take a handful of undead with them. Some screamed as they were pitched across the air and others were simply there one moment and gone the next. I glanced at Reit but he had his normal cocky shrug. I looked up the rolling hills and saw Hizzous standing there, smirking at me with a look that beckoned me to forth. This was the challenge. This was the showdown.

I was not going to disappoint.

With the speed in my boots I shot forward, bounding across the hills as I dashed towards him. Hizzous quickly notched three arrows and fired them at me. I dodged one and slapped aside the remaining two. Every second I spent looking at him was another degree my rage grew. I wasn't just mad at Hizzous, I hated him. The sight of him made every inch of my skin come to a boil. I *fucking* hated him.

"Come at me, Rake," Hizzous yelled as he shifted his bow into a double-bladed sword. "Let my pain come to an end."

Our steel collided with a loud clash and spark. Hizzous let out a loud maniacal laugh. It was a bone chilling laugh that sent a shiver down my spine. I deflected his attack with Whaitiri Edge and dove in with Splinter's Bite. My longsteel never made contact as the sniper spun quickly, bringing the opposite end of his sword around to slap mine aside. I moved my steel quickly as I pivoted and struck again. Hours of Adelaide's training came rushing back. My body knew where to be and how to move but so did Hizzous. His speed matched mine. Every opening I saw, I took. I'd thrust my longsteel in but somehow he'd slap Splinter's Bite aside. With each deflect his bowblade emitted a crimson glow. Hizzous' foot shot up and connected with me directly into my chest. I stumbled back and saw Hizzous' blade spinning at my neck. I activated my ring and blinked away. I didn't get a chance to recover as the sniper blinked towards me.

Oh right, he *also* has a blink ring.

I blinked again, landing atop another hill. Hizzous blinked after me. I blinked a third time and Hizzous blinked as well. I landed on a third hilltop, only this time I was ready for the sniper. I arched my arm back and waited. As the air began to shimmer, a sign of an incoming blink, I thrust with Splinter's Bite. As Hizzous materialized my blade dove through his chest and began to feast. Hizzous didn't scream and he didn't shout. He only laughed.

"What da fuck is wrong with you?" I yelled. Hizzous just laughed as he pulled himself off the steel.

"Only the living can be *wrong*. The dead are free of such burdens," Hizzous cackled. His eyes still looked chaotic and mad, devoid of sanity. "I am dead. I feel no pain, I feel no suffering and I feel no doubt and neither will you."

"You're not making any sense," I said as he slapped my longsteel away once again with a crimson glow. "Who did this to you?"

"I was promised no pain," Hizzous said, his body twitching as he spoke. "But pain still came. You still cast pain upon me. Now I will abolish pain. Nobody will ever feel pain again, not you and not me. Pain will be but a choice."

Guilt.

"Hizzous," I pleaded. "Please stop. You've hurt people and you still are. Let me help you. Let me make up for the pain you once suffered. Let me heal you."

"There is no healing the dead. They are beyond such things but perhaps the dead could heal us," Hizzous said. "Perhaps, I can save others from the pain you caused me."

Guilt.

I wanted to further plead but I couldn't; try as I might, I couldn't find the words, I couldn't find any words. I just stood there, with my blades held high, and let the overwhelming guilt roll over me.

Suddenly the Corrax Gate came alive and the center began to glow with a shimmering white light. It was like the light at the end of a tunnel.

"Fear not, Rake," Hizzous cackled. "You will not see the world after I abolish pain. You will not live long enough."

"You can't beat me," I snapped, words finally returning to my lips.

"I don't have to. This world is filled with your past mistakes. There are things here that hold hate for you in quantities far greater than I." The gate shimmered as a large form began to step through. "I found the one thing that hates you the most and I have summoned it here. I searched the afterlife for your greatest nemesis, your greatest foe and your greatest mistake and I have summoned it here." A man stepped through the gate and I froze. I recognized him immediately. It was impossible not to. Hizzous stepped back and pointed to the man. "I will not finish you, Rake. He will."

Standing before me was Steelion.

Chapter 07

"...." – Link, (The Legend of Zelda)

Steelion: just the sight of him was enough to send me into a fit of anxiety. My body shook and my mind melted. Guilt took free reign of my being and turned me into mush. I stared as he approached me, the warrior with his namesake armour coving his body while he firmly held a hand-and-a-half sword in one hand. He pointed at me, let out a massive roar and charged. I tried to raise my blades and take a combat position but I couldn't find the strength or motivation.

I had killed Steelion and now he was here for his revenge. He was here to balance the scales and I was going to allow him. I wasn't going to fight him, not again.

"Rake!" He roared as he bounded across the hills.

Guilt's grip on my mind and body grew tighter with each bound Steelion took. Guilt flashed before my eyes with the memories of our final encounter. I saw the look as I bested him. I saw the look as my dagger dove into his neck.

"Rake!!"

Guilt showed me the dreams I had of Steelion. Over and over he appeared before my eyes and told me to stop killing everybody. It was true. I had killed many since the Glitch and none had weighed more on my conscience than Steelion. He stormed at me, with his sword held high. I knew how Steelion fought and I knew what came next. He would leap high into the air and bring his sword down upon me and I was not going to fight it.

"Rake!" He yelled as his strong legs pushed him into the air. I closed my eyes and awaited the final strike. Perhaps, if I was lucky, death in this realm would free me from VCO but I wasn't counting on it. "Duck!"

I dropped to my knees and dove forward into a roll. I pulled myself back to my feet and whipped my head around. My eyes went wide as Steelion's hand-and-a-half, gripped in both hands, came down across Hizzous' chest. The sniper screamed and rolled away. Steelion didn't give him a chance to escape as he charged forward and let loose a flurry of one-handed attacks. His blade moved like a blur as each attack attempted to assault the sniper. Hizzous spun his double-bladed sword and quickly deflected each, his blade giving a crimson glow as the two steels connected. Steelion kicked the sniper back and tapped his chest. From beneath his armour his heart began to glow, dimly at first but rapidly growing brighter. I knew what this was. This was *Reactor Love*. I dropped my head and covered my eyes. Seconds later a blinding light filled the field, blinding those who weren't apart of his party. Screams of pain emerged from the Nethall as the blinding light seemed to burn their skin.

From behind me the gate glowed once more and a dozen men and women, of various races from both factions, emerged ready to fight. In the lead was a female paladin. She glanced over at Steelion.

"Mow them down!" Steelion yelled. The paladin nodded. She pointed her hammer forward.

"Charge!" She yelled as she bolted down the hill. The men and women behind her followed suit. Steelion's army charged into the Nethall and struck with a vengeance. An Elven hunter caught my eye. He wasn't staying back and shooting from afar, he was charging in beside the melee fighters. He fired as he ran. The hunter carried three arrows in his hand, flipping one up the bow string, drawing back, firing and flipping up another - all in the blink of an eye. When he reached the Nethall horde he ducked beneath a swiping claw and fired one arrow in the undead's leg, pinning him to the ground. He quickly pivoted, fired another arrow into a second Nethall's neck and then used the final arrow to drop a third. The hunter grabbed four more arrows from his quiver and started spinning in a circle. At each quarter of the spin he'd notch an arrow and fire it. By the time the spin, was finished four arrows had been fired and four undead had been felled. The dude was fucking Legolas.

"Rake!" I snapped my head back to Steelion. "Get up and Fight!"

I pushed myself to my feet and grabbed both blades. I pivoted towards Hizzous but found him screaming in anger. His body convulsed as he twitched and shook.

"No! No! Nooooo!" Hizzous cried out. "Rake; attack Rake. He is your hate, he is your pain. Attack him. Kill him."

"I'll get to him," Steelion growled. "You have a great deal more to answer for, Fog Lord."

"No, no, nooooo!" Hizzous morphed his blade back into a bow and drew two arrows. He fired a red-tipped arrow at me and a purple-tipped one at Steelion's feet. The purple-tipped arrow dove into the ground as I slapped aside the red-tipped arrow with Whaitiri Edge. Only then did I realize my mistake. The moment my blade made contact with the red-tipped arrow was the moment it detonated. The explosion pitched me across the air and skipped me across the ground. I winced as I rolled to my feet. I glanced at Steelion and found him rooted to the ground with vines that sprouted from the purple-tip arrow. I glanced towards Hizzous but found him gone.

"Fuck!" Steelion yelled as he cut away his vines. He looked down at the battle and saw the Nethall in retreat. He swore again, just louder. Steelion looked over at me and stormed over. I tried to pick myself up off the ground but pain and fear made the task nearly impossible. I lay there, paralysed by my own terror and anxiety. Steelion stood over me and scowled. I stared up at him and suddenly was reminded of the warrior's stature. He was a giant of a man and appeared doubly so as I lay on the ground.

I gulped in fear. Steelion offered me a hand. I stared in confusion as a smile crossed the warrior's lips. I took the hand and felt his enormous strength lift me to my feet.

"It's good to see you, old friend," Steelion said. "I've been waiting for you."

Dafuq?

"Steelion," a voice called out. The warrior looked over at the paladin. "The Fog Lord's numbers are escaping. Should we pursue?"

"No, it's not worth it," Steelion said with a shake of his head. "Set up our perimeter and fire up our flares. We have five here. Let's see if we can find any more wanderers." The paladin nodded and started to walk away. Steelion stopped her with a word, "Yasna."

"Sir?"

"Good work."

"Thank you, sir."

Yasna walked away. I looked back at Steelion. My hand hung by my belt, my fingers danced over the hilt of my blades like a nervous gunslinger, ready to draw and fire on a moment's notice. I wasn't sure what was going on but I was not going to be caught off guard, not again.

"You look scared," Steelion said.

"Last time we saw each other you did *try* to kill me," I said cautiously.

"True but you *actually* killed me," he retorted. Guilt hit me like a Wal-Mart shopper on Black Friday. I expected a pissed off look from Steelion but instead I got a smile. It wasn't a creepy joker-smile or an unsettling grin, it was a genuine smirk. "You always were better than me at this game."

"Enough of the bullshit, Steelion," I snapped. I was tired of the *Rachael-Ross will they or won't they* routine. "What the fuck is going on? Are we going to fight or not? I'm not anxious for a rematch but if we're going at it again, I'd like to know now."

Steelion shook his head. He dropped to a knee and looked up at me. With a look of sorrow in his eyes he pleaded.

"I'm sorry for what I did to you, Rake. Can you ever forgive me?"

Two hours passed before we left the hilltop. For two hours Steelion's men patrolled the neighbouring area as his Orc warlock fired spell into spell into the air, each burning brightly enough to be seen for miles. Steelion explained that they were looking for people like us, the deceased PC's that patrolled the Grey Lands. When the two hours had passed, Steelion recalled his army and then led us through the Corrax Gate into Helruss' realm. The difference was instant. It was like going from a Willow filter on Instagram to Valencia. Everything looked brighter and more vibrant. There was colour in the sky and life on the ground. I still looked horrible but that was to be expected. Nobody looks great in Valencia.

Helruss' realm was filled with grass and flowers. I could see forests, villages and farms and in the distance I could see a vast mountain range. It was nothing like I expected. I imagined a world of bones and skull like some gothic nightmare. I was imagining the Crypt King; I wasn't expecting Fólkvangr or Elysium. Steelion led us across the field towards the village.

"This is Helruss' realm," he started. "The Death god's job is to judge each soul that crosses here and send them to their final resting place. Those who were good get sent here, to Völusá. Those who were great get sent to the Aeolisian Halls, high atop the Elysium Mountains." Steelion pointed to the massive white-caps that littered the sky. He moved his finger across the sky and lowered his hand as he pointed to what could only be described as a burning tear in the mountain. "That is the Cronus Scar. Below it is VCO's literal hell. Those who are bad get sent there."

"That is a *massive* oversimplification," Reit defended.

"The Grey Lands are--" Steelion's words were quickly interrupted.

"Those that escape Death or unsuccessfully bargain with the reapers get sent to the Grey Lands," Reit explained. "There they stay, their souls deteriorating until they become a monstrous echo of what they once were."

"Who's this?" Steelion asked. I ignored his question.

"So what does this all have to do with you?"

"When PCs die they end up in the Grey Lands. There is no food in the Grey Lands. People are starving to death. I've been trying to help them," Steelion explained as we entered the village. "Völusá is an affluent land, full of riches and food. So I go into the Grey Lands and try to find anybody I can and bring them here."

"When did the Fog Lord get involved?" Geist asked.

"I found him a while back. He was on his own. He seemed sound enough when I brought him back here. Then..."

"Then he snapped?" Steelion just nodded.

"He killed started killing PCs," Steelion said. "By the time we figured out who was to blame, eight were dead and Hizzous had fled. He ran into the Cronus Scar. The next time we saw him he was in the Grey Lands, summoning the fog and ruling the undead. He takes pleasure in torturing people and driving them insane."

Steelion led us into the village. It was like something out of a Viking show. There were wooden huts and stone buildings. Weapons and shields decorated the outsides. Furs and skins hung from various clothes lines. As we entered, each soldier looked to Yasna.

"Our next excursion is in two days," the paladin called out. "Be ready. Until then, enjoy."

The men and women cheered as they dispersed. Yasna looked to Steelion. He nodded. "If you four want to follow Yasna, she'll find you rooms. I need Rake for a bit."

"I'm staying," Reit said. He turned to Scáthach. "Care to get us a room?" The druid just nodded and left with Ziena and Geist. Reit looked back to Steelion. "What else do you have to show us?"

"Seriously, who is this guy?"

"Not important right now," I said. Steelion sighed. He led us further into the village. He moved to a large stone building in the rear. It was one of the largest in the village. I expected it to be a party hall, a Valhalla if you would, but it was far from it.

"Many die in the Grey Lands before I can save them. They starve to death, are killed by the Nethall or are consumed by a paenido," Steelion said. "But those who are saved are not....well. Some succumb to the maddening."

Steelion opened the building's door and let us in. The hall was filled with dozens of rooms. Each was filled with a PC. They were of various races and both factions. They were crazy and screamed like lunatics.

"I don't know why but people are going insane here. They are becoming---" He pointed to the various cells. "I don't know what to do." For a moment we just stood there and listened to their screams. One by one their voices echoed through the halls.

"Help me!"

"The Fog, fear the Fog."

"Mommy!"

"The pain!"

"Cobie! Where is my Cobie?"

"I'll fucking kill you!"

"Kill me. Please kill me."

"I don't know what's causing this," Steelion said somberly. "I don't know how to help them."

"People aren't dreaming," Reit said. "It's what's causing the emotional imbalance above and the insanity down here." Reit explained to Steelion about the *Looking Glass system* and the lack of REM sleep.

"Seriously, who the *actual* fuck is this guy?" Steelion asked. I glanced at Reit and he nodded in approval.

"This is Reit," I started. "But you'll know him better as Casper Ramirez."

My room was simply that. It had four walls, a ceiling and a door. It wasn't much but it was all I needed. It also had a bed. I stared at the wooden bed and cringed. It did not look comfortable. I looked like a piece of crap bed that was going to give me back pains. I sighed. It was going to be better than nothing. I kicked off my boots and sat down. I blinked in surprise. The bed was soft, hella soft. I lay down upon it and gasped. This bed wasn't just comfortable, this bed was hella comfortable. It was the greatest bed in all creation. I smiled as I closed my eyes.

A bang on my door jolted me awake. My body told me that I had been asleep for a while. I winced in regret as I climbed out of the bed and made for the door. I pulled it open and saw Steelion standing on the other side.

"We need to talk." That was an understatement.

Steelion escorted me to the great hall. We both sat down. He placed a meal before me and accompanied it with a mug of ale. I took a sip of one and a bite of the other. My stomach reminded me that I was hungry, hella hungry.

I had to stop saying hella.

I started to scarf down the food.

"We need to talk about my death," Steelion said. He took a long sip before speaking again. "It wasn't your fault. It was mine."

"I killed you," I said quickly. "I should have found another way."

"There wasn't another way. I see that now. I left you no other option." Steelion bit his lip as he fought for words. "Did I ever tell you I have four brothers? I have three older and one younger. We all pretty much hate each other. Most of us can't even stand to be in the same room with each other. Each of us is a piece of work. We'd fight, fuck and steal our way into trouble. In school, the teacher would squirm the moment they saw our names on their list. 'You're an O'Conner boy. You're trouble.'

"Our hatred of each other and our attitudes were all because of our Pa. He's a piece of shit that only cares about his kids depending on what they can do for him at that moment. He's a con artist who owes a lot of people a lot of money and if one of us can make him a few extra bucks, then we become his favourite. The whole dynamic is fucked up. Our Pa has brainwashed us into being dependant on his praise and approval and doing whatever it took to get it. There was no second place, there was only being the best at what we did and proving ourselves to the old man."

"Jesus, that's fucked up, man."

"When I was fourteen, I was selling illegal smokes at school. Pa would buy them for a dime a dart and I was selling them to assholes at school for a buck each, just so Pa would hate me less than the other four." Steelion took another sip. "I got into VCO as an escape but when I learned I could make money from it, I dove in head first. I needed to make as much as possible so my younger brother Seamus, the only brother I actually like, didn't have to suffer the same way I did. He's still in school. I don't want him selling darts like I did. I don't want him suffering Pa's wrath like we did.

"When the Glitch hit I had trouble controlling my emotions. I was filled with so much rage. I was the strongest in VCO and nobody was going to take that from me. I beat down the gangs and took control. I took out Browntown and was unbeatable. Then you showed up. You were Stov. You had beaten me time and time again. You were always better but not now, not anymore. Now you were Rake and you were tiny and a nobody. I would finally have my revenge."

"Then I beat you," I said sheepishly.

"Then you *fucking* beat me, again." Steelion said with an exasperated sigh. "I only saw red. I was not going to be happy until I ripped your head from your shoulders." Steelion looked down into his mug and shook his head. "I forced your action. I forced you to kill me. It wasn't your fault, it was mine and for that I'm sorry. I'm sorry for everything."

We sat in silence for several moments before I spoke. "How did you get from rage to Mr. Calm?"

"I ended up in the Grey Lands. I was just pure rage.

I endlessly fought the Nethall in the most brutal and violent manner. I was like the Hulk, a being of pure rage, combat and killing," Steelion explained. "I needed for nothing. I always had food on me so I never starved."

"Always the chef," I teased. He laughed back. Steelion always had food on him and it was always the good stuff. He was the guy who maxed out his cooking skill.

"Then I ran into her." Steelion pointed to Yasna. She was a female Elf. She had a crew-cut haircut that screamed Carol Danvers. "She found me and calmed me down."

"Sun's getting real low?"

"Exactly," Steelion shrugged. "She showed me something other than rage. She showed me....Banner."

"Wait, are you two....."

"Nope."

"Oh." I paused and stared into my own drink. It was my turn to emote. "I have been so racked with guilt. You haunt my dreams, Steelion."

"Those aren't dreams," he corrected. I glanced up at him confused.

"Yeah they are. You're in the Crypt Walker's throne room and you tell me to stop killing everybody. Wait, how do you know they're not dreams?"

"One: Reit said we can't dream," Steelion said. "And two: I sent you that vision."

"What the hell? What do you mean you sent me a vision? And why would you tell me that? What the fuck?"

"I have been using a seer and shaman to try and communicate with you. Communicating between the living and the dead is not an easy thing to do. The message got blurred."

"What were you trying to tell me?"

"I was trying to warn you to build an army. I was trying to warn you to get ready for a war."

"The Brotherhood? We stopped them."

"I wasn't warning you about them. Something has caused an unbalance here and an old bad is returning," Steelion warned. "The Undead are back. Rake, stop the Crypt

Walker. He's killing everyone."

"What are you talking about?"

"His prison is about to break," Steelion said. "The Crypt Walker is returning."

Chapter 08

"...." – Claude, (Grand Theft Auto III)

I walked the village alone. This place was called Fargismál and it was peaceful location. Its citizens were the good folk who got to live out their eternal days in peace. Many of them enjoyed the decadence of the afterlife. Food, drink and carnal pleasures were plentiful in Völusá and its people had no hesitation about partaking. From what Reit spoke of, the peaceful but decadent lifestyle here paled in comparison to the hedonism and orgies that existed in the Aeolisian Halls. High atop the Elysium Mountains was the great hall. The Halls were the final resting place for the greatest of Aspumer's warriors. They were Helruss' army and they rested and partied until they were needed, until the Red Horn of War was blown and the battle continued once more.

I glanced up at the mountain. If I was going to be stuck in the land of the dead like some Manolo Sánchez (*The Book of Life* was much better than *Coco*) then I was going to have to make my way up that mountain. That type of party seemed like my type of scenario. All I had to do was survive the Crypt Walker. And with that mental reminder, my mind reverted to the problem at hand. Digressions were nice but they did little to solve the problem. The Crypt Walker was returning.

VCO's first expansion, *The Ashen Downpour*, dealt with Helruss' archon. Diaduss was corrupted by Vörissa, became the Crypt Walker and launched an attack on the living with his army of the dead. His goal was to abolish all life and leave Aspumer in the hands of the dead.

I had fought the Crypt Walker numerous times during the *Assault on Death's Keep* raid. He was a pain in the ass back in the day and I doubted now, with the Glitch in full effect, he'd be any easier. How the hell was I going to stop him this time? Was the Crypt Walker going to be gentle on a man they called the Reaper? I doubted it.

"Rake?" I turned around and saw the Elf paladin approaching me. I gave Yasna a nod. "You looked worried. I take it Steelion dropped his bomb?"

"Hell of a bomb," I said with an exasperated sigh. *"Hey, Rake. I'm not evil anymore because there is a bigger evil out there and they sucked up all the evil so now I'm good.* The worst part is after that conversation with Steelion, now I have to do two things that I don't want to."

"And they are?"

"I now have to go down into the Cronus Scar and stop the Crypt Walker," Rake said. I threw up my hands in a frantic wave and screamed. "And if I'm going to forgive Steelion then I kinda have to forgive Bearcules and I don't want to do that either 'cause he's a tool and I really fucking hate him. FML."

"I don't know who that is," Yasna said with a shrug. "But you're dead. Why do you care about the land of the living?"

"Because everybody I love and care about is there."

"Good," Yasna said with a relieved smile. "We need more people and from what Steelion says, you're the best one to have in our corner." She paused for a moment. "What did you do that has him all enamoured with you?"

"I used to be Stov."

"The legendary mage? But why are you in a rogue's body?"

"This is my bank-alt," I admitted. "This was the body I got stuck in."

She laughed for five full minutes.

I was so done with that reaction.

"T..t..the way I see it," Yasna said between giggles, "we only have one option. We have to go down through the Cronus Scar and stop the cage from breaking."

We stood around the large table staring at Yasna's *magical* journal. Hers looked identical to mine, an installed app that had access to the VCO wiki. The only difference between the two was she was updating hers with intelligence of the dead realms. One by one, I looked around the table and saw the faces looking back. Ziena and Geist stood side by side, holding hands. Reit stood by the table as Scáthach choose to stand a few paces behind him. Steelion did the same with Yasna, choosing to stand a few paces behind her. Also joining us at the table was the Legolas hunter - whose name I learned was Badënov - and a Dhampir Revenant called Alluca.

The entire situation felt like a massive deja-vu. Mere months ago I was standing at a similar table with similar people, discussing our attack on the Crypt Walker's Keep. Now I was here discussing an attack on the Crypt Walker's Cage. Even the PCs were similar. Yasna was Slashlore, Steelion was Scova, Geist was Punchocalypse, Ziena was Fleyming, Scáthach was Tialla and the quirky Reit was Skith. It felt like everything was a parallel to before. Was this intentional? Was this fate? Or was the Crypt Walker linked to the mystery of the Glitch?

My mind raced as I ran through VCO's timeline. When the Crypt Walker was slain, his soul and body returned to the land of the dead to spend eternity. Helruss couldn't let his archon roam free in the land of the dead. He needed a place to lock up the villain. Left with no option, Helruss travelled into the demon realm and sought an audience with the Infernal Council.

The demon realm was actually the realm of fire and the home of Vörissa. It was a vast realm that held demons, devils and the oni. The three hell-factions were constantly at war but they were still ruled by the Infernal Council, a table that sat three from each hell-faction and was ruled by Vörissa. Since the goddess' fall, the final chair was filled by Vörissa's archon, Yazasha.

With the permission of the Infernal Council, Helruss commissioned the Hellforge, a collection of brilliant - albeit evil - craftsmen, to construct a cage from which the Crypt Walker could not escape. The denizens of the Hellforge agreed but needed more resources then were available in their realm. With the blessing of the remaining gods, they seeded the mortal realm with the infernal resources. The world was littered with new materials and clockwork creatures were sent to collect them. The resources were collected and the cage was built but the Infernals were not to be trusted. The Hellforge Assembly were a cunning lot and had planned for their sudden but inevitable betrayal. Their clockwork creatures attacked the outlying islands as they tried to build a foothold for the eventual Infernal invasion.

In game terms, the *Hellforge Assembly* expansion brought new Infernal materials, new clockwork foes and Infernal foes, new lands to explore and a level boost. The expansion held some popular dungeons but overall the expansion was viewed as one of VCO's least successful. While the gameplay was solid, many questioned the choice to add steampunk elements into a fantasy game, citing that it felt like it didn't fit in VCO's world. The unpopular *Hellforge Assembly* was followed by *Babellian Ascent*, a monstrously popular expansion that dealt with the return of Vörissa and her attempt to conquer the Heavens.

What this all had to do with the Glitch was beyond me. There was some aspect I wasn't seeing and it was frustrating.

"Rake!"

I snapped back to reality and noticed everyone staring at me. Somebody had just asked me a question and I had missed it due to my thoughts. I raised an eyebrow and let out a confused *guh*. Yasna rolled her eyes.

"I asked if you were ready."

"Yeah, go ahead," I quickly admitted before sheepishly adding an apology.

"We're going to descend through the Cronus Scar," she began. "The Scar is not a pleasant place to be. It is filled with torture and pain. The worst of the worst go there to be punished. It is filled with Helruss' servants, his peacekeepers and the undead remnants of the Crypt Walker's army. This will be a fight."

[Many trials will appear before our gaze. Without skill, those trials will become impassable hurdles. I wish not to witness an impassable hurdle.] Badënov said.

I looked at Steelion and raised an eyebrow. He smiled and quickly answered. "He's a foreign player. He doesn't speak English. What you're hearing is the auto-translate."

The auto-translate was a feature that allowed players from across the world to understand each other. It was a brilliant feature that had the unfortunate drawback of making the different language speaking players sound like robots.

"The cage was meant to be eternal," Reit said. "Something or someone is breaking it from the outside."

"We need to find out what is doing that and make them stop." Yasna continued. She took a deep breath and exhaled slowly before speaking again. "This is a dangerous mission. No one knows what happens if we die here. The working theory is that this is the absolute end of the line. There is nothing after this.

"I'm saying this out loud because I need each and every one of you to decide for yourself if you're going down the scar. I can't, and won't make you join this mission. You have to choose for yourself."

"I'm in," Steelion said.

"I ain't got anything better to do," Alluca sassed.

"I cannot let the Crypt Walker roam free. I'm in," Reit said. He turned to Scáthach. The druid nodded in return. "Scáthach's in as well."

"I'm in," I said.

[The decision to join you has been made by myself,] Badёnov said.

All eyes fell on the last two, the married couple. The Fenririan and Orc didn't say anything. They silently eyed one another. They spoke without words, using a telepathic language that only existed between couples. Geist took Ziena's paw into his hand and both nodded. Ziena turned to the group and nodded. "We're in."

"Good," Yasna said. She rose to her feet. "Get some food, get some drink and most importantly, get some sleep. We descend tomorrow."

Chapter 09

"...." – Serge, (Chrono Cross)

Stepping through the Cronus Scar, I didn't know what to expect from the land below. Was there going to be a three-headed dog? Was there going to be heinous looking demons torturing the ill fated? Was there an eternal flame that would burn us all alive? As I descended the cold, stone stairs, I found my hands often dropping to my belt. My fingers would dance over the hilts of my blades. At every sound, I fought the urge to draw both. Whaitiri Edge meant a lot to me. Even Splinter's Bite, formerly a placeholder blade, had grown on me. My blades were like my limbs, they were a part of me.

After what seemed like an endless amount of stairs, my foot touched down on the stone floor. We had finally arrived in the land below. We walked forward and passed through a massive stone archway. Yasna held her hammer tightly as her footsteps became slow and cautious. Nobody knew what to expect in the land below and none of us wanted to be caught off guard. We walked forward, our boots stepping across the smooth crimson-stone.

A blood curdling scream filled the air and both blades leapt to my hands. I held my steel aloft as I pivoted in circles. Where did that scream come from? I started to scan the horizon when I began to notice the citadels and buildings in the distance. Each was a beacon of pain and suffering for some unfortunate souls.

"We're going there," Reit said with a point. I followed

his finger until I saw a massive spiralling spire. It wasn't built with the same dirty brown-stone that make up the rest of the buildings. This was a porcelain tower, with a grey fence that surrounded it, that stood out in the hope-deprived land below. "I imprisoned the Crypt Walker in that tower. I called it the Bautisica Spire."

"Then what is that spire?" I pointed far in the distance, in the opposite direction, to a near identical tower. This one was onyx black compared to the porcelain white.

"That is the Torixica Spire. That is where the Crypt Walker tore his way into the mortal realm. That is the other side of *Under Way*."

"What can we expect from the Bautisica Spire?" Steelion asked.

"Helruss will have his guards," Reit said. "They will be archons, like the Crypt Walker, but of a lesser breed. They will allow none aside from Helruss to approach the cage. They cannot be swayed, they cannot be tempted and they are loyal to only Helruss."

"Then how is the cage in danger?" Yasna asked.

"I fear that they may have fallen," Reit said. "We may not have much time."

"Then we ride," Alluca said, bearing her fangs. "And we kill anything that stands in our way."

My blades moved quickly as I slapped aside a jagged spear. My longsteel dove forward and past the shield. The hungry blade dove deep into the clay-skinned hide. The creature, an Archon Foulsoul, was a monster patrol that searched the land below for wayward souls or those trying to escape. The patrol stumbled onto our party, assumed us escapees and attack. We decided to fight back. The Foulsouls looked like Orcish Spartans with darker coloured skin. Some carried a shield and a spear while others carried greatsteel.

I withdrew my steel and slid back. Whaitiri Edge twisted as it once again slapped aside the thrusting spearhead.

Splinter's Bite sliced forward but bounced harmlessly against the beast's shield.

"Archons are unlike anything you've ever fought," Reit yelled over the heat of battle. He raised his own shield as a greatsword swung towards him. Steel collided with steel and Reit felt his legs buckle. "They are stronger, tougher and they heal at an outstanding rate."

"Are you trying to kill us?" Steelion asked.

"Fucking Gygax!" I yelled. Steelion and I both smirked. Gary Gygax, the creator of *Dungeons and Dragons*, often believed that it was a DM's job to kill his players and often made his adventures, like *Tomb of Horrors*, to be the hardest of the hard.

Alluca dashed past me and slashed at the archon's leg. My foe buckled and I thrust once more with Splinter's Bite. The steel snaked around the shield and dove into its shoulder. I removed the blade. The beast's wounds were already starting to heal, the skin knitting together right before my eyes. Alluca slashed the archon's back with her scimitar and pressed her palm against the opened wound.

"Die!" A blast of sickly green magic ripped through each wound as the Foulsoul screamed. Seconds later it fell to the ground, twitching. I stepped forward and, with a swing of my longsteel, separated the creature's head from its body. Alluca looked at me and smirked. "Next?"

Alluca was a Revenant like Skith. Unlike Skith, she was less of a brute and more of a dexterous fighter. She used a smaller blade - a scimitar - to better suit her more vibrant fighting style. She didn't use big strikes. Instead she used a greater number of smaller strikes. She'd spin, and twist and somehow her blade would pull across the exposed weak spots of her foes. She bared her Dhampir fangs with a grin. Dhampir were fast, almost as swift as Elves, and they had the ability to consume the blood of their enemies. Most times they offered small boost of health but for those who focused on their consumption, they had access to far more abilities.

I turned to my left and saw the swift hand-a-half blade

of Steelion moving like a blur. It struck with a flurry of swift slashes before the warrior grabbed the weapon with both hands and brought the blade down in a massive strike, cleaving the Foulsoul in two.

Reit stunned the archon with a slam of his shield and followed it up with a hammer to the side of the creature's skull. The archon fell but another charged from behind it. Reit called upon the spirits to fuel his magic. With a point of his hammer and a tap of his fingers, Reit called a lightning spell. It was meant to be a single bolt. Instead a massive line of electricity, fifteen feet wide, ripped through the air. It tore the archon in two and scorched the area around it. The remaining archons screeched and fled. Badënov dropped one with a well placed arrow but the other three escaped. Everybody else just stared at the shaman.

"Overkill much?" Geist asked, his breathing heavy as he sheathed his blade.

"I...I..." Reit's voice trailed off. He stared at his hammer. He looked as stunned as the rest of us and maybe even a little scared. Suddenly he looked up, his trademark giddy smile on his face. "It got the job done, didn't it?"

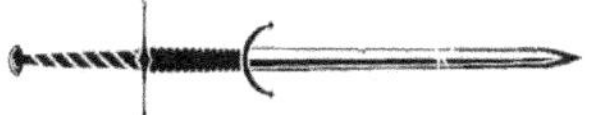

"I had a thought," Ziena said. The Fenririan slowed her pace to match that of the dwarf's. "This whole *land below* world, you did create it, right?" Reit nodded. "Did you write the Crypt Walker's return?"

"This is something new. I wrote the *Land Below* arc to create a new archon for Helruss. The PCs were going to quest and help find the new archon. It was going to be an NPC you met during this game. He was going to be revealed to have a *sliver of divinity.*"

My ears perked up. This was a lore conversation and it was far more interesting than anything Geist was saying to me. "And his first time Scrooge ever dove into his money was *Four-Color Comics* No. 386 way back in 1952. So I mean the new *Ducktales* (Whoo who) show is good and all but---"

I stepped away from Geist and listened as Ziena and Reit talked.

"A sliver of divinity is basically a dilution of blood from archons to the mortal races like Dwarves, Man, Orcs and whatnot. In order to become the new archon, you needed a sliver of divinity." Reit shrugged. "The story was that the archons were unstable without a high-tier archon leading them. You help quiet that instability by finding a new archon for the God of Death."

"Why didn't you put it in the game?"

"It's wasn't fun," Reit admitted. "After completing it, I tested it. It turned out to be a grind. It wasn't engaging or exciting. It was basically a dull *who done it* that you end up watching. So I put it on the back-burner until I could find a way to make it better."

I opened my mouth to speak but paused as the sound of a familiar hiss reached my ears. It was like water escaping from a radiator and it meant only one thing. I snapped my head around as a familiar menacing fog rolled in. Scowling, I swiftly drew both blades. The sound of a growl forced me to dive into a roll. I saw a set of baleful swipe where I once stood. The Nethall were back.

"Form up!" Yasna yelled. She held her hammer firmly as a swarm of undead appeared. They had marched from the Bautisica Spire, a thought I loathed. Yasna stepped in and swung her hammer hard. She connected with a Nethall neck and smirked at the satisfying crack. The undead fell but Yasna paid it no heed. She had already forgotten about it. She was focused on the next.

Alluca summoned forth Helruss' magic and gripped the mind of the nearest undead. She stole away control and turned the undead against its own kind. The renegade Nethall fell two undead before being destroyed. Alluca just smirked as she watched.

Steelion gripped his blade with two hands and swung firmly. His blade slashed hard, cutting through the decrepit hide before he pivoted and cleaved through another.

Ziena and Geist quickly worked as one. The Fenririan would move the undead together as the Orc would strike them down with his greatblade. The two still fought with a hint of hesitation. The trauma from the Pale Forest was still fresh in their minds but somehow they found the strength to push forward.

My blade felled the last of the initial swarm; smaller swarms were no match for our party. I looked beyond and saw the Spire in the distance. The porcelain tower was only an hour away but something felt off. I squinted for a better look. For a moment I saw movement in the grey fence that surrounded the Spire but that made no sense. Fences did not move but the more I looked the more I realized that they were indeed shifting and weaving. Suddenly, as if by some command, the fence suddenly disconnected from each other and each plank started to move toward us. Then it hit me. That wasn't a fence. That was literally hundreds of Nethall standing side by side. They were waiting for us and now, they were coming right at us.

"This is about to get worse," I yelled. Yasna glanced down at the tower and cursed. She eyed Steelion for guidance. He said nothing. I decided to speak up. "We need a plan, now!"

Steelion and I have always had our issues. We are friends but more like asshole friends. Yet all that aside, and ignoring the attempted murder by him and that actual murder by me, I always knew that when push came to shove, Steelion had a plan. It wasn't always a good plan but nine times out of ten, a bad plan is better than no plan.

"Range: drop what you can before they reach us," Steelion barked. There was no hesitation in his voice. "Alluca: grab a paenido and start some chaos. Yasna: consecrate. Geist, Reit and Rake: You're up here with me. Ziena: keep them from flanking us. Scáthach: keep us fighting. We're punching through this horde and making our way to that tower. "

Scáthach held her hands before her face as she summoned forth her magic. The spell was a ball of magical moonlight, the same one I had seen earlier. The druid was preparing a starfall spell.

Badënov notched an arrow and waited. He couldn't fire until they were in range but he was going to be ready.

Yasna dropped to one knee and began summoning magic of her own. In lore, paladins found their magic through prayer. In the game nobody prayed. It wasn't needed but as I watched the paladin, down on one knee, I swore I saw her lips moving. Was Yasna actually praying and if so, to whom?

"Do you remember us fighting the dragon-abomination waves?" Steelion asked me as I readied my blades.

"You mean that *horrible* launch event for the Scaleborn Scism?" I asked. Steelion nodded. The dragon-abominations were monstrous clones that had been magically created by one of the great dragons. They attacked one of the smaller cities with numbers in the thousands. Hundreds of PCs united to fight them. The event was long and tiring and did not give great loot.

"I stand by my work for that event," Reit said proudly.

"Well you shouldn't," Geist said.

"Are you thinking about Charlene?' I asked Steelion. He just nodded.

"I don't know why but she just jumped into my mind." I saw the look of confusion on our party's faces. A quick glance at the Nethall horde told me we still had a few moments before they were on us. So I explained.

"Steelion is dating this girl name Charlene. She wants to learn more about his interests and joins VCO to play with him. She gets pretty good at it for a normie," I begin. "She chooses to be a healing monk and the three of us - and others we know - enlist in the defense and jump at the chance to do the event. Steelion starts dying, like a lot. He gets mad and starts running his mouth. Charlene gets pissed and decides to stop healing him. Things escalate and get worse. Long story short: they break up over that event."

"It was a stupid event," Steelion growls.

"You're just an idiot boyfriend," I corrected.

"Says the guy who has lost how many girlfriends by obsessing over this game?" I scowled. I don't like it when my insults are turned back around on me. Steelion raised his blade and nodded at the horde. "They're in range. Take them out."

Scáthach's ball of moonlight energy floated into the sky and splintered, forming dozens of shards. Each shard rained down on the ground, each causing great devastation upon impact. Dozens of undead were pitched into the air while dozens more perished.

Badënov pulled back on his drawstring and fired off his first arrow. One Nethall fell. The archer quickly notched and fired a second, then a third and a fourth. Arrow after arrow fired from his bow, each dropping the unlucky undead that happened to come in contact with it.

With a final syllable, a large circle of divine energy erupted from Yasna's hammer. The area around it began to emit a golden glow. Yasna stood up and held her hammer firmly. Consecrated ground wouldn't stop the undead but any foolish enough to step in it would definitely feel pain.

Steelion pointed his blade forward. The steel began to shimmer with energy before a beam fired from its tip. The energy crossed the battlefield and tore through the chest of a Nethall. The undead fell to the ground, still, as dozens more trampled over it.

Alluca reached out with her revenant magic. Her magic was like magic tendrils that wrapped around the bulbous form of a paenido. For a moment there was a battle of wills but the revenant was a warrior; she was one of Helruss' chosen. She would not be bested by the very thing she was created to slay. She controlled the creature like a puppet. With a pull of one string, she would turn the creature on its allies and with the pull of another, the beast would smash the nearest grouping of undead. Over and over she repeated the action, felling many before they even got close. Eventually the paenido would fall but the damage they caused to their own was devastating.

Reit stood at the front and raised his hammer. With a look of hesitation and fear, he summoned his magic. He summoned forth a massive ball of lava and pointed it forward.

Then it exploded.

Chapter 10

"...." – Commander, (Commander & Conquer: Red Alert 2)

I don't know what happened but I suddenly found myself on the ground with a massive ringing in my ears. It was the type of ringing you saw in *literally* every *Call of Duty* game. The world seems silent; chaos and death is all around you and all you hear if that annoying ring as reality slowly returns to your ears. Then some character looks directly into the camera - at you - and tells you to get up while offering a hand to do so. You grab it, get handed a gun and proceed to commit the worse genocide since Nolan North decided to enter Dubai.

I looked up and there he was. Steelion was standing over me, like my own personal Reznov, offering me a hand up. He pulled me to my feet. He said something to me but all I heard was the damn ringing. I shrugged and glanced around. Our party was scattered across the field. Each of us was burned and most of us were lying on our backs.

"---nd get your ass in this fight!" The ringing had stopped and sounds had returned. I blinked in confusion. Steelion, his armour scorched from the explosion, quickly repeated himself. "I said, *hurry up and get your ass in this fight.*"

Steelion spun and swung his sword. The hand-and-a-half blade sliced through the neck of a Nethall before Steelion pivoted and cleaved through the body of a second. The first thing I saw was Reit, on the ground, trying to pick himself up. Alluca was casting another set of tendrils, stealing control of a nearby Nethall. She turned the undead minion against its own before grabbing Badënov and pulling him to his feet. The archer swiftly drew three arrows. One after another he'd flip them into his bow and fire.

Yasna scrambled to her knees and called upon another prayer. A wave of healing magic rippled across her body. Her wounds quickly knitted together as she cast the spell once again. This time she targeted Geist.

Geist glanced around for his sword but it was nowhere to be seen. He cursed. The undead were here and he had no blade at his disposal. The Nethall charge the group, each wincing in pain as they crossed the consecrated ground. With a roar Geist lunged at the first Nethall. He ducked beneath the set of baleful claws that swung for him. Geist grabbed the chain that dragged behind and gave it a pull. He pulled the Nethall off of its feet and began to spin. With a throw last seen in the Mario-Bowser fight in *Super Mario 64*, Geist release the chain and flung the undead towards the others. A set of claws slashed across Geist's back. He screamed in pain and disgust. How did he allow an undead to sneak up on him? The claws struck again, tearing through his Orcish flesh and drawing blood. Geist slammed his fist into the undead's face and knocked it back. A third undead tried to strike with its chain but a flying foot knocked the beast back. Ziena flew across the battlefield looking like Liu Kang. Her flying drop-kick sent the undead away from her husband and flying across the field. She spun her quarterstaff, keeping further foes from approaching, before she snapped the weapon forward, like a striking serpent, catching the undead in the neck and felling the beast with a satisfying snap.

"You dropped this," Ziena said as she materialized a greatsword. Geist took the weapon with a grin. He leaned in and gave his wife a kiss on her furry cheek.

"What would I do without you?" he asked.

"Let's not find out," she retorted.

Reit knelt by the fallen Scáthach and checked her

wounds. The druid was out cold and on the verge of death. Reit could have healed her - shamans had healing magic in their arsenal - but for some reason he did not. He called out for Yasna. His voice was angry and scared but his face was filled with sorrow and helplessness.

"Cover me." Yasna yelled as she slid next to the druid. I dashed towards them, my blades at the ready, and slashes at the pair of undead that was following her. Whaitiri Edge dove through the neck of one Nethall while Splinter's Bite ripped the heart out from within its chest.

I pivoted towards the horde as more descended upon me. My Edge snapped up to deflect the flurry of claw slashed as I ducked beneath the swinging chains. My longsword struck again and again. When one fell, another would stand in its place.

"She's up!" Yasna yelled.

"We have to move," I called back. Our plan went to shit the moment Reit's spell exploded and we lost positioning. "Steelion: do something!"

"Geist and Rake: get up here with me. We're going to cut a hole," Steelion yelled. "Reit and Yasna: take a flank and cover us. Badënov and Scáthach: keep in the middle and give us support. Alluca and Ziena: cover our rear. Don't let them take us from behind."

We grouped up as he said and we began our push. Geist and Steelion each swung with their large steel as I weaved in and out, striking with both my blades. Those who attacked our flank met with the skull crushing hammers of either Yasna or Reit and those who crept up from behind fell to the lighting-fast strikes of Zeina's quarterstaff or Alluca's scimitar. All while an arrow shot out or a spell knotted a wound back together.

We fought for what seemed like hours, our blades and spells carving through one undead after another until we stood before the Bautisica Spire. Two porcelain doors stood tall and daunting. They towered over us, reminding us of our small place in the world. Steelion and Yasna pushed open one door as the rest of us dashed inside. They closed the door behind us.

Each of us paused to catch our breath. I let out a sigh of relief as I slid to the floor and dropped down with a plop. Each of us silently looked at each other before a collective giggle filled the room as it morphed into a billowing laughter. None of us knew why we were laughing, we just were. It was like relief and exhaustion combined into one and all that was left was the laughter.

"Holy shit balls," Yasna said loudly.

"Amen," Steelion said.

"You know what that just reminded me of," Ziena said as she looked at her husband. Geist raised an eyebrow. "It reminds me of that time I stood outside our niece's school to pick her up. The bell rang, the doors opened and hundreds of kids ran outside directly at us."

[A comparison of children to a wave of undead is an accurate one,] Badënov said.

"What the hell was up with that spell," I asked suddenly, staring at Reit. The shaman shook his head.

"I...I don't know," he replied; stammering a few words. He looked at Scáthach. The Druid just nodded back. "Everything is weird down here. The voices are louder and the magic is....." He looked at his hands. "It's unreliable."

"The voices?" Alluca asked.

"The voice of the spirits," Reit explained. "Shaman magic comes from the spirits and suddenly they have a voice."

"Shit," Steelion said. "You're in the fucking underworld. No wonder they're so loud."

"Are you going to be able to control it?" Geist asked. Reit glanced down at his hands and stared silently. He eventually responded with a slow nod.

I climbed to my feet and looked around. The Bautisica Spire's interior wasn't what I expected. I was expecting a prison, dark and dirty and full on Oz. I expected something between Magneto's prison and Hannibal's cell. What I got was the ballroom from *Labyrinth*. The walls glimmered with polished pearl and sparkled with a hint of magic. I thought the decorations on the wall were random squiggles but as I walked closer I noticed that they were not random. They were engraved with arcane runes.

I missed being Stov. I missed being famous. Stov was a legend. Stov was a household name. Everybody knew the name and Stov was a legacy within the game. Some thought that Stov was Casper himself. But what I missed the most about being Stov was the prestige that came with being a mage. I missed the magic, I missed the knowledge and wisdom and I missed being able to do what no other class could. I ran my fingers over the runes and sighed. There was something special about being the one class that could cast ritualistic magic.

Warlocks and druids, among others, could cast magic but they couldn't cast ritualistic magic. That honour belonged solely to the mage class. Ritualistic magic wasn't combat magic and it wasn't portal magic. It was the type of magic that took a crap ton of channeling to complete. In any book or movie, when the mage is summoning great deals of magic to finish the boss while the melee grunts fight some minions, that was ritualistic magic. The interior walls of the Bautisica Spire were covered with ritualistic magic. Someone had gone through a lot of trouble to keep their prisoner trapped within these walls and they were using very powerful ritualistic magic to do so.

"Where to?" Steelion asked. Reit pointed to a white spiraling staircase. It was a large staircase that seemed to endlessly climb. Steelion just shook his head. "Please don't say what I think you're about to say."

"He's gonna say it," Ziena added.

"Please don't say it," Geist added. "Please don't say those two letters."

"Up," Reit finished.

Everybody groaned.

The stairs seemed endless. We took them, one after another, in our ostensibly endless climb. My legs were killing me and I made sure everybody knew. The worst part was, I was in far greater shape than anybody else. All that training with Adelaide had made me a machine but if that was true, then these stairs were John Connor. It would explain why my legs felt like they'd been dipped in molten steel. When we reached the top, each of us dropped to the floor. We all moaned and groaned and whined about our pain but at least we were doing it together.

The top floor of the Bautisica Spire had walls like those below. They were polished pearl and were engraved with the same arcane runes. Yet unlike the room below, there stood five large alabaster pillars with a tombstone in the middle of them. The floor was also littered with corpses. I walked over and examined the first. Most were Foulsouls but some were higher ranked archons. Reit pointed down a long hallway.

"The prison is in there," Reit said.

"Then that's where we need to go," Alluca added. Yasna nodded and started leading the way. I started to follow but paused. My eyes were drawn to the pillars. Why were they here? My body gravitated towards them. I paused at one of them and ran my fingers across its surface. I felt the feeling of raised letters. I glanced at them. NFHAZC. What did they mean? I moved to a second pillar and saw more written there. RAJAAC.

"Rake, we have to get out of here," Geist said.

"We are standing in the spire that acts as the Crypt Walker's prison," I said quickly. "In the middle stand five pillars. Now each of these seems to have random letters on it. Now, why would that be?"

"It's a hint," Steelion said. "No, it's a hint wrapped in a puzzle." Steelion moved from pillar to pillar, looking at each of the letters. He pulled out a pencil and some paper and he began to write each of the letters down.

"What are you guys doing?" Ziena asked.

"VCO is a wide and vast world and it is filled with secrets and hints," I said. I pointed to Reit. "That man has filled the world with treasure and surprises. Steelion and I are treasure hunters. We know a hint when we see it. This group here could probably go and stop whatever is trying to free the Crypt Walker but it won't be easy. Whatever this hint is, it will probably make our fight just a little easier."

Steelion handed me the notepad. I gave it a glance. He had written on it all of the letters etched upon the pillars. NFHAZC RAJAAC ATAYHD AEFXLJ TPRY. He quickly showed it to the others.

"It's gibberish," Alluca said. Steelion just shook his head.

"It's a cipher." There are many different types of treasure hunters in VCO. Each seems to specialize in a different field. I was a lore junky. Scova was a math nerd. If there was a math based problem, she had it solved in no time flat. Steelion was a code breaker. I had never seen anybody see a code and break it as fast as him. "It's obviously a substitution cipher. The only question is what type."

"A basic cipher takes one letter and replaces it with another," I said out loud. "We just have to figure out which letter is swapped out for which."

I glanced at Reit but he shook his head. "This is different than when I built it. I made a puzzle using prime numbers. I don't know what this is."

"There are five blocks of words. There are five pillars," Steelion said. I could see his mind racing. The relationship between Steelion and I had always been strained. We were each too competitive for our own good. Yet as I watched his mind work, and the smile that crossed his lips as he did, I was reminded of what it was that drew us together in the first place: the joy of solving a puzzle. "It's a playfair cipher."

Steelion looked around and saw stunned faces. He quickly began to explain. "A playfair cipher uses a five by five grid. You start by putting in your code word. Then you fill in the rest of the alphabet. From there you split your message into groups of two. Then you follow a set of rules that will determine what letter replaces yours."

"Can you break it?" Alluca asked.

"Not without the code word. It's virtually impossible to do so."

I walked past the pillars and paused at the tombstone. I knelt before it and looked at the writing. Naked Shame Can Harm Both Oaths. The words were gibberish but everything else had been as well. I looked back at Steelion.

"What is that grid again?" I asked

"Five by five," he replied. I glanced back at the tombstone. Perhaps five was the magic number. I counted the letters of the inscription and stopped at the fifth one. D. I counted five more. E. With a smile I continued onwards. A. T. H. I looked at my newly formed word. It was obvious.

"The code phrase is death," I called out. Steelion nodded. He scribbled on his notepad as he quickly deciphered the text.

"Light will defeat the darkness," he read aloud.

"Well that seems obvious," Geist grumbled. "What a waste of time."

"Light is spelt wrong though. It's L-I-T-E," Steelion added. "There are never typos in puzzles."

"The Blade of Lite," Reit said in a shocked tone. He put both hands over his mouth as his eyes went wide. "They put them in."

"Care to explain?" Yasna asked. Reit grumbled for a moment. He looked over at Scáthach. The druid just nodded.

"I had a storyline I was working on for the next expansion. It was going to be the return of Vörissa's god-spark. Vörissa was the goddess of power and war. She was also the goddess of chaos. In order to defeat the carrier of the chaos-spark, the players were going to have to find the swords of Lite and Nite, two blades that worked in perfect balance and order." Reit stroked his chin. "The two blades would be wielded by NPC and they would fight alongside a raid of PC as they defeated the carrier."

"Because only order and balance can defeat chaos," Ziena said. She looked at her husband. "That makes logical sense, unlike Flipism."

"You leave Flipism out of this," Geist defended.

"Where are these blades?" Yasna asked.

"The Blade of Lite resides here, in the world of night," Reit said. "It is held by a high archon called Castimiri. The Blade of Nite is in the land of the living, in the world of light."

"Who is Castimiri?"

"She is the highest ranking archon. She is a champion of Helruss," Reit said. "I don't know where she is."

"Well this was useful," Alluca snapped. "Let's push forward."

Steelion nodded. He was thinking the same thing I was. This puzzle didn't come with a treasure but it came with a hint, one we wouldn't want to forget. Yasna rounded us all up and started us forward. We carefully made our way down the long hallway. In the distance we could hear the sound of a battle. A fight was occurring in the cage room. We picked up the pace. With each step the sounds of battle got louder. We ran until we reached the two large doors. They were supposed to be large and foreboding, the magic gates to the Crypt Walker's prison. However, the unsettling doors were little more than splinters.

"This isn't good," Reit said as he stared at the broken doors. "This isn't good at all."

Chapter 11

"...." – Kirby, (Kirby's Dream Land)

The cage room was large and vast, with a mystical cage in the center, but stepping into the cage room was like stepping into a warzone. Dozens of Foulsouls and archons were currently in a large scale battle against the hordes of Nethall. Swords clashed with claw as the archons defended the cage. Flying archons were being ripped from the sky by the undead gargoyles while the Solomon Grundy-esq undead were ripping apart the Foulsouls. The archons were fighting with all of their might, each warrior felling nearly a dozen undead, but they were still falling to the undead horde. The undead had the numbers. Flying in the center of the room was a large female archon. She held in her hands a glowing hand-and-a-half blade. The archon looked broken and bruised and had several red-tipped arrows protruding from its body. She desperately flapped her wings to stay in the air but with each flap, the strength in her body poured out.

"There," Reit pointed. "She is Castimiri."

Steelion's eyes followed the high archon but mine followed a different path. I knew those arrows and I knew who fired them. I scanned the room until I spotted him. Standing at the far end was Hizzous.

"Boss?" Yasna asked.

"We protect the cage," Steelion barked. "Help the archons and cut down the undead. Stay together and don't be a hero. We can't afford to lose a single one of us. Rake: I need-

----Rake?"

I was already gone. I activated the speed in my boots and bolted through the undead horde. I sliced at any who I came across but I never stopped. I was looking for one person and one person only: Hizzous. I knew going off on this was stupid, that thought occurred to me mid-run, but I had no other choice. If I killed the Fog Lord, then the Nethall would vanish. Hizzous glanced over and saw me approaching. He pivoted and brought his bow around to aim at me. He quickly notched an arrow. With lightning speed he drew back and fired. I easily slapped aside the arrow using Whaitiri Edge.

"Come at me, Rake!" He challenged.

"This ends today!" I yelled.

Hizzous fired two more arrows. I slapped one aside and ducked beneath the second. I sprung forward and slashed. Hizzous morphed his bow into a blade and swung it to collide with Spinter's Bite. The bowblade let off another crimson glow as the two steels collided. I switched my boots to stone and struck with a spinning kick. The blow collided with Hizzous' chin and sent his flying backwards. I switched back to speed and bolted forward. My longsteel dove in but Hizzous slapped it aside, his bowblade glowing with each strike.

"Everything ends today," Hizzous cackled.

"You're mad," I yelled. "Why do you try and free the Crypt Walker?"

"I plan to free us all," the sniper cackled. My blades moved swiftly as I struck. I would lead with Whaitiri Edge and follow through with Splinter's Bite. With each strike of the Edge, Hizzous would dodge but with Splinter's Bite the sniper would bring his bowblade across to block and each time the two steels met, the bowblade emitted a crimson glow. Why was he ignoring one of my blades? When he was on the attack, Hizzous' bowblade struck not at me but at my longsteel but I didn't know why. What was with that crimson glow? My mind raced. A crimson or red glow on a weapon usually meant fire. Both Reit's and Scáthach's respective weapons had a red glow when they summoned fire or lava. It was an evocation spell, a form of magic meant for destruction. If he had a destructive spell on his bowblade he should have been aiming for me, with hopes of finishing me with a strike. So why, then, was he focused on my longsteel?

The solution hit me a moment too late.

Hizzous slammed the bridge of his double-sided bowblade across my face. My head snapped back and my body kind of froze. For a moment I found my vision blurry and my body unresponsive. He had got me with a stun. He slammed me against the wall and pressed his boot down onto Spliter's Bite, pinning it to the ground. He quickly drew an arrow from his quill and jabbed it into my shoulder. I screamed as I tried to move, to escape, but found myself unable to do so. The arrow had me pinned to the wall.

"The only reason anybody feels pain is because they allow it," Hizzous whispered in my ear. "I will free you from all pain. I will free everybody from the pain."

"Why?" I gasped.

"Because I am tired of being trapped in this game and I am tired of pain." Hizzous shook his head. "There is only one escape from this game and only one escape from pain. You couldn't free us, Reaper, so I will do the job for you but first I will take everything from you, just as you did from me."

Hizzous released my blade and took a step back. He summoned a crimson glow onto his bowblade and arched his blade back. With an evil smirk, he swung his bowblade and slammed it against my longsteel. The bowblade flashed a bright burst of crimson light and the sickening sound of steel breaking filled my ears. I glanced down and stared at the broken blade that resided in my hand.

Hizzous had destroyed Splinter's Bite.

I stared in shock. There was nothing special about Splinter's Bite. It wasn't as rare as Whaitiri Edge but it was still a magical weapon and more importantly, it was mine. I had grown attached to the blade. It was the duo of Bite and Edge, the trademark of Rake. It was like my stability had just vanished with my trademark. I looked up as Hizzous prepared a second strike, this one at my neck.

A pair of arrows slammed into his side, forcing the sniper back. Hizzous screamed. He spun around as two more arrows dove at him. Hizzous blinked away as the two arrows passed through nothingness. I glanced over at Badënov. The Elf slid in next to me.

[Injuries do not look fetching upon your form,] Badënov said. [Freedom comes by my hand if you permit it.] I nodded as Badënov pulled the arrow from my shoulder. I glanced across the room and spotted Hizzous in the far corner. He stood, with his arms out, as strands of fog began to swirl around him. In the distance I heard the sound of a hiss, like water escaping from a radiator. The swirling fog began to spread across the floor, like a flooding basement.

"Shoot him," I yelled at Badënov. The hunter spun around and fired two arrows but neither connected. They harmlessly bounced off the strands of magical fog that leapt up to protect him. I glanced at Steelion. "Attack Hizzous, now!"

"I found salvation in the afterlife and the truth of my origin. I possess a sliver of divinity within me, enough to hold the power of the Crypt Walker and the corruption of Vörissa. I possess enough divinity to become the Fog Lord." Hizzous cried out. The menacing fog began to thicken and spread. Steelion and Yasna bolted towards him with Reit and Alluca close behind. Badënov notched a few more arrows and let them loose. No attack reached Hizzous. A burst of fog shot outward and pitched everybody in the room - PC, Undead or otherwise - against the nearest wall and hard. "I am here to free the Crypt Walker so that he may free us from the game; so that he may free us from the pain."

Fog began to form in his palm like a DBZ energy blast. Hizzous flicked his hand towards the cage and sent the blast of fog at it. Fog dove into the cage's lock and seeped through the bars. For a moment nothing happened. Hizzous' arm twitched as he desperately tried to focus but still nothing happened. Then the cage exploded. The sound was deafening and the blast was blinding. When we regained our senses we saw him standing before us. The Crypt Walker was free.

He stood nearly ten feet tall. His body was muscular and strong, covered with armour made from dirty grey bones but his face was a hollow skull, with sickly green energy glowing from the eye sockets. He looked like a cross between *Mortal Kombat*'s Shao Khan and the grim reaper.

"I am free," he bellowed in a hollow voice that seemed to echo through my brain. "My reign continues."

"Not as long as I stand," Castimiri called out. The archon pushed herself to her feet, spread her wings and held her blade in two hands. She willed forth the magic in her blade and the steel began to glimmer a golden glow. "I am Castimiri, High Archon and devotee to Lord Helruss. I am the wielder of the blade of Lite and it is my duty to stop you from ever taking another step in the land of the living. I face you now, with my blade at the ready, and will end you where you stand."

"Brave words, little ant, but a myrmidon like yourself has no chance against I."

"Be that as it may, I face you still." Castimiri bolted forward, using her wings to push her faster.

"Why are you so eager to throw away your life?" The Crypt Walker summoned a large scythe. He brought it around as the Blade of Lite slashed at his chest. The arctic blue blade parried the archon's strike.

I forced myself up from the ground, my body objecting at the decision, and tried to watch. Their speed was remarkable. The archon and the Crypt Walker moved faster than I could follow. They were like blurs, dancing in the mist.

A pained cry and a loud thud signaled the fight's end. Castimiri lay on the ground, clutching her chest. She did her best to cover a gaping chest wound with her hand but it was to no avail. The Crypt Walker had won. He marched over to the fallen angel. Castimiri looked up with a pained look on her face.

"My lord will come for you," she promised. "He will

be here and he will end you.”

“I desire his company, I crave it.” The Crypt Walker slammed his foot into Castimiri chest and pressed down. “Call for him. Beckon your master forward. It is time he and I were reunited.”

“I...” The Crypt Walker interrupted Castimiri’s protest with a press of his heel. Castimiri cried out.

“Call him.” Castimiri held open her left palm. A ball of magic formed. It grew in size until it was the same as a softball. The ball rose from her hand, hovering slightly before zooming off into the distance. The Crypt Walker let out a hollow laugh. “Well done, ant. You have signed the warrant of your master’s death.”

I felt a tickle on my neck and spun around. A black feather floated down from above. I looked around stunned. The entire room seemed to be filled with the falling rain of feathers. Each was black as midnight and they numbered seemingly as infinite. I looked around, confused. Suddenly the feathers began to move. They began to circle in the air, spinning around until they formed a feather tornado.

“I once granted you leniency for your crimes,” a voice cried out. Unlike the Crypt Walker’s voice, this was loud and booming and everybody heard it, whether they wanted to or not. “You were my archon and I cared for you deeply. I was blinded by that emotion. I will never let that occur again.”

The feathers vanished, leaving a humanoid form in their wake. It stood as tall as the Crypt Walker but was completely different. The body was a humanoid raven, with a long black beak, frail hands with talons at the end and midnight black feathers that covered its body. An onyx coloured cloak sat atop the form but it blended into the body in such a way that none knew where the cloak ended and the feathers began.

This was Helruss, the God of Death.

I couldn’t believe my eyes. There, standing before me, was a god of Aspumer. I had seen Vörissa, she was a raid boss, but this was different. Helruss was never written into VCO. He was never an NPC. He was simply a creature that revenants saw before they turned. They couldn't talk to him or interact with him. He was simply there.

"Hello, Helruss," the Crypt Walker said in his hollow tone. "I have had a yearning for this meeting. It was all I thought of during my time in the cage."

"Now we stand face to face," Helruss said. "What do you desire to say?"

"I have practised what I wished to say to you, over and over, but now it seems unfitting." For a moment there was a hint of hesitation in the Crypt Walker's voice. "Now that you stand before me, I can only come up with one word."

"And that is?"

"Goodbye." The Crypt Walker held out his hand and slammed a ball of magic energy into the death god's chest. Helruss dropped to one knee and clutched his chest in pain. The Crypt Walker backhanded the god and sent him falling to the ground. I stared in shock. He had just bitch slapped a god. I didn't even know that was possible.

"I spent only a decade in that cage, in your prison, but to me an eon had passed. During that time you have grown weak and you know not why." A sinister hollow laugh echoed through the chamber. "We are linked, you and I, through the same spark of divinity. I am simply an echo of you. I draw my strength from you but in my eon of imprisonment, I discovered a way to draw even more. Once I was the shadow, cast from your divine form. Now the roles have reversed. I possess more of your power than you do. You are now the echo; you are now the shadow."

Helruss spun upward and slammed his palm into the Crypt Walker's chest. The archon went flying backwards. The god climbed to his feet.

"I am not as weak as you foresaw." Helruss walked towards his former disciple. He drew a dark blade form his cloak and held it by his side. "I taught you everything I know. I gave you the powers you hold dear. Now I will take them from you. You forget that you cannot kill me but I can kill you."

"And you forget, Master, that I am not alone."

A blast of fog slammed into the death god's back. Hizzous held both hands up in the air as he commanded the fog. Like Bugs Bunny at the opera, he controlled the fog with the movement of his hands. The sinister tendrils wrapped around the god's limbs and pulled him to the ground.

"I thought myself forever trapped in your cage, Master," the Crypt Walker explained, mocking the last word. He climbed to his feet and walked towards the trapped god. He nodded at Hizzous. "Then I discovered this wayward soul. He held a sliver of divinity in him and a mind broken enough to channel Vörissa's corruption. He became my disciple. He became my Fog Lord."

"Let...me...free..."

"He wields a combination of your power and of Vörissa's. I gave him such a gift and promised him his one desire." The Crypt Walker placed his palm onto Helruss' chest. "In return I got my one desire. I got to rid the world of you."

Helruss screamed as magic flowed from inside of him, through the palm and into the Crypt Walker. For a moment I felt horrified. A god was dying. A god was suffering and screaming in agony. If a god could suffer and feel the pain of the world then what hope did us mere mortals have?

"I will take your divinity. I will take your magic. I will take your spark. Everything you are will exist in me," The Crypt Walker declared, laughing maniacally as he drained the god.

Steelion leapt to his feet and charged forward. Reit and Alluca were right behind him. I rolled to my feet and bolted after them. The Crypt Walker was only a raid boss and I had defeated many of those. He was only an archon and I had spent the last few hours cutting down any that stood in my way. We could stop the Crypt Walker; we could save a god.

Hizzous turned towards us and flicked his hand in our directions. Four tendrils of fog emerged and launched at us, stabbing us through the chest and pushing us backwards into the wall. I tried to scream but the impact of the smash robbed me of air. I tried to move but the tendril had me pinned. I had to do something but movement was impossible. Unless.... I winced at the thought. I had a plan but it was far from a good one. There was still my Feore Shell armour.

I activated the armour and my body became an impassable mist. I should have shot forward but I knew from experience that when dealing with the fog, I wouldn't. Instead my mist-body would merge with the fog. It was a dangerous tactic and it hurt like hell but I was out of choices. The fog tried to disperse my body throughout. Unbearable pain through every inch of me as my body was literally being torn apart. I focused my thoughts.

Guilt; I felt nothing but since the Glitch. I had killed Hizzous and I had killed Steelion and I was responsible for others who died.

No. The thought ripped through my mind. *You have taken a life but you are not responsible for their actions. You did not make Steelion attack. You did not make Hizzous murder.*

It was not my duty to carry the weight of other's choices. I had enough weight of my own to shoulder. Hizzous had made his choice and now he had to live with the consequences.

I focused on my thoughts and tried to ignore the pain. I willed my body forth, traveling through the fog tendril and emerging on the other side. Pulling my body together, I reassembled above Hizzous. I tackled the startled sniper the ground and pinned him there.

"I don't know what happens when we die here," I growled. I materialized the broken remnants of Splinter's Bite and thrust it into the side of Hizzous' skull. "So let me know when you find out."

Hizzous was dead -- again.

I scanned the room. The fog was dissipating. I glanced at Helruss. The god's frail corpse fell to the ground and shattered. Standing where the Crypt Walker once did was a new form. It was a combination of the two. He stood tall and still had the body of Shao Khan but the bone armour was replaced by a set of amour adorned with black feathers. The human skull that once resided atop the Crypt Walker was replaced by the skull of a raven and the long cloak that was once worn by Helruss now adorned this new form.

"I am neither Helruss nor the Crypt Walker. I am something new. I am perfection. I am the Death Walker." He glanced over at us. None of us knew what to do. He raised his hand and prepared to snap.

"Mr. Stark," I said, suddenly afraid. "I don't feel so good."

"You will interfere no longer." He said. "Any last words?"

"Babe," Geist said as he crawled to his wife. He pulled her close and held her in his large Orcish arms. "I love you."

"I love you too," she replied with a sob.

"Your kind, tenacious to the end," The Death Walker snapped his fingers and that was when we all died.

Chapter 12

"...." – Deputy, (Far Cry 5)

I had two thoughts when I opened my eyes. The first was *Holy shit, I can open my eyes* and the second was I *will kill the first person who makes a Thanos joke*. I looked around and saw us all in the room, alive. I looked around. Steelion, Reit, myself and the rest of the PCs were okay. We were in the exact position we had been when the Death Walker snapped his fingers. The corpses, both archon and undead, that once littered the room were gone. Castimiri stood in the center of the room, one hand on her chest and the other held high in the air. A fading golden glow came from the aloft limb.

"W...w...what?" I stammered.

"Your kind is not like others. Your kind is different. You are not what he expects," she said through pained grunts. "I did what I could to protect you." Her tired legs gave way and she crumpled to the floor, crying out. I tried to bolt to her but, somehow, Steelion was faster. He slid next to her and caught her in his arms.

"Hush," Steelion said. "You'll be okay."

"I....I...." Castimiri's eyes fell shut. She opened them a few seconds later to see Scáthach standing over her. Scáthach silently knelt down and summoned her druidic magic. Nature flowed through her hands and into the angel's body. The archon's wounds slowly knitted together. Castimiri stared with wonder in her eyes. "W..w..what do angels call those that save them?"

"I am no one of consequence," Scáthach said. I blinked in surprise. Her voice was musical, like a chirping bird. "I am but a tiny nightingale, singing to the stars and knowing that she will never be heard."

"Sing, pretty bird," Castimiri said as she took Scáthach's hands into her own. "Sing and know that this time the stars have heard your voice."

"Are you well enough to stand?" Scáthach asked. The angel nodded. Scáthach helped Castimiri to her feet.

"My wounds are....." she trailed off as she searched for the word. "Archons don't heal like your kind does but it will suffice. My magic, however, is not sufficient enough to fight."

"Let us do that," Scáthach declared with a determination in her voice.

"Where is the Death Walker," I asked.

"He has taken his undead army and united them with the Foulsouls," The angel explained. "He has created the largest army in all of history and now marches them to the Torixica Spire. He means to march once more on the living world. He means to rid Aspumer of all life."

"We need to stop him. We need to find his army and...." Steelion voice trailed off. Logic had taken hold and he was now thinking the same thing I was. There was no way we'd survive against an army that big. He quietly repeated his words. "We need to stop him."

I glanced back at Helruss' corpse. What was left of the god was little more than a pile of broken and shattered bones. It was moments like this that I'd expected to forget that I was trapped in a video game, reality lost to the faux one that had been built around me, but instead it only reinforced the truth. VCO was just a game and its creator stood behind me but even Reit had no clue what to do next. A red sparkle caught my attention. It was the flicker of light coming from something buried beneath a pile of bones and ash. The rest kept talking as I walked over to the bones.

"Even if we face him," Yasna said, "wouldn't he just

kill us again with a snap?"

"The Death Walker's power is not absolute. The absorption has weakened him," Casimiri explained. "In his current state I doubt he has the power to do that again."

"We still can't face him," Steelion said. "We don't have the numbers. We need troops."

I stood over Helruss' corpse and stared down at the pile of bones. I whispered a small apology as I knelt down beside it. I brushed the bones aside until I saw. My eyes widened in surprise. I grabbed the once hidden item and held it aloft.

"Reit," I called out. "Is this what I think it is?" Reit looked over and stared at the red horn that rested in my hands.

"Y..yes," he stammered. He dashed over to me and took it. He let out a whistle as he admired it. "This is it; this is Helruss' legendary Red Horn of War."

"What good does it do?" Alluca asked.

"It gives us an army," I said began.

"It gives us an army of the greatest of Aspumer's warriors that party atop the Elusium Mountain in the Aeolisian Halls," Steelion finished. He smirked. "Now we have the numbers. We just need to warn the living. I could try another communication spell."

"When did you learn magic?" I asked.

"I didn't," he explained. "I found a series of orbs that could communicate between the living realm and the dead realm. They're called Realm Glass. It's what I used to try and speak to you."

"They were terrible at their job," I admitted.

"They work better when each person has an orb," he admitted.

"An army forms as we speak," Castimiri said. "We have done what we could to signal the living world and they prepare to march against the undead arrival. The five armies of the Descendents stand at the ready. They will face the threat as it emerges from beneath but they are not prepared. They know not what will come to face them."

"Then we need to face them," Yasna said. She glanced

at Steelion and got a nod of approval. Her face tightened as she barked orders. "Search the room and find what you can. Replenish what you need and ditch what you don't. We have to move fast. By the time we reach UW we'll be coming out into a battle. There will be no time to waste. We'll need every spell and steel we can get." Yasna glanced at Reit. The shaman shook his head.

"My magic is too unpredictable," he explained. "The spirits are too loud."

Castimiri opened her mouth to speak but paused as the sound of flapping wings filled the air. Five more archons - three men and two women - landed next to her. They quickly bowed. "Where are the rest?"

"They have sided with the Death Walker," the lead male said. "He is our Lord now and they follow him. They are drawn to him. Even now, as we speak, I fight the draw to join him." Castimiri looked at the others. The five nodded as well. "We will oppose him and aid you as we can. Do you need me to look at your wounds?"

Castimir shook her head. For a second I swore I saw her cheeks redden. "I am fine for now." She pointed to us. "Get them suited. They mean to face the Death Walker."

The lead male looked over at me and my group. "What do you need?"

[I need arrows,] Badënov said. He held up Hizzous' bowblade. [Do any of you possess some form of objection to my acquisition of this blade?]

None of us objected. I raised my hand. "I need a longsteel."

A female archon stepped forth. She drew a longsword and handed it to me. "My name is Dikaya and I am a Scourge Hunter. It is my duty to hunt those who dare defy death. I would be honoured if you used my blade."

The blade was coconut coloured steel with a boysenberry coloured handle. It was heavier than Splinter's Bite but still within my limit for use. I gave the blade a scan and studied its stats. It was stronger than Splinter's Bite but still paled in comparison to Whaitiri Edge. What did bring a sparkle to my eye was the blade's undead bane enchantment. That meant the blade had increased hit and damage towards undead. That was definitely going to come in use. I glanced over my shoulder and saw Reit talking to the second male archon.

"Try not to control to the spirits," the archon said. "Instead, listen to them. They grant wisdom and power. They will aid in your spells."

"They all yell at once," Reit replied. "It's like trying to talk over kids."

"Steelion," Castimiri called out. I pivoted around and saw the angel waved him over. Steelion approached. She held out the Blade of Lite. "I need you to wield this. This blade must lead the charge but I have not the strength to fight."

"A...are you sure?" he asked, trying not to sound too excited. Castimiri nodded. Steelion bowed his head in thanks.

"The armies have met," the female archon said. "They are holding strong and awaiting the Death Walker's march. Do you wish to see?" I nodded. The archon held up her arms and summoned a ball of magic between the palms of her hands. The ball grew in size. I peered inside. An image of the area outside *Under Way* came into focus. I saw hundreds of men and woman standing in formation, five armies at the ready. At the head of each race's army was that nation's leader. Leading the Enclave army was none other than Slashlore.

"My Queen," Slashlore said with a bow of his head. Queen Theresa Archona looked at the paladin. She gave him a nod. The Witch Queen was dressed not in her normal royal gear. She was dressed in an anchor-grey coloured breastplate with shamrock dyed slacks. A charcoal coloured, open-front skirt fell to her boots. A combat staff rested in her arms. "It is always good to see you, My Queen. I wish it was under better circumstances."

Theresa looked up at the sky. I hoped she was looking for me but I was in the opposite direction. The normally blue sky was covered by grey clouds. Flakes of ash rained down from above. "As do I."

"We all do," A skippy voice added. An old gnome strutted forward. He was covered from head to toe in clockwork armour, each cog adorned in a golden colour. On his back was an eccentric crossbow. This was King Toshel Gearrigger. "This ash is deplorable."

"I spend a great deal of time in caves and mines," a new voice said. The Dwarves were once ruled by a monarchy but that had long since been dissolved. Now they were ruled by a council known as the Masons. High Mason Jozuth Redaxe, the leading member of the council, wore a set of full plate armour, stained a mahogany red. Held carefully in his hand was a scarlet two-handed battleaxe. He gave a nod to each of the ruling three. "I see very little of the sun so I find it ironic that I long for it. I wish it free of the clouds that contain it."

"Irony is a peculiar mistress," a female voice added. She was Lord Guard Lanmina Nightpride. She was a lithe bodied Elf with flowing alabaster hair, scarlet eyes and wore studded leather armour, green as the forest foliage. Atop her head was a wide brim hat that matched the leather armour and had a wine coloured feather sticking out. On her belt hung a rapier with a fine edge, a strong enchantment and a point so sharp it could almost pierce time. The Elves used to be ruled by a crown. They became obsolete and were replaced by a younger generation, or as they were referred to, the New Guard. Seven sat on the Guard's ruling board and Lanmina sat at the head. "Irony has also allowed us to have such varied company. One time this meeting of the Eternals would consist entirely of kings. Now we have but one king, one queen, a High Mason, a Lord Guard and now a President. We are the Eternal no longer. I think it ironic that we've been using the name Descendents of the Eternals for years but only now have we finally achieved its accuracy."

"How goes the foundation of your kingdom, President?" Gearrigger asked.

"It is a struggle, Your Majesty. We are slow going," he admitted. "Coming to a consensus is frighteningly difficult.

We cannot even agree on a flag."

"Flags are important, child," The Mason added.

"We have people eagerly designing them," Slashlore admitted. His voice quickly fell into a mumble. "But all they keep suggesting are chocolate starfish and penis drawings."

"You need a flag," Lord Nightpride said. "Every army needs a banner to fight under."

"Bah," the Mason scoffed. "A banner is all fine and well but it ain't what people fight for. Each man and woman here to fight do so 'cause they know what is right. What ye need is to remind them of it. When the fighting gets heavy and their strength starts to waiver, call out a cheer and remind them what they fight for." None of them argued that. I knew Slashlore's mind raced. What could he call out that every Enclave member, every gamer, would instantly recognize? Somehow *we pay $15 a month for this shit* didn't seem to cut it.

Queen Archona looked past Slashlore and spotted Lady Adelaide Bullmourn. Adelaide stood beside Scova and Garruil, the three discussing the upcoming battle. The Witch Queen waved Adelaide over. "Lady Bullmourn, does your presence here mean the Whispers are among us?"

"They are, my Queen," Adelaide said. She wore a ninja's keikogi with a matching tabi. She kept a ninjatō on her back and several kunai on her belt. "The Whispers are not soldiers but we stand with you."

"Not with the Enclave?" The Witch Queen asked. "What of the fiery one there?"

Adelaide, to her credit, did not blush. She stood there stoically, showing no emotion. "I am here for all of my allies, your Highness." The Witch Queen just smiled.

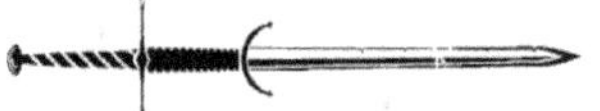

The sound was unnerving, even from my vantage. It started quite low and then it started to grow. It was an undead groan that echoed across the battlefield, coming from the doors of *UW*. A gnome scout pointed at the approaching horde and called out a warning.

"The undead have come," Slashlore said with some nerve. He looked at Tialla and Scova for support.

"We didn't stop the undead from coming, it came. Somehow or other, they came just the same," Scova said. "How could it be so? They came without necromancers, they came without hags. They came without magic, horns or flags."

"Have I ever mentioned that I hate you?" Slashlore said, a small grin crossing his lips. He looked over the battlefield when Tialla's voice kicked in.

"He puzzled and puzz until his puzzler was sore," she rhymed. "Then Slashlore thought of something that he hadn't before. Maybe fighting the undead wasn't a chore; maybe fighting the undead, meant a little bit more."

"I hate you most of all," he snapped. "You're supposed to be on my side, *General* Tialla."

"That's not how I remember it."

Skeletons and zombies marched into view as gargoyle looking undead circled in the air. Hundreds were clearly visible and these were just the vanguard. Slashlore silently gulped.

"Steady yourselves," a commanding voice cried out. Queen Theresa Archona stepped up. Her staff glowed and her speech carried across the miles of battlefield. It didn't matter how far away someone stood, they heard her with perfect ease. "We stand here today, ready to fight. We do so not for honour or duty. We fight not for resources or political reason. Today we fight to live and to protect everything and everyone we love. We fight here, today, so our friends, our families, our loved ones and our children can continue living tomorrow. If we fail here today, then everything will be wiped out.

"Ready your spells and steady your steel. Tighten those fists and raise those shields. Death marches forward no further. Death will claim us no longer. Today, we beat death!" Roars claimed the sky like a monstrous thunder.

"Glory is eternal!" The Witch Queen pointed her staff forward. The humans charged forward.

"No gear ticks alone!" King Toshel Gearrigger called out. The Gnomes charged forward.

"Immortality grants us wisdom," Lord Guard Lanmina Nightpride called out. The Elves screamed the reply alongside her. "By wisdom's guidance!" The Elves charged forward.

"Our clan, our town or wherever we roam," High Mason Jozuth Redaxe called out. The Dwarves roared the reply alongside him. "Dwarves fight for what they call home!" The Dwarves charged forward.

The Enclave army stood at the ready. They were waiting for the signal to attack. Slashlore looked out over the army. He spotted familiar faces and new ones. Everybody was here to fight and they all needed him to lead him. They all needed him to inspire him. A smirk crossed his face as the perfect cheer rolled across his mind.

"Alright, let's do this. Leeeeeerrrrrooooooooyyyyyyyy......" Hundreds of eyes snapped over at Slashlore. Each started out in disbelief. Was he actually saying that? But then they turned. Smiles crossed their faces and hundreds of Enclave members screamed the reply alongside him. "Jeeeeenkiiiinnnnnnsss."

I had to admit, it was the perfect chant. It united the Enclave but more importantly it reminded us of the truth that had gotten so easily missed. Despite the bodies we wore, we were not Dwarves, Elves, Gnomes or VCO humans. Aspumer was not our world. We were all gamers and we were trapped there. This was not our home but we would defend it. We were here to do what gamers did best: be big damned heroes.

The Enclave charged forwards.

Slashlore led the Enclave charge. He reached the undead and slammed the first skeleton with his shield. The bone walker shattered and Slashlore moved to the next. He slashed at the closest zombie, his axe cleaving it in two.

A pair of shadow tendril leapt from the ground, grabbed a pair of zombies and squeezed until the bodies popped. The tendril tossed them aside. From behind the lines,

Tialla stood. She waved her hands like a conductor, summoning more shadowy tendrils. A large bear bolted past the priest, letting out a loud roar as it barrelled into the horde. Bearcules felled one undead with a powerful swipe of his claw and bit into another with his powerful jaws. A Dwarf leapt over the druid. He hit the ground with a downwards ground punch that sent ripples across the battlefield. Dozens of undead fell over. The Dwarf pivoted to his feet and fired another powerful punch. His fist slammed into the chest of an unsuspecting zombie and sent the undead corpse flying backwards.

"Kamé-Doken Blast!" A ball of ki energy formed in the Dwarf's hands and fired outwards. It ripped a hole through the undead horde. Punchocalypse smirked. He was in a fighting mood.

"I'm not letting a monk outdo me," Scova said. She flipped up her hand and fired a blast of fire. It ripped through the horde, incinerating the unlucky few that got caught in her path. The slash of a blade came down beside the mage. Scova looked behind her to see two zombies fall. One was cleaved in two by the cut of a blade and the second was damaged by a flurry of high speed blows.

"Don't lose focus, Little Flame," Adelaide said. She pivoted to her left, slashed again and fell a second one. "Everything can change in a heartbeat. If you don't behave, I will have to punish you."

"Is that supposed to be a deterrent?" Scova pivoted to her right, Keshim's Fang felling a zombie with a burning slash.

"Just imagine what I'll do if you behave," Adelaide sternly said. Garruil rolled her eyes as she fought, her fist moving in the usual blur.

"I love how they talk," Anize said as she ran past.

"Don't get any ideas," Noran added as he kept pace. Both rogues struck with their blades, their steel slicing through undead hides as they tore through the battle ground. A pair of undead gargoyles swiftly swooped down, slashing at the pair. Noran quickly dodged. Suddenly a trio of sickly green balls crashed into the first one. The creature screeched as it crashed into the ground. Fleyming raised her hands again and began to form another spell.

"Yippie!" a small voice cried out. "It's fighting time!"

Skith - Son of Zook - rode atop his un-orc. The eight-foot undead orc had putrid flesh falling off of its body and a massive club in his hand. Skith rode atop the un-orc, slashing with his cleaver-glaive as they both charged into battle. Montra ran beside the Gnome. Her hands were quick and decisive. Each blow she fired was carefully chosen. She didn't obliterate the undead like Punchocalypse nor did she overwhelm them with speed like Garruil. Montra's blows would shattered the spinal cord or shattered a leg. No magic could keep a skeleton upright without a leg or spine.

Slashlore couldn't help but smile. His army was succeeding. The undead had the numbers but each of his soldiers was worth ten or more undead. This battle would soon be won.

That's when the tide of the battle turned.

Chapter 13

"...." – Hero, (Dragon Quest VIII)

Bearcules was the first to fall.

Slashlore's army was one of five that stood against the undead horde. They were expecting a massive army of low level zombies and skeletons. What they got were the Death Walker's elite. The zombies, skeletons and gargoyles were the first wave. They were the vanguard, slated to be defeated. The Nethall were next in the attack line. The humanoid beasts, with long skeletal limbs and baleful claws, were next onto the battlefield. They led the wave of dangerous, powerful undead like the paenido and the brutish Solomon Grundys. They were unexpected.

Slashlore's face dropped as the Nethalls came into view. He hadn't seen them since......ever. They were before his time in VCO. He'd only heard about them and read about them online. Now they marched on him with troops numbering in the tens of thousands. He silently gulped as he charged the Nethall. He raised his shield just long skeletal limbs slashed at him. The baleful claws scrapped across the paladin's shield. Slashlore was protected from the attack but the strength behind it still pushed him back a few paces. He swung with his axe and the edge sliced through the Nethall's decrepit hide but the creature didn't fall. He raised his axe to strike again but was forced to pivot as a second Nethall dashed towards him. Slashlore barely had enough time to raise his shield as the undead shoulder-tackled him. The blow sent him skipping across the ground like a bowling pin. A trio of Nethall descended on the paladin and assaulted him with attacks. Slashlore rolled onto his back and used his shield as cover.

A powerful fist slammed into a Nethall's chest and sent the beast flying. Punchocalypse pivoted around and brought his foot across. It caught a second undead and knocked him off of the prone paladin. With a rising uppercut that would make Little Mac jealous, Punchocalypse knocked the third Nethall off. His feet touched down on to the ground for only a second before the monk pivoted around and summoned forth his ki. A glowing ball of energy formed between his palms but he never got the chance to fire it. A pair of gargoyles swooped down, diving like peregrine falcons, grabbed Punchocalypse by the shoulders and carried him off. Slashlore rolled to his feet and willed the magic in his shield. Using his best Chris Evans, he flung the glowing shield into the air. The shield connected with one of the gargoyles and Punchocalypse fell free. A chain as thick as an arm snapped across the paladin's face and tossed him to the ground. An undead roar echoed across the battlefield as a paenido stumbled forward.

Two tendrils of shadowy energy leapt forward. They slashed at the paenido but did little damage. General Tialla bolted across the battlefield. She needed to be close to heal both Slashlore and Punchocalypse. A circle of shadows formed around the body of Slashlore. His wounds began to knit together but the spell came to an abrupt halt when a pair of baleful claws slashed across her back. She dropped to one knee. She looked out across the battlefield as the charging paenido. Tialla pushed up to her feet but lasted only a few seconds before another set of claws forced her back down.

Bearcules barreled across the field, the druid letting loose a roar of his own. He slammed into the paenido with the full strength of a charging bear and forced the creature to one knee. Bearcules roared again, his battle cry pulling threat from those around him. Undead turned towards him, each carrying a look of hunger upon their faces. He roared a third time, wanting all of their attention on him. Bearcules stood up on his hind legs and swung with his massive claws. His strikes were big, wide and devastating to any in its path. With one swoop of his arm, his claws would rip at two or three undead. Bearcules summoned forth his magic and pushed it through his body. Each thread of fur morphed into a thread of iron. The paenido swung with his gargantuan chain, the links slammed against the bear's hide with a loud clang. The druid didn't even flinch. He lunged at the undead and slammed both paws into the undead's enormous gut. The claws sliced through the glacial blue skin but the undead still stood. Bearcules let out another roar and struck again. He willed the druidic magic through his veins, calling upon nature to boost his strength and hold steady his constitution. His blows became stronger, each strike seeming to force the paenido back a few paces. He glanced over his shoulder and eyed the field behind him. Tialla was back on her feet. She stood over Slashlore, a circle of shadows forming beneath him. Bearcules roared again, pulling all threat in the nearby area towards him. He needed it all on him. Only that way could he save Slashlore, Tialla and Punchocalypse. Only that way could he balance his own ledger. Bearcules slammed into the paenido and gored the creature. Suddenly a devastating punch slammed into Bearcules' side. The druid felt his iron fur dent upon the impact. He dropped to all fours, limping from the blow. Bearcules looked over at the gigantic Solomon Grundy undead. The creature struck again with a backhanded slap and sent the bear skidding across the ground. Bearcules tried to climb back to his feet but several Nethall chains lashed out, each wrapping around a leg and pulling it out from underneath the druid. Bearcules slammed back into the ground. A murder of gargoyles descended upon him. Each ripped and tore into the druid's body, tearing into the iron and rending it apart. The paenido stood over the fallen druid, watching as Bearcules, in his last breath of life, morphed back to an Elf. The undead's chest opened up like a set of massive teeth and ingested the druid whole. In one swallow, the paenido absorbed Bearcules and his powers.

Bearcules was dead.

Slashlore screamed out in agony. The paladin had just watched the Enclave's sheriff die. He just watched a friend die. He just watched a friend sacrifice his life for Slashlore's. The paladin didn't want to watch another die, he wanted to swear that he wouldn't allow any more to die but that was a foolhardy premise. This was war. More were going to die. Slashlore just hoped it wasn't somebody else that he cared about.

Scova was the next to fall.

With a thunderous march, the archons entered the battlefield. The foulsouls marched first as the winged angels took to the air. The Enclave had never seen these creatures before. They didn't know what their weaknesses were.

"Any thoughts?" Scova panted. Slashlore shook his head.

"Cut them down," Adelaide sternly said. "We fight them like we fought everything else, Little Flame."

Scova and Adelaide ran to meet the foulsoul march. Skith, son of Zook, and Garruil ran beside them. Skith let out a whoop of excitement as he rode his un-orc. Scova's blade met the foulsoul steel. She twisted Keshim's Fang and pushed the archon's steel aside. The mage's burning blade cut twice as it ripped across the foulsoul's chest. The creature screeched but did not fall. Scova summoned forth a tongue of fire and wielded it like a whip. As Scova Belmonted all over the battlefield, Adelaide moved in and out of vision. She was quick, like Goku quick, and her blade was faster. She cut at one, vanished, reappeared a second later near a different foulsoul and slashed at it all before vanishing again. Beside her was Garruil. The monk couldn't move as fast as Adelaide but her strikes were far swifter. Her hands and feet were literal blurs as she pummelled any foe stupid enough to engage her. In only three seconds she'd dodged a blade from one foulsoul, slapped aside a spear from the second and somehow still had time to throw one hundred punches and kicks between the two of them.

Skith struck hard with his cleaver-glaive as his un-orc pummeled away with its undead fists. Blow after blow smashed against the foulsoul's face. The gnome leapt off of the un-orc and dove his glaive into the beast's neck. He twisted, ripped it free and leapt back to the un-orc's back. The foulsoul, already forgotten by the pair, fell to the ground. The pair moved to the next foe but the un-orc suddenly screamed and fell to one knee as an archon blade ripped across its chest. Scared and in pain, the un-orc violently flailed about, accidently pitched Skith from its back. The Gnome skipped across the stones in surprise. He rolled to his feet and glanced at the foulsoul's blade. It was glowing. Skith eyed the un-orc's wound. It was also glowing. Skith swore. That foulsoul had an undead bane weapon. Skith ran towards his ally but was knocked back by the power strike from an archon's club. The Gnome struggled to stand, his eyes wide with terror as the bane weapon tore again and again into the un-orc. Each slash ripped a little more of the beast apart. Before the Glitch, if the summon was defeated it would just take a cool-down time to re summon it. Now there was no telling what would happen.

The archon raised his club once more. He swung at Skith's skull but the Gnome quickly rolled out of the way. Skith raised his hand and summoned forth sickly green magic. Suddenly the archon's body froze. Two seconds later the creature screamed in agony. Skith had used the Revenant magic to boil the archon's blood. It wouldn't kill him but it would stun the creature. Skith grabbed his weapon and gave it a solid swing. The strike separated the archon's head from its body. Skith panted, he always preferred to kill with his weapon over a spell. He looked over just in time to see the un-orc explode in a ball of dust. Skith screamed in sorrow.

Adelaide ran her blade through the back of an archon and quickly twisted away. She brought her ninjatō up to block a foulsoul spear but the thrust was too swift. The spearhead ripped into her shoulder. Adelaide winced but ignored the attack. It was the first wound she'd received today but she knew it wouldn't be her last. The ninja twisted away and lashed out with her foot. The kick stumbled the foulsoul back a few paces. Adelaide drew a kunai and fired it at her foe. I knew countless hours had made her accuracy something to be feared but somehow she missed. The kunai flew wide. Just before the point of release, Adelaide felt a surge of weakness flow through her arm. It had affected her throw. She glanced down in surprise but swore as realization hit. She looked at her shoulder as a drop of blue liquid rolled down. That spear had been covered with poison. The foulsoul thrust again. Adelaide called upon her speed to dodged but found it lacking. The poison had robbed it from her. Adelaide desperately tried to twist out of the way.

Scova flicked her flame whip to her left and wrapped around the neck of an attacking foulsoul. She pulled the creature closer and slashed with Keshim's Fang; the flame blade sliced through the foulsoul's neck in a single slice. Scova looked over her shoulder just in time to see a spear run through her lover. She screamed and her blonde hair burned a brighter fiery-red. The mage morphed into a ball of fire and shot forward. It was a quick burning blink that put her right beside the foulsoul. Scova slashed with Keshim's Fang and cut the spear in two. She pivoted quickly and slashed again, running the flaming blade across the foulsoul's chest. She summoned forth a ball of fire and planted it deeply into the foulsoul's body. A second later the ball exploded and the creature burned from inside. Scova turned around to see Garruil standing over Adelaide. The monk held a dagger in her hand and an opportunistic look upon her face. Scova bolted towards Adelaide. Garuill looked up and noticed the mage. She flicked the dagger away and backed up to defend the pair. Scova grabbed her lover and examined the wound. It was through Adelaide's lower gut. Scova sighed in relief. Adelaide would survive.

"Be...be..." Adelaide stammered. Scova tried to shush her but the Lady would not listen. "Be....hind....you."

Scova spun around just in time to see the tip of a sword rip across her neck. Scova tried to cough but found herself gurgling instead. The archon smirked as she pulled the blade away only to run it through Scova. It dove into the mage's chest and emerged out the other side. Scova fell beside Adelaide. Scova willed her body to move, she begged it, but it did not respond. The burning hair suddenly was extinguished and it returned to her normal blonde colour.

The archon stood over her with a blade at the ready. In one strike it would all be over. The archon would kill her and she'd make Adelaide watch. Scova looked over at Adelaide. The ninja tried to get up but the poison wouldn't allow it. The ninja had enough strength left for one more movement, one more action.

Adelaide reached over and took Scova's hand into her own. She coughed as she spoke. "I love you, Cobie."

"I love you too, Adelaide," Scova replied. She smiled. She didn't want to die but if she had to, she was glad it was with Adelaide. She tried to keep her eyes open but she couldn't. She wasn't strong enough to face death head on.

The sudden sound of a metallic plink caught her attention. It was a sound she was familiar with but she hadn't heard it in a very long time. It was the sound VCO made when a player in their friends list logged on. But how? Since the Glitch nobody had logged into VCO. So who was logging in now? She looked over and saw the words floating in the air.

Rake has logged on.

With electricity flowing through my body, I bound across the battlefield. Dikaya was in my right hand and Whaitiri Edge in my left. I slashed at any I came across but I had one target to get through and damn anyone who was dumb enough to get in my way. I spotted the archon standing above the girls and I slammed into him, hard. Take my normal quick speed, add in the boots and stack on top of that the power and speed of the Kahail set and I was moving at some insane speeds. Now take that speed and put it into a body check. I ain't great with physics but something tells me that no matter how big or strong that archon was, he wasn't going to stand a chance against me. I body checked him at full speed and sent him flying. I didn't look where he landed, I didn't care. I pulled off my Third Eye headband and looked at the two. Adelaide pointed to Scova. I understood and immediately pressed it against her skull.

"Activate Second Wind," I pleaded. Scova just lay there. I couldn't activate it for her and I didn't have any other healing spells. I needed her to save herself. "Scova, please, activate it."

The headband let out a small shimmer as the magic started. The wounds on both her chest and neck knitted back together. Scova coughed and spat up blood. She wasn't fully healed but she wasn't dead.

"Rake?" she said. I spun around. Dozens of Nethall, undead and foulsouls were converging on me. I scowled. I summoned every ounce of electricity still in me and put it into a burst attack. Lighting exploded outwards, consuming every foe in my immediate area. Once upon a time I thought myself Ben Affleck in *Daredevil*. That was no longer true. I was Thor and this was me entering the *Battle of Wakanda*.

I glanced up and locked eyes with Garruil. She was clearly shocked to see me. For a moment we just stood there, string each other down. Every inch of my body wanted to rip her apart but now wasn't the time. I watched as Garruil backed away, vanishing in the battle. I knelt by Adelaide. She was alive but not for much longer. The poison was eating her. I needed a healer. I looked around and in the distance spotted Montra. The monk was currently fighting a foulsoul. I called out for her. She snapped her head over at me and stared in shock. She dropped her foe and quickly dashed over.

"I heard you were dead," she said.

"You and everybody else," I said in my best Plissken. I pointed to Adelaide. "She's poisoned, badly." Montra nodded. I looked at Scova. "Where is Slashlore?"

"Over there, why?" I followed her point until I saw Slashlore fighting beside the Witch Queen.

"Shit is about to get worse. Stay with her and keep them alive," I said. There was no sense getting Scova to follow me. Nobody could separate her from Adelaide now. "Meet me when you get the chance."

I bolted away. Without the *Kahail Set* I was limited to just my speed and the boots. That would have to be enough. I bounded across the battlefield, stopping only when I arrived beside the two leaders.

"I wondered where you were, Rake," The Witch Queen said. She spun around, blocked a foulsoul attack with her staff. She quickly spun her staff, struck the attacker twice and then blasted it with a spell. It quickly became dust. "You're late."

"Traffic was a bitch," I smirked. I glanced at Slashlore. "I need you to do what you do best. I need you to lead us."

"What do you mean?"

"Something bad is coming out of that raid and we are not prepared."

"The Crypt Walker, I know."

"No, this is much fucking worse than the Crypt Walker," I snapped.

"Worse?" Slashlore swore. "How the hell can we stop worse?"

"Listen to me. Everything on this battlefield are nothing but adds," I said quickly. "The raid boss is coming out." Suddenly the spark of understanding took hold. Slashlore smiled. He waved over Tialla. She paused, looking at me with surprise.

"We need side tanks and side healers dealing with these adds," he said quickly. "We'll need main-tanks ready to deal with the boss. Split up the DPS. Keep range firing and high damage melee ready to run. If they're good at cleave, put them on the adds."

"Yes, Mr. President," Tialla said. She paused and eyed me. "Welcome back."

"In the meantime," I said with a smirk. "I brought back-up."

A metallic plink filled both of our ears. We each looked at the words in the sky.

Steelion has just logged on.

The sound of a horn blared across the sky. Every person, no matter where they were, heard the sound. It was clear, it was powerful and it sounded valiant. I smirked as I looked across the battleground. Standing at the entrance to UW was Steelion. He held a glowing sword in one hand and the Red Horn of War in the other. He took a deep breath and blew the horn once more.

"Is that Steelion?" Slashlore asked.

"I died and I went to the land of the dead. Not only did I find some old friends and some new ones, but I found an army as well."

From high atop the Elysium Mountains they came. Each dined and partied in the Aeolisian Halls, living a hedonistic life until the moment the Red Horn of War was blown. Then they would descend to the battlefield to fight the Great War. From the clouds the warriors rained down. They were warriors and Vikings, paladins and barbarians and each rode great mounts and descended upon the battle like the great Valkyrie of lore. They were the greatest soldiers in all of Aspumer and Helruss' personal soldiers. They were the Aeolisian Army. They followed whoever held the horn and that meant they followed Steelion. The legion of Aspumer's best rode forward, trampling over the horde of undead. Their weapons quickly cleared through the minions, mowing them down like grass on a warm summer's day.

"Slay the undead and fell the archons," Steelion cried out, holding his blade forward. "Today we fight to save Helruss and all of Aspumer."

I took a deep breath in and readied myself for battle. The fight was far from over. A familiar form stood beside me. I glanced at Scova. The mage was back on her feet, her blade held in her hand at the ready.

"What are you doing here?" I asked. "Why aren't you with Adelaide?"

"I love that woman and want to stand by her," Scova explained, "but she would not respect me if I did not fight. So whatever it is we're about to fight better hurry the hell up 'cause I ain't staying away from her for long."

"Then let's go be heroes," I said.

"Hero ain't on my resume," she replied, her blonde hair re-igniting into flame.

We both dashed into battle.

Chapter 14

"...." – Jack, (Harvest Moon)

Anize charged the Solomon Grundy. Her blade slashed quickly, ripping through the brute's left leg. The creature spun around fired a fist in her direction but the rogue had already vanished. Noran appeared a few seconds later, flying through the air and striking with a diving slash. His blades tore across Grundy's face but the creature didn't fall. Grundy pivoted with a backhanded swipe but Noran was gone. Anize reappeared, her blades cutting through the other leg. Grundy stumbled but didn't fall. The brute tried to move to the left. Suddenly a staff shot out. It snapped against the Grundy's leg and forced it to the right and directly into the path of a greatsword. The blade came down hard and cut the legs out from underneath it. Grundy fell forward onto the waiting blades of Anize and Noran. The rogues looked up to see a Fenririan and an Orc.

Geist roared as he turned towards a new foe, his blade cleaving a skeleton in two. Ziena just smirked at the rogues. "Try and keep up."

The xenomorph atop Montra's shoulder spat as swiftly as it could. Each gob of acid burned through hide and bone. One spit would weaken the skeleton's bones and her punch would finish the job. The monk pivoted back, ducking beneath the deadly swipe from a set of baleful claws. She brought her foot and snapped it across the Nethall's face. The undead spun in the air as it crashed to the ground. Two more rushed her. She leapt into the air and performed a butterfly kick. Her feet knocked the undead back. Montra hit the ground and spun once more, sweeping the legs of the second Nethall out from underneath it. It too crashed to the ground. She moved back to the first and fired with a flurry of punches. Her fists were glowing but as each blow struck the decrepit skin the glow seemed to leap from her and flow towards the nearest ally. With each strike against a foe, she healed the nearest injured ally. It wasn't much per hit but with the speed at which she punched, it quickly added up.

"Duck!" Montra didn't look to see where the voice came from; she just dropped to the ground and rolled to the side. Steelion leapt over her and brought his glowing blade across the hide of an unlucky Nethall. The Blade of Lite ripped through the undead flesh with little resistance. He cleaved the undead in two. He looked back at Montra and offered his hand. "Grab on!"

Montra grabbed the warrior hand and held tight. Steelion pulled the monk into the air as she spun. Montra's foot spun around, kicking the charging undead trio. Each skeleton shattered upon the impact. Montra returned to the ground and pressed her back up against Steelion's.

"Nice move," she said.

"Nice legs," he replied. Both looked over their respective shoulders and glanced at one another. A smile of approval crossed both their lips. "I'm Steelion."

"Montra," she replied as both leapt back into the fray.

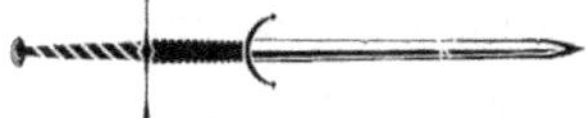

Punchocalypse slammed his fist into the chest of the nearest foulsoul. The archon screeched as its chest collapsed. The monk pivoted around and cocked his fist for a second punch. He never got the chance. The angry cry of a charging gnome zoomed past him. Skith darted past the monk and slashed with his cleaver-glaive. The gnome was furious;

gone was the jovial attitude and his RPing was nowhere to be found. Skith was mad and he was ready to take it out on someone. His first slash came down hard on the foulsoul's leg. The limb buckled and the foulsoul dropped to one knee. Skith stuck again, his cleaver-glaive diving deep into the creature's neck. Skith kicked the body to the dirt, growling as he sliced at a second. His attacks were brutal and savage. He screamed and roared as he brought the weapon down, time after time. With each stab of his cleaver-glaive, he'd give the blade a twist. He wanted to make each strike hurt.

A Dhamphir leapt across the field. She landed atop a foulsoul and bit deep into the archon's neck. She drew blood from the form and felt her body strengthen. Alluca back flipped off the body and gracefully landed on the ground. She bolted forward, with greater speed in her legs, and ran her blade through the foulsoul's chest.

A pair of arrow flew through the air and ripped into two gargoyles. Badënov ran through the field, notching more arrows with each step. The Elf dropped into a slide, fired two arrows into the back of a Nethall and slid between its legs. He notched another arrow and fired it upwards through the Nethall's skull. Badënov rolled to his feet and notched two more. He aimed his bow upwards and fired both. Two more gargoyles dropped from the air.

Yasna slid in beside the archer and swung her hammer. It collided with a skeleton and quickly shattered it. The paladin quickly called forth her magic and sanctified the ground around her. A gold circle of magic surrounded the area around her. Two zombies stumbled towards her but suddenly started screaming as their hides began to burn. She knocked one back with a solid kick, the zombie toppling to the ground, and swung her hammer at the second. A sickening cracking sound was heard as the hammer shattered the second zombie's spine.

A paenido let out a bearish roar and swiped with a

newly formed claw. I glared at the undead brute and scowled. This paenido had consumed Bearcules and now had some of his abilities. I hated Bearcules but he had just sacrificed his life to protect others, others I cared about, and I wasn't about to let that go unanswered. This death wasn't like mine; there was no coming back when a paenido ate you. I pointed Dikaya at the undead.

"He's the next to go," I declared. Scova just nodded. I bolted forward and Scova kept pace. Our faces were stern and serious. We were no longer having fun. Scova slowed just a bit and I crossed over in front of her. I ducked underneath the bear-claw swipe and slashed with Whaitiri Edge. My steel made a clang of contact as it scraped across the undead's iron fur, another druid gift. I scowled and pivoted to the side. Scova leapt in with Keshim's Fang and slashed at the face. Her flaming steel burned through the fur and tore into the hide. She dropped to the ground and rolled to the side, avoiding a bear swipe. I leapt back in, this time striking first with my longsteel. Dikaya tore through the paenido's hide and burned into its flesh. The creature screeched in pain. I struck again with my undead bane and received another screech in reward. The paenido let out a magical roar and for a moment I felt my resolution waiver. I felt the urge to flee but I fought against it. Suddenly a bear-swipe collided with me and knocked me back into the air. I landed with a heavy thud. I scowled, more disappointed with myself then anything. The roar was a magical stun and I had fallen for it.

Scova dashed forward and pressed her palm near the undead's chest. In her best Vegeta, she smirked and blasted the paenido with a gut blast of fire. The undead cried out but still struck. A fist slammed across Scova's face and dropped her to the ground like Rocky in the first half of every final fight. I rolled to my feet and charged but the undead was ready for me. Its chain swung at me and knocked me aside. I skipped across the ground, hating each and every rock I felt in the process. Scova flipped back up and fired a pair of fire darts. They collided with the paenido's face and exploded.

The paenido didn't fall. It just stood there, unfazed as fire ravaged its body and consumed its flesh.

"So grappling is out," I said, looking at the burning body.

"I think it was always out," Scova replied. "I don't know about you but I was in no rush to go hugging that thing."

"What now?"

"Hit it hard?" she suggested.

"Hit it really hard, " I added, "together."

We both bolted forward. The paenido summoned a blast of moonlight energy and fired it at us.

"Crap Baskets!"

We both dodged the blast, feeling its effect as it detonated behind us. Scova took the lead. She held up her hand as she ran. Dozens of small flame darts emerged from her fingertips and fired forwards the undead's face. It was some *Robotech* level volley of missiles. The paenido held up its arm to block the assault. Scova stepped aside as I bolted past her, attacking with both blades. Dikaya slashed across the burning gut and Whaitiri Edge dove in deep. I withdrew both blades as the undead swung at me with its large fist, I rolled back and Scova leapt in. Keshim's Fang dove into the wound I'd just made. Scova pumped as much of her own magic into the blade causing its flame to grow brighter and wilder than ever before. The paenido tried to back away but Scova wouldn't let him escape. With each step he took back she took forwards, plunging the longsword in deeper. I ran in from behind and struck with Dikaya. My longsteel sliced through its neck, separating its head from its shoulders. The head dropped to the ground and the undead body erupted into flame. Scova and I stood there, panting for air, as the paenido burned before us.

A chill filled the air. I noticed it and Scova noticed it. It came with a sense of approaching dread. I glanced across the battlefield as the chilling dread rippled across. Then the ground shook. It was only a slight tremor but I suddenly felt like the kids trapped in the Jeep during *Jurassic Park*. I snapped around to the entrance of *UW*. A petrifying form stepped out from the entrance. Each step rocked the ground.

The Death Walker had arrived.

He raised his hand and a wave of fear rippled across the air. I was suddenly filled with an urge to flee. Despite my command not to, my legs started to retreat. I wanted to run, I needed to run. All around me, hundreds upon hundreds of fearful soldiers began to flee.

"Fear not!" The voice was commanding and clearly heard regardless of location. Queen Theresa Archona, leader of the Descendents of the Eternal, stood firm. She held her staff high in the air. Glowing magical light began to circle her staff. "We will not flee, not this day."

With a dramatic thud, she banged her staff on the ground. The magical light exploded and the spell rippled across the air. It touched every ally on the field, undoing the damage the fear spell had caused. As the spell glimmered across me, my fear vanished. It was like a haze that was sitting on my bravery had lifted and I was thinking clearly once more.

"What is that thing?" Slashlore asked. We began to form up on our paladin.

"That is the Crypt Walker and the God of Death, fused," I said. I glanced at Punchocaplyse. "I thought you were done."

"End of all life is hard to ignore," Punchocaplyse said sternly. "I thought when you came back from the other world you were supposed to return with new wisdom not a new big bad."

"The spirit bomb exists in VCO," I quickly replied. Punchocaplyse grabbed me by the shirt and hoisted me into the air.

"You better not be fucking with me," he snapped. "I'm so fragile right now."

"I mean it's not *the* spirit bomb but it's close enough so VCO doesn't get sued but I'll tell you that later," I promised. I looked at Tialla and Slashlore. I pointed at the Death Walker. "We need you two to lead us. We need to stop that."

The two nervously looked at each other. They silently nodded. Slashlore looked back on the field. "Is he even killable?"

"Any god that walks upon the mortal realm is killable," Reit said. "Besides, Helruss is within that body. If we weaken it more, he may take control."

"How do you know he's still in there?" I asked.

"He gave us the horn," Reit said. "The Crypt Walker would never give us that option."

"Who is this guy?" Slashlore asked.

"I'm Casper Ramirez," he said quickly.

"As in..."

"Wait.....do you mean?"

"Bullshit!"

Slashlore quieted the voices with a raise of his hand. "It doesn't matter who he is. Right now we need to focus on the battle." For a moment it was like a glimmer of sparkle ran across Slashlore's face. This was his kickass moment. This was his great leader moment.

"If you have a plan, Mr. President, then put it in action," the Witch Queen said.

"Aye, lad," the Dwarven King said. "Put me to work."

"I will follow your lead, Mr. President," High Lord Lanmina Nightpride said. King Toshel Gearrigger gave a smile and a nod. Slashlore bowed back to the four.

"Steelion, Yasna and Skith: You're with me. We'll be playing tank. Keep him occupied and keep him confused. Shift and rotate. Tialla: organize healers. I want them showering this battle with heals," Slashlore said. "Queen Archona: you're in charge of range. Line them up and keep them firing. I don't care if it is arrows or spells. King Gearrigger: I don't want to be attacked from above. If it flies, bring it back to the ground. High Mason Redaxe: keep the minions off of us while we tear down the big guy. High Lord Nightpride: We'll need every enhancing spell possible to strengthen us. Start staggering the spells and keep us going. We need to be faster, tougher and stronger than ever before. Everybody else...." Slashlore glanced at me. I nodded. "You're with the Reaper."

"We hit him hard and we hit him fast," I said quickly. "Stick and move. We do not want to be caught flat-footed. Hit and move." I pointed to Reit. "We need the biggest and baddest spell you have."

"It's going to take time," Reit said. "The voices.... they're loud."

"We'll give you cover." I promised. Reit nodded. He dropped to a sitting position and closed his eyes. He began to meditate. I looked at Scova. "Burning Typhoon: let it rip."

Scova walked forward and held her hands in the air. Clouds began to assault the sky. They weren't white or grey clouds, as was normal. They were a combination of red and orange, like the clouds were aflame. They began to cyclone, eventually causing four flaming tornadoes to touch down on the battlefield. The fiery spirals of death each ripped a swath of destruction through the undead horde and barrelled towards the Death Walker.

Scáthach stepped up next. She held her staff horizontally in both hands as moonlight magical energy swirled around her body. A few moments later the magic shot upwards, into the sky. The moonlight splintered, forming dozens of shards. They rained down onto the ground, like starfall, each causing a great devastation upon impact.

"Power up," I commanded. "It's time to end this."

I summoned a blast of electricity and caught it with my blade. Lightning shot around my body as my *Kahail Set* reacted. Scova's blonde hair ignited into a brightly burning flame. All around me, rogues, monks, warriors, revenants and druids activated every trick and spell they had to buff themselves. It was like a million different monkey-men had just gone Super Saiyan. When everybody was ready, we all looked to Slashlore. We were waiting for a sign to charge.

A clicking sound flew above us. I glanced up and saw a tiny gnome riding a yellow cloud. The gnome had black hair, a red staff and a belt attachment that gave him a tail. I smiled. Of course he was here, he was Aspumer's greatest warrior. When the horn was sounded, he came. Tinygoku had returned.

Slashlore pointed his axe forward.

"Charge!"

Chapter 15

"...." – Logan Walker, (Call of Duty: Ghost)

A volley of arrows arced across the sky. They crashed down upon the Death Walker. Some bounced off his armour; some were swatted away with a flick of his wrist but a few hit home. The Death Walker didn't flinch.

The spells were next. Fire, ice and other slammed against him. Darts, balls, explosions and javelins slammed into him. The Death Walker didn't flinch.

Slashlore led the charge. He and all the other tanks slammed into the Death Walker at once. Shields, axes, spears and swords collided against the merged god. The damage was incalculable by pre-glitch standards. The Death Walker didn't flinch.

Me and the DPS crew were next. Daggers, swords and fists slammed into the foe that stood before us. We used every first-attack bonus we had for the biggest hit we could. The Death Walker didn't flinch.

The Death Walker glared at the numbers that toiled below him. He roared and every feather on his armour rippled. He dropped into a combat stance and readied his first attack. The battle had begun.

Final Boss: The Death Walker

Tactic: Tank and Spank

Slashlore slammed his axe against the Death Walker's leg. He pivoted away and tossed his glowing shield at the Death Walker's skull. Skith moved in next, running up

Steelion's outstretched blade. The warrior flung the gnome forward. Skith hollered as he did a diving attack, stabbing his blade deep towards the Death Walker's chest but met only his armour. The Gnome bounced off and fell to the ground.

Fire slammed into the Death Walker's face as Scova yelled. Keshim's Fang struck quickly, the fire desperately trying to feast on the God's flesh. She quickly summoned another tongue of flame, holding the burning whip in one hand and her blade in the other. Whip and blade struck together. She was a dancing swirl of fire, constantly twisting and turning as the fire weapons struck time and time again. She was the burning typhoon.

"Kamé-Doken Blast!" A ki blast slammed against the ground and shot the dwarf upwards into the air. Punchocalypse flew toward the god. His fist glowed as he barrelled towards the Death Walker. He collided with a massive shockwave as his punch landed with the gigantic figure. For a second, the Death Walker seemed to stagger. We had caused it some damage. It was beatable. Punchocalypse hung onto the Death Walker's body for dear life as he fired punch after punch into the divine form.

The Death Walker slammed his foot down and we went flying backwards. A ripple of death traveled outwards as plants and grass suddenly died. The swiftest of us were back on our feet in seconds and shooting forward. The slowest of us were up a few seconds later. Steelion was first to reach him but a backhanded slash set him flying backwards. Deathly magic rippled through the ground as jagged spikes ripped up from the earth. Screams filled the air of dozens of us suddenly felt our inside being stabbed. Sadly, I was one of the unlucky. Since the Glitch, I had been shot, stabbed and had my neck sliced opened. I was now familiar with the feel of cold steel tearing into my body. It was not a familiarity I wanted to have but it was one fate had thrust upon me. So when the spikes, blacker than night, jetted up and tore into me, I was expecting the cold feel of steel. Instead, what I felt could only be described as a forceful claw gripping my soul and trying to rip it from me. There was pain but the draining feeling was worse. I slashed at the spike with my blades, striking them over and over until they shattered. I dropped to the ground. My hand shot out to brace myself but it suddenly came in contact with a pink bulb atop a green stem. I looked down and saw a flower that had yet to bloom. Dozens of them were scattered across the field. As if on cue, they all bloomed and the green glitter of druidic magic floated upwards. My wounds were quickly knitting together. I looked back and saw Scáthach. The druid was on healing duty.

I glanced back at the Death Walker. A trio were fighting him as Yasna was casting a spell. Ziena's staff was a blur in her paws, striking out as a serpent as she forced the Death Walker to his left. Geist let out an Orcish roar as he charged in. His greatsteel slashed hard. There was little chance in missing a target as large as the Death Walker so the Orc had put everything he had into damage. He struck with a three-hit combo then ducked. Tinygoku leapt over him and stuck with a flurry of blows. A red aura glowed about him. He wasn't going Kaio-ken but he was being boosted. I glanced back to see Footkneebra in the back line, using spell after spell to boost the forward front and her current recipient was the legend himself. Tinygoku's punches weren't as strong and devastating as Punchocaplyse's but he did fire more of them. He attacked with a flurry then dodged, slapping aside the Death Walker's punch. I blinked in shock. Tinygoku could actually dodge a move like that. The Death Walker's fist had moved so fast that I barely even saw it and not only was Tinygoku able to see it coming; he slapped it aside like it was nothing.

The ground around Yasna began to glow, consecrating the area. She gripped her weapon tightly and charged, yelling out an intimidating scream as she struck with the glowing hammer. The blow caught the Death Walker's attention. He swung with a backhanded slap but Yasna saw it coming. She backpedalled but realized her mistake a second too late. The Death Walker wasn't trying to slap her, he was trying to get his hand into position. A blast of deathly energy erupted in his hand. He blasted her directly in the chest and sent her flying. He pivoted to his left just as Tinygoku leapt into the air for a powerful Superman punch. He raised his hand and let out another blast. Tinygoku was sent flying high into the sky until all that was left was a sparkle in the distance.

Team Rocket's blasting off again.

Balls of energy formed around the Death Walker's skull. They hovered there for a second before shooting outwards. Each found a random target and exploded in their vicinity. Dozens more screamed in pain. The Death Walker raised his hands and pulled from the ground dozens of new skeletons. These ones had shields and swords like they were fighters in Killer Instinct and marched upon the battlefield. It was a common thing for bosses to summon adds to trip us up. These ones were just stronger.

"Leave these for us," High Mason Redaxe bellowed. "We ain't letting one of them through."

High Mason Redaxe led a charge of Dwarves. They collided with the armoured skeletons and quickly pulled them away from battle. Legions of Dwarves bravely fought the adds, leaving the big bad for us.

I bolted forward, weaving in and out of the small skeletons battles, and leapt at the Death Walker. Dikaya dove first but only scratched the feather adorned armour. Whaitiri Edge slashed next but only caught the afterimage of his cloak. I landed and pivoted around, bringing both blades across in a double slash. Both of my steel slashed across its leg. The Death Walker turned to kick me but I blinked away.

Two blinks left.

Badënov charged in. His hands moved quickly as he notched an arrow and fired, one after another. His rate of fire was incredible. One arrow would barely leave the bow before another was notched. He leapt over a blast of death magic and transformed his bow into a blade. He slid between the Death Walker's legs, slashing at his shin with his double-bladed sword. Both sides tore flesh as he passed. Badënov flipped to his feet and slashed at the Death Walker's back.

Swirls of deathly magic circled around the Death Walker before shooting out. Each swirl dove into a random target, infesting them with a corpse plague. The plague was a damage over time debuff that lasted twelve seconds before fading away. The only problem was this plague had two additional features. The Death Walker formed a lance of death energy in his hand and dashed forward. He moved faster than I could track. Next thing I knew, he was standing in front of Yasna, the spear stabbing through her chest. She dropped to the ground and the spear dissipated, activating the first alternate ability of the corpse plague.

Death Lance: if it connects with a foe it causes all instances of Corpse Plague to reset the timer and leap to the nearest un-infected foe.

The Death Walker leapt at Geist. His fists were fast as he slammed them into the Orc. The warrior held strong, blocking what he could with his greatsteel and taking the damage from what he couldn't. Geist struck back, finding an opening and swinging hard against it. His steel collided with the god but bounced off of its armour. The Death Walker slapped Geist aside and summoned another death lance. He drove it through Geist and the plague leapt again.

Badënov leapt in again, his bowblade slashing at the Death Walker's arm. He was infected but it wasn't slowing him down. Badënov hit the ground and morphed his blade back into a bow. He grabbed four arrows in his hand, notched one, drew back, twisted into a spin and fired. For each quarter of a turn he made, Badënov fired another arrow. His shots dropped two skeletons and put two arrows into the Death Walker. The god summoned a ball of deathly energy in each of his palms and clapped his hands together. This activated the second function of the corpse plague.

Burning Infestation: when activated, each target that is infected by the corpse plague shall have the plague burn up inside of them and receive fire damage.

Screams filled the air as dozens burned from the inside. I roared as I dashed forward. Punchocalypse ran beside me, giving me a wink as he charged in. I led the way, my longsteel moving quickly, slashing twice before my shortsteel dove in next. I rolled to my left as Punchocalypse charged in. He slammed his glowing fist into the Death Walker's chest and once again the god stumbled just a bit.

"Hit him now!" The Witch Queen cried. I grabbed Punchocalypse and pulled him aside. From the back line, a seemingly endless line of mages and caster readied their spells. "If pain is life, then let us make him feel alive."

A flurry of spells erupted forward. Several fireballs landed beside the Death Walker and exploded. Hundreds of arcane bolts and sickly green darts flew through the air and ripped through his body. Shards of ice leapt up from the ground and impaled him as lightning tore down from above and shocked him. The forces of nature, the spirits, arcane energy and even the blessing of Helruss himself were united in their assault on the Death Walker.

For a moment the battle seemed to pause. The Death Walker dropped to one knee. The coordinated blast had hurt him and badly. With a look of anger and rage, the Death Walker stood back up, more determined than ever to slay us all. He held out his hand as a scythe formed in it. That was the Morrigan Scythe. We hadn't defeated him; this was just the second phase of the battle.

Tactic: Survive

I bolted in. Yasna and Badënov ran in beside me. Yasna struck with her hammer and pulled threat. Badënov filled his back with arrows before morphing the bow back to a blade for a melee strike. I slashed with both weapons in a crossing slash. All three attacks landed but they did nothing. An enraged look crossed the Death Walker's eyes and I swore. In VCO, an enraged look like that meant an increase in damage and attack speed. The Morrigan Scythe slashed with blurring speed. The first trio of attacks landed on Yasna. She blocked one with her hammer but the other two collided with her armour. She was relatively unharmed but even with armour each blow still felt like getting hit by a truck. She skidded across the ground. He turned to me next. I held Whaitiri Edge at the ready. My defensive blade was quick in deflecting the scythe's strike, Dikaya leaping in to assist when possible, but even with a successful block, I still slid back with each strike. I was so focused on his scythe that I missed his foot. His boot leapt up and caught me in the chest. I was lifted off the ground and pitched into the air, landing a few moments later, hundreds of feet away, my lungs gasping for air. I tried to climb to my feet but found my body unresponsive. I was hurt, bad. I looked back at the Death Walker. Badënov's bowblade moved quickly, the hunter trying to protect himself, but it was not quick enough. Morrigan tore across Badënov's chest. Then it pulled across Badënov's neck. The hunter's head fell to the ground, bouncing along the dirt, and the body followed a few seconds later.

Badënov was dead.

I screamed and tried to stand up once more but my body would not respond. A circle of shadowy energy formed around me. Seconds later my wounds began to knot together once more. I glanced at Tialla. The shadow priestess was doing what she did best. She was controlling the battle as she healed those that fought. I stood up and began to run. I heard a clicking sound and felt a tiny, albeit strong, hand grab me. I looked up and saw Tinygoku atop his flying cloud.

"Thanks for the save," I said with a smile. There was something epic about being scooped by the legend himself. Everything about Tinygoku, from the orange suit to the black hair and yellow cloud, triggered every ounce of childhood nostalgia for the show and character I loved and still love. The only problem was that somebody was about to get sued for the blatant rip-off. It was going to be City of Heroes all over again. Unless......

Tinygoku is a fan-based PARODY.

Dragonball, DragonBall Z, Dragonball GT and *Dragonball Super* are all owned by Funimation, Toei Animation, Shueisha and Akira Toriyama.

"We're not done yet, Reaper," the legend said as we flew forward. I smiled. We were far from done. I pointed to Steelion on the ground. He was running beside Scova and Slashlore. Tinygoku changed his direction accordingly. I dropped down to the ground and ran beside them. The Death Walker sliced Morrigan in the sky and opened a small portal. It looked like a tear in the sky. A wave of flying gargoyles poured out. They were headed right for us.

"Take aim!" King Toshel Gearrigger yelled. A long line of Gnome archers aimed upwards. They waited for the command to fire. "Rip them from the sky."

A volley of bolts and arrows shot into the air. The arrows ripped through their wings; the gargoyles tried to stay in the air but each spiralled downwards as they crashed into the ground. We leapt over the fallen foes and continued our charge.

"I'll keep him busy," Tinygoku said. "You hit him hard."

Tinygoku zoomed ahead. He leapt from his cloud and attacked with a flurry of blows. The Gnome dodged and weaved through the scythe's slashes and counter with strikes of his own. A powerful punch slammed into the Death Walker's back. He spun around to see Punchocaplyse readying himself for another strike. The Dwarf leapt over Morrigan and slammed another fist into the god's chest. The Death Walker readied another combo attack when Tinygoku launched a volley of his own. Twelve punches landed in blurring speed, each pummelling the god's side. The Death Walker let out a wide arcing strike with Morrigan and caught both of them. The monks tumbled backwards, each badly injured. A glow of healing energy suddenly surrounded both of them as Montra drop kicked the Death Walker. She fell to the ground, rolled up behind the god, pulled herself back to her feet and fired a quick burst of punches. Each blow caused another wave of healing to occur. A staff suddenly shot out, catching the Death Walker's leg. Ziena forced the god to his left, directly into the path of Punchocalypse's oncoming fist. The god stumbled back slightly, just as Tinygoku fired another barrage of fists. The four monks moved as one. Ziena forced the Death Walker into position, Punchocaplyse landed a deadly blow, Tinygoku kept the god confused and Montra healed them all. They moved quickly, struck swiftly and kept the god guessing. I was beginning to think monks were a little OP.

A stomp of the Death Walker's foot sent the four monks flying. Swirls of deathly energy circled around the Death Walker once again. Each flew outwards, diving into random foes. One dove into me. It was like a stinging sensation that didn't go away. It was like a bad tooth-ache; strong enough to be noticeable but not strong enough to stop me.

Slashlore slammed his shield into the Death Walker and twisted away. My blades came down quickly across his upper body. Darts of fire flew from behind us, ripping into the Death Walker's chest. Scova quickly summoned a flame-thrower of flame and showered the god with flame. Steelion stepped in next. He held his hand-and-a-half sword with both hands and slashed hard. The Blade of Lite ripped into the Death Walker and for the first time since the battle began, the Death Walker looked at us directly. We were not simply some gnats flying about, we were a real threat and it was all because of that blade.

Steelion struck again but this time the Death Walker was ready. He blocked the blow with Morrigan before slashing in retaliation. The blow ripped across Steelion's torso and sent him back. Slashlore stepped in again, striking with his axe. The blow pulled the Death Walker's threat. Slashlore had just enough time to raise his shield as Morrigan came searching for him. The sound of steel scratching steel filled the air. Two tendrils of Tialla's shadow energy ripped up from the ground, it dove into the Death Walker's chest and exploded. He roared and fear rippled through our bodies once more. I fought every urge to flee, pushed through the desire to retreat and instead I attacked. Scova and Steelion were frozen, stunned by the shout. Slashlore pushed past the two and slammed with his shield. The Death Walker spun with Morrigan. I had barely enough time to bring Whaitiri Edge up to block the blade but not enough time to block the weapon's blunted staff. The butt of the weapon slapped against me and knocked me on my back. The Death Walker kicked Slashlore and sent him skidding into the dirt. He rushed over and raised his foot to stomp. One kick would be enough to crush his chest and kill Slashlore. A charging Solomon Grundy slammed into the god and punched him with his large fists. I rolled to my feet and glanced behind me. I saw Alluca standing, her tendrils of magic wrapping around the undead. She was finding the strongest undead and turning them against the Death Walker. The god reached up and touched the Grundy on the forehead, turning it to dust. He glanced in Alluca's directed and bolted forward. A lance of deathly energy formed in his hand. He rammed it through her chest. I suddenly felt a swirl leap from my body and dive into Steelion's. The plague was spreading again.

I glanced back at Reit. The shaman was still sitting, quietly meditating. Swirls of gold, glowing energy circled his sitting form. Three undead moved towards the undefended shaman. I cursed and started to move towards him but stopped when I saw the sheen of a swift moving blade. Three swift strikes from a katana dropped the zombies before they even got close. I let out a sigh of relief as I recognized Shuteye, my personal con-artist samurai. You know things are bad when even Yajirobe comes out to fight.

The Death Walker bolted forward, sliding across the ground, and slammed his shoulder into Steelion. The warrior went flying backwards. The god pivoted, grabbed Alluca and slammed her onto the ground like a pog from the 90's. He slashed Morrigan in a sweeping arc and caught Tinygoku and Scova with the blade. Both fell backwards. A lance of deathly energy formed in his hand as the Death Walker charged at me.

He thrust the lance at me but at the last second I blinked away.

One blink remaining.

Unfazed at his miss, the Death Walker stabbed the lance behind him, catching Geist in the chest. I suddenly felt a swirl leap from my body and dive into Skith. The plague was spreading again. The god summoned a ball of deathly energy in each of his palms and clapped his hands together. The Burning Infestation triggered and I fell to the ground. Fire burned up inside of me and I screamed in pain as my inside melted. I twitched at the ground, searching for relief from this incomparable pain. I whimpered, I screamed and I may have cried. I'm proud of none of my reactions but when you're under that much pain, you have little say of how you react.

Almost as quickly as the pain arrived, it vanished. I was left on the ground as a twitching mess. I looked up and saw Steelion, Scova, Skith and dozens upon dozens of others all reacting like I was. Fuck; we were so screwed. I tried to climb to my feet just as the Death Walker slammed his foot into me. I was pitched back, skipping across the ground like a bouncing ground ball except there was no Vladdy Jr. to catch me. My body came to a halt and I winced. Tinygoku crashed down beside me. I glanced at him.

"We done yet?" I asked.

"Not yet we...." The gnome tried to stand up but his tiny legs gave way. He crashed back down with a tiny thud. He was like me, a quivering ball of pain, just tiny. He looked up at me with a wince. "I'm beginning to have doubts in your plan."

"Fuck," I laughed. "I'm surprised you still consider this a plan."

"Drink up, me hearties, yo ho." A pair of potions fell beside each of us. I looked up and saw Shuteye. I popped the cork and chugged it down. Pain began to vanish and wounds began to heal. I pushed up to my feet. Shuteye nodded to Reit. I glanced at him. The golden energy that circled him had nearly formed a complete dome, with only a few gaps remaining. "He's almost done. We just need to hold him off."

Across the field, hundreds of us lay just like I did, injured and slowly getting up. I could see that resolve was vanishing. We were losing and we were losing bad. There was hope but we needed a few moments more. I looked around the battlefield. Archons were doing battle against Steelion's summoned army. I glanced over at our troops. I had an idea. I bolted across the field and slid next to Steelion.

"I have a plan," I said.

"Your last didn't work well," he replied.

"We need a few moments more but we won't last that long." I pointed to the archons and the Aeolisian Army. "Turn them against the Death Walker."

"If we pull the army, the archons will overrun us."

"Turn them both," I clarified. "You wield the Blade of Lite. Only the best of the archons ever wielded it and now you do. Show them you're worthy. Show them that they should follow you."

Steelion looked hesitant for a moment but reluctantly nodded. He stood up and held the blade in both hands. He willed the blade to life, putting as much of his own energy into it. With each ounce of strength he put in, the blade began to glow a little more. Suddenly, he thrust the blade upwards into the sky as the steel let out a burst of light. The burst was followed by the sound of a horn, its cry reaching across the battlefield. Both Aeolisians and archons froze, some mid strike. Both sides glanced at the warrior. Eons, according to lore, had passed since one form held both sword and horn and now they were both being held and wielded by a mortal. Steelion didn't make a speech. He simply pointed the blade at the Death Walker and spoke a single word.

"Attack."

Both armies obeyed. They turned and charged. Aeolisians and archons assaulted the Death Walker and attacked as one. Blades came from the ground, from upon a mount and even from the sky. Steel after steel slashed at the Death Walker. Morrigan was a blur as the Death Walker fought back. He deflected, blocked and countered. His scythe danced as he sliced through archons and Aeolisians.

As the battle raged, I called for a group up. Everybody came to me and we readied ourselves. I glanced at Shuteye. "Is he ready?"

"I am," Reit's said. I glanced at the now complete dome of gold energy. It suddenly shrunk and poured directly into his hammer. Reit stood up and marched forward with a determined look in his eye. He pointed the hammer at the Death Walker. "The spirits have spoken; your time has come to an end."

A blast of golden energy fired from the hammer. It wasn't a small beam, like a Freeza finger blast. This was a massive blast that kind of felt like it could destroy Alderaan all over again. It blasted across the battlefield and tore into the Death Walker's chest and out the other side. We all stared in shock. We could literally see behind the Death Walker from the hole in his chest. The Death Walker roared as the hole quickly mended itself. I nearly crapped myself. If that didn't stop the Death Walker, what would? He took a step forward but suddenly dropped the ground as his knee buckled. The Death Walker wasn't beaten but he was weakened. We could end this, right here and now.

"Charge!" I cried out as I bolted forward. The thundering sound of running boots followed me. Suddenly a rainbow of glows covered us as enchantment after enchantment were cast. Suddenly I was fast, I was stronger and my strikes would do more damage and leave a DOT when I was done. I glanced back.

"Our strength is now your strength," High Lord Lanmina Nightpride called out. "End this now."

My blades were the first to land. The Death Walker was back on two feet with his scythe in his hand. Whaitiri Edge deflected Morrigan's slash as Dikaya dove first. It thrust through his shattered armour and into his divine flesh. The blade dug deep and I gave it a twist, I wanted this to hurt. I withdrew the blade and pivoted away. Scova was there with her palm raised. A blast of flame seared through the flesh.

Morrigan slashed at the mage but the steel only met Slash-lore's shield. The paladin stepped in with a slash of his axe but he was not alone. Standing on his shoulder was Skith. The gnome leapt off and plunged his cleaver-glaive into the Death Walker's neck. He stood atop the god as he plunged his spear over and over into the creature's neck.

Orbs of deathly energy formed around the Death Walker's skull and fired outwards. They collided with the allies and exploded in damage. A sickening circle of necromantic energy formed around his feet and I suddenly found myself in pain. He had cast a similar spell to Yasna but instead of consecrating the area, he had desecrated it and any foe who stepped in there received damage.

Punchocalypse ran in and fired another of his devastating punches but this one wasn't to the chest or head, this time the Dwarven monk punched at the Death Walker's leg. The powerful blow crippled the leg and forced the Death Walker back to one knee. Montra slapped her foot across the Death Walker's skull and sent a wave of healing across her allies. Circles of shadowy energy suddenly appeared as more of Tialla's healing came in. Geist roared as he leapt into the fray, his greatsteel coming down in a powerful slash. Alluca appeared behind him, a trio of swift slashes finding a home in the Death Walker's side. The Death Walker raised his hand and a ball of energy exploded. I blinked behind him and avoided the blast.

I was out of blinks.

The blast should have pitched everybody dozens of feet back but with all the blessing and boosts, they flew only a few feet at most. Punchocalypse stepped up and started summoning a ball of energy in his palms.

"Kamé-Doken --"

"You're not doing this alone, kid," Tinygoku said. He stood beside Punchocalypse and formed a ball of his own.

"Blast!" Punchocalypse yelled as he and Tinygoku fired their blast forward. Two beams shot forward and collided with the Death Walker's torso. The blast sent him staggering back, into my awaiting blades. Whaitiri Edge and Di-kaya danced as finely and swiftly as I could ever ask of them as they tore at the Death Walker from behind. A trio of Tialla's shadowy tendrils leapt up from the ground and wrapped themselves around the god to pull him down. The Death Walker struggled against the grapple but his strength was fading. Scova stepped up and fired another blast of fire into the god's face. She dove out of the way as Steelion charged in. The Blade of Lite was glowing now, leaving a golden trail as it swiftly slashed. Steelion used the hand-and-half blade with one hand, giving his strikes speed. His strikes were a blur, his glowing blade looking like a glow stick at a rave, and each slash caused exponentially more damage upon the Death Walker. Steelion suddenly pivoted away as Punchocalypse rushed in with another powerful punch.

The god roared and backhanded Punchocalypse out of the way. He erupted in anger and magic. The sudden burst of energy sent Skith flying off of the god's shoulders. The Death Walker pivoted around and summoned a blast of energy pointed in my direction. I tried to blink out of the way but found my ring unresponsive.

I was out of blinks.

I felt like a Tracer would after she'd been hacked by Sombra: helpless. Suddenly a large form tackled me to the ground just as the blast erupted. It flew above me, harmlessly blasting off into the horizon. I panted in fear. I had felt the heat of that blast on my face. It had only missed me by inches. I looked at my rescuer: Steelion.

"You ready to end this?" he asked. I nodded. We both grabbed our blades and charged in.

Steelion moved first. He swiftly slashed twice. They were thin slashes but pulled the Death Walker's attention. The Death Walker slashed with Morrigan but the warrior was gone. In his place was Whaitiri Edge. The shortsteel blocked the scythe as my longsteel dove in for the chest. I stabbed as quickly as I could before I ducked beneath the god's fist and pivoted away. Scova was next in line. Keshim's Fang went for the limbs, burning the flesh upon contact. She and I struck as one; she went for the left leg and I went for the right. Both of the legs buckled under the strikes of our steel. The Death Walker dropped to both knees only to find Steelion standing over him with the Blade of Lite in both of his hands. Steelion didn't say some joke or make some final glib remark, a wasted opportunity in my mind; he simply remained silent as he brought the blade across the Death Walker's neck. With one final strike he separated the skull from the shoulders and watched as it fell to the ground. The skull bounced along the ground as the body collapsed. We all stood there for a moment, wondering what would happen next. Then the body exploded.

I awoke several moments later, hundreds of feet away. I scrambled to my feet and found that the battleground was covered in shadows and flowers as a golden glow rained down from above. The healers were working over-time. I looked at where the Death Walker had stood and saw only a crater. In his place was a pile of ash. I smiled and fell back to the ground, exhausted.

The Death Walker was dead.

Chapter 16

"...." – Sir Douchebag, (South Park: The Stitck of Truth)

The party was beyond epic. Five nations, united as one, drank, sang and screwed the night away. Slashlore debated the wisdom of a celebration when many had died but the Queen insisted; we celebrate now and mourn tomorrow. So we partied. The Elves set up tents on the battlefield and the Dwarves used the ancient magic of their kin to summon copious amounts of food and booze. The Gnomes set off fireworks and the humans provided music. We had survived the *Battle of Death's Return* and now we celebrated at the *Feast at Death's Crater*.

"We need more kitchens," Scova said as her and Adelaide approached me. "It never feels like a real party unless we all end up in the kitchen."

I would never understand Scova. I glanced at Lady Adelaide. "Have you seen Garruil?"

"Not since your arrival," she admitted. "Why?"

"She was the one who killed me," I revealed. "She is your betrayer within the Whispers."

Adelaide looked at me with a stern look. She took in a deep breath and let out a long exhale. "That is troubling, to say the least, but there is little I can do about it this eve. Tomorrow, I will begin the hunt for her. Until then, I will celebrate the return of my apprentice and the victory we have won this day."

I smiled. There was a reason that she was the wise

one. Adelaide and Scova kissed and I suddenly felt like the third wheel once again. I was tired of being alone. I didn't know how long I'd be in this game but perhaps I didn't have to solo it. Perhaps it was time to find some companionship beyond a single night.

I looked across the battlefield and saw Tialla, drinking with Slashlore. I shook my head. That door was closed. I kept scanning until I saw Footkneebra. The succubus wouldn't even meet my gaze. I had burned that bridge during the heist. I looked for Montra. I spotted her and Steelion passionately making out. They didn't care that people were watching. They were simply enjoying each other. Montra grabbed Steelion and pulled him towards the nearest tent. I smirked in surprise. I would have never seen those two getting along. Who did this leave? Who was out there for me? Was it somebody I had yet to meet or was there somebody standing before me that I could not see?

"Hello, Rake," the Witch Queen said as she approached me. I bowed and she nodded. "Welcome back to the living, Reaper."

"Thank you, Your Highness."

"We are grateful for your return but please don't make dying a habit," she said as she walked away. "Some of us would prefer you stick around."

What the hell was that?

I spotted Skith walking around with a skull in his hand. I raised an eyebrow and approached him.

"Okay, what in the actual crap is that?"

"This is my un-orc," he replied. "He was mostly vanquished in the battle. I will feed him flesh and bone until he is rebuilt. Then we will be together once again." I smiled and nodded and slowly backed away. Skith and his un-orc were the creepiest version of Groot and Rocket, ever.

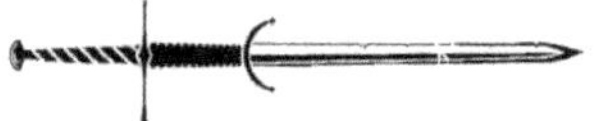

Morning came with a hangover and the sound of battle and I wasn't sure which was worse. The Horn of War rang out and snapped me awake. I dove out of my tent wearing only my boxers with a blade in each hand and desperately snapped my head around in search of a threat. Standing in the center of the crater stood the Death Walker. Somehow, he had survived. Without thought or preparation I bolted for him. An equally unclothed Steelion charged beside me.

"I mean no threat," his voice boomed. We skidded to a halt. "I am Helruss once more."

"Then why do you look like that?" Reit asked, approaching from behind. Somehow the shaman had enough time to get fully dressed.

"The fusion remains but the consciousness of the Crypt Walker was destroyed. Our powers have combined but this form is...." His voice trailed off as he studied his own hand. "I have come for two reasons. The first is to thank you and yours. If it were not for your swift actions, death would have overtaken all. This I cannot allow."

"And the second?" I asked.

"I need one to serve as my second in command." My jaw dropped. Death was hiring? Was he looking for an assistant or perhaps an apprentice? Holy Mort, Mr. Pratchett! "The Crypt Walker's corruption has left my realm is disarray. My forces are scattered and war will come to the land of the dead. I looked to one of you, heroes, to lead my army. I look to one of you to restore balance."

Please don't be me. I just got back to the land of the living. I really didn't want to die again. Reit suddenly stepped forward. "I volunteer."

"You...." The death god said, "Are insufficient. I require one with a stronger sliver of divinity. I require him." Helruss pointed at the half-naked Steelion. "You have a strong sliver within you. You controlled the Aeolisian Army, my army, you wield the Blade of Lite and you earned the loyalty of the archons. It is you I request. I cannot demand it of you but I would greatly desire it."

I glanced at Steelion. He looked back at me. I had just gotten him back. We had patched things up, I brought him back to life and he saved mine. Now I was going to lose him once again.

Steelion didn't hesitate. He simply nodded and stepped forward. "I accept."

"Wait..."

"It's okay, Rake," Steelion said as he turned towards me. "I can help down there. I can save others who died today. I can try and learn about the Glitch from the god's side and I can find Badёnov. If that archer's down there, I'll find him." I tried to argue but Steelion shook it off. "I screwed up in the past. Now I get to make it right and, more importantly, now I get to do something you never will."

We both hugged, holding each other for a moment and silently said our goodbyes. I chuckled and really wished both of us were wearing a lot more clothes. The hug broke and Steelion looked back to Helruss.

"Ready yourself, warrior," he said. "Soon we will depart."

Five minutes later, both of us were dressed. Steelion walked up to Montra and handed her an orb. "It's called Realm Glass. It can be used to talk to me across the realms of living and dead."

"Thanks," Montra said. "I'll only use it for emergencies."

"Or whenever you wanna chat or whatever," Steelion said with a smirk. Montra smirked back. The warrior walked towards Helruss and bowed. Yasna walked beside him.

"Where you go, boss," she said, "so do I."

Scáthach walked up beside them. Reit walked up and grabbed her hand. "You're going?" She nodded. "Why?"

"I have an angel to find," she said. Reit released her hand and smiled. The two hugged.

"Good luck, Scáthach." She thanked him with a nod.

Tinygoku walked up next. Punchocalypse approached him. "Why are you going? You don't have to leave."

"I was one of the best in this game and because of that I get to live in Aeolisian Halls. Do you know what they do up there? They drink, party and they boink like nobody's business. I ain't leaving that unless there is a good fight to be had." He smirked. "Take care, kid. This world needs more monks like us." The two bumped fists and, I swore, the world gently shook at their power.

The four stood there and waved as they faded out of existence. They were gone. Suddenly a small chest appeared before each member of the Enclave. Atop each was a note of thanks from Helrus. We eagerly opened our respective chests. People cheered and boasted as they showed off epic gear. Mine, however, contained a small low level ring. It was called the ring of memories and only offered a tiny bonus to armour. I examined the ring. I had never seen it before. It was a gold ring where the gold had been tarnished and faded. It looked like the ring version of the Holy Grail but on the inside was a small etched raven, the symbol of Helruss. I waved over Reit.

"What is this?"

"I honestly don't know. This is my game and I don't have a clue." Reit frowned. "Wow, that is getting to be real annoying."

A few hours later, after breakfast, we began to tear down the camp. Ziena, Geist and Alluca waved me over. "We're heading out," Ziena said. "We have a warchief to find."

"We need to find out who won our civil war," Geist explained. "We need to be with our kind."

"You're PCs," I reminded them. "You're gamers. You're already with your own kind."

"If you honestly think the Descendent and the Damned are the same kind," Alluca said with a laugh, "then I don't think you're playing VCO properly."

I smirked. Ziena and I hugged, than Alluca and I hugged. I offered Geist my hand but he grabbed me with his large Orchish hand and hugged me tight.

"Y'all have a long walk," I said with an evil smirk.

"And I don't think Alluca has heard of Flipsim."

Geist's eyes went wide and Ziena scowled. "I hate you, Rake."

"If you think I care what one of the Damned think, then you haven't been playing VCO properly." All three of us smiled. I watched them turn and walk away. I watched them walked into the distance. I watched long after I couldn't see them, hoping and praying that they'd make it back okay.

Days had passed since the *Battle of Death's Return.* I had aided in the cleanup of the undead, hunted down the last Nethall and even found some of the few archons stranded on the living realm. When all of that was done, I returned to the Havenhold library, ascended the stairs and stopped at the door. I tapped the doorknob and heard the distinct sound of the door unlocking. I pushed open the door and looked around. It was a large room with a sturdy desk, a large bed, an armoire and dozens of books placed on a set of three bookshelves. Underneath the bed was a brown chest with an enchanted padlock. This was my room. I was back in my room. I fell back onto my bed and smiled. I had only been gone a couple weeks at most but it had felt like it had been a year.

I was just happy to be home.

I sat up and looked around. A small stain of blood remained in the center of the floor. Whoever found me - dead me - had done their best to clean up but blood has a way of leaving a reminder that it was there. I glanced at my desk. My copy of *Delusionary Illusion: Manifesting Reality through Belief* was gone. Garruil must have taken it when she killed me. I kind of expected that. I had no clue who Lthena Oakenhide was or how to find her but, for the first time, in a long time, I had a lead.

But that was a tomorrow problem.

A lot had changed since I'd last entered this room and a lot still remained the same. We were still stuck in a game and were fighting for our lives but the Enclave was now a united government accepted by the Descendents of the Eternal. Death wasn't as bad as we once thought. If we died in the land of the living we went to the land of the dead. There was no proof that anybody would be able to return like I did, and if you died down there then that was it, but at least we knew now that there was a chance of survival after we died up here. People needed to know what they could do to increase the odds of survival down there; they needed to know what to do to make it out.

But that was a tomorrow problem.

It wasn't just me that escaped the death realm. Dozens of others had made it out when the Death Walker died. Those that had succumbed to the maddening, those once kept in cages in the Völusá village. The insane were freed as well and they needed help getting back on their feet. There was no way of knowing what the Grey Lands did to their minds. I barely made it out with my sanity. They needed to be looked after, for their protection and ours.

But that was a tomorrow problem.

I walked to the wall and materialized Dikaya. I unequipped the longsteel and hung it on my wall. An undead bane weapon was great for the day but I needed a new sword to act as my main weapon. I was going to have to go treasure hunting. I smirked. I couldn't wait.

But that was a tomorrow problem.

I pulled off my armour and my tunic and tossed both on the floor. I would clean up later. Kneeling by my bed, I pulled out my chest. I opened it and stared at its contents. Lying before me was all of the gear and equipment that I had collected as Stov. Everything the mage didn't have in his bags or on his person was in this chest and it stared up at me.

"I thought I locked that door," I said without looking up.

"And yet you do not draw weapons to defend yourself?" a female voice said.

"I am beyond exhausted. If you were trying to kill me, I don't think I could stop you," I smirked. "I've died once and come back, I'm kind of curious if I could do it again."

"Hello, Rake," a familiar voice said. I recognized it as the voice of Queen Theresa Archona. I turned around. The Witch Queen stood in my room. Her bodyguard Gine was nowhere to be found.

"I am happy to see you, your Highness," I said with a bow.

The Queen wore a long berry blue dress, with a golden trim. The dress had a high collar, a shoelace style fastening that pulled the dressed closed over her white blouse and split side that showed off her ample legs and matching boots. She held her usual staff in her hands. It was a stunning ensemble that made me want to drool.

"I have come to see how you are adapting to your return from the afterlife."

"It is.....unsettling," I admitted. "I died in this room. I was betrayed by a friend and had my throat ripped out. I'm happy to be back but it is going to take some time to adjust."

She nodded. "If there is anything I can do, please let me know." I thanked her. I looked past the Queen's cinnamon hair and purple eyes and found my gaze locked on her staff. The Witch Queen's staff was made from a bone white metal that twisted and turned upon itself as it got closer to the lilac jewel that glowed on the top. The Witch Queen's staff was famous but, compared to a PC's, it was weak. I knelt by my chest and withdrew a staff. As Stov I had used many staves but none were more recognizable then the Green Wood Staff. It looked like simple wood but as it reached the top it curved like a question mark. Hovering, under the bend, was a shamrock coloured gem.

"I wish to give you this gift, my queen," I said as I offered the weapon to her. "This is more powerful than your current weapon and it should greatly increase your magical potential."

As Stov I had used it for a great many years before discovering the *Jötnar Set*. I no longer needed it. Hopefully she could use it. Theresa's eyes went wide.

"How did you get that weapon? It belongs to the mage Stov," she said suddenly. She took the staff and went quiet, deep in thought. "I once told you I was saved by the mage Stov and I awaited his return to aid us in this time of need. He seems not to be returning."

"He cannot return," I said. She eyes me suspiciously. "My people are not from this world."

"I know of this. You create new bodies to use when you cross from your world," the Queen finished. "I don't completely understand the process but I have accepted it as fact. Why do you mention this now?"

"Some create more than one body, each with their own name and skills. Some want to be rogues like me part of time but want to study magic the remainder. They make two bodies to do this." I could see understanding slowly crossing her face. Most of the NPC had a difficult time understanding the idea and I was putting a new spin on an already difficult concept. "Since the Glitch, my kind has been stuck to one body each. We can no longer switch like we used to. I had another body in this world but I can no longer return to it. I am stuck only as Rake." I took a deep breath as I said the next bit. "My other body was a powerful mage. My other body was Stov."

The Witch Queen just stared at me. I had just revealed to her that I was her teenage crush. I was the hero that saved her from capture. I was the mage that inspired her down a path of magic. I expected a reaction but I got none. She just stared at me, silently.

"Your Highness?" I asked.

"Please do not refer to me as a Queen," she said finally. She took a couple paces towards me stopping only when our faces were but a hair's length apart. "For I am about to do a very un-queenly thing."

Queen Theresa Archona rose up on the tip of her toes and pressed her lips against mine in a passionate kiss. I was shocked and surprised both at the kiss and at the peach taste on her tender royal lips. I broke the kiss and looked down at her. I was about to cross a line from friendship into more and it was going to be with my lore crush. I was kissing the Queen of Havenhold and leader of the Descendent of the Eternal. I brushed the cinnamon hair from her eyes, leaned in and kissed her. She kissed back and we both made our way to my bed. I fell on top of her and clothes immediately started to vanish as passion overtook us both. I was about to make love to the NPC Queen. This was going to be complicated, dangerous and just trouble upon trouble in many different ways.

But that was a tomorrow problem.

Epilogue

The noise was thunderous. It echoed across the land and deafened anything else in the vicinity. Thousands upon thousands of players stood in formation. Each banged along to the same rhythm. Two knocks on their armour and a stomp of their feet. Over and over they repeated the actions until the sound was all that could be heard.

Knock, knock, thump.

Knock, knock, thump.

They stood in four massive squares, the troops endlessly echoing backwards. Four races meant four formations. One was a division of Orcs. Warriors, warlocks, rogues or hunters; it didn't matter; they were all there tapping out the same rhythm.

Knock, knock, thump.

Knock, knock, thump.

A division of Dhamphir stood next to them. They seemed like frail beings beside the Orcs, but they were just as vicious and just as deadly. Their fangs protruded out as they hungrily stared up at the dais, tapping out the same rhythm.

Knock, knock, thump.

Knock, knock, thump.

The Fenririans were next. An endless number of wolfmen and wolfwomen stood at the ready. Their claws were bared and a look of excitement echoed throughout as they tapped out the same rhythm.

Knock, knock, thump.
Knock, knock, thump.

The Changelings were the last in line. Each seemed almost nondescript in their appearance but their desire for blood was far greater. Those who could blend in with their enemy became all the more dangerous. They steadily tapped out the same rhythm.

Knock, knock, thump.
Knock, knock, thump.

A female Orc walked onto the stage and held up her right hand; the rhythm came to an instant halt. The Orc was dressed in fine armour and she proudly displayed the scars of her past battles. Her name was Idracab and she was the War-chief.

"The civil war is over," she called out. Her voice boomed and echoed endlessly. "We have survived and we are now unified. We are strangers to this world but we will not be victims to it. What stands before me is proof that we will conquer this world and we will find a way home. This is the greatest army ever to exist in this world or ours. We are the Coalition of the Damned and you are my Legion.

"Everything in this world is trying to kill us, be they monsters, dragons, NPCs or the Descendents but we will not falter. Hostilities exist. There is no blinking at the fact that our people, our territory, and our interests are in grave danger. With confidence in our Legion and with the unbending determination of our people, we will gain the inevitable triumph.

"To the Decedents of the Eternal I say this: enjoy this moment of peace and prosperity and cherish the civility you currently have because the Damned are coming for you and the Legion marches your way. War has come to VCO and we will not stop until we are victorious!"

My name is Rake and I'm *still* stuck in a MMO. It wouldn't be so bad except Garuill is out and about, the Damned are looking for a fight and I still have no clue on how to get home.

Where's a GM when you need one?

HELP!

RAKE WILL RETURN

SEASON TWO ON SALE SOON!

APPENDIX

THE GODS

1) **Erothos:**   God of Light,healing and lore.
2) **Apeus:**   God of magic, cunning, trickery and charisma.
3) **Helruss:**   God of Death, balance, order and balance
4) **Vörissa:**   Goddess of Power, war and fire
5) **Torrina:**   Goddess of Life, Nature and strength
6) **Atella:**   Goddess of all

THE FACTIONS
DESCENDANTS OF THE ETERNALS
Greatness is Eternal!

Races

- Humans
- Elves
- Dwarves
- Gnomes

Important People

- Queen Theresa "The Witch Queen" Archona
    Queen of the Humans

- King Toshel Gearrigger
    King of the Gnomes

- High Mason Jozuth Redaxe
    Leader of the Dwarven Masons

- Lord Guard Lanmina Nightpride
    Leader of the Elven New Guard

- Lord Dorian Bullmourn
    Leader of the Whispers,

THE FACTIONS
COLLATION OF THE DAMNED
For the Damned!

Races

- Orcs
- Dhampir
- Fenririans
- Changlings

Important People

- Idracab
    Warchief of the Damned

- Geist
    Warchief Bodyguard

- Ziena
    Warchief Bodyguard

- Rozé
    Arcana Assassin

THE FACTIONS
THE ENCLAVE
Leeerrroooyyyy Jeeeennnkkkiiinnnsss!

Races

- All Player Characters

Important People

- Slashlore
    Enclave President

- Tialla
    General of Enclave Military

- Rake "The Reaper"
    Champion of the Enclave

- Bearcules
    Enclave Sherriff

THE EXPANSIONS

- The Ashen Downpour
- Hellforge Assembly
- Babellian Ascent
- Scaleborn Scism
- Sound of the Cuprric Echo
- From Perdition to Rapture (forthcoming)

THE CLASSES

- Druid
- Hunter
- Incubus
- Mage
- Monk
- Paladin
- Priest
- Revenant
- Rogue
- Shaman
- Warlock
- Warrior

AUTHOR NOTES

VCO was a passion project for me. For years I have wanted to do a serialized ebook series and bounced around various ideas for a while. It wasn't until I hit upon doing a trapped online genre that a plot came together. I made a few mistakes doing this book and have instantly learned from them. This will make season 2 even better and I can't wait to show that off to the world.

VCO wasn't done alone. I had lots of help and lots of people I need to thank. This was the first time I cast such a wide net looking for beta readers. I got lots of great feedback from several people. I won't try listing them all because I will forget some of you and I'd hate to do that. Just know you are all important to me.

Friends: Cliff, Lenny, John, Mike, Brandi, Kayla, Andrés, Sam, Tay Tay and more. Thanks for all the support. You make a guy feel loved! I feel like you've each given me your energy and I've used it to make my book into *a very similar to but legally different* enough Spirit Bomb.

Boss Man: VCO's biggest supporter and motivator. Sorry the ending took so long.

Family: You are my biggest supporters! Thank you!

Little Bunny: You've changed me in ways I can't even comprehend. You're always pushing me forward in reading and writing. Thank you so much!

Mom: You have had a massive influence on my career as a writer. Thank you and I love you.

Val: You did the covers and art for this series. There is more of you in VCO than anything else. I literally think one of your fingers is trapped between pages 309 and 310.

Zid: I do as thy commands.

All Hail!

My name is Benedict Thompson and I am a superhero. With a single Touch, I can read an item's past. I can tell who used that pen before you, I can describe how that shoe was made and I can describe everything that has been done on that motel room bed.

The problem with having superpowers is that people want you to actually use them.

I just want to watch TV but here I am dealing with a movie-quoting assassin, murderous celebrities, kidnapped children and secret government conspiracies.

My family's in danger, my life is in ruins and worst of all, my TV is being ignored.

I miss my TV.

NOT EVERY

SUPERPOWER

IS A BLESSING

THE BENEDICT FORECASTS

Author **Larry Gent** transports you into a world spies, espionage and superpowers. Each book is an action-packed thriller that'll keep you on the edge of your seat.

Winner of the silver medal in the *Best in Halifax* award, the Benedict Forecasts deleve deeper into the ever growing Lycotta mystery

WHO IS MAC?

The mysteries of the Visegar Company, Polaris Industries and the Lycotta gene grow deeper with the introduction of the deadly young raven called Mac.

> The Prague Riots
> The Port Alexander Explosion
> The Clockwork Killer

She shows up at each and brings death with her. Who is Mac and what is her connection to all three?

The TOP SECRET Mac Files

Book 1: She Who Trains Under Death
ON SALE NOW

The Lycotta-Verse expands with a look behind the Visegar curtain and a glimpse into the evil that dwells beneath.

TO ARMS, SOLDIER

LIGHTYEARS TO GO
BEFORE I SLEEP
ON SALE NOW

Allana Guiver was the Legendary Soldier that all of history knew. She won the great war but lost everything she knew and loved doing so.

400 years later, Major Guiver wakes up from cryo-sleep to find a world she doesn't reconize.

Earth is gone, humanity floats through space on a massive ship searching for a new home and a new alien threat wants to rid the universe of every human.

Humanity needs their Legendary Soldier but how do you ask a woman who gave up everything to give up more?

YOU'RE NOT DONE YET

WHAT'S WORSE THEN BEING STUCK IN A VIDEO GAME AND NOT BEING ABLE TO LOG OUT?

My name is Rake and I'm stuck in a MMO. It wouldn't be so bad if I was in my max level main but I'm not. I'm stuck as my level 1 Rogue. I'm stuck in my bank alt.

Now I'm running for my life, I'm fighting to stay alive and I'm trying to figure out how the hell to get out of here.

Where's a GM when you need one?

HELP!

BEING STUCK IN YOUR BANK ALT!

Ⅴörissa's Ⅽatalyst

—ONLINE—

Patch 1.01: New Game+
Patch 1.02: Escort Mission
Patch 1.03: Corpse Run
Patch 1.04: In Another Castle
Patch 1.05: Silent Protagonist

In this new series by Award Winning author Larry Gent, we dive in the action and mystery of the *Stuck Online* genre.

Follow Rake and company as they fight in a harsh digital world. If they're smart, they'll keep their lives. If they're lucky, they'll keep their sanity and if they're both, they just may find a way to log out.

SEASON TWO
COMING SOON!!

STORIES WORTH STAYING UP LATE FOR

 @midnightreadingpublishing

 @MR_Publish

Photo by Lisa Liteplo

ABOUT THE AUTHOR

Larry Gent is a is a bottomless well of know-legde on historical wars in worlds that are, sadly, fictional.

Larry is an enthusiastic gamer whose dreams as a child was to be either a detective or a TARDIS Repair Man (it's like a VCR repair man except you just see the ending of the movie first). He got into writing to give back to the worlds he's enjoyed so much from.

A Perth, Ontario native, he lives in both Ottawa and Halifax where he works as a freelance writer and full-time dreamer. He lives with his wife Valérie and his owner Zid the cat.

Website:	Larrygent.com
Twitter:	@42webs
Instagram:	@xan_in_the_hat